MW00710965

# Virginia Woolf

# Virginia Woolf

## Feminism and the Reader

*Anne E. Fernald*

Best wishes from a neighbor to
a neighbor of a friend! ☺

A. E. Fernald

2006

palgrave
macmillan

First published in 2006 by
PALGRAVE MACMILLAN™
175 Fifth Avenue, New York, N.Y. 10010 and
Houndmills, Basingstoke, Hampshire, England RG21 6XS
Companies and representatives throughout the world.

PALGRAVE MACMILLAN is the global academic imprint of the Palgrave Macmillan division of St. Martin's Press, LLC and of Palgrave Macmillan Ltd. Macmillan® is a registered trademark in the United States, United Kingdom and other countries. Palgrave is a registered trademark in the European Union and other countries.

ISBN-13: 978–1–4039–6965–1
ISBN-10: 1–4039–6965–5

Library of Congress Cataloging-in-Publication Data

Fernald, Anne E.
    Virginia Woolf : feminism and the reader / Anne E. Fernald.
       p. cm.
    Includes bibliographical references and index.
    ISBN 1–4039–6965–5 (alk. paper)
       1. Woolf, Virginia, 1882–1941—Criticism and interpretation.
    2. Woolf, Virginia, 1882–1941—Knowledge and learning.
    3. Woolf, Virginia, 1882–1941—Books and reading.
    4. Feminism in literature. I. Title.

PR6045.O72 Z5-Z999
823'.912—dc22                                        2005057636

A catalogue record for this book is available from the British Library.

Design by Newgen Imaging Systems (P) Ltd., Chennai, India.

First edition: September 2006

10 9 8 7 6 5 4 3 2 1

Printed in the United States of America.

*To my parents, Graham and Greta Fernald*

# CONTENTS

# ACKNOWLEDGMENTS

This book has been long—too long—in the writing and, in consequence, my debts are great. In the years since I first imagined a book on Woolf, I have taught at five different institutions. One community, however, has been constant: the global one of Woolf scholars. Thus, my first and deepest debt must go to Virginia Woolf and the readers whom she has inspired. In particular, I thank Mark Hussey and Vara Neverow for turning a virtual community into an annual conference: from the very first conference at Pace University in 1991, I have been welcomed, challenged, and encouraged.

These conferences have been my intellectual home, and, through them as well as through other gatherings, I have met, talked with, and befriended many great thinkers on Woolf. It is marvelous and humbling to remember how deeply even single conversations have enriched my work. It is wonderful to remember the many who read my work and talked to me about this project over the years. My debts are too great to count or repay. I would like to single out Jessica Berman, Julia Briggs, Beth Rigel Daugherty, Maria DiBattista, Jay Dickson, Jeanne Dubino, Jed Esty, Christine Froula, Jane Garrity, Jane Goldman, Sally Greene, Leslie Hankins, Ed Hungerford, Jeri Johnson, Andrew McNeillie, James Najarian, Beth Rosenberg, the late Lucio Ruotolo, Brenda Silver, and Alice Staveley for sharing their intellectual gifts with me. Most recently, my writing group has been a lifeline, so I thank Manya Steinkoler and Sarah Zimmerman for great conversation and for reading, reading, and reading some more.

This project began in Harriet Chessman's graduate class on Woolf and Stein at Yale and continued as a dissertation under the direction of David Bromwich. I thank them for their support as I began to shape admiration into prose. David in particular has continued to encourage my eccentric path. Friends from those years at Yale, especially Doug Mao, Jesse Matz, Jeff Bowman, Mary Bly, and Lisa Rabin, continue to challenge and inspire. Margery Sabin and the late Bob Garis have continued as mentors long beyond my days as an undergraduate at Wellesley.

Chapter 2 has its origins in a far different essay for Sally Greene's collection *Virginia Woolf: Reading the Renaissance* (Ohio University Press, 1999). Thanks to Sally for believing in that piece and to the editors at Ohio University Press for permission to print a substantially revised version here. A somewhat shorter version of chapter 3 first appeared in *Feminist Studies* 31.1 (Spring 2005) 158–82. I thank editor Sharon Groves and all the editors at *Feminist Studies*, especially Suzanne Raitt, for their generous hard work and for permission to reprint it here. A shorter version of the introduction appears in Blackwell's online journal, *Literature Compass* © 2006. <http://www.literature-compass.com>. I thank the editors for permission to reprint it. Finally, I gratefully acknowledge permission to reprint "Papyrus" by Ezra Pound from PERSONAE © by Ezra Pound. Reprinted by permission of New Directions Publishing Corp.

My colleagues at Harvard, Purdue, DePauw, and now Fordham have been generous with their time and advice. My students have continually reconfirmed my interest in Woolf and her world. Financial support from Yale, the Purdue Research Foundation, and DePauw University provided time, travel monies, and research assistance. I further extend thanks to my assistants Angela Laflen of Purdue for her work on the Addison chapter and Kevin Rasp of DePauw for his work on Hakluyt. Their discoveries and our discussions gave those chapters depth.

Throughout this long journey, my family has been my foundation. My husband, William Morgan, saw the possibilities in my ideas before I did and has continued to push me to make this book its best. My sister, Sarah Fernald Fulton; my parents, Greta and Graham Fernald; and my daughters, Olivia Jane Fernald Morgan and Isabel Sophia Fernald Morgan, have, together with my husband, provide the home from which I write.

# Abbreviations

Citations of works by Virginia Woolf are noted parenthetically throughout using the following abbreviations. Unless otherwise noted, citations are to the *unannotated* Harcourt editions. The date of first publication is given here. Following standard practice in Woolf studies, I have reproduced the spelling and punctuation of Woolf's diaries and letters as transcribed and published by her editors.

| | |
|---|---|
| ARO | *A Room of One's Own.* 1929. |
| B&B | "Byron and Mr. Briggs." 1979. |
| BTA | *Between the Acts.* 1941. |
| CDB | *The Captain's Death Bed and Other Essays.* 1950. |
| CDML | The Crowded Dance of Modern Life. 1993. |
| CR1 | *The Common Reader.* 1925. |
| CR2 | *The Second Common Reader.* 1932. |
| CSF | *The Complete Shorter Fiction.* 1989. |
| D | *Diary.* 5 vols. 1977–84. |
| DM | *The Death of the Moth and Other Essays.* 1942. |
| E | *Essays.* 4 vols. 1986–94. |
| F | *Flush: A Biography.* 1933. |
| GR | *Granite and Rainbow: Essays.* 1958. |
| JR | *Jacob's Room.* 1922. |
| L | *Letters.* 6 vols. 1975–80. |
| LS | *The London Scene.* 1975. |
| M | *The Moment and Other Essays.* 1948. |
| MB | *Moments of Being: Unpublished Autobiographical Writings.* 1985. |
| MJB | "Memoir of Julian Bell." 1936. |
| MD | *Mrs. Dalloway.* 1925. |
| MWG | "Memories of a Working Women's Guild." 1931. |
| ND | *Night and Day.* 1919. |
| O | *Orlando: A Biography.* 1928. |
| P | *The Pargiters: The Novel-Essay Portion of* The Years. 1977. |
| PA | *A Passionate Apprentice: The Early Journals, 1897–1909.* 1990. |
| 3G | *Three Guineas.* 1938. |

TTL     *To the Lighthouse.* 1927.
VO      *The Voyage Out.* 1915.
W       *The Waves.* 1931.
WE      *A Woman's Essays.* 1992.
WW      *Women and Writing.* 1979.
Y       *The Years.* 1937.

# Introduction: Woolfian Resonances

From her girlhood in her father's library to the end of her life, Virginia Woolf read widely and with passion. She was also an unusually subtle feminist thinker. These, for me, are the two most important facts about her. This book investigates the relation between these two facts—her reading and her feminism—arguing that her revisionist reading constitutes the fundamental shaping force of her feminism. That Woolf was a great reader needs little qualification; she is one of the best-read writers in the history of English literature. The publication of annotated editions of her novels, of her letters, diaries, and reading notebooks, of studies cataloguing her allusions, and the ongoing project of publishing a scholarly edition of her works have all made it possible to trace the appearance of the history of literature in her work.[1] My other central focus, on Woolf's feminist thought, does need further explanation in spite of the continuing stature of *A Room of One's Own* (1929) and *Three Guineas* (1938). It was not until the 1970s and 1980s that the feminist Woolf emerged as central to critics. The work of American feminists, Carolyn Heilbrun and Jane Marcus prominent among them, challenged the stereotype of Woolf as a delicate aesthete. At the same time, the publication of Woolf's complete letters and diaries made the details of her life, including her many feminist alliances and activities, available to all. Soon after, Alex Zwerdling's still essential *Virginia Woolf and the Real World* (1986) and the essays of Gillian Beer advanced our grasp of Woolf's engagement in the social and political world.[2] Still, even those persuaded by the sincerity of Woolf's feminist commitments must account for insensitive and snobbish remarks. I contend that what critics have seen as inconsistencies in Woolf can more properly be explained by our unease with her ambitions as an artist (and her consequent willingness to make less than sisterly judgments about women writers whose work she did not admire) and our imprecision about the extent and kind of contribution Woolf made to feminism. Initially, critics were inclined to see Woolf as an aesthete and an apolitical snob. It is easy to see why.

Her bourgeois upbringing gave her a somewhat narrow, even Arnoldian, aesthetic that she never fully escaped. Furthermore, the intellectual milieu of Bloomsbury encouraged the intense individualism that she made central to her feminism. Woolf, who once wrote an essay entitled "Am I a Snob?" (1932), was indeed a snob, and her snobbery persisted to the end of her life: she nourished this quality even as she acknowledged more communitarian ways of knowing and connecting. Yet her snobbery was not only—or even mainly—about class; part of her unforgiving judgments of others emerges also from her effort to distinguish good writing from bad and, more importantly, good from great. Woolf's desire to be a great writer with no humiliating qualification of "for a woman" not only conflicts with contemporary feminism's communitarian aspirations, but also marks the first time in English literature that a woman stated her ambitions without apology, the screen of a persona, or the protection of a pseudonym.

In an essay published in 2000, Beth Rosenberg laments the lack of scholarship on Woolf as a literary historian. She attributes this neglect, accurately I think, to the necessary emergence of a more political version of Woolf and goes on to suggest that it may be time to return to the literary, to reexamine what kind of literary historian Woolf was. In doing so, she calls for a new literary history, one that attends to historical context without encasing Woolf in her own era, like a fly in amber.[3] I share Rosenberg's desire to return to literary history, but, in doing so, I do not want to leave the political Woolf behind. My book seeks to bridge the divide between the literary and the feminist Woolf. As one critic argues, "Woolf figured the sheer pleasure of reading . . . as the most potent of forces in humanity's long struggle toward civilization, sociability, and peace."[4] In short, Woolf experienced literature and feminist politics as continuous; more importantly, her political stance derives from her reading and remaking of the literary past. Understanding the durable connection between feminism and art may help us develop a feminist literary history that is subtle and committed enough to welcome the unexpected, the experimental, and the original without compromising either feminist goals or artistic ambitions.[5]

In examining the aspects of Woolf's feminism as they are manifest in her responses to her reading, this book presents a model of feminist literary history that benefits from and moves beyond the strict historicism of Margaret J. M. Ezell and the feminist psychoanalytics of Sandra Gilbert and Susan Gubar. Until quite recently critics have had only a few models through which to explain writers' relationship to their past: prominent among them are T. S. Eliot's "Tradition and the Individual Talent" (1919) with its notion of tradition as earned, Virginia Woolf's "we think back through our mothers if we are women" (1929) (ARO, 76), and Harold Bloom's *The Anxiety of Influence* (1973).[6] These models, whether tutelary or familial, impress us now with their limitations as much as they do with their intuitions. Even as a Woolf scholar working on the question of Woolf's literary history, I have found that her idea of thinking back through our mothers needs explanation, expansion, and revision. This book represents my attempt to move beyond metaphors of family and apprenticeship and to rethink literary history and tradition, restructuring the investigation in feminist terms and with a feminist's eye to the intricacies of reading.

Questions of tradition are particularly vexed for women. In societies with rigidly defined gender roles, such as the Victorian Britain into which Woolf was born, tradition is passed down from mother to daughter and from father to son. To be crushingly blunt, this often meant that the women learned the recipes while the men learned the rhetoric.[7] Questions of tradition are also particularly vexed for modernists. Modernism announced itself as a break with the past, belying the intensity of many modernists' obsession with what came before. Eliot's fragments and Joyce's reconstructions are but two of the best-known examples of modernists making their art from the past. Still, modernism's backward glance was always self-conscious, even surreptitious.[8] In fact, once we begin to think about the question seriously, we can see that each modernist, in his or her quest to "make it new," developed a strikingly original stance toward the past. I argue that this sense of tradition as an invention rather than as an inheritance is the distinguishing mark of English (and global) modernism.[9]

For a woman modernist, the vexations of tradition multiply. For Woolf, literary tradition was at once a source of pleasure and a constant reminder of her culture's low estimation of women's intelligence. This tension shaped Woolf's active, revisionist form of literary history. She worked simultaneously to recover the lost voices of women and to learn from and take pleasure in what was useful, interesting, and beautiful in the art of men.

In developing a feminist theory of tradition, I draw on Wai Chee Dimock's idea of resonance. Her article "Toward a Theory of Resonance" positions itself against Harold Bloom's idea that texts survive because of their success in the battle for immortality. Instead, Dimock links "literary endurance . . . not to the text's timeless strength but to something like its *timeful* unwieldiness," to "its tendency to fall apart, to pick up noise, to break out in a riot of tongues."[10] Transforming the physics of resonance into a metaphor for the way we read literature, she demonstrates the important ways cultural "background noise" can make the previously inaudible audible, and how this, in turn, transforms the meanings of texts over time. Sometimes a noise in a particular frequency jumps into prominence when juxtaposed against a competing buzz. Thus, Dimock offers, the religious right's homophobia allowed Eve Sedgwick to hear the queer resonances in a passage from *Billy Budd* while that same passage merely emphasized the contrast between characters to a critic in 1971.

Texts, for Dimock, remain important beyond their immediate context because of their adaptability, the way language (and readers and the world) change around them. She writes,

> The literary, it seems, comes into being not only through the implied reader . . . but also through the reader not implied, not welcome. This includes both the reader who turns a deaf ear to a particular tone of voice and the one with ears newly and differently sensitized, who now hears nuances the author did not.[11]

Dimock's metaphor of resonance embraces and celebrates literary adaptation rather than viewing it as part of an Oedipal struggle. Such a model honors both precursor and successor. It does not envision influence as a kind of competition, nor does it indulge in the bluff geniality of E. M. Forster's vision of all great writers ranged together in the British Reading Room.[12] Resonance not only acknowledges the centrality and importance of intertextuality, but it also puts historical contexts ahead of family romance. Furthermore, it refuses to privilege a single historical moment—the moment of writing or publication— in favor of allowing the text to be relocated variously in a multitude of richly constructed contexts. In short, the theory of resonance has tremendous potential for the construction of a feminist theory of intertextuality. In the case of this book, three contexts play a significant role in my analysis of literary resonance and intertextuality: the original context of the source text's literary production, the context in which Woolf received, read, and wrote (including, often, the Victorian incrustations she sought to clear away), and the context of this study itself. Postcommunitarian, historically specific, international feminism permits my analysis of Woolf's individualism as a phase in feminist literary history.

Woolf read knowing that she was "the reader not implied, not welcome." This book analyzes Woolf's persistence in the face of this fact, emphasizing her resistance to existing literary histories that would exclude her, her revision of them, and her creation of a new, more accommodating literary history that makes room for her at the center, even as it admits the possibilities of its own undoing. Woolf's revisionist literary history also reaches outside the realm of the literary, speaking to feminist goals in the realms of education, professionalization, and international politics (especially peace work). Her resistant and revisionist method speaks to some of the major literary theorists of the twentieth century. As my work shows, Woolf's writing complicates and questions Benedict Anderson's theories of the nation as imagined community, and it offers to us a thorough feminist critique of Jürgen Habermas's account of the rise of the public sphere. The "thinking back through our mothers" that Woolf proposed in *A Room of One's Own* inspired the landmark feminist literary history on which we now depend; without it, countless projects recovering lost voices might not have been undertaken. A twenty-first-century feminist theory of literary tradition must build upon this foundation and press on further. It must teach us to persist in our reading and in our feminism, to recognize the limitations of great writers, and to embrace and delight in their gifts. It must recognize that gifts and limitations coexist in the same author, in the same text, and in the same sentence.

There are good reasons, beyond the narrowness of the Oedipal model, to resist it and all familial metaphors, including "we think back through our mothers." Still, a complete refusal to acknowledge family metaphors would certainly entail denial of some very important— even central—facts of our literary history. There is no doubt that many writers have engaged in a kind of Oedipal struggle with their precursors. The brilliance of Harold Bloom's *The Anxiety of Influence* depends on this fact. Furthermore, there is no doubt that Woolf herself was engaged, at a very deep level, in an Oedipal struggle with her own biological father, with Shakespeare, with Jane Austen, and with the fact of a literary past. However, precisely because family is so powerful, so inevitable, and so central, I want to try to imagine a version of literary history that would not rely on family metaphors. What might that look like? What might we learn about our own history from this thought experiment?

One place to start thinking about how Woolf reimagined the literary past is "Milton's bogey," the strange allusion at the end of *A Room of One's Own*. The phrase Milton's bogey is both prominent and undeveloped. It occurs without warning in one of the last sentences of *A Room of One's Own* where Woolf urges young women writers to "look past Milton's bogey, for no human being should shut out the view" (ARO, 114). Since Gilbert and Gubar emphasized it in *The Madwoman in the Attic*, we grasp the multiple feminist possibilities embedded in the phrase:

> For who (or what) *is* Milton's bogey? Not only is the phrase enigmatic, it is ambiguous. It may refer to Milton himself, the real patriarchal specter or—to use Harold Bloom's terminology—"Covering Cherub" who blocks the view for women poets. It may refer to Adam, who is Milton's (and God's) favored creature, and therefore also a Covering Cherub of sorts. Or it may refer to another fictitious specter, one more bogey created by Milton: his inferior and Satanically inspired Eve, who has also intimidated women and blocked their view of possibilities both real and literary.[13]

Like Gilbert and Gubar, I have found the phrase itself worth pausing over. Following and loosely adapting Gilbert and Gubar, I take the phrase to mean the version of Genesis presented by *Paradise Lost*, combined with the image of Milton himself forcing his daughters to read and write for him. As they note, the word *bogey* means a devil, an evil spirit, or a goblin. The phrase Milton's bogey like the phrase Frankenstein's monster contains the potential for confusion within it. Just as people often confuse the monster *for* Frankenstein, readers may confuse the bogey for Milton. And, of course, that is part of the message of both Woolf and Mary Shelley: the creator bears some responsibility for the monster he has created.

The problem of interpreting the phrase Milton's bogey, however, lies in reconciling the rejection of Milton therein with the intense engagement with him earlier in the text and elsewhere in her work.[14] Gilbert and Gubar fail to note that, although it may have much older origins, *bogey* only appeared in print in the late nineteenth century.[15] There is a second sense of *bogey*, unmentioned by Gilbert and Gubar, from golf, which emerged shortly thereafter. According to the *OED*, English golf clubs in the 1890's established a course score—what we would now call *par*—against which players began to measure their own performance. When a golfer protested against the practice, he drew on a song about the bogey man popular at the time, complaining that he felt like he was playing a bogey, an imaginary opponent.[16] The phrase stuck, eventually taking on its current meaning of one stroke over par. This meaning, too, resonates with Woolf's use of the word.

The sentence in which the phrase Milton's bogey appears is long and complex. Looking past Milton's bogey is the fourth of five conditions, which, if met, may make it possible for Shakespeare's sister to return and write her masterpieces:

> For my belief is that if we live another century of so—I am talking of the common life which is the real life and not the little separate lives which we live as individuals—and have five hundred a year each of us and rooms of our own; if we have the habit of freedom and the courage to write exactly what we think; if we escape a little from the common sitting-room and see human beings not always in their relation to each other but in relation to reality; and the sky, too, and the trees or what-ever it may be in themselves; if we look past Milton's bogey, for no human being should shut out the view; if we face the fact, for it is a fact, that there is no arm to cling to, but that we go alone and that our rela-tion is to the world of reality and not only to the world of men and women, then the opportunity will come and the dead poet who was Shakespeare's sister will put on the body which she has so often laid down. (ARO, 113–44)

Interestingly, it is not a deposition of Milton's bogey that she seeks, but a *looking past*. To look past something is far less violent than to destroy it—as she does with the Angel in the House in "Professions for Women"; it is even less dramatic than casting it aside. Looking past something implies coexistence and independence whereas looking through term than looking through which turns the thing—Milton's bogey—into a lens or, perhaps, a phantom. Milton's bogey is an imag-inary opponent, to be looked past for a clear view of the fairway, of the best shot to the hole, of the sky. An imaginary opponent, devil or otherwise, can spur one on to a better performance, or, if not con-tained, he or she can completely throw one off the game. One may admire an imaginary opponent, but he or she is not a god. Milton's bogey is just another player. In making him so, Woolf is free to admire and dislike whatever she chooses in his work. What Woolf does with Milton in *A Room of One's Own*—drawing extensively upon "Lycidas," alluding to *Paradise Lost*, contrasting Milton's access to the library with her inability to enter because of her sex, and making his poetry into a bogey man—suggests in miniature the kind of resonant feminist response that I chart throughout this book.

Once the writer has overcome her bogeys, she still has to get her work published. The marketplace was as important to Woolf as the imagination and loomed as importantly in the near distance. In "Professions for Women" (1931), an essay arising out of *A Room of One's Own* and anticipating *Three Guineas*, Woolf recounts the story of how a young woman (at first *she*, then *I*) transforms herself from an amateur to a professional:

> But to tell you my story—it is a simple one. You have only got to figure to yourselves a girl in a bedroom with a pen in her hand. She had only to move that pen from left to right—from ten o'clock to one. Then it occurred to her to do what is simple and cheap enough after all—to slip a few of those pages into an envelope, fix a penny stamp in the corner, and drop the envelope into the red box at the corner. It was thus that I became a journalist; and my effort was rewarded on the first day of the following month—a very glorious day it was for me—by a letter from an editor containing a cheque for one pound ten shillings and sixpence. But to show you how little I deserve to be called a professional woman, how little I know of the struggles and difficulties of such lives, I have to admit that instead of spending that sum upon bread and butter, rent, shoes and stockings, or butcher's bills, I went out and bought a cat—a beautiful cat, a Persian cat, which very soon involved me in bitter disputes with my neighbours. (WW, 58)

What interests me here is the swift move Woolf makes from being a reader to writing for pay and the lack of discussion of craft or artistic ambition (topics that Woolf wrote eloquently about in many other places). Here, Woolf emphasizes the deep and important satisfactions of earning money. At the same time, the money goes, as she states, not to rent but to buy a cat. And not a Manx cat (the local exotic from the British Isles that she punned on in *A Room of One's Own*) or a Siamese cat (from far off East Asia), but a Persian cat from the Near East, a region that attracted her friend and lover Vita Sackville-West and excited Woolf's imagination. A Persian cat is fluffy and exotic and, as such, aligned with pleasure and the feminine things so often dismissed as trivial by men: "Speaking crudely, football and sport are 'important'; the worship of fashion, the buying of clothes 'trivial' " (ARO, 74). As such the cat stands for the many moments in Woolf's diaries that document the economic exchange of writing: sales for this book went toward a car, that one paid for the privy. In *The Pargiters*, we learn that the cat, "<in being of the male sex> soon involved me in rows with all my neighbours" (P, xxix).[17] This tomcat becomes another Woolfian representative—a miniature, mammalian flâneur, free to act out sexually in ways that Woolf is not. The Persian cat celebrates the idea of choice and freedom, the way earning money lets women choose the pleasures in their lives. At the same time, by dismissing idea of rent, Woolf distances herself from those professional women whose economic realities are harsher. This distance is not only snobbery but also a reminder to women about what they might aspire to: men have, for all these years, spent their extra money on cricket or football; likewise, women who earn money may also begin to imagine pleasant uses for it.

Read together, Milton's bogey and the Persian cat demonstrate the need to read Woolf's career holistically, keeping in mind the conundrums of literary predecessors, publication, and women's proposed stance toward both—as professionals and as private women. Reading with Dimock's resonance in mind clarifies Woolf's Milton and our Woolf, not to mention our continued ambivalence about professionalization. Woolf consistently sought to make it possible for Shakespeare's sister to be recognized and to nominate herself *as* Shakespeare's sister. Christine Froula makes a similar point about Woolf's letters to her brother Thoby when he was at college: "This aspiring Shakespeare's sister is not too much abashed to criticize Shakespeare's characters or to pit her judgment against Thoby's."[18] For all her well-documented anxiety about lacking formal education, Woolf, from the first, sought to match her intellect and imagination against the best rivals available: her brother and Shakespeare himself.

In focusing on the intersection of Woolf's feminism with her reading, I have focused on how her pervasively feminist outlook affected and was affected by her development as a writer. Each chapter traces a single aspect of Woolf's feminism as it develops from the beginning of her career to the end, looking at her feminism in the contexts of nation, the imagination and memory, the public sphere, and fame. Thus, we travel across Woolf's writing life four times, with different emphases and outcomes each time. This recursive structure resists a simplified determinism and results in a rich portrait of the development of Woolf's thinking. Patterns do emerge. The first half of the book, emphasizing imagination, is also the most closely engaged with her reading in her girlhood. By contrast, the second half of the book, on the more public life of a writer, analyzes Woolf's reading of writers she first encountered early in her professional life.

Different novels emerge as central in my discussion of each aspect of Woolf's feminism. For example, her engagement with the classical Greek tradition was a passionate intellectual investment, and it emerges most vividly in two novels that are also widely considered her best, *Mrs. Dalloway* and *To the Lighthouse*. Before her lessons in the Greek language, however, when she was a young child, Woolf gobbled volumes of Richard Hakluyt's collection of Elizabethan travel narratives. Thus it is perhaps to be expected that Hakluyt's work, so central to the formation of her imagination, rang in her ears when she wrote her first novel, *The Voyage Out*. More surprising—and, ultimately, more telling—is the fact that she did not return to Hakluyt in her last novel, *Between the Acts*. There, Woolf's Elizabethan world is no longer global but local. Documenting Hakluyt's influence on her career through the 1920s casts into sharp relief the significance of his fading from sight in the final decade of Woolf's life and checks the current critical impulse to depict her as more communitarian and more liberal as she aged: she certainly did not look beyond England's borders in her last book. Again, one might expect that Woolf's reading of her eighteenth-century journalist precursors would emerge as an important theme in *Night and Day* and *The Years*, her most realist novels, but the public sphere's centrality to *Mrs. Dalloway* and *Orlando* show her engaging with ideas of what it means to be a woman in public in the 1920s, at the very moment of her emergence into fame. Finally, fame itself is the subject of the final chapter on Woolf's reading of Byron. *Jacob's Room* and *The Waves*, both so centrally occupied with a young man's death, are natural places in which to find Woolf weighing the relationship between martyrdom and fame. Yet, *Mrs. Dalloway* does not contain significant allusions to Byron. Woolf's most profound meditation on a soldier's death eschews the light, Byronic touch.

Woolf's nonfiction is equally important to this study. Three of the chapters—on nation, the public sphere, and fame—culminate with readings of *Three Guineas*. *A Room of One's Own* shadows the book, playing a prominent role in both the introduction and the epilogue. *A Room of One's Own* and Woolf's 1925 essay collection, *The Common Reader*, as much as her novels, form the heart of the book. More than many recent critics who have singled out Woolf's later writings for special praise, I have consistently found her writing to be most interesting, most engaging, and most complex at the height of her career.[19] Indeed, for this study, the year 1925 is something of an *annus mirabilis*, which saw not only the publication of *Mrs. Dalloway* but also the essays "On Not Knowing Greek" and "The Elizabethan Lumber Room."

Taking Woolf's commitment to feminism as my starting point, I examine the shifting nuances of her feminism in response to the central political questions of her art. Through her reading and translation of Greek literature, Woolf found the source of English patriarchal nationalism, but through her reading of Aeschylus, Sophocles, and Sappho, she found a lineage of antimartial, feminist pride within the Western literary tradition. Through her reading in the British Library's Reading Room, Woolf encountered the regulated national memory born in the Renaissance and embodied in Victorian architecture, but through her reading of Elizabethan travelogues collected by Richard Hakluyt, Woolf found a miscellaneous collection offering imaginative freedom and bearing witness to the power and value of the idiosyncratic, exploratory, and serendipitous memory over the official, possessive, and organized one.

When she turned from the tradition that both nourished and excluded her to the public world she hoped to enter as a great writer, her reading continued to influence her. In her readings from the eighteenth century, Woolf found an earlier version of the gender wars that marked her own period, but in her reading of Addison and his exploitation of the spectator's stance (quiet in the streets, opinionated in print), she found a strategy that she could make her own. Finally, through her reading in Romanticism, she found many connections between that aesthetic and her own: the high valuation of friendship, siblings, and companionate marriage; the intense devotion to art; the passionate belief in ordinary citizens speaking out on political issues; and the commitment to putting into words the sublime moments of ordinary life. Still, only through her reading of Byron did she find a way to court fame and stand clearly for a political point of view while preserving the privacy needed to create art.

Out of the hundreds of writers that Woolf wrote about in her career, I focus on four: Sappho, Hakluyt, Addison, and Byron. They function here as synecdoches, useful metaphors for how Woolf's engagement with a period in the literary tradition helped her understand and refine her own attitude to a particular aspect of feminist thought. That is, since Britons regularly understood their nation through allusion to Greek literature, we can witness Woolf's feminist resistance to mainline nationalism through observing her allusions to Sappho. There is also a strong modernist precedent for such selectivity. In 1932, Woolf published an essay series on the turn from the eighteenth century to Romanticism entitled "Four Figures." (These essays were originally published serially in the *New York Herald Tribune* and reprinted in the *Second Common Reader*.) Woolf focused not on Wordsworth, Coleridge, Shelley, and Keats, but on William Cowper, Beau Brummell, Mary Wollstonecraft, and Dorothy Wordsworth. Woolf's choice of these figures is deeply indebted to Lytton Strachey whose *Eminent Victorians* (1918) set the standard for choosing influential but not monumental subjects as a means of illuminating literary and cultural history. In focusing on Sappho, Hakluyt, Addison, and Byron, my book echoes this modernist methodology, hypothesizing that figures just to the side of their age's greatness (for even Byron's fame did not seriously threaten Wordsworth's reputation) provide a richer cultural context for studying Woolf's resonant rethinking of tradition.

Unlike Strachey's and Woolf's works, however, my book does not offer profiles but rather uses these four unlikely figures to gain a purchase on the development of Woolf's art and her feminism. Other figures could—would—lead to different arguments. I chose these four because together their importance to Woolf gives a rounded picture of her feminism and separately her admiration for each is something of a surprise. A writer so private about her own sexuality might not be expected to love Sappho; few readers today ever come across Hakluyt's name, let alone read his collection multiple times; and Addison's and Byron's deeply entrenched patriarchal viewpoints make them unlikely models for a feminist. Yet Sappho keeps our attention trained on the fragment; Hakluyt emphasizes abundance and miscellany, and he also exemplifies the depth of Woolf's reading; Addison, through the idea of the spectator, points to the contrast between print journalism and the coffeehouses as Samuel Johnson could never have done; Byron brings together the pathos of early death with the pleasures of wit. I hope that this method of tracing a writer's engagement with a precursor as an index of her intellectual development will feel as rich to others as it has to me. Too often critics tracing a writer's reading stop short of the kind of synthesis at the heart of this study, in which reading, writing, and political opinion inform each other. For me, once we know what someone—Woolf—has read, then the really interesting questions begin. Those questions need not be strictly literary; they can, as I hope this book shows, extend to the whole range of a writer's engagement with humanity.

In following Woolf's eccentric historicism and letting these four figures stand synecdochally for her reading of the literary past, I demonstrate how she creates resonances and feminist possibilities for her art far beyond what other critics, following Woolf's story of Shakespeare's sister, have recognized. Chapter 1 explores Woolf's three main uses of the Greek past: (1) the national, in which she uses her knowledge of Greek to establish a connection with the English gentleman; (2) the feminist, in which she celebrates a pantheon of heroic women, linking them to her contemporaries; (3) and the aesthetic, in which the celebration of the Sapphic fragment demonstrates her commitment to adapting and transforming the past. While drawing from Benedict Anderson's idea of the nation as an imagined community and Partha Chatterjee's revision of the nation as fragmented, I offer a new way to understand how Woolf retained and transformed a tradition she loved into a source of resistance to patriarchy. Her admiration of the ancient Greek canon tempers both her occasional nationalist as well as her feminist moments under the sign of the fragment. Recognizing education as ideology, Woolf replaces patriarchal Greece with a fragmented Sapphic one. She celebrates the aesthetic of the fragment in order to disrupt complacency about "our" nearness to or distance from Greek culture.

Chapter 2 turns from grander ideas of nation to more local English ideas of memory and imagination; in particular, it examines Woolf's sense of the role of exploration and empire in stocking the mind and the English language of the Elizabethan era with images. For Virginia Woolf, memory is inseparable from writing. Following the social history of her day, Woolf believes that writing only becomes a significant cultural force in England between the period of Chaucer and Shakespeare. In "The Elizabethan Lumber Room" (1925), she documents the transformation of English from the humble, pragmatic language of ordinary folk into the more worldly and historically self-aware language of Shakespeare. In doing so, Woolf singles out Hakluyt's special role in bringing English to maturity. Hakluyt, more an editor than a writer, collected an enormous compendium of travel documents—narratives of voyages, charters, requests for funding, accounts of battle—in the late 1500s. His work, eventually running to well over a million words, documented England's quest to emerge into an empire, and serves as a source of images, knowledge, and memory for English poets, especially those who did not travel much abroad, including Shakespeare and, much later, Woolf herself.

Chapter 3 turns from the worlds of nation and memory to those of authorship. Through Woolf's ambivalent identification with Joseph Addison, author and editor, with Richard Steele, of *The Spectator* (1711–12, 1714), this chapter charts Woolf's emergence into the public sphere. At first, Woolf accepts the prevailing mainstream model—still close to an eighteenth-century one—of anonymous publication (as was then the practice at the *TLS* (Times Literary Supplement), her most frequent early outlet for reviews). From 1919 onward, however, as her career becomes more established, she looks more critically at prevailing practices, expressing increasing feminist skepticism about the place (or lack of place) for women in the public sphere. In *Three Guineas*, Woolf's skepticism reaches its greatest intensity. Even there, however, in advocating the notion of an Outsider's Society, she does so in the context of an imaginary letter to a male barrister. In short, from the beginning, Woolf seeks to participate in the public sphere, and even when most disenchanted with its politics and most vocal about her own feminism, she works to maintain communication with mainstream (and male) readers.

From the challenge of going public, we turn in Chapter 4 to the challenge of fame. What better figure through whom to explore Woolf's complex attitude to fame than Lord Byron who was, arguably, the first celebrity poet? As a celebrity, his life and his reputation act as cautionary tales for Woolf, who maintains her privacy not by being reclusive but through carefully managed publicity. Two of Woolf's diary entries from 1918 and 1930 offer extended meditations on Byron. Readings of these two entries along with analyses of Byron and Byronism in *Jacob's Room* and *The Waves* form the basis of Chapter 4. The chapter concludes with a discussion of Woolf's changed perspective in the 1930s. Then, Byron serves primarily as a negative example: his martyrdom comes as an increasingly dangerous example, particularly in light of the Spanish Civil War. Through Byron one sees Woolf's shifting attitudes to fame: its effect on one's financial and intellectual independence, its intrusions into one's privacy, and its political clout (and responsibility).

Finally, in the epilogue, I once again work synecdochally, turning to Woolf's surprisingly resonant appearance in the works of three mid- to late-twentieth century African writers: Doris Lessing, Nawal El Saadawi, and Ama Ata Aidoo. Although Woolf's own views about Africa were often especially parochial and racist, these three important women writers from three very distinct regions of Africa (the south, the north, and the west) have turned to Woolf and transformed Woolfian thought much as Woolf herself did with Sappho, Hakluyt, Addison, and Byron. My starting point is the moment in *A Room of One's Own* in which the narrator reads the newspaper, noting that the front page alone betrays the complete dominance of patriarchy in the mainstream print culture of Woolf's day. In texts by each of the three African authors, the female narrator experiences a similar "splitting off of consciousness" (ARO, 97) while reading the newspaper. The newspaper, then, serves in each of their texts as a metaphor for an encounter with patriarchy. My focus on women writers from Africa underscores one of Dimock's points: one mark of literary endurance is the continuing resonance of a literary work for "the reader not implied, not welcome." One of Woolf's limitations may have been her inability to imagine African readers or writers; one of her strengths, however, is their ability to imagine, revise, and respond to her.

Ultimately, I seek to contribute to the current revaluation of Woolf's feminism through this eclectic historicism, shaped by Woolf's reading and gesturing toward the many readerships of Woolf. If Woolf once found readers who elevated her aesthetic achievements while denying her political significance, many more recent American critics have sought to transform Woolf from a writer "ethereal and remote" to one "polemical and close."[20] While the former assessment of Woolf is dying out, the latter branch of Woolf criticism remains troublesome in its insistence on her radicalism in all things, her rightness, her anticipation of the most advanced views that we ourselves hold on feminism, gay rights, antifascism, animal rights, and access to education for the economically disadvantaged. For though all of these ideas exist in Woolf's writing, there is much else, including racism, snobbery, and impatience with group politics.

In recent years a more measured assessment of Woolf's politics is beginning to emerge. This view admits her contradictions and limitations while exploring her vision and her strength. Just as recent critics like Brenda Silver, Christine Froula, and Julia Briggs have reemphasized in various ways the centrality of reading to Woolf's literary life and her feminism, I also assert that Woolf's importance to educated women around the world derives much more from her legacy as a feminist artist and theorist—from the goals she set for herself as a reader and writer—than from her feminist social activism.

Woolf's feminism, which was fundamental to her character and always evolving, was expressed in the goals she set for herself as a writer: to challenge the hegemony of the Oxbridge education with its patriarchal canon not by overthrowing that canon but by revolutionizing the way we read; to be a great artist, of course, but to make a living through her art by finding an audience and selling books. Nearly everything Woolf did as a writer was done to first clear space for her imagination to roam and then establish a place for herself amidst the great writers of the literary tradition. She took the craft of writing seriously. She also saw how very few women had had the opportunity to do the same and, if they did, how few got treated with the kind of respect such artful dedication warrants. Woolf emphasized imaginative freedom, access to education, and the extension of recognition to women's achievements. Her sense of irony led her to puncture the pretenses of her society, to show how the old assumptions held hidden corruptions, how those corruptions were damaging for all and were especially corrosive for women. From the Dreadnought Hoax of 1910 to the pageant she presented within her final novel in 1941, Woolf worked to tease her countrymen and women out of their most cherished beliefs. She was able to do so in large part because she read her own literary history skeptically and critically, making it her own, reshaping and abandoning it as she saw fit, concerned not with orthodoxy but with how texts resonated for her. Woolf's interest in reading that is at once generous and critical teaches us how to read her, allowing us to continue reading even as we hear things that no longer please us quite so well.

# CHAPTER 1

# O Sister Swallow: Sapphic Fragments as English Literature in Virginia Woolf

*For it is vain and foolish to talk of knowing Greek, since in our ignorance we should be at the bottom of any class of schoolboys.*

Virginia Woolf

*There is a great gulf fixed between us and them, which no willingness to make allowance for the difference of ages and countries would enable us to pass.*

Benjamin Jowett

*How far removed is their hidden meaning from revelation, how close can it be brought by the knowledge of this remoteness?*

Walter Benjamin

In the feminist pamphlet *Three Guineas* (1938), Woolf linked gender and citizenship, writing, "As a woman, I have no country" (3G, 109). Today, we hear in that phrase not only a refusal of nationalism-as-patriotism, but also a gesture toward a new global citizenship, which is differently constituted to welcome women and is imagined in opposition to mainline nationalism. For some time critics have made this into Woolf's most important statement on nationalism.[1] They have emphasized the link Woolf makes between the resistance of antifascist women and Antigone's refusal to obey Creon. But this progressive, antipatriarchal sense of the legacy of Greek literature was not always Woolf's. Early in her career, she acceded to the bourgeois habit of using her knowledge of Greek as cultural capital. Aware that few women knew Greek, she willingly distances herself from working women in order to forge an alliance with educated men, a gesture she explicitly repudiates in *Three Guineas*. At the same time, her female tutors introduced her to a counterhistory of Greek heroines while providing a living model of how the discipline of Greek can be open to all. To explore how Woolf went from this bifurcated but otherwise conventional bourgeois Victorian idea of the classics to the antinational vision of Antigone in *Three Guineas*, this chapter takes a close look at major texts from the mid-1920s: *Mrs. Dalloway* (1925), *To the Lighthouse* (1927), and the essay "On Not Knowing Greek" from *The Common Reader* (1925). During these years, Woolf emphasized our distance from Greece: how little we know of the ancient Greek language and culture and the mystery of our continued fascination and attraction with it nonetheless. Her metaphor for this imperfect knowledge was the distinctly modernist one of the fragment, invoking at once Cubist aesthetics, archaeology, and the slow and interrupted work of translation. This emphasis on the fragment enabled her to explain the coexistence of competing and incompatible invocations of Greece in the England of her day. If we only know Greek imperfectly through fragments, it can at once symbolize many things: heroism, access to education, mourning, and sublime poetic achievement. Finally, it becomes possible for Woolf to imagine that emphasizing the fragmentary nature of our understanding might shift the resonance of Greek literature. If others could share her sense of Greek as fragmented, they might not so confidently link it to England and British Empire, and the importance of Greek could shift from national to international. Critics have recently emphasized how Woolf's "view of Greece is intertwined with her view of the British empire."[2] Taking Woolf's anti-imperialism for granted, this chapter looks at her more complex relationship with her own Englishness, especially at her changing sense of the connection between the classical Greek canon and the English ideas of nation. Understanding this evolution explains how Woolf's feminist reading of Greek allowed her to continue to love it even as she rejected nationalist English Hellenism.

Woolf's beliefs that "as a woman I have no country" and that she is a solidly English writer coexist because of her reading of Greek. Like her Victorian forbears, Woolf studied Greek, read Greek, and alluded to Greek throughout her life. In her own death-ridden childhood, Greek lessons were her therapy: an intense mental labor to distract her from and alleviate her sorrow.[3] Ironically, these lessons also showed her the cultural function of Greek women as mourners bound by tradition to lamentation and, in a violent civilization, certain to be touched by untimely death and its attendant grief. When Woolf translated the *Agamemnon* of Aeschylus in preparation for writing "On Not Knowing Greek" (1925), she, like generations of readers before her, found "heroism itself" and "fidelity itself" (CR1, 27), and found those qualities admirable. Yet she wrote both "On Not Knowing Greek" and *Mrs. Dalloway* in 1925, in the aftermath of World War I, a war she opposed. She explored the ravages of shell shock in *Mrs. Dalloway* through the character of Septimus Smith, whose delusions include thinking that he hears the birds singing in Greek.[4] The link between Greek and mourning persists to the end of her career: the title of the serialized American publication of *Three Guineas* (1938) was "Women Must Weep—or Unite Against War," and, inside that text, Woolf refers on several important occasions to Antigone. She recognized Greek literature's part in the patriarchal and martial past; she knew how the Greeks, accepting the inevitably of violent death, relegated women to the role of weeping for and burying their men, and she still always loved Greek literature.

Throughout her career, Woolf explores and challenges the classist, sexist, and martial-imperial slant of much classical education. In doing so, she consistently seeks to separate Greek itself from the uses to which the educated English society put it. This emphasis on ancient Greece itself, however, in no way tempts Woolf to concoct her own counternarratives refuting the dominant ones as, for example, H. D. did. Instead, she celebrates the impossibility of knowing Greek except through fragments. In this way, while insisting on the consequences of hero worship—especially loss and grief—more than heroism itself, Woolf also attempts to undo the damaging association of Greek with nation- and empire-building while retaining a place for Greek literature in the imagination—hers and England's.

## Greek Lessons, 1897–1924

In 1897, when she was 15, Virginia Woolf began to study Greek. She studied first at King's College with Dr. George Warr; shortly thereafter, she began private lessons, first with Clara Pater (who also tutored her in Latin) and then with Janet Case, with whom she formed a lasting friendship. These lessons were the young Virginia Stephen's chief experience of "paid for education" (3G,4), begun as therapy, suitable mental labor for an intelligent, grieving girl. (Her mother had died in 1895; her half-sister Stella died in 1897.) The lessons continued off and on for four years. From the beginning, she strove to find a balance between her love of poetry and the accuracy demanded by tutors and translators. For example, of Case, Woolf writes, "she used to pull me up ruthlessly in the middle of some beautiful passage with 'Mark the *ar*' " (PA, 182). She might complain that the translator "Jebb splits [Greek] up into separate and uncongenial accuracies" (L, 2.221), or feel "generally humiliated to find how much Jebb is able to see," but she also expresses a writer's confidence: "my only doubt is whether he doesn't see too much" (D, 1.184). Woolf's formal study of Greek literature as a young woman culminated in a trip to Greece in 1906. Her diary of that trip records, with alternating comedy and wonder, the mood of a young woman checking modern sites against ancient reading. Overall, studying Greek was central to Woolf's intellectual development. Andrew McNeillie asserts that Woolf's "aesthetic values" are based more in her "extensive independent reading in Plato, her fascination with 'Greek' " than in Walter Pater or G. E. Moore.[5] Very early on, "Woolf entertained the Hellenist idea of a direct mental link between the ancients and the English, between those at the beginning of civilization and those at its culmination," a position she would come to revise as early as 1912 (with the publication of her first novel) and would eventually reject.[6]

Allusions to Greek literature appear throughout her career: Woolf's brother Thoby "is a Greek God" (L, 1.72) as is Jacob Flanders, the protagonist of *Jacob's Room*. She translated Aeschylus's *Agamemnon* in 1925. The ghost of her friend the classicist Jane Harrison makes an appearance in *A Room of One's Own* (1929). In the 1930s, she plays with varying significations of Antigone, from the lauded masterpiece to an antiauthoritarian polemic: *Antigone* is a work of "great literature," translated by the luckless Edward Pargiter in *The Years* (1937) while it is invoked as a play about an antifascist, feminist heroine in *Three Guineas* (1938). And in her last novel, *Between the Acts* (1941), Isa tries to write poetry in spite of being a big-boned woman who had "never looked like Sappho" (BTA, 16).[7] This, then, is the bare outline of Woolf's engagement with Greek. Other critics have filled in the details both of Woolf's early education and her many allusions; more is being done by those working with her Greek notebooks and translations. My purpose here is to suggest the fruit of that intense engagement, to show how Woolf's radical feminist rejection of nation emerged from her critique of the English habit of linking ancient Greece with modern England.

When the Stephen family prescribed Greek lessons for their daughter, they were participating in a centuries-old tradition of classical education for the English elite. Greek in particular was seen as a suitably impractical genteel pursuit. Though Latin had its uses for the aristocracy and intelligentsia as recently as the seventeenth century, it had been many centuries since knowledge of classical Greek was, in any strict pragmatic sense, useful. In the eighteenth century, rather than abandon an impractical curriculum, gentlemen and the tutors to their sons found a new justification for classical education: "their 'useless' knowledge comes to stand . . . as a pure sign of their noble status."[8] At the same time, translation made classical literature more widely available, meaning that, in John Guillory's words, "For us, Plato and Aristotle, Virgil and Dante, are great works of literature *in English*. The translation of the 'classics' into one's own vernacular is a powerful institutional buttress of imaginary cultural continuities; it confirms the nationalist agenda by permitting the easy appropriation of texts in foreign languages."[9] The increasing availability of translations meant that the English could simultaneously widen the range of cultural sources appealing to the Greek past (as in such celebrations of translation as Keats's "On First Looking into Chapman's Homer") while buttressing the prestige of classical texts. During Woolf's lifetime, as the study of classics in England advanced to keep pace with German scholarship, the confidence reported by Guillory began to wane. Ultimately, seeing ancient Greece as distant came to be the highest mark of intellectual sophistication. Late Victorian Hellenism, for all its innovations, continued the long-standing tradition of educating elite Britons in the Greco-Roman tradition. Becoming an English citizen was still bound up in an educational system that was focused on Latin and Greek, and the content of Latin and Greek literature taught the English what it was to be a citizen.[10] Those who single out Greek literature for praise as distinct from Latin were part of a large liberal minority seeking to confirm the value of classical education without endorsing the militarism and imperialism associated with Rome.[11] Virginia Woolf participated actively, intensely, and creatively in this national practice of valuing a classical education and the liberal Victorian practice, which was begun by John Stuart Mill and continued through, for example, Walter Pater, of reserving special admiration for Greece. Citizenship, in a Greek rather than a Roman context, connotes the city-state, not empire, and thus, for English liberals who were uneasy or ambivalent about imperialism Hellenism could be imagined as compatible with what would become a "Little England" mentality.

Woolf's most conventional Hellenism resides in her descriptions and memories of travel. When she first visited Greece (at the age of 24), Woolf sensed that, at its roots, village life in Greece and England had much in common. On that trip, she noted that "the narrow streets of Athens reminded us of St. Ives" (PA, 330) and that "the coast is very steep, & gray; like Cornish cliffs" (PA, 338). These analogies persist throughout her career. In 1932, on her second trip to Greece, she returned to the analogy, reflecting "I could love Greece, as an old woman, so I think, as I once loved Cornwall, as a child" (D, 4.97). She believes that in both the Greek village and the English village, "life is simply sorted out into its main elements" (CR1, 24). She does not emphasize the noble lineage of tragic figures. Instead, she distills the plots into local drama. What interests her about the characters is not their nobility, but their familiarity—with each other and to her as a reader: "Queens and Princesses . . . stand at the door bandying words like village women, with a tendency . . . to rejoice in language, to split phrases into slices, to be intent on verbal victory" (CR1, 25). For Woolf, the way readers imagine a world wholly different from England is no less extraordinary for being quite simple. When we read Sophocles

> at once the mind begins to fashion itself surroundings. It makes some background, even of the most provisional sort . . .; it imagines some village in a remote part of the country, near the sea. Even nowadays such villages are to be found in the wilder parts of England, and as we enter them we can scarcely help feeling that here, in this cluster of cottages, cut off from rail or city, are all the elements of a perfect existence. (CR1, 24)

This could be a description of Rodmell, the small Sussex town in which Woolf spent much of her adult life. Thus, Woolf makes the familiar gesture of transplanting Greek literature onto English soil.[12] But where other writers make such connections unconsciously, with confidence that England is the sure inheritor of Greek civilization, Woolf asks us to pause over the distortion involved: "It is the climate that is impossible. If we try to think of Sophocles here, we must annihilate the smoke and the damp and the thick wet mists" (CR1, 24). Returning from Greece in 1932, Woolf again delights in the ephemeral similarity that is not sameness: "just for a moment England & Greece stood side by side, each much enlivened by the other" (D, 4.100). Crucially, England is not the inheritor of a Greek tradition here; rather, it is simply similar to Greece. In Edward Said's terms, the relationship between the two nations is not dynastic but adjacent.[13]

Even in this rather conventional connection between Greece and England, we see the elements of Woolf's more surprising insistence on distance. Thus, for example, in a 1931 essay, working women in England have "no Greek hills or Mediterranean bays in their dreams" (MWG, xxiii). Shakespeare's words may run in their veins, as part of their natural English inheritance, but one has to have the education to read Greek and the money to travel to Greece in order to feel and know the connection between England and Greece. For Woolf, this lack of a connection simultaneously indicts social inequality and cancels her own ability to befriend or even align herself with women of such unfurnished imaginations. Elsewhere, she contrasts the "cruelty in Greek tragedy," "the lightning-quick, sneering, out-of-doors manner" with "our English brutality" (CR1, 25). This difference, Woolf proposes, evolved out of the need to communicate with a large outdoor audience. Thus, in contrast to the English theatrical tradition, the Greeks favored familiar stories with lots of drama and dancing that is quite different from the English theatrical tradition. To understand the Greeks, she seems to say, we first need to imagine a place that is not so different from our own home, and then to attend carefully to the details of difference, and imagine their significance.

If women of the English working class cannot share her thrill at the connections between England and Greece, men of her own class can. And Woolf was not above using her knowledge of Greek to insist on her right to participate in male-dominated intellectual discourse. A letter of February 25, 1918 to her friend Saxon Sydney-Turner exemplifies this willingness to use Greek as cultural capital. In that letter Woolf juxtaposes praise for Aeschylus, Sophocles, and Shakespeare with a classist, racist rant against Leonard Merrick, whose novels she was reviewing.[14] In associating Shakespeare with the classics in contrast to Merrick, one of the "mortals," Woolf claims as her own the most conventional kind of literary good taste.[15] Woolf's elaborate letter aims to mend a rift in their friendship:

> Dearest Saxon,
>
> Neither of us (I speak for myself at least) was "hurt" by the silence between us . . . but a sense of your being possibly unhappy did hang about us and make us wish . . ., to see you, or hear of you or have you in the room. I don't think that being happy makes one want ones friends less—Is this partly selfish? Perhaps it is; but not all your craft shall persuade me that my feeling for you has more than a thread of vice in it; the rest is heavenly true. (L, 2.220)

The tone here is of a patient friend addressing an oversensitive, even wounded, one. Woolf gently defends herself and reassures Saxon of her ongoing affection. She continues in a new paragraph, writing "Perhaps you don't realise those ['the rest is heavenly true'] are Shakespeare's words. I'm thinking of reading Measure for Measure this afternoon" (L, 2.220).[16] What Woolf is doing here—gently soothing her friend's feelings, admitting to a thread of vice, but no more—sets the tone for the complexity of her deployment of cultural capital throughout the letter. Woolf continues, "Still the classics *are* very pleasant, and even, I must confess, the mortals"—like Leonard Merrick (L, 2.220). Later in the same letter she writes of her dissatisfaction with Jebb's edition of Sophocles, adding, "I can remember Jebb coming to dinner with us . . . I there and then saw and perhaps said that he had the soul and innumerable legs of a black beetle" (L, 2.221). Since she has already professed to her enjoyment of "the Electra, which has made me plan to read all Greek straight through" (L, 2.220), such comments—about the inadequacies of a translation (and the translator) or the pleasures of a middlebrow writer—come after her assertion of her cultural authority.

Her remarks on Jebb remind Saxon—who got a Double First in the Classical Tripos at Cambridge—that her Greek is good enough to comment on the merits of a translation.[17] As such, they reestablish the intellectual basis of their friendship. Misunderstandings aside, Woolf emphasizes that she shares with Saxon a commitment to reading—especially the serious reading of Greek. In contrast, her comments on Merrick do not affirm her interest in reading popular fiction; they link literary quality and race. Woolf makes Merrick a scapegoat:

> a poor unappreciated second-rate pot-boiling writer . . . whom I deduce to be a negro, mulatto or quadroon; at any rate he has a grudge against the world, and might have done much better if he hadn't at the age of 20 married a chorus girl, had by her 15 coffee coloured brats and lived for the rest of time in a villa in Brixton, where he ekes out a living by giving lessons in elocution to the natives. (L, 2.220–21)[18]

This essentializing, racist, mock-critical "insight" is followed by the taunt, "Now if this were about a Greek writer, it would be what is called constructive criticism, wouldn't it?" Woolf knows she is being ugly here and defies her imagined censors. She defends herself by arguing that the kind of judgment she is making—that personal and economic factors hamper Merrick's art—passes as "constructive" when applied to the Greek, the safely dead. Still, she does not write such criticism of Greek literature. In fact, nowhere in Woolf's writings on the Greeks, be they formal or informal, is she so nasty in connecting biography and literary output. Furthermore, as Woolf herself notes elsewhere, for the thin-skinned writer, there is really no such thing as "constructive" criticism. She writes unsympathetically (and inaccurately) about how Merrick's (imagined) race and taste in women have made him angry in ways that hamper his writing—an argument that she would come to adopt on behalf of women writers in *A Room of One's Own*. Woolf's joke about her cruelly reductive judgment of Merrick casts an unflattering light on her willingness to play with stereotypes. Susan Sellers calls this kind of mockery "the expression of what is outlawed from social intercourse," but that may give Woolf too much credit.[19] In *The Years* (1937), Sarah Pargiter and her cousin North overcome their discomfort with each other by agreeing that the Jew down the hall is dirty. In this episode, I think critics are right to see Woolf investigating the phenomenon of scapegoating, rather than practicing it. Decades earlier, however, Woolf makes a similar gesture in her own voice by making a scapegoat of Merrick to smooth the tensions between Saxon and herself.

None of this racial and class prejudice shows up in the finished *TLS* review where Woolf brushes aside Merrick's (middlebrow) reputation to look at what it is like to read the books. There she judges him on how well he seems to have achieved his writerly goals. In spite of all of her nastiness in private, the review insists on the pleasure of reading him. In so doing, she transforms an aesthetic contrast into an adjacent pleasure. Instead of seeing Merrick and Sophocles as distant points on a linear scale, she sees them as very different writers whose books are shelved together in the same library. This more populist notion of reading gets further development in "Phases of Fiction," "On Being Ill," and other essays on reading. Woolf's prejudices and her efforts to confine them to her private writings are not news. The crucial gesture for our purposes, however, is her use of Shakespeare and the Greeks— the conventional contrast to the middlebrow—to reestablish intimacy with a friend. Here, Woolf's Greece is the Victorian Greece—imperial, connected, and prestigious.

So ingrained is the British habit of seeing itself as linked to (if not, in spite of all the obstacles of time and space, descended from) ancient Greece that even in an essay committed to praising Woolf for her resistance to imperialism, Gillian Beer connects the British Empire to the Greeks: the island is to the English imagination "as the city was to the Greeks."[20] The fiction of the island nation, in which a democratic government arose naturally from the terrain, fostered England's sense of kinship with Greece. This sense of kinship persisted into Woolf's day and, as Beer's ready analogy shows, our own. Beer's continuing unconscious assumption that there is a connection between twentieth-century England and ancient Greece suggests that there is still reason to discuss Woolf's relation to nationalism in the wake of Beer's work. For Beer, Woolf desires to be connected to her fellow citizens while circumventing the trappings of nation. Thus, the momentary, accidental community of people trying to decipher sky-writing in *Mrs. Dalloway* becomes a model of how "Virginia Woolf's disaffection from the heavily bonded forms of English society often expresses itself paradoxically . . . as affection and play."[21] Beer quotes a 1941 letter to Ethel Smyth in which Woolf insists that her love of English literature is her "only patriotism" (L, 6.469). Of this, Beer writes, "Woolf's insistence on her own 'unpatriotic' relation with England is nearly always formulated in relation to a concession."[22] For Beer, this signifies her resistance. But the concession of patriotic feeling interests me. In conceding the existence of some fragment of England that does make her proud to be English, Woolf is not simply rejecting patriotism, but trying to find a way to express national feeling that does not compromise her antipatriarchal, anti-imperial, and pacifist views. Although Woolf was opposed to patriotism, especially in its official manifestations, she was also eager to claim her kinship with Shakespeare and was quick to note her distance from anyone who seemed not quite English. Woolf's opposition to nationalism was neither simple nor total. Furthermore, sometimes the alternative expressions of national pride she finds are just outright expressions of racial and class bias.

Late in her career, Woolf again uses her knowledge of the classics to forge an alliance with men of her class—a tactic that stands in tension with her feminist politics. Throughout *Three Guineas* (1938), in spite of her claim to belong to no nation, Woolf speaks as an *English* woman and addresses her appeal to the barrister, a fellow countryman. When Woolf ironically describes her astonishment that she, a woman, was asked how to prevent war, she tells a joke with a distinctly English set of cultural references. She writes that such a request from a barrister to a woman is as if "the Duke of Devonshire, in his star and garter, stepped down into the kitchen and said to the maid who was peeling potatoes with a smudge on her cheek: 'Stop your potato peeling, Mary, and help me to construe this rather difficult passage in Pindar' " (3G, 85). This passage plays with upper class assumptions, making a joke of both the Duke and the barrister: she knows that both love to imagine themselves reading Pindar, famous for his heroic odes, that both still see the classics as worthy moral teachers for the young and as honorable leisurely pursuits for the middle-aged, and that neither "gentleman" imagines that a female servant shares any of these feelings.[23] "Mary" is not the primary subject of this meditation, but Woolf portrays the lack of shared education as the central barrier in communication across class and gender lines. Woolf knows that she can, however wickedly, forge an alliance with educated men through reference to the classics.

If these were Woolf's only comments on Greek literature, they would hardly be distinguishable from her other belletristic opinions. But with Clara Pater and, more importantly, Janet Case, her tutors, and Jane Harrison, her friend, Woolf learned to associate the study of Greek with feminism. In fact, it was the brilliant and formidable Case who first introduced Woolf to feminist politics.[24] So, through her female tutors, Woolf focused on these aspects of the canon that her brothers might have overlooked while replicating the homosocial atmosphere that was central to classical education in Britain. The feminist legacy of Pater, Case, and Harrison, however, does not take the form of a straightforward recuperation of Greek heroines. Instead, their intellectual independence combined with Woolf's aesthetic to help her grasp the centrality of mourning and grief to the women of ancient Greece and to transform the fact of Sappho's fragments into a protest against using literature as propaganda.

## Not Knowing Greek, the 1920s

Woolf's most sustained piece on Greek literature is the 1925 essay "On Not Knowing Greek," written specially for *The Common Reader*.[25] The essay begins with a discussion of the historical, linguistic, and cultural gap between ancient Greece and twentieth-century England. Again and again in the essay Woolf asks whether there is anything to the English national obsession with ancient Greece. What kind of a massive illusion is it, she asks, to feel close to a people from whom "we" are not descended and about whom we know so little? As she discusses drama and poetry (genres between which she makes little distinction here), she connects the Greek setting to English village life and then quickly moves on to discuss the alienation created by the Greek aesthetic of simplicity. From the drama, she moves to discuss dramatic elements in Plato's dialogues, and finally the *Odyssey*. With each turn, she rejects what initially feels familiar to her (English) contemporaries about Greek literature—Greek villages remind us of English ones, we feel like students in Plato's academy, or we race through Homer like "children . . . wanting to find out what happens next" (CR1, 37)—to emphasize our distance from ancient Greece, how little we know, how different we are. Two things emerge as certain, however: that the Greeks understand sorrow and that we only partially understand them. Throughout her discussions of drama and poetry, philosophy, and epic, she consistently values unsentimental and operatic mourning without equivocation. Thus, she ends her section on drama with Cassandra's opening expression of woe, and ends her discussion of Plato by considering Greek fearlessness in the face of death, and the essay with the observation that "there is a sadness at the back of life which they do not attempt to mitigate" (CR1, 38). This special emphasis on mourning has feminist origins, but Woolf's emphasis on our distance from the Greeks, on the fragmentariness of our knowledge of them, adds another layer of grief: we mourn not only with them, but also our distance from them. However, even as the fragment seems to trap us in grief, it offers a way out, an escape from women's traditional roles as mourners into something modern and revolutionary.

Richard Jenkyns calls "On Not Knowing Greek" Woolf's "curious" essay on the Greeks, "half a reaction against the Victorian style of Hellenism, half a reassertion of it."[26] Her transformation of her inheritance continues the strand of liberal Victorian classicism that celebrated the diversity, openness, and possibility represented by Greek literature.[27] Both paradoxically and predictably, this liberal inclusiveness depends on the difficulty of learning Greek. Whether or not one knows it well enough to assess a translation's merits becomes either a bar against one or an initiation rite for another. Anyone who can pass that bar can lay claim to belonging to the category of the educated elite (including, e.g., the otherwise excluded Jews and women, as Leonard and Virginia Woolf well knew). When, in 1905, the young Virginia has "Tea with Violet & was blown up for my journalism. Promised to translate a bit of tough Greek, as a penance" (PA, 229), she accedes to the long-standing cultural valuation of Greek. But her frustration with her Greek teachers' interest in grammar over beauty and her ambivalence about R. C. Jebb's translations emphasize her belief in a writer's way of reading over the scholar's. Furthermore, her questions about what "we" know, what we can reconstruct, of Greece contain the implicit assertion that Woolf herself belongs in that (elite, largely male) we.

"On Not Knowing Greek" draws special attention to the cultural role played by Greek women. In ancient Greece, women performed the public and private rites of burial and mourning and this fact about Greek women was of special significance to Woolf, as several critics note.[28] Aware of this tradition and of the healing role that Greek played in her own death- and grief-filled youth, Woolf pays special attention to the connection between women and grief, noting the intensity of both the dramatic sufferer and the stoic griever. Of Electra's intense and intensely private grief, Woolf writes, "in a play how dangerous this poetry" (CR1, 28). That is, how can we attend to the plot in the presence of a daughter's grief over her loss first of a sister (sacrificed by her father) and, then her father (murdered by a vengeful, grieving mother)? Part of Woolf's question here is dramaturgical wonder: How does the play move forward after Electra has spoken of Niobe, "who evermore weepest in thy rocky tomb?" (Jebb, qtd CR1, 28). How can the actress embody "the horror of her position, an unwed girl made to witness her mother's vileness"? (CR1, 26). Electra's imagined gesture, "as if she swept her veil over her face" (CR1, 28), reopens one of the original questions that Woolf asks of Greek literature: what do we mean and what do we experience when calling these texts "immortal." If Electra's words sound profound rather than maudlin to us, why is that so? Woolf is trying to account for emotional intensity: "But it is not so easy to decide what it is that gives these cries of Electra . . . their power" (CR1, 26).

Interestingly, she depicts the Greeks as facing grief with an image of the very military heroism she typically deplored: "They could march straight up, with their eyes open; and thus fearlessly approached, emotions stand still and suffer themselves to be looked at" (CR1, 34). Her depiction of the Greeks as hunters of their own timid emotions combines a residual Victorian admiration for courage with her modern interest in psychological self-knowledge. What Penelope, Antigone, Electra, and Clytemnestra all show is the power of inconsolability, the fidelity and courage of a mourning that never ends. What they say is without irony, unlike World War I poets Wilfred Owen and Siegfried Sassoon for whom "it was not possible . . . to be direct without being clumsy" (CR1, 34). The modern response contrasts with that simple, original bravery: "In the vast catastrophe of the European war our emotions had to be broken up for us, and put at an angle from us, before we could allow ourselves to feel" (CR1, 34). These modern fragments, unlike the Greek, are distortions and diminutions. In the continuing, extended mourning period after the war, Woolf proposes the words of the Greeks as an alternative to irony, pomposity, and mawkishness. The mourning here is distinctly anti-Victorian in its rejection of sentimental soft-focus weeping and its emphasis on the violence preceding grief.

"On Not Knowing Greek" employs a pattern of violent imagery to describe the experience of reading Greek literature. Throughout the essay, Woolf uses images of cutting and slicing to describe

Greek: "split phrases into slices" (CR1, 25), "gashes and ruin" (CR1, 25), "cut each stroke to the bone" (CR1, 25), "one slip means death" (CR1, 26), "struck down" (CR1, 27), "a fragment of their speech broken off" (CR1, 27). This imagery, though violent, refuses to glorify battle; instead, it laments the lost connection to the past and celebrates aesthetic risk. Much has been made of Woolf's pacifism, but these images show how far her pacifism is from passivity. Though she loathes war and shrinks from physical combat even as a young child (MB, 71), her pacifism is active and engaged. Her imagery recognizes violence and strives to channel violent impulses into language. These sentiments emerge with the greatest force during World War II. In "Thoughts on Peace in an Air Raid" (1940), Woolf wonders what might we give men to substitute for the guns we want to take away: perhaps the answer, embedded in this much earlier essay, is *words*.

Woolf's meditations on grief, both personal and more broadly cultural, are mixed with the anxiety that characterizes much high modernism. Thus, added to her grief—and to the grief of any modern person, she implies—is an emotionally crippling self-consciousness. In contrast to the emotional complexity of her own day is the sense she gets, in reading Greek tragedy, that the cries are unencumbered by embarrassment. Thus, she quotes (in Greek) Cassandra's opening line, "O woe, woe, woe! alas! Apollo, Apollo!" (CR1, n. 244) and comments, aware of her very English shrinking at public notice, "Dramatic they had to be at whatever cost" (CR1, 31). Because Greek literature is not Christian, it offers far different solace to the grieving: "There is a sadness at the back of life which they do not attempt to mitigate . . . it is to the Greeks that we turn when we are sick of the vagueness, of the confusion, of the Christianity and its consolations, of our own age" (CR1, 38). Woolf clearly learned from the risks she saw in Greek tragedy. She, too, refuses to console. Her offstage depiction of tragedy is one aspect of this. Her lack of sentimentality over death and disappointment is another. When, in *To the Lighthouse*, Mrs. Ramsay dies, her husband walks down the corridor: "[. . . his arms, though stretched out, remained empty.]" (TTL, 194) and the dramatic gesture avoids Victorian excess by being enclosed in square brackets. Elsewhere, grieving characters in her novels do not know what to do with themselves; none of the usual consolations work—or even appear. Characters may, like the Pargiter children in *The Years*, be shocked at their own lack of feeling; they may, like Louis in *The Waves* or Septimus in *Mrs. Dalloway*, be numbed by the intensity of their loss; or they may, like Mrs. Flanders in *Jacob's Room*, be left holding an empty pair of shoes.

If Greek was consoling to Woolf, it does not quite play the same role for her characters. In *Mrs. Dalloway* (also 1925), Woolf writes that Septimus reads, "Aeschylus (translated)" (MD, 88). As Septimus and his wife walk through London to his doctor's appointment, the narrator reviews his history. He volunteered early in the war "to save an England which consisted almost entirely of Shakespeare's plays and Miss Isabel Pole in a green dress" (MD, 86). Any young man of those days whose knowledge of Shakespeare comes from his reading and "Miss Isabel Pole," not Cambridge, is unlikely to have Greek. Not knowing Greek, Septimus is excluded from the very different distraction from grief it offers. For, though Greek literature does not console (CR1, 38), it was to Greek that Woolf turned after her mother's death. With Septimus, Woolf sympathetically acknowledges the social bar to learning Greek, retains her faith in its imaginative value, and criticizes the nationalism in education that leads intelligent but poor young men to volunteer to fight for the imaginary England of Shakespeare and Aeschylus. Thus, a phrase ("Aeschylus [translated]") that at first may seem snobbish and distancing, in the context of Woolf's other writing, comes to be an expression of wary solidarity. Reading Aeschylus links Woolf to her character as surely as Shakespeare connects Septimus to Clarissa. But reading it in translation makes Septimus vulnerable to what John Guillory calls "imaginary cultural continuities." His night school education did just what orthodox educators hoped and expected: reading Shakespeare and the Greeks taught Septimus the patriotism that made him willing to volunteer to fight in the war. After the war, Septimus finds it difficult to read anymore. Language no longer intoxicates him. Instead, he feels that "the secret signal [of literature] . . . is loathing, hatred, despair" (MD, 88). In his wasteland, language ceases to heal; it corrodes. Only too late does Septimus perceive the message of despair in Greek. That message, Woolf implies, might have been clearer to him if he had translated Greek himself; the experience of translating forces the reader to confront not inheritance but fragmentation, not continuity but distance.

Woolf begins "On Not Knowing Greek" not with mourning but with unknowability. The first sentence explains the essay's title: "For it is vain and foolish to talk of knowing Greek." At first this seems a literal statement, a meditation on the author's ignorance, perhaps with a feminist slant, as she notes, "For it is vain and foolish to talk of knowing Greek, since in our ignorance we should be at the bottom of any class of schoolboys" (CR1, 23). But the context here rapidly becomes more inclusive as "we" expands to include anyone—even schoolboys—and ignorance is not of the Greek language but of Greek culture, its climate, and its emotions. Thus, in her opening comments, Woolf defines her subject through unknowability and desire. What is remarkable about "On Not Knowing Greek" is *not* the sense she is excluded based on gender, but that everyone is excluded. The title (and her refusal to translate the Greek she quotes) expresses her supreme self-confidence as one who knows classical Greek as well as anyone. Her point is that even the greatest, most imaginative, most learned reader of Greek cannot *know* Greek. Ultimately, as we will see, the unknowability of Greek has the potential to reconcile the gender-divided worlds of war and mourning.

Our distance from the Greeks becomes the essay's most prominent theme. Woolf asks, "Are we reading Greek as it was written when we say this? are we not reading wrong? losing our sharp sight in the haze of associations?" (CR1, 35). These questions about "reading wrong" are the questions of taking the work of art on its own terms to which Woolf held herself responsible throughout her essays. For Woolf, readers must not only account for how and why literature speaks to them, but they must also consider how their reading might differ from that of the author's contemporaries. Greek literature is the only ancient literature that Woolf writes about in any detail, and for her it represents our limitations in imagining a world wholly different from our own. Woolf worries that we are "losing our sharp sight in the haze of associations." That particular fear—that our sense of Greek might be hazy—reveals much about her aesthetic. It may partake of the renewed scholarly interest in Greece, but it most certainly rejects the nineteenth-century prettified Greece. By focusing on the difficult, the fragmentary, and the distant, Woolf adopts the ultimate expert's position—that our ignorance exceeds our knowledge—and uses it to dismantle the complacency of mainstream truisms about Greek. In so doing, she makes an argument that nicely reflects the double consciousness of women classicists in the early twentieth century, where knowledge admits them (partially) to an elite in which they are unwelcome and politically disenfranchised.

Woolf was writing just after what Hugh Kenner had called "Renaissance II," when Victorian archaeological discoveries and the adoption of rigorous German academic standards permitted the classics to "assume a more nearly scientific character."[29] One unintended result of this was a heightened awareness of the fragmentariness of our knowledge of the ancient world and, for many modernists, a growing admiration for the aesthetic of the fragment. Where their teachers had focused on cataloging potsherds and textual fragments, the imagination of Woolf's generation was caught by the fact of how much of the urn and the text had gone missing. To better understand how Woolf's allusions alter the resonance of ancient Greece to better fit her feminist art, it may help to compare them with the allusions of some of her contemporaries.[30] For example, Ezra Pound's 1916 poem, "Papyrus" suggests the younger generation's infatuation with the romance of what cannot be known:

> Spring . . .
> Too long . . .
> Gongula . . . [31]

The dramatic, mock-philological punctuation and the strange "Gongula," the name of one of Sappho's pupils and lovers, conjure up the image of a papyrus fragment. At the same time, the first syllable of "Gongula," a homonym for "gone," simultaneously invites and prevents a reading of the poem as simply "Spring, too long gone." The melancholy sentiment of a season and a love just beyond reach nicely echoes the subject of Keats's "Ode on a Grecian Urn," offering a fittingly modernist conclusion to a century of English lyrics on the ancient world. Poems like "Papyrus" combine a very modern idea of the fragment with an ancient artifact: the fragment.

Not surprisingly, Woolf's use of the classics shares some important features with H. D.'s: both women insist on their right of access to Greek unmediated by male translators and editors, and both reserve special admiration for Sappho, whom they recognize as a forbear. Though Woolf consults her Jebb and H. D. her Wharton (whose eccentric translation and study of Sappho was then the standard), both women translate Greek for themselves.[32] Nonetheless their emphasis differed in important ways. For H. D., studying Greek presents the possibility of recapturing a wholeness, a pre-patriarchal linguistic purity in which being a lesbian was not only accepted but also celebrated.[33] In her poetry, she alludes to and ventriloquizes Sappho, writing, for example,

> At least I have the flowers of myself,
> and my thoughts, no god
> can take that.[34]

Though Woolf, too, finds such autonomy and clarity in reading Sappho's fragments, and though she, like H. D., admires Sappho for her free expression of her mind and body, Woolf's cautiousness—about both translation and sexuality—means that she never attempts such a bold revisioning. Instead, she focuses on the importance of retaining our sense of distance from the Greeks.

In this Woolf finds an ally in Gertrude Stein, who shares Woolf's insistence on the utter difference of great ancient masterpieces: "The manner and habits of Bible times or Greek or Chinese have nothing to do with ours today but the master-pieces exist just the same and they do not exist because of their identity . . . they exist because they came to be as something that is an end in itself."[35] Stein, an ambitious woman like Woolf, explores this idea in part to explore what a master-piece is and to make her bid for having written one. And, different from Woolf, she believes that art's greatness lies in its possession of a durable transcendent kernel that distinguishes it from the other works of its own time. But Woolf has a political point to make, too: that we must be responsible students of historical context. Again and again she reminds us that we cannot simply apply the ideas of Antigone or Plato to our own world, even though we can see modern analogs to her brave defiance, his brilliant teaching.

The contrast between Woolf's Greek women and those of other male modernists are stark. Her heroines are about as unlike the beautiful and stupid Ledas and Helens as can be that overpopulate Yeats's poetry. Though Woolf, like Yeats, admires the intensity of Greek heroines and though she, too, sees that these single-minded women are "the greatest bores" (CR1, 27), she most certainly does not wish that modern women "think opinions are accursed."[36] Yeats's noble women are spoiled by their political power that consists of charismatic influence, not thought. Thus, in "No Second Troy," "simple" has a cruel double meaning: "What could have made her peaceful with a mind / That nobleness made simple as a fire . . . ?"[37] Yeats does not call Helen/Maud Gonne "simple" in order to put down aristocracy—his own sympathies were even more aristocratic than Woolf's—she is simple because she is a woman. Unlike Yeats, T. S. Eliot spends his energy depicting and savoring women's vulnerability, where all we hear of the nightingale is " 'Jug Jug' to dirty ears."[38] Though Philomel, raped and transformed into a nightingale, may have an "inviolable voice," we hear her song through "dirty ears." Less nasty, but still objectifying, is Joyce's massive revision of Penelope, Odysseus's weaving and waiting wife, into the passionate "yes" of Molly Bloom. More Woolfian is Joyce's comic revision of stuffy translations. In *Ulysses*, the narrator intones, "And lo, as they quaffed their cup of joy, a godlike messenger came swiftly in" that he renders as "Little Alf Bergan popped in round the door."[39] Here, Joyce riffs against pretension, an impulse Woolf shares when she objects to a Victorian translator's "wan": "Professor Mackail says 'wan,' and the age of Burne-Jones and Morris is at once evoked" (CR1, 36).

The symbolist poets, more than the classicists, taught the moderns to see fragments as a symptom of the alienation of modernity. This newfound appreciation of the fragment as modern offered a new way to appreciate the fragmentary texts of the classical world. Since so much of the ancient world survives only in fragments, the modernists could claim allusions to classical literature as modern. So, as Woolf writes, wryly parodying the critics of her day, hers was "an age of fragments" (CR1, 234). But, for Woolf, in spite of moments of nostalgia for more, it is good that it is so. The fragment precludes grand theories, replicates the sense of being lost, of being in the midst of shards of civilization too various to organize. As Woolf wrote on her first visit to Greece, "There is a great deal to tantalise you in these Greek ruins; innumerable fragments & scarcely one whole piece anywhere" (PA, 324). For Woolf the fragments remind her of historical contingency. "On Not Knowing Greek" is full of questions designed to unsettle preconceived notions about the ancient world: "Are we reading Greek as it was written when we say this?"; "what remains visible to us?"

Woolf's contribution to the modernist reconsideration of England's Greek inheritance is less Utopian, less idealized, and more historical than that of most of her peers. In focusing on the "chasm" that separates us from the Greeks, Woolf shows how literary inheritance can be reshaped. She speculates on the attraction of this incomplete knowledge. Since we cannot know Greek, she writes, "All the more strange, then, is it that we should wish to know Greek, try to know Greek, feel for ever drawn back to Greek, and be for ever making up some notion of the meaning of Greek" (CR1, 23).[40] The attraction of Greek is also the problem. Translation itself is a fragmentary endeavor: "We can never hope to get the whole fling of a sentence in Greek as we do in English" (CR1, 35). Our imperfect knowledge means that even when a text is whole, our understanding of it remains fragmentary. For their part, Woolf writes, "Translators can but offer us a vague equivalent; their language is necessarily full of echoes and associations" (CR1, 36). Translations, embedded in their own time, do not bring us closer to the Greeks.

Frequently, Woolf's discussion of the difficulty of Greek zeroes in on the specific problems of translation. She demonstrates the intensity of this difficulty by quoting, in Greek, the notoriously difficult-to-translate lines 418–19 from *Agamemnon*, of which she writes, "The meaning is just on the far side of language" (CR1, 31). These lines in which the chorus describes Paris's cooling toward Helen are rendered as "and in the hunger of his eyes all loveliness is departed,"[41] but Woolf neither shares a translator's version nor does she discuss how she herself translates them. It is more important to her to get across the idea that this line eludes translation than it is to make a case for her own version, or any version. When she does briefly discuss a translation, it is Shelley's Plato. Of it, she only notes that he "takes twenty-one words in English to translate thirteen words of Greek" (CR1, 35), which leads to the general observation that, in Greek, "Every ounce of fat has been pared off" (CR1, 35). This economy of Greek makes translation difficult and makes the original powerful.

In this, Woolf's notion of translation may be compared to Walter Benjamin's. He, too, sees the translation as fundamentally engaged in "coming to terms with the foreignness of languages."[42] He praises Hölderlin's translation of Sophocles, originally reviled as a "monstrous example of . . . literalness," because it, like the best translation, "does not cover the original, does not block its light."[43] He even echoes Woolf's language of jumping through space, writing that Hölderlin's "meaning plunges from abyss to abyss."[44] The crucial difference, however, between Woolf and Benjamin lies in their contrasting sense of the importance of the fragment. Where Benjamin's translator uses fragments of language to reconstruct a vessel, Woolf pauses over the fragments themselves and marvels at the untranslatability of words.

For Benjamin the incommensurability of any two languages is a veil covering the "suprahistorical kinship of languages."[45] Benjamin insists that ultimately there are knowable objects behind the words:

> The words *Brot* and *pain* "intend" the same object, but the modes of this intention are not the same. It is owing to these modes that the word *Brot* means something different to a German than the word *pain* to a Frenchman, that these words are not interchangeable for them, that, in fact, they strive to exclude each other. As to the intended object, however, the two words mean the very same thing.[46]

Woolf wants us to pause over the strangeness of foreign words. For her, *Brot* is not *pain*, nor is *thanatos death*. That languages "strive to exclude each other" supercedes any possible deep kinship between the original and the translation. Woolf is not interested, as is Benjamin, in "the intended object" or in meditating on an ideal "pure language," however unattainable.[47] In the sentences immediately preceding her dismissal of a Victorian translator's "wan," she writes,

> Then there are the words themselves which, in so many instances, we have made expressive to us of our own emotions, θαλασσα, θανατος,

ανθοες, αστηρ, σεληγη [sea, death, flower, star, moon]—to take the first that come to hand; so clear, so hard, so intense, that to speak plainly yet fittingly without blurring the outline or clouding the depths, Greek is the only expression. Translators can but offer us a vague equivalent. (CR1, 36)[48]

Neither Woolf nor Benjamin desires a modern translation, one dressed in the most up-to-date clothes. But Benjamin's beliefs lead him to see the translation itself as a work of art, enriching the language. For him, translation is "charged with the special mission of watching over the maturing process of the original language and the birth pangs of its own."[49] For Woolf, it is not the translation that adds to the language, but the experience of translating. Although her imagination is enriched by her reading of Greek, she does not claim that any translator for a moment enriches (or could enrich) the English language. The effect of Greek is limited to the individual who translates.

In bringing her feminist, modernist aesthetic to her understanding of Greek, Woolf developed her own version of what Page DuBois calls an "aesthetics of the fragment." Closely related to Woolf's ideas of translation, the notion of the fragment has even greater reach: fragments refer to the choppy, interrupted, assisted reading of the student of Greek and to the imperfect, incomplete, often corrupt texts she attempts to translate. DuBois, like Woolf, asks us to look at the fact of the fragment before projecting it into its whole state. She compares the fragments of text to the mutilated "bodies" of statues.[50] DuBois wants us to pause over failure before we imagine what Benjamin called "intention."[51] Calling statues "bodies" and comparing ellipses to "stopped mouths" force us to consider the challenge of coming into voice.[52] For DuBois, the fragment offers many pleasures. It provides a *frisson* of survivorship in which reading a fragment brings a ghost of the distant past into our present.[53] It also offers rich interpretive latitude as a fragment, taken on its own, can be a partial poem, asking us to contribute to the process of inferring what its whole once was.[54] Moreover, any one fragment offers a rich array of intertextual resonances, for connections can be based on a single word or image.[55] And, since so many of Sappho's fragments in particular are about the absent, the distant, the unattainable, their very fragmentary nature only intensifies the poem's aesthetic.[56] DuBois describes the fragments of Sappho in a language much like that one might use to describe the subject of lyric. In DuBois's telling, Sappho, the first lyric poet, sets the agenda for the genre not only through her poetry but also through its imperfect preservation.

Given the importance to modernism of both the fragment and the lesbian, it makes sense that Sappho would be a hero for modernists generally and Woolf in particular. Though what we have of Sappho's poetry is predominantly homoerotic, it is a diverse collection, including love lyrics addressed to both men and women, celebrations of marriage, and lamentations for the young women friends lost to marriage. As others, including Woolf, have noted, to know everything about Sappho is not to know much. There is, for example, no historical support for the fable that it was her unrequited love for a ferryman that led to her suicide; her suicide itself is a fable; in short, a lot of interference stands in the way of understanding or simply imagining her. If her poems are autobiographical (already a guess), then we still do not know how much weight to put on her various loves: lesbian, heterosexual, and maternal. For Woolf, whose own sexuality was complex and intensely private, Sappho's appeal lay as much in our lack of knowledge about her as in the fact that one of the main things we do know is that she wrote beautifully about women's love for each other.

The fact that mainly fragments of Sappho's poems survived by no means implies that she wrote in fragments or meant to be remembered in fragments. There is a fragment of Sappho's that reads, in its entirety, "I say someone in another time will remember us."[57] This is both true and untrue. She *is* remembered. Still, we only possess a few complete poems of hers; every fragment that has survived has done so by chance, by virtue of its quotation in another work or a randomly saved piece of papyrus. This is the rupture at the heart of Sappho's appeal. Sappho, who meant so much to Woolf and means so much to us, is a construction. As such, the fragment of Sappho nicely illustrates the emerging modernist sense of reality as wholly constructed by language.

This has important political implications. Even if a fragment contains a suggestion of politics, simply by virtue of its brevity, that suggestion—of rebellion, fealty, or ambivalence—never develops into an ideology. Moreover, what little we know of Sappho's politics is antimartial. In Homer, epic similes connect the world of war to the domestic and small, for example, comparing an army to ants. Sappho, by contrast, used epic similes to undo martial discourse, displacing war imagery into an erotic context, using metaphors from the battlefield to describe love.[58] This combination of pacifism, sublime poetry, love of women, and mystery makes Sappho the ideal Greek ancestor for Woolf. A recent article on Woolf's use of epic simile makes a parallel point showing how Woolf "raise[s] everyday activities to the level of the heroic . . . the converse of deflating old values of heroism."[59] In short, Woolf does with the epic simile precisely what Sappho does herself. Woolf's connection to Sappho is a crucial symbol of her intense involvement with words and her deep skepticism of state-sanctioned language. Sappho's poems as we have them may represent the greatness of the Greek language, of poetry, of the sublime, of women's desires, but they cannot be pressed into the service of official state nationalism, Greek or English.

Woolf's aesthetics of the fragment reaches its fullest articulation not in an essay but in *To the Lighthouse* (1927). At the end of the dinner party in that novel, Mr. Ramsay and Augustus Carmichael recite the sentimental Victorian poem "Luriana, Lurilee" to honor Mrs. Ramsay and the evening. As she listens to the words, they detach from their context, become fragments, and, as such, become transcendently beautiful: "The words (she was looking at the window) sounded as if they were floating like flowers on water out there, cut off from them all, as if no one had said them, but they had come into existence of themselves" (TTL, 166). For Mrs. Ramsay, their beauty comes from her ability to hear them as separate, "cut off from them all"; the words are at once natural, "like flowers on water"; inhuman, "as if no one had said them"; and self-contained, "they had come into existence of themselves." This combination transforms a Victorian poem into a fragment, capturing all of the fragment's appeal. The artificial gesture of ending dinner with a recitation comes naturally to the elders in the party, and Woolf makes us experience it as natural through Mrs. Ramsay's perceptions[60]: "Her husband spoke. He was repeating something, and she knew it was poetry from the rhythm and the ring . . . in his voice (TTL, 166). This intuitive listening, resolutely responsive to sound, uninterested in author, title, or even sense, has a purpose. Mrs. Ramsay understands that retaining her title of "the happier Helen of our days" (TTL, 43) depends on her willingness to inhabit the images of the poems that the men around her read and write, even if "disgraceful to say, she had never read them" (TTL, 43). Though she submits to being an image, she refuses to read the results of male image-making.

When Mrs. Ramsay reads poetry on her own, she continues the impressionistic, nonlinear characteristics of her listening[61]:

"Nor praise the deep vermilion in the rose," she read, and so reading she was ascending, she felt, on to the top, on to the summit. How satisfying! How restful! All the odds and ends of the day stuck to this magnet; her mind felt swept, felt clean. And then there it was, suddenly entire; she held it in her hands, beautiful and reasonable, clear and complete, the essence sucked out of life and held rounded here—the sonnet. (TTL, 181)

This account of the experience of reading moves from fragment to whole by a circuitous route. There is nothing about mountaintops in the line from Shakespeare's Sonnet 98 that inspires Mrs. Ramsay's meditation, yet she makes that link, "ascending . . . on to the summit," and the idea of mountain climbing alludes to her own and Mr. Ramsay's love of walking.[62] Her terms of praise are ordinary: the poem's greatness lies in it being "satisfying" and "restful." It is both comic and fitting that a housewife praises poetry for gathering up the clutter of the day and sweeping the mind clean. Nevertheless, Mrs. Ramsay has an aesthetic experience that, in Woolf's own terms, is granted to few. Of Aeschylus, Woolf writes, "To understand him it is not so necessary to understand Greek as to understand poetry. It is necessary to take that dangerous leap through the air without the support of words" (CR1, 30). That is the leap Mrs. Ramsay takes, first in her metaphoric connection of the red rose and the summit, then in her sudden grasp of the "entire in her hands . . . clear and complete . . . the sonnet." The metaphoric leap required of all who want to understand poetry alludes to the fabled suicidal leap of Sappho herself.

Like Mrs. Ramsay's way of understanding poetry, or the song from Shakespeare's *Cymbeline* that confirms the connection between Septimus Smith and Clarissa Dalloway, breaking off fragments to transform and inhabit them sidesteps the political and aesthetic orthodoxies Woolf resists. Metaphors "rise up and stalk eyeless and majestic" (CR1, 30).[63] Mrs. Ramsay, Mrs. Dalloway, and Septimus all turn Shakespeare into fragments, a habit that strengthens the associative link recurrent in Woolf between Greek, known to us so often in fragments, and Shakespeare.[64] Those who understand Aeschylus, Sappho, or Shakespeare grasp a meaning that is beyond words.

Nonetheless, though the experience of understanding Shakespeare can be as intense as Greek, it is different: "we bruise our minds upon some tremendous metaphor in the *Agamemnon* instead of stripping the branch of its flowers instantly as we do in reading *Lear*" (CR1, 35). For Woolf, the whole that Mrs. Ramsay grasps from the Shakespeare sonnet is instant because an English woman reading English poetry can grasp the meaning without thinking. Though her experience is sublime and rare, her status as a native speaker of English, not her intellect or her study, grants her access to the experience. Though Shakespeare's words are as beautiful and fragile as flowers, Aeschylus's have all the sublimity and endurance of a block of marble. Woolf offers the disturbing image of bruising our minds, conjuring a doltish student straining to understand, pressing her forehead against the intractable difficulty of an ancient metaphor. Whereas *To the Lighthouse* may help us to understand the fragment's centrality to Woolf's reading, "On Not Knowing Greek" insists on the greater challenge of the Greek fragment.

To understand poetry, "[i]t is necessary to take that dangerous leap through the air without the support of words" (CR1, 30). And for Woolf, part of the difficult pleasure of reading and studying Greek is that sometimes all that a student can translate are fragments. In order to understand, Woolf writes, "one must be able to pass easily into those ecstasies," and yet, to pass easily "is exactly what we cannot do" since translating is such hard work, and "the choruses . . . must be spelt out" (CR1, 29). Though, in reading Plato, Socrates may lead us to "the greatest felicity of which we are capable," "such an expression seems ill fitted to describe the state of mind of a student to whom, after painful argument, the truth has been revealed" (CR1, 32). The task of translating is drudgery followed by epiphany. The student is at once the modern student (cold rooms, long hours of solitary labor) and the student of Socrates or Sappho's academy (where learning occurs through challenging conversation). The contrast between the discussion depicted in Plato and the experience of trying to read it, upsetting at first, turns into a reminder of the elusiveness of truth and the importance of the quest for it. While Socrates's and Sappho's students sit with their teacher, rigorously yet companionably arguing their way to truth, Woolf and other solitary students sit alone in their rooms, with only a dictionary and a Greek grammar book to aid them.

Woolf's account of bruising our minds against a metaphor strongly implies that fragments do not always lead to peak aesthetic experiences. In fact, they can also injure. Once again *To the Lighthouse* provides a useful illustration. There, Mrs. Ramsay thinks about her habit of breaking off fragments of language:

> And [she] would lift up on it some little phrase or other which had been lying in her mind like that—"Children don't forget, children don't forget"—which she would repeat and begin adding to it, It will end, it will end, she said. It will come, it will come, when suddenly she added, We are in the hands of the Lord.
>
> But instantly she was annoyed with herself for saying that. Who had said it? Not she; she had been trapped into saying something she did not mean. She looked up over her knitting . . . searching . . . into her mind and heart, purifying out of existence that lie, any lie. (TTL, 97)

Where earlier the fragment of poetry purifies, here Mrs. Ramsay must purify herself against an unbidden fragment, which is, for her a "lie."

As she lets her mind wander, she moves from one of her own credos— "children don't forget"—to two general spiritual tags—"it will end" and "it will come." The "it" might represent childhood, death, or even the fine weather needed for a sail to the lighthouse. In any case, these short, vague, repeated phrases seem to reassure her, assuaging her anxiety that James will not ever forget his disappointment. However, this ready-made reassurance easily slides into Christian cant and, once it does, Mrs. Ramsay snaps to attention, combing her mind clean. Elsewhere, Lily Briscoe too struggles with a dangerous fragment: Charles Tansley's "women can't write, women can't paint" haunts her, seeming to confirm her own self-doubt. These slogans must be overcome, and Lily and Mrs. Ramsay eventually defeat them through internalizing, repeating, and rejecting them. What Woolf depicts in Lily and Mrs. Ramsay is not a feminist political program, but the acts of everyday resistance that enable women to carry on under patriarchy.

For Woolf, great readers and writers do not succeed with verbal precision but with imaginative leaps. Early in "On Not Knowing Greek," Woolf compares Sophocles to Jane Austen, a context shift that attempts in argument the kind of leap that Woolf celebrates. Of both authors, she writes that they chose "the dangerous art where one slip means death" (CR1, 26). This image of a writer balancing atop a cliff again alludes to Sappho. It evokes the idea of aesthetic commitment so intense, of an aesthetic so unforgiving, that to fail would be to die.

## GLOBAL GREEK, FROM THE 1930S TO 1941

So far we have discussed two phases of Woolf's writing on Greek: her study of it as a young woman and her consideration of the fragmentary nature of our knowledge in the 1920s. As we have seen, Woolf's early introduction to Greek not only taught her another literature, but also showed her the effects of a segregated educational system. Woolf quickly recognized that the discipline of Greek that, for her, represented freedom—a welcome mental labor, a break from both grief and the indignities and molestations of the marriage market—played a far different role in the lives of men of her social class. For them, Greek offered confirmation of social orthodoxies rather than freedom from them. In the 1920s, Woolf responded to the gulf between her own liberating education and the more orthodox understandings of it by emphasizing how little any of us know about Greece. Through the ideas of not knowing and of the fragment, Woolf asserts her right to participate in the conversation about the meaning and significance of

Greece. Rather than claiming expertise, she demotes anyone else's right to claim it. In doing so, she dodges her own anxiety about inadequacy because of her sex and lack of formal education. At the same time, she refuses to accept the opinions of others as intrinsically more valuable than her own. In particular, her discussions of translation, focusing on cultural and historical gaps rather than continuities, set the stage for the more political questions of nationhood that emerge as central to *Three Guineas* (1938).

*Three Guineas* marks Woolf's most comprehensive repudiation of the myths of nationhood. This feminist, antifascist pamphlet takes the form of a series of embedded letters, solicitations for donations, and Woolf's speaker's reply to them. The three guineas of the title represent her three linked donations, to a women's college, a society for professional women, and a society for the prevention of war. From the very opening lines of this text, she links identity to education, expressing wonder that an educated man—the fictionalized barrister, working on behalf of a group for peace—should appeal to an uneducated woman—the narrator. After decades of relative neglect, the current understanding of *Three Guineas* calls it radical, important, and long undervalued. In fact, the text that failed either to prevent war or to persuade friends to pacifism in the face of war has found a second life in feminist and pacifist theory in recent decades. Critics who rate *Three Guineas* highly take the allusions to Sophocles' Antigone in the text as central to Woolf's development of a feminist theory of preventing war. Putting Woolf's high valuation of *Antigone* into the larger context of her lifelong engagement with Greek demonstrates more fully how this early engagement contributes to her most radical feminist reading. Knowing both the centrality of Greek lessons to Woolf's education and to English education more generally at the time helps us see links between Woolf's critique of Cambridge education in *Three Guineas* and her praise for Antigone. In turn, these links demonstrate how Woolf was able to persist in her admiration for Greek even knowing the pernicious uses to which classical education had been put.

John Guillory describes how literature in translation once created "imaginary cultural continuities."[65] As he argues, these continuities were often put in the service of what we might now call bad nationalism— patriotism and a sense of cultural supremacy. But, as Woolf saw, other literatures—especially Greek—could also become a marker of internationalism. In "On Not Knowing Greek," Woolf articulated an engaged response to Greek literature that was curious and alert to connections and differences. In *Three Guineas*, she demonstrates the political possibilities of such a vision. Education is a central theme in the book. For Woolf, the drive to war emerges from a drive to defend "our civilization," "our land," "our country," and private property; furthermore, young men learn these values at school. Antigone emerges as central in part because Woolf's discussion of her is the only extended discussion of a literary text in the book. In contrast to *A Room of One's Own, Three Guineas* turns away from literature. Instead, the narrator relies on what she calls "psychology," her common sense and ability to read human motivation in analyzing newspapers, photographs, and memoirs. Central to the method of *Three Guineas* is Woolf's response to her own pretended or assumed lack of preparation and resources to answer the barrister's question. Woolf argues that the current educational system "breeds neither a particular respect for liberty nor a particular hatred of war" (3G, 33). Moreover, we can predict that helping women attend university would likely make women more warlike:

> Again, if we help an educated man's daughter to go to Cambridge are we not forcing her to think not about education but about war?—not about how she can learn, but how she can fight in order that she may win the same advantages as her brothers? Further, since the daughters of educated men are not members of Cambridge University they have no say in that education, therefore how can they alter that education, even if we ask them to? (3G, 31)

For Woolf, Cambridge, as it was then constituted, encouraged the very proprietary, competitive behavior that leads to war. As Beer and others note, throughout her work Woolf connects the "militarism bred in men through their education and the coming of the Second World War."[66] Unfortunately, Woolf fears, women's economic disadvantages will only make them more complicit in the system. In the face of these practical needs, Woolf still urges women to cultivate what she calls *indifference*: "the daughters of educated men should give their brothers neither the white feather of cowardice nor the red feather of courage" (3G, 109). Not just courage and cowardice, but nation itself may be of little interest to women: "When he says . . . 'I am fighting to protect our country' and thus seeks to rouse her patriotic emotion, she will ask herself, 'What does "our country" mean to me an outsider?' " (3G, 107). In short, Woolf argues that men, in professing to be fighting for ideals, are in fact fighting to preserve their status, property, and power.

*Three Guineas* moves between this dark realism and hope. If Cambridge does not prevent war, women educators "must rebuild your college differently . . . it must be an experimental college, an adventurous college" (3G, 33). *Three Guineas* never directly endorses a syllabus, curriculum, or even a reading list, but it does ask women to "practise the profession of reading and writing in the interests of culture and intellectual liberty" (3G, 90). Woolf defines that latter phrase as "the disinterested pursuit of reading and writing the English language" and "the right to say or write what you think in your own words, and in your own way" (3G, 91). The problem that Woolf addresses lies not in the curriculum's content but in the pedagogy, the method of teaching espoused by the major universities. Literature itself is not corrupted—or even, in her view, corruptible—the problem lies in the ideology and method of the old institutions. The "experimental" and "adventurous" curriculum that she describes is all about reading for oneself, making up one's own mind, reading critically, thinking about the source of information and the hidden motives that source might harbor, about how "the money is spent" (3G, 112). This habit of taking an existing part of civilization— Cambridge University—and imagining it in its ideal guise has its roots in Greek, too: in Plato's *Republic*. The heroine of this kind of thinking also resides in Greek literature: Antigone.

Woolf does not explicitly connect this discussion of education to the subsequent one of Antigone. However, our attention to Woolf's study of Greek helps make the connection clear. Woolf reveres Antigone's independence of mind, her ability to distinguish between the laws and the Law, her confidence in her own intelligence: all the qualities that she dreams of in the ideal university for outsiders. Furthermore, Woolf explicitly states that Antigone's situation is a powerful analogue for her own: "Let us shut of the wireless and listen to the past. We are in Greece now; Christ has not been born yet, nor St. Paul either. But listen: . . . That is the voice of Creon, the dictator. . . . Pictures and voices are the same today as they were 2,000 years ago" (3G, 141). After all her cautious rhetoric in the1920s, Woolf returns in the 1930s to the equations between Greece and England of her own youth, but this time, they are in the service of pointed feminist pacifist propaganda. And, in fact, she concedes in the endnotes, "though it is easy to squeeze these characters into up-to-date dress, it is impossible to keep them there" (3G, 170 n. 39). Woolf admires Antigone and recognizes that, to work as a contemporary inspiration invoking Antigone's story carries risks. In *Three Guineas*, she insists that we simultaneously see how suffragettes and antifascists are Antigones, and that insisting too much on this analogy, though politically valuable, cripples art.[67]

In rethinking her relation to her nation, Woolf has more than just herself in mind: she is trying to think for her sex. Woolf defied men's right to explain what was important about Greek literature and civilization. Her own defiance connects her to the great heroine of defiance: Antigone. Woolf admires Antigone's refusal to accept Creon's authority as king, her fidelity to the memory of her brother, and her fatal disobedience of Creon. Woolf's references to Antigone reinforce her conviction "that the anti-patriarchal and anti-authoritarian aspects of the Western tradition are the truly noble legacy of the sons of educated men, a legacy more completely enacted by their sisters than themselves."[68]

If Woolf's pacifist feminism seems to contradict her pride in being English, she was not the only one in her circle to hold such views. Her friend Jane Harrison, the pioneering Cambridge classicist, expressed her bemused dismay at her own lingering prejudices:

> In politics I am an old Liberal, with a dash of the Little Englander and the Bolshevik. I hate the Empire; it stands to me for all that is tedious and pernicious in thought; within it are always and necessarily the seeds of war. I object to nearly all forms of patriotism. But when I search the hidden depths of my heart, I find there the most narrow and local of parochialisms. I am intensely proud of being a Yorkshire woman.[69]

The phrase "Little Englander" suggests an appealing liberal fantasy: the possibility of shrinking England back to a single vulnerable island.[70] The phrase "Little England" refers to an anti-imperialist nationalism, one that centers its pride on the identity of the British Isles rather than the larger empire. (Ireland, Scotland, and Wales are not, at this point, always excluded from the category of England.[71]) Retreating from the Empire, little Englanders could imagine a way to take pride in a smaller (and more vulnerable?) nation. Though Little Englander is not a phrase used by Woolf, it is a stance she works her way toward by the end of her life. As a feminist and an intellectual, Harrison is acutely aware of much the same thicket that Woolf attempts to negotiate. Ultimately, however, Harrison admits to only a "dash" of little Englander, anchoring her pride in Yorkshire. Her tone in this passage is both pragmatic and abstract: the Empire is not a geopolitical fact but a symbol of "all that is tedious and pernicious in thought." Ultimately, Harrison ducks nationalism in favor of regionalism, whereas Woolf attempts to puzzle out her feelings for her own Englishness head on.

Though always critical of the empire, Woolf is often untroubled to call herself English, as when she writes "English fiction . . . bears witness to our natural delight in humour and comedy, in the beauty of the earth" (CR1, 154). Nonetheless, Woolf endeavors to separate a love of nation from patriotism, to find a way to take pride in being English without affiliating herself with the official nation. During World War II, the bombing of London makes her think of "my England" that "if a bomb destroyed one of those little alleys with the brass bound curtains . . . I should feel—well, what the patriots feel" (D, 5.263). Throughout her career Woolf remains confident that in calling a writer "English" (or not) she evokes a meaningful shared identity.[72]

The refusal to console makes Greek literature "useful" to those still grieving after World War I, but it does not address the problem that she was addressing in the late 1930s of preventing the next world war. For that, Woolf returns most directly to the connection between grief and nationalism: when *Three Guineas* was published in the *Atlantic Monthly*, it was given the title "Women Must Weep—or Unite Against War." Her title recognizes women's complicity in a martial society while presenting them with an impossible (though patriarchally sanctioned) choice: grieve or fight. Her text proposes a third way: prevent war. Woolf treats grieving as yet another of the messy social tasks that have been women's domain. And, as she did with child-rearing, nursing, cooking, cleaning, and boosting egos, she demystifies grieving and the role it plays within patriarchy. In a just world, Antigone would not mourn alone. Without patriarchy, there could be no abduction of Helen by Paris. If women had a voice, daughters would not be sacrificed to get a good wind. For Woolf, the recognition that "there is a sadness at the back of life" (CR1, 38) is not one that women should shoulder alone. Instead, women and men should work together to reduce life's most violent evils—especially war—that increase life's sorrow.

Throughout *Three Guineas* Woolf insists on the connection between nationalism and violence, citizenship and sexuality, and education and outlook. She demands that, since the nation interferes in their lives, women must articulate their relationship to the nation; at the same time, since the nation refuses privileges to women, women must remain indifferent when it asks for loyalty. Woolf questions the value of citizenship for women. National identity is connected to citizenship; this connection poses a lingering question for anyone new to the privileges of citizenship: "Why seek to be nationals?"[73] Whether the question "why seek to be nationals?" comes from gays, lesbians, and queer theorists (as with Robert Caserio and Lauren Berlant), or from writers of colonial and postcolonial perspectives (as with Woolf and Partha Chatterjee), its answer is not simple. One might think—as occasionally *Three Guineas* seems to suggest—that the safest course of action would be to reject the privileges of being part of a nation since these privileges come at such a high price. However, turning one's back on the nation carries its own serious political dangers.[74] Outsider and subaltern communities must negotiate a delicate balance in the pursuit of citizenship: they must monitor a state hostile to their identity and behavior, participate in its daily life, protest its actions, and retain the distinctive values of their outsider community all the while.

Woolf retains her pride in Englishness while proposing a community of outsiders. She works toward a private, nonofficial, anti-institutional national identity. Though Woolf wrote more extensively about Aeschylus, Sophocles, and Plato, what unites her comments on the entire canon of Greek literature is her interest in the fragment. For this reason, I have pushed Sappho to the fore, especially in my discussion of the crucial turns in Woolf's thought in the 1920s. Everything in Woolf's oeuvre points to Sappho's centrality as a precursor. So, what does Woolf's modernist admiration for the Sapphic fragment make us think about nation? My question revises Woolf's main questions in "On Not Knowing Greek." There, she asks, given all that we do not know about the Greeks, what is it that the words communicate nonetheless? For Woolf the response is that, in reading Greek we approach something about "the insoluble question of poetry and its nature." For theorists of nationalism Partha Chatterjee and Gyanendra Pandey, "the 'fragmentary' point of view . . . resists the drive for a shallow homogenisation and struggles for other, potentially richer definitions of the 'nation' and the future political community."[75] Woolf, too, works toward a richer definition of nation through fragments, one that accepts mystery and difference without leading to violence. In the end, though her elitism may trouble us, her transformation of the even greater elitism of imperial and martial classics stands as a model.

Nations get built through myth and ritual, and the English have leaned heavily on the Greeks in constructing their own story. In her study and discussion of the Greeks, Woolf at once reminds us how flimsy (and thus malleable) that habit of mind (once thought a foundation) is and suggests, as an alternative, an antifascist, feminist model of reading and thinking. In doing so, she constantly forces us to acknowledge that at the center of nationhood is women's grief. Through fragments, Woolf unravels the imaginary nature of England's affiliation with ancient Greece, constantly disrupting the English elite's complacency about their kinship.

Greek to Woolf still means something like civilization, but the civilization of reading, not of conquering. And a kinship with Greece can be earned by anyone with the intelligence, passion, and opportunity to learn. It does not run in one's veins like blood. When Woolf writes about her nation, she is anti-imperial and antipatriotic, but when she writes about English literature she slips into praise of her own nation and race. Greek literature checks her prejudices. Her admiration for Sappho and Sophocles' *Antigone* suggests an alternate route to some thing we still might want to call civilization, one that is imaginative and passionate but not sentimental. It is not that Woolf cannot find support for her own views in Greek literature, it is only that she knows that her opponents, too, could find support for theirs. As she writes of Creon and Antigone, though "it is easy to squeeze these characters into up-to-date dress, it is impossible to keep them there" (3G, 170). In the end, the Sapphic fragment stands as a reminder against arrogance even as her words testify to the endurance of beauty and the possibility of choosing love over hatred. And for Woolf, the survival of those fragments, when so much else was lost, confirms the power of her own pacifist feminism and suggests that it might one day be possible to be proud of those fragments of English society while deploring all that she deplored. Or even the outlandish hope that, in the end, what will survive of England might be the very best of her own words.

# CHAPTER 2

# The Memory Palace and the Lumber Room: Woolf's Renaissance Miscellany

*The mind has been called a* lumber-room, *and its contents or its printed products described as* lumber, *since about 1680.*

Nicholson Baker

Like most social historians of her day, Virginia Woolf traced the emergence of literature as a significant cultural force in England to sometime between the ages of Chaucer (c. 1343–1400) and Shakespeare (1564–1616). For her, print culture became dominant only when men and women outside the court had access to enough books to make reading for pleasure an engrossing pastime. In her essay "The Pastons and Chaucer" (1925), she imagines the impact of literacy on the Pastons, a well-to-do Norfolk family, emphasizing how a love of reading led to the neglect of family business.[1] But it is in "The Elizabethan Lumber Room" (also 1925) that she documents the transformation of the English language from the humble, pragmatic language of ordinary people into the language of Shakespeare. Woolf's originality lies in her claim that the agent of that transformation was Hakluyt's *Trafficks and Discoveries* a huge collection of the narratives of voyages, mostly English, mostly by sea. Woolf locates the cultural memory of English literature in Hakluyt's volumes, whose lively miscellany contrasts with later, patriarchally sanctioned attempts to bring memory into order. My purpose here is not to assess the validity of Woolf's claims, but to trace their origins in her reading and, more importantly, their effect on her feminist understanding of memory and imagination, both individual and cultural.

Richard Hakluyt (1552?–1616) collected and edited hundreds of travel narratives for publication in *Principal Navigations, Voyages, Trafficks and discoveries of the English Nation Trafficks and Discoveries*). In the dedication, he describes his first sight of a "Cosmography, with a universal map" read alongside Psalm 107.23–24 ("They that go down to the sea in ships, that do business in great waters; These see the works of the LORD, and his wonders in the deep"). This sight, Hakluyt writes, "took in me so deep an impression, that I constantly resolved, if ever I were preferred to the University . . . I would by God's assistance prosecute that knowledge and kind of literature."[2] The first edition of *Trafficks and Discoveries* appeared in 1589, just a year after England's defeat of the Spanish Armada; ten years later, the publication of the vastly expanded second edition, running to over 1.5 million words, marked England's emergence as an imperial power. Although little commented on today, Hakluyt was a major cultural force throughout the history of the British Empire. Reprinted many times since its initial publication, it was reprinted twice in the first decade of the twentieth century.[3] In addition to reading Hakluyt several times, Woolf read and reviewed two influential accounts of his significance, one by James Anthony Froude (1818–94) and another by Professor Walter Raleigh (1861–1922).[4] Froude called Hakluyt's work "the prose epic of the English nation"; Walter Raleigh called Hakluyt "a zealot of the map and of the flag."[5] Raleigh faults Froude for casting the work too narrowly "as an aspect of the Protestant Reformation."[6] The secular Raleigh sees many other plausible themes to investigate: "the fascination and the power of gold; the doom of the races of America, met by them with a tragic simplicity; the pathos of Christian missions; the romance of map-making; or the tardy growth, when all else had failed, of the idea of colonization."[7] Raleigh's list, with its racist "tragic simplicity" of the Americans, its boyish lust for adventure ("the power of gold," "the romance of map-making"), and its depiction of colonization as an inevitable (and last ditch) outcome of economic development, and Froude's more single-minded vision of religious destiny capture Hakluyt's continuing appeal for many readers. Both accounts indicate the usefulness of *Trafficks and Discoveries* for purposes of nation- and empire-building. But neither one explains Virginia Woolf's admiration.

Hakluyt's "agenda" is so malleable because his chief purpose was to compile a *useful* work, to be of service to the queen.[8] He was a capitalist with a deep interest in geography and exploration. When Stephen Greenblatt calls Hakluyt's collection "intensely patriotic and staunchly Protestant," he melds the views of Froude and Raleigh.[9] In spite of Greenblatt, indications of religious faith vary widely among the narratives;

Spain is a consistent enemy, however, and in many accounts, it is hard to discern the difference between anti-Catholic and anti-Spanish sentiments. As for Hakluyt's own views, the chapter headings are factual and unobtrusive: Hakluyt notes the date, purpose, and destination of each voyage with minimal editorializing on either the faith or the race of the people encountered there. Among those writing on his work, there is much variation in the short titles that critics prefer: of these the more political critics favor "principal navigations" (emphasizing the imperial ambitions of the project), whereas Alice Fox, the only other Woolf critic to discuss Hakluyt, uses "voyages" (emphasizing her strong interest in Woolf's development and thus, in Woolf's first novel, *The Voyage Out*).[10] Two of Woolf's three reviews on Hakluyt, however, were called "Trafficks and Discoveries" (the third was a short notice entitled "Richard Hakluyt"), and although she probably did not title these herself, this title best suits her interest in the collection's celebration of both new encounters and new trading partners. For this reason, I have used "Trafficks and Discoveries" as my preferred short title.

Woolf was not alone in dating England's coming into consciousness to the early days of the Elizabethan age: the modernists generally (especially her friend T. S. Eliot) took a keen interest in reviving and celebrating the Elizabethans. The modernists, less convinced in progress than their Victorian forbears, saw, in the Elizabethan age, a parallel age of discovery in which the learned heroically attempted to understand a dizzying array of disparate, often incompatible, observations. However, just as Renaissance thinkers varied widely in their approach to burgeoning knowledge, so too did the modernists choose different intellectual and philosophical precursors. T. S. Eliot's admiration for Renaissance metaphysics, especially Donne and Marvell, is the best-known celebration of bringing order into a world of doubt. His view was endorsed and supported by academic studies such as E. M. W. Tillyard's *The Elizabethan World Picture* (1943). James Joyce's admiration for Giordano Bruno, the author of several influential memory treatises, represents a less orthodox encyclopedism.[11] But no one has yet examined why, in this atmosphere, Woolf turned not to Donne (on whom she wrote a rather uninspired essay for *The Second Common Reader*, "Donne After Three Centuries" [1932]) or Bruno, whom she never mentioned, but persisted in her long-standing admiration for the travel narratives compiled by Richard Hakluyt.[12] In choosing Hakluyt, Woolf does not simply choose the Renaissance writer with whom she agreed, but she chooses how to read him as well, deliberately transforming his practical capitalism into an analogy for the imaginative flourishing of Elizabethan poetry.

For Woolf, the Renaissance ideal was not a complete organization but a wonderful completeness.

A common distinction used to characterize Renaissance epistemology is one between empiricism and abstract reasoning. Although this distinction suggests a continuity that stretches from Aristotelians versus Platonists to Anglo-American empiricism versus continental reason, of more significance to my argument is the wide range of approaches *within* empiricism. Significantly, among Anglo-American modernists who sought Renaissance precursors, none chose Bacon; in the end, Eliot and Joyce, like Woolf, sought the inspiration of a more imaginative worldview. In addition, a deep divide separates the Protestant metaphysics of Donne from the cabalistic ambitions (and heresies) of Bruno. More important for my argument (because it is more important to Virginia Woolf) is the less philosophically rigorous but still culturally central empiricism represented by Richard Hakluyt, Thomas Browne, and Michel de Montaigne. Of the three, her admiration for Hakluyt offers the richest possibilities. Hakluyt makes no attempt either to organize or to complete his collection of travel narratives. As a critic notes, there is no *fin* at the end of his work: "the most obvious work performed by Hakluyt's texts is *accumulation*."[13] Like other collections of the period—the commonplace books of quotations that, for Montaigne and others, gave birth to the essay and cabinets of curiosity—Hakluyt's work seems to have focused more on gathering the narratives than on editing, analysis, or commentary. Crystal Bartolovich analogizes Hakluyt's work to the cabinets of curiosity while noting his seeming inability to make the link explicit:

> While gathering material for *Principal Navigations*, Hakluyt examined at least two "Wonder Cabinets," or curiosity collections. Attempting to describe the relationship between the collections of objects he had viewed in the cabinets and the collections of texts he was in the process of assembling, he generates a list. . . . The reader is confronted with a string of words, as if describing the wealth of the new world demanded a certain verbal excess.[14]

In the face of abundance, Hakluyt cannot analyze; he simply and enthusiastically makes a new list. This charmingly unpedantic response is precisely what Woolf values in *Trafficks and Discoveries*. Like a cabinet of curiosities, his collection of texts takes her back to a moment of wonder.

Woolf consistently singles out the special role of Hakluyt in bringing English to maturity: for her, it is thanks to Hakluyt's narratives that "we find the whole of Elizabethan literature strewn with gold and silver; with talk of Guiana's rarities, and references to that America . . . which was not merely a land on the map, but symbolised the unknown territories of the soul" (CR1, 43). Nonetheless, what Hakluyt meant to Woolf changed considerably over the course of her career. She first read Hakluyt as a young teenager and returned to him as a source for both plot and setting in her first novel, *The Voyage Out* (1915), in which she strove to imagine a female voyager. In "The Elizabethan Lumber Room" (1925) and the essays and reviews that led up to it and, to a lesser extent, in "The Mark on the Wall" (1917), Woolf retreats to the ventriloquized space of an anonymous or male narrator, and, from within that neutrally male voice, she shifts the emphasis from conquest to discovery. In doing so, she alters Hakluyt's importance: instead of preserving a record of the rise of England, he has assembled the textual equivalent of an Elizabethan lumber room, a dusty storehouse of junk and treasure. The shift is a stage in her larger antipatriarchal feminist vision. In the third phase, manifest in "Street-Haunting" (1926), *A Room of One's Own* (1929), and the "London Scene" essays (1931–32), Woolf integrates her feminism with her love of the stuff of travel: the stories and the souvenirs. This integration bypasses the mode of acquisition (piracy) in order to celebrate the beautiful things acquired. Finally, at the end of her career, in *Between the Acts* (1941) and "Anon" (both published posthumously), there is a retreat from the philosophically complex celebration of exploration and acquisition in the late 1920s to a nativist, little England position, taking an isolationist turn from travel and adventure to domestic pastoral, imagining the Elizabethan age as less international and more local. Ultimately, Woolf's solutions to these problems of memory and imagination, empire and capitalism are incomplete and unsatisfactory. They bear witness to some of the limitations of her feminism.

## Early Voyages Out, to 1915

For Woolf, the greatest writer of English literature by a very wide margin was Shakespeare: "Shakespeare stands out, Shakespeare . . . has had the light on him from his day to ours, Shakespeare . . . towers highest when looked at from the level of his own contemporaries" (CR1, 48).[15] For most of her career, the greatest literary mystery was not how English moved from anonymous pastoral songs and fables to Chaucer, but how, out of this culture of Chaucer, Shakespeare emerged. She believed that "masterpieces are not single and solitary births" (ARO, 65) and that even the greatest writers emerge from (and bear the marks of) a knowable culture. But that belief alone could not account for the fantastic explosion of linguistic and imaginative wealth in Shakespeare. Woolf finds the answer in Hakluyt: travel, exploration, and trade. The capitalist and imperialist expansion of England in the sixteenth century brought material wealth, and these riches enriched the imagination. This is a large-scale, national version of an argument she makes at the individual level in *A Room of One's Own*: that "intellectual freedom depends on material things" (ARO, 108). But in the case of the English Renaissance, Woolf feels that material abundance and variety fed not the intellect but the imagination.

Virginia Stephen's first publication on *Trafficks and Discoveries* was a 1906 review of Professor Raleigh's *The English Voyages of the Sixteenth Century*, a work originally published as a commentary within the final volume of the 1903–05 edition of Hakluyt. She praises Raleigh's "luminous and authoritative comment" (E, 1.123), a view she would later retreat from. In this brief review, Woolf sets out the major themes of her lifelong engagement with Hakluyt: amazement at the sheer scope of Hakluyt's work, fascination with the character of an ordinary seaman, love of the lists of commodities, and a sense that all of these might inspire poetry. For, although she writes that "it is not, as Professor Raleigh goes on to remark, in literature that we must look for the influence of the Elizabethan voyagers" (E, 1.121), she does not seem to believe it. Even in this early essay, under the influence of just having read Raleigh, Woolf sees clearly that "wherever you open the book you may find some rough phrase to be tuned to such melody, and as you go along you may be your own poet" (E, 1.123). Certainly, Woolf read *Trafficks and Discoveries* as her own poet, borrowing "rough phrases" to tune *her* melody.[16] For her, Hakluyt provides a storehouse of language, and as the years went by and as she developed a greater critical distance on Raleigh, she came to believe that he was wrong about Hakluyt and poetry. She believed, in fact, that the work's greatest influence was its influence on literature.

After the 1906 review, Woolf's next substantive engagement with *Trafficks and Discoveries* was also her most literal: in *The Voyage Out* (1915), she drew on Francis Drake's description of Guiana, among other narratives, to set the stage. Alice Fox's study of Woolf's Elizabethan sources charts how "the successive drafts of the novel written over a five-year period reveal the author's developing awareness of how best to use Hakluyt's *Voyages*" and how "the very plot of the novel resembles countless narratives in Hakluyt."[17] As in many

Elizabethan voyages, not everything ends happily for the principals: Rachel Vinrace does not triumph but dies, like "the Elizabethan voyager Sir Hugh Willoughby, who died on his voyage out" and for whom her father, Willoughby Vinrace, seems to have been named.[18] The voyage here is one of discovery and exploration that ends in senseless death. Rachel and Terence would seem to be voyaging together—in Terence's fantasies, anyway—to a new vision of marriage. But Rachel's relief that, while engaged, she need not think about marriage, herself, or Terence, and her hallucinations while dying suggest a solo voyage, one fraught with perils. As Fox notes, "Rachel's milieu is depicted as Elizabethan, and only the naïve Evelyn Murgatroyd would see that as propitious. . . . Woolf's later portrait of Judith Shakespeare in *A Room of One's Own* puts the lie to Evelyn Murgatroyd's romanticizing."[19]

Evelyn's attempts to try on the role of an adventurer, though comic, are more suggestive than Fox allows them to be. She arrives in South America unaccompanied by husband or father, having read adventure stories like those collected in Hakluyt. Her abundant ideas of herself—she changes fantasies and boyfriends with manic frequency— attest to the way that her reading has expanded (and excited) her imagination: "With a feather drooping from a broad-brimmed hat, in white from top to toe, she looked like a gallant lady of the time of Charles the First leading royalist troops into action" (VO, 129); "I'd have liked to be one of those colonists, to cut down trees and make laws and all that" (VO, 192); "I'm tired of playing . . . I'm going to do something" (VO, 248). Woolf plays these moments for comic effect: Evelyn's politics are egotistical, conservative (she is a royalist, an imperialist, and a woman of action), and incoherent (she later wants to enact reforms for unwed mothers). Nevertheless, Evelyn is portrayed as energetic and full of ideas: her character suggests possibility; she embodies the gap between a young woman's energy and her lack of opportunities for meaningful action. The feminist point here is muted; instead, Woolf's social commentary emphasizes the absurdity of a woman with nothing to do. If Rachel is a clueless and blank female voyager, Evelyn tries to be a pirate. Woolf treats one woman's failure with sympathy, and the other's with mockery. In neither case can she imagine how a woman could undertake a voyage—in any era—and prevail.

Although reading Hakluyt enriched Woolf's imagination in the ways she imagined it enriched Shakespeare's, her characters do not have a similarly enriching experience of travel. Evelyn responds to the new landscape as an English*man* should, wanting to be an empire-builder, a pirate, buying into the nationalist rhetoric even as she pants for revolution: "If I were you . . . I'd raise a troop and conquer some great territory and make it splendid" (VO, 136). More pragmatically capitalist, St. John remarks that an English businessman could make his fortune without much effort, continuing the imperial habit of seeing the developing world as a business opportunity. Meanwhile, Rachel's father, Willoughby Vinrace, does not respond to the landscape at all: a minor character and a failure as a father, his inert presence symbolizes the failures of the English sea captain. When Helen Ambrose thinks cynically (if accurately), "Willoughby, as usual, loved his business and built his Empire, and between them all she would be considerably bored" (VO, 23),[20] Woolf resists the cultural pressure to celebrate such men. In contrast, Professor Raleigh, writing in 1905, praises the type:

> The character of the English sailor is the most inalterable and valuable of national assets; while the British Constitution has moved from precedent to precedent, he has remained the same. His life is a hard one, but he takes it as it comes. . . . He is careless of the graces and ornaments of life. Though he has a warm heart, he is no humanitarian. Danger is his daily companion, and he has learned . . . that a seaman is useless unless he is resolute to the degree of madness.[21]

Here, an English professor openly prefers unthinking manly stoicism over the powerful, reasoned flexibility of the Constitution. Raleigh's admiration is studded with cliché. The sailor "takes it as it comes," "danger is his daily companion," and he is "resolute to the degree of madness." Froude's sense of the English sailor is even more enthusiastically stereotypical: "Drake's cannon would not have roared so loudly and so widely without seamen already trained in heart and hand to work his ships and level his artillery."[22] Perhaps Froude's and Raleigh's clichés are justified since the sailor himself has not changed in 300 years. Yet Raleigh's and Froude's sailors do not interest Woolf nor do they match wholly with the accounts we read in Hakluyt. The difference between Woolf's and the men's accounts can partially be explained by the huge cultural shift separating 1905 from 1915. Still, much of the difference may also be attributed to Woolf's acuity, her commitment to questioning culturally accepted myths. The captains in Hakluyt may be resolute—as is Willoughby Vinrace—but the sailors (and many of the narratives in Hakluyt are written by sailors rather than captains) are smaller and more malleable than Froude's and Raleigh's descriptions imply: they get scared, seasick, and homesick; they are amazed at cultural differences; they negotiate with their captors; they use their wits to escape; they delight in making a good trade; and they love plunder and piracy. In short, they are small-time capitalists, opportunists, crooks, and adventurers, hoping to benefit from experience.[23] As Woolf says, "they had, as we have, a mixture of motives" (E, 2.330). The whole point of Hakluyt for Woolf is not unchangingness but change: the voyages of the sixteenth century changed England forever; they made Shakespeare possible.

In *The Voyage Out*, only the elderly Mr. Pepper seems to benefit from the voyage.[24] Looking over the deck of the *Euphroysne*, he remarks on earlier voyages; his reading (of Hakluyt, presumably) has prepared him for the sight of the South American coast and he draws on that reading to interpret the moment. His privileged status as a reader contributes to his appreciation rather than distancing him from it, giving him a doubly meaningful experience:

> [T]hree hundred years ago five Elizabethan barques had anchored where the *Euphrosyne* now floated. Half-drawn up upon the beach lay an equal number of Spanish galleons, unmanned, for the country was still a virgin land behind a veil. Slipping across the water, the English sailors bore away bars of silver, bales of linen, timbers of cedar wood, golden crucifixes knobbed with emeralds. When the Spaniards came down from their drinking, a fight ensued, the two parties churning up the sand, and driving each other into the surf. The Spaniards, bloated with fine living upon the fruits of the miraculous land, fell in heaps; but the hardy Englishmen, tawny with sea-voyaging, hairy for lack of razors, with muscles like wire, fangs greedy for flesh, and fingers itching for gold despatched the wounded, drove the dying into the sea, and soon reduced the natives to a state of superstitious wonderment. (VO, 88–89)

Pepper's musings, of little interest to the others, closely mimic stories from *Trafficks and Discoveries*—in this case, we can trace many details to Francis Drake's circumnavigation of the globe.[25] But Woolf's account contains an ironic detachment unthinkable in 1577 or even in 1905.

In order to grasp Woolf's transformation of Drake's voyage, we need to go back to the account in *Trafficks and Discoveries* and then to Froude's and Raleigh's interpretations of it. The anonymous account of Drake's voyage in *Trafficks and Discoveries* matter-of-factly details Drake's "carnival of plunder."[26] An English sailor boards a Spanish ship, strikes "one of the Spaniards, and said unto him, *abajo perro*, that is in English, go down dog"; later, "our general rifled the ship."[27] The 1577 account is unselfconscious. Spanish is useful insofar as it helps defeat Spaniards and the captain's job is to "rifle the ship." In a deadpan voice, this sailor gives an account of bullying and piracy. Centuries later, Froude turns this into a moment of heroism and, strangely, gentlemanly restraint: "A Plymouth lad who could speak Spanish knocked down the first man he met with an '*Abajo, perro*' 'Down, you dog, down!' No life was taken; Drake never hurt man if he could help it."[28] Where the Elizabethan narrative simply translates *abajo perro*, Froude embellishes adding an extra "down" for effect. The "lad" intimidates; Drake refrains from murder. Later in the 1577 narrative, they find "a Spaniard lying asleep, who had lying by him 13 bars of silver" and they "took the silver and left the man."[29] The treasure ship *Cacafuego* carries "80 lbs weight of gold, and a crucifix of gold with goodly great emeralds set in it" that they take. They loot a few more ships, mug some Spaniards on shore, and the general deems himself "sufficiently satisfied and revenged."[30] In his 1895 account, Froude is keen to reestablish Drake's reputation as a hero:

> We English have been contented to allow Drake a certain qualified praise. We admit that he was a bold, dextrous sailor, that he did his country good service at the Invasion. We allow that he was a famous navigator, and sailed round the world, which no one else had done before him. But—there is always a but—of course he was a robber and a corsair, and the only excuse for him is that he was no worse than most of his contemporaries.[31]

This chumminess characterizes Froude's book; he continually justifies the actions of Drake and others by reminding his readers that times were different. Raleigh, slightly less savage, shares much of Froude's enthusiasm and notes with some regret that "these early exploits of Drake are barely recorded in Hakluyt's compilation" since Hakluyt "shows a certain tenderness of conscience with regard to sheer piracy."[32] Religion, too, gets different treatment over the years. The 1577 narrative claims that, with the gift of good English wool, the indigenous Americans "supposed us to be gods and would not be persuaded otherwise."[33] Froude, committed to a more orthodox theology, omits the incident. (His focus is on the triumph of the Protestant Reformation: Englishmen encouraging idolatry hardly fits the pattern.) Raleigh, by contrast, banishes doubt, reporting that Drake "was solemnly crowned by the Indians as their king."[34] In sharp contrast, Woolf has the "natives" "reduced . . . to a state of superstitious wonderment." For her, the English are not gods but at best wondrous, and at worst, simply strange.[35]

Thus, to return to Woolf's version of the incident in *The Voyage Out*, when Woolf has Pepper recall how the English sailors "bore away" great heaps of goods, she both suppresses the violence and resists the heroism. Although she does not go so far as to condemn the voyage—and she makes that emerald-encrusted crucifix as appealing as ever—she refuses to celebrate piracy. Where the 1577 narrative boasts of a sailor's ability to curse in two languages, Woolf depicts them as dirty, greedy, barbaric and unfeeling men. The men are "tawny with sea-voyaging, hairy for lack of razors," and, in that parallel construction, Woolf offers a comic deflation of the English seamen—strong, yes, but also smelly. She insists on the romance of the tale, accurately calling the small ships barques; where they "anchored," the less-threatened *Euphrosyne* simply "floats." The land was not simply sparsely inhabited but "a virgin land behind a veil": a phrase that fuses the tropes of exotic landscape as feminized sublime, the veiled Oriental woman (no matter that we are in South America), and Elizabeth, the Virgin Queen. The catalogue of treasures is balanced and calculated to entice all consumers, with luxury items framing humbler commodities: "bars of silver, bales of linen, timbers of cedar wood, golden crucifixes knobbed with emeralds." In this context, the crucifix ceases to be a sign of Catholic idolatry (as it partly was to the Elizabethans) and becomes sheer treasure. Most striking of all, the drunken, bloated Spaniards are Woolf's invention, and her description of the brutish English sailors, while derived from clues in *Trafficks and Discoveries*, is far from either the sailors' self-presentation or that of Froude and Raleigh. Thus, instead of a story of bravery, hints of imperial greatness to come, or the superiority of Protestant piracy to Spanish empire-building, Woolf tells a roughly comic story of Spanish gourmands versus English ruffians. Overall, whereas Woolf emphasizes the ordinary sailor and the abundant variety of things brought back to England, Froude focuses on mastery, success, and destiny and Raleigh on adventures and the magnitude of the courage of the sailors. Though there are boilerplate sentences about the true English character that could be in any work, Raleigh's and Froude's pulses really start to race when talking about piracy. They relay stories of glass-eating and, though Professor Raleigh expresses regrets at plunder, he, like Froude, talks about it a lot. None of this plays a role in Woolf.

## IMAGINARY VOYAGES, 1916–25

Mr. Pepper's appreciation of the landscape in *The Voyage Out* anticipates the use that Woolf would make of Hakluyt in the next phase of her career. In the late 1910s and early 1920s, Woolf's comments on Hakluyt emphasize the experience of reading over the voyages. Much as Woolf loved reading travel literature, she was not enough of a traveler herself to write it convincingly, and, after *The Voyage Out*, her subsequent allusions to *Trafficks and Discoveries* emphasize the impact of Hakluyt's text on readers back home over the voyages themselves. In this period, Woolf's writing on travel was nearly silent on questions of gender: it is as if she let the problem of the female traveler lie fallow.

Woolf wrote several essays and reviews from 1916 to 1923 from which she drew for her 1925 essay, "The Elizabethan Lumber Room."[36] In them she celebrates the process of exploration over the moment of discovering, wandering over taking possession, and imaginative over actual travel. During the same period, her essays and reviews strive toward a perspective that she might later label androgynous: she combines the confident authority of the professional journalist with the outsider's perspective of the feminist intellectual. Yet, even in this retreat from an attempt to imagine a female traveler, she continues to question the grounds on which travel had been admired. For example, she continues to downplay conquest and piracy and insists on the centrality of trade, and she finds the correspondence between merchants and their agents abroad "as good reading as the more heroic passages which have become famous" (E, 2.333). Decades later, Stephen Greenblatt explores the existence of an alternative to Columbus's drive to possess and occupy and the possibility of "circulation or wandering as an alternative to ownership," and of "a refusal to occupy."[37] This is the side of travel literature—the side represented for Greenblatt by Mandeville and Montaigne—that Woolf admires and emulates in Hakluyt.

Woolf continues her work to scrub Hakluyt of his Victorian encrustations, particularly chauvinism, while developing her views on how his narratives contributed to Elizabethan poetry. While she typically stresses poetry's dependence on diverse and abundant material, in one review, she even goes so far as to imply the superiority of mental travel over actual travel: "The navigator and the explorer made their voyage by ship instead of by the mind, but over Hakluyt's pages broods the very same lustre of the imagination" (E, 2.91–92). Even here, it is only a suggestion, offered as part of an effort to elevate Hakluyt's centrality not for heroism or empire but for the "lustre of the imagination." Woolf's persistent admiration for Hakluyt comes as a surprise even to her: "I have spent the week (but I was interrupted 2 days, & one cut short by a lunch with Roger) over Hakluyt: who turns out on

mature inspection to justify over & over again my youthful discrimi-
nation" (D, 1.224). In the face of all the changes at the turn of the
twentieth century, including all those of 1910 and World War I, Woolf
still delights in reading Hakluyt.

This section traces Woolf's transformation of Hakluyt in four ways:
first, by way of further comparison with Professor Raleigh, whose thesis on the impact of the voyages on poetry Woolf extended; second,
through a reading of Woolf's story "The Mark on the Wall," wherein
she shows her intense antipathy to system and her great affection for
imaginative openness; third, through a reading of "The Elizabethan
Lumber Room," emphasizing the analogies she makes among voyaging, collecting travel narratives, and composing richly imagined texts
(here, Browne's *Hydriotaphia, or Urne-Buriall*). Finally, we see the
first glimmer of a solution to the neglected question of gender, travel,
and imagination in Elizabeth Dalloway's bus ride to East London.

To better understand the differences between Woolf and her
Victorian precursors, we need further comparison with Froude and,
especially, Raleigh. To do that, it helps to imagine the plight of the
overwhelmed reviewer. The second edition of *Trafficks and Discoveries*
ran to over 1.5 million words. Clearly, selection is necessary for any
commentator: as Woolf notes, "these magnificent volumes are not
often, perhaps, read through" (CR1, 39). And for Woolf, writing a
brief review, the temptation to highlight what had already been high-
lighted must have been great. It was, in fact, her habit in writing
reviews to stick close to her source, borrowing heavily. Woolf's review
of Froude, by contrast, opens by damning him with the faint praise,
"readable" (E, 2.329), then barely mentions his *English Seamen in the
Sixteenth Century*, and urges people to read *Trafficks and Discoveries*
instead.[38]

Though Woolf quickly dismissed Froude, it took her longer to
shake off the influence of Professor Raleigh, for whose book she initially expressed gratitude. Raleigh devotes a full one-third of his study
to the topic of greatest interest to Woolf: "The Influence of the
Voyages on Poetry and Imagination." And Woolf borrowed liberally
from and extended his thesis. In a 1917 review, she argues that poetry
joined the worlds of court and sea, that "the world of Shakespeare is
the world of Hakluyt and of Raleigh; on that map Guiana and the
River of the Plate are not very far distant or easily distinguishable from
the Forest of Arden and Elsinore" (E, 2.91–92). For Professor
Raleigh, the Elizabethan age was one of "the great ages of the world"
in which "a new prospect" extends "the horizon of experience": "All
preconceived notions and beliefs . . . were made ridiculous by the new

discoveries. . . . All things became possible."[39] As Woolf would insist that "masterpieces are not single and solitary births" (ARO, 65), Raleigh, too, insists on the "hidden causes" that led to England's emergence as a naval and literary power: "The English naval power, like the English drama, seemed to be the growth of a single night. In either case, hidden causes had been at work."[40] To demonstrate the differences between them, this section analyzes their treatment of three narratives: one admired by both and then each writer's paradigmatic choice. Both Woolf and Raleigh highlight the story of the *Squirrel*'s sinking, but while one of Professor Raleigh's favorite stories is of the sinking of the *Revenge*, Woolf repeats (three times) a more homely anecdote, of a "worn-out man" whose parents recognize him as "the boy who had left years ago to sail the seas" by "a wart upon one of his knees" (CR1, 40; CDB, 159–60; E, 2.332).

In spite of Raleigh's capacious thesis about the literary benefits of travel narratives, he emphasizes only direct metaphors of sea voyages as the manifestations of Hakluyt's influence. He gets distracted by Shakespeare's misapprehension that hour glasses run out in 60 minutes. (They run out in only 30.[41]) Although he claims that Elizabethan literature's abundant catalogue derive from Hakluyt's influence, he does not analyze any. In fact, every time it seems that Raleigh is going to show us the interesting and unexpected ways that the voyages worked on the imagination, he turns from literature to anecdote: "The fantastic adventure of the age and its intimate connection with grave historical events may well be seen in the career of the notorious Tom Stukeley," whose story he proceeds to relate.[42] When Raleigh turns to Hakluyt himself, the cult of manliness persists. He makes the work of the scholar heroic, praising the *physical* exertion of hunting down stories and manuscripts: "It was to speak with the only surviving witness of this voyage, one Master Thomas Buts, that Hakluyt, at a much later date, traveled two hundred miles on horseback."[43]

The story of the sinking of the *Revenge* in 1591 is one of the most literary in *Trafficks and Discoveries*. (Sir Walter Raleigh [1552?–1618], who did not witness the event, wrote the account.) Alone and besieged by 15 Spanish ships, the commander of the *Revenge*, Sir Richard Grenville, kept fighting for 15 hours, sustaining much damage to his own ship but causing even more to the Spanish fleet. Finally, with defeat inevitable, Grenville urged the master-gunner to help him in sinking the *Revenge* so that no English ship could fall into Spanish hands. With the English sailors begging for surrender and survival, Grenville was forced to surrender to the Spanish authorities, in whose custody he died. For both Sir Walter Raleigh, who wrote the account, and Professor Raleigh, Grenville's tale is one of honor; both men have special respect for how Grenville's determination earned the admiration (and, ultimately, the mercy) of the Spanish. The story of the *Revenge* is violent and gripping. Unlike many of the anonymous or forgotten authors represented in *Trafficks and Discoveries*, Raleigh writes with a dramatist's ear. Three hundred years later, the account moves Professor Raleigh, who writes that Grenville's peers saw his actions "matched only by poetry in its strongest and highest flights."[44] Keen as she was to find the poetry in *Trafficks and Discoveries*, the story of the *Revenge* does not even figure in Woolf's accounts.[45] Woolf admired Sir Walter Raleigh only as a prose stylist, not a hero. In her review of his works, she faults him for being "always eager to justify his own daring, and to proclaim the supremacy of the English among other peoples" (E, 2.92). She offers this justification for her continued admiration of sea stories: "if we had to justify our love of these old voyagers we should not lay stress upon the boastful and magnificent strain in them; we should point, rather, to the strain of poetry" (E, 2.93). Here, to illustrate the kind of poetry one finds in Elizabethan tales, she digresses from her review of Professor Raleigh's book to retell the story of Sir Humphrey Gilbert and the sinking of the *Squirrel*.

In fact, the story of the *Squirrel* is one that both Woolf and Professor Raleigh admire. Edward Haye's account of Sir Humphrey Gilbert's Atlantic voyage is less novelistic and more miscellaneous than the story of the *Revenge*. As with many other accounts, no transitions cushion the shift from speculations about future profit or lists of commodities to be found from accounts of fierce storms and death. Thus, for example, in the same report that offers the famous description of Gilbert's last moments, Haye also writes of Newfoundland, "Iron very common, lead, and somewhere copper. I will not aver of richer metals."[46] On this arduous and tragic journey, Gilbert sailed on the *Squirrel*, one of the smaller ships in his fleet because it was "the most convenient to discover upon the coast."[47] The tiny overloaded frigate was ill-suited for the early September sail back to England. Nevertheless, Gilbert insisted on remaining with his ship:

> Monday the ninth of September, in the afternoon, the frigate was nearly cast away . . . yet at that time recovered: and giving forth signs of joy, the general sitting abaft with a book in his hand, cried out unto us in the *Hind* (so oft as we did approach within hearing) we are as near to heaven by sea as by land.
>
> That same Monday night, about twelve of the clock . . . the frigate being ahead of us . . . suddenly her lights were out, whereof as it were

in a moment, we lost the sight, and withal our watch cried, the general was cast away, which was too true.[48]

Professor Raleigh writes, "Gilbert's last speech is his sufficient memorial: perhaps it was ringing in Robert Burton's memory, when, writing of the remedies for discontent, he paraphrased Gilbert's great saying."[49] Woolf uses the story four times: in her 1906 review, in her 1917 essay on Sir Walter Raleigh, in the posthumously published 1919 essay "Reading" and, finally in the 1925 essay "The Elizabethan Lumber Room." In "The Elizabethan Lumber Room", the story exemplifies the proximity of God, a key difference, for Woolf, between the Elizabethans and the moderns[50]: "God was as near by sea as by land, said Sir Humfrey Gilbert, riding through the storm. Suddenly one light disappeared; Sir Humfrey Gilbert had gone beneath the waves; when morning came, they sought his ship in vain" (CR1, 40).

Because of her suicide by drowning, much has been made of Woolf's lifelong interest in stories of drowning, from "A Terrible Tragedy in Duck Pond" (1899) to her interest in the soldier in the channel during World War II (M, 130–31), but it is Raleigh, not Woolf, who connects Gilbert's courageous words to Burton's *Anatomy of Melancholy*. In "The Elizabethan Lumber Room," Woolf includes her very brief account of the *Squirrel*, and what it reminds us about faith in the era, in a catalog of hardships balanced by extravagant hope. The hope, she asserts, fuels continued voyaging, as men ask themselves "what if the passage to the fabled land of uncounted riches lay only a little farther up the coast?" (CR1, 40). The idea that success lies just a bit farther ahead fuels many of the accounts in *Trafficks and Discoveries*. It is a prime justification for captains in search of financial backing and a frequent speculation of sailors returning disappointed. Deploying the era's vague hyperbole with gentle irony, Woolf captures the poignant hope that Hakluyt expresses in moments such as this one from his preface: "True it is, that our success hath not been correspondent unto theirs [the Spanish]: yet in this our attempt the uncertainty of finding was far greater, and the difficulty and danger of searching was no whit less."[51] As a reader Woolf loved these stories, but as a citizen she saw clearly how they worked as recruitment literature: "These are the fine stories used effectively all through the West country to decoy 'the apt young men' lounging by the harbourside to leave their nets and fish for gold" (CR1, 41).[52] These ordinary sailors, seduced by stories, interest Woolf. She recognizes the lure and love of gold for these men and also recognizes the more immediately pragmatic capitalist impulse of the financial backers who saw "how necessary it is to find a market abroad for English wool" (CR1, 41). The Elizabethans had a major wool surplus, and, as Hakluyt writes, "our chief desire is to find ample vent for our woolen cloth."[53] With her comprehension of both the role of advertising ("fine stories . . . to decoy 'apt young men' ") and market forces, Woolf transforms the Victorian Hakluyt into a modern one. Some of this not only involves complicity in hiding violence—particularly of the slave trade—but it also involves being forthright about capitalist ambitions and the usefulness of romance in recruiting sailors.

Everything that Woolf found interesting in Hakluyt worked against the Victorian vision of him: for her, his collection is eccentric, individual, and suggestive. To make the contrast with Raleigh complete, we turn to an incident that is absent in his accounts but is central to hers: the return of a sailor, unrecognizable but for a wart on one knee. Woolf's ability to take something small and ugly, like the sailor's wart, and use it as the germ of a story is central to her modernist method:

> And sometimes a ragged and worn-out man came knocking at the door of an English country house and claimed to be the boy who had left it years ago to sail the seas. "Sir William his father, and my lady his mother knew him not to be their son, until they found a secret mark, which was a wart upon one of his knees." But he had with him a black stone, veined with gold, or an ivory tusk, or a silver ingot, and urged on the village youth with talk of gold strewn over the land as stones are strewn in the fields of England. (CR1, 40)

The wart functions as a mnemonic device on the sailor's body for his parents, and also for Woolf's essay, standing for the many amazing and suggestive stories in *Trafficks and Discoveries*. The story of a sailor's return reminds us that such returns are never as simple as one, in a sentimental mood, might like them to be: people return changed, often damaged, even traumatized. The sailor in "The Elizabethan Lumber Room" returns half-starved. His body, altered almost beyond recognition by the privations of the voyages, bears an earlier mark: the wart. In spite of these signs of suffering, his return's chief effect is to encourage further journeys. The stories he returns home with and their seductive powers demonstrate the power of words. The imaginary picture of "gold strewn over the land" seems more real and incites more action than the actual suffering man. Woolf again explores the theme of a sailor's return in "Three Pictures" (1929): three connected vignettes of village life depict a sailor's joyous return to his pregnant wife and his subsequent death, days later, of fever.

These stories, once committed to paper (as the story of the sailor with a wart was by Hakluyt himself), became the stuff of *Trafficks and Discoveries* and, centuries later, inspired English writers.

The Elizabethan voyages themselves could not have an effect on literature until there were accounts of those voyages. And for Woolf, Hakluyt's unobtrusive editing gave writers maximum imaginative freedom. As she asks us to imagine the scenes she sketches of a sailor's homecoming or of "savages" living chastely under the gaze of their captors on board a ship (CR1, 42),[54] she asks us to share her delight in imagining the narrative possibilities, to imagine in each the germ of *Twelfth Night*, *The Tempest*, or *Othello*. *Trafficks and Discoveries* inspires Woolf because it is suggestive, not didactic. The narratives are relatively unadorned, sticking close to the events—sometimes devolving from reportage to mere lists. As we have seen—and in spite of her admiration for Sir Walter Raleigh's prose elsewhere—Woolf does not gravitate to his or other polished narratives in Hakluyt. Instead, she looks to rougher accounts, to stories that suggest more, which retain the vivid simplicity and colloquialisms of their day. These are the stories that lodge in her memory that ignite her imagination. The notion of writing as a trigger for memory and imaginative flight governs Woolf's best experimental writing. In "The Death of the Moth," she charts the movement of a reader's eyes back and forth between the book and the world. As was the case for Woolf herself and for Mr. Pepper in *The Voyage Out*, a mind enriched by reading is more receptive to and observant of the world. But it is in "The Mark on the Wall" that we can best see her imaginative power. There Woolf develops the multiple significances that can lie within even a detail as humble as a wart.

Yet what Woolf makes of that mark in her 1917 story "The Mark on the Wall" says much about the effects of historical context on the imagination. The story, written against the backdrop of World War I, begins with the narrator shaking off a childishly militaristic "automatic fancy" "of red knights riding up the side of the black rock" (CSF, 83), triggered by the fire in the grate. When she sees the mark, which is new to the narrator and as yet free of significance, she is relieved to be free of the automatic fancy. Such fancies, always irritating to Woolf's characters,[55] indicate the potential of memory: our minds are attracted to and retain elaborate images. However, automatic fancies emerge from collective memory, not from individual imaginations. Woolf's ultimate refusal to give the mark significance emphasizes her distance from any universalizing or generalizing turn of mind. Woolf's resistance to institutional or culturally endorsed memory is integral to her resistance to all patriarchal structures, especially the war machine. In "The Mark on the Wall," she demonstrates how deeply the habits of mind are affected by culture and how fiercely women must resist patriarchy. "Generalizations," she writes, "are very worthless. The military sound of the word is enough" (CSF, 86).

The mark permits the mind to wander freely, and even the antiquarians, who are, in her imagination (and from her reading), "retired colonels," have given up their fealty to Whitaker's Almanack and the Table of Precedency and feel "agreeably philosophic in accumulating evidence on both sides" (CSF, 87). Their wives, meanwhile, busy with the details of housekeeping, "have every reason for keeping that great question of the camp or the tomb in perpetual suspension" (CSF, 87). Because the mark is, in the end, a snail, it will move, though its presence there once, now recorded in the story, will always inspire the memory of the thoughts surrounding it. But what are those thoughts? "I can't remember a thing" (CSF, 89), says the narrator, refusing summary. The narrator's refusal of summary and the colonels' and their wives' (differently motivated) acceptance of ambiguity emphasizes how completely the mark refuses incorporation into a system: it stands for too many different things. Preeminent among them is its usefulness as a site of inquiry; as an inspiration for imaginative adventures, it allows the mind to wander freely, unhampered by the need to possess. Then, just after the narrator asserts that she cannot remember, someone enters and reveals that the mark is just a snail. The snail, as Woolf presents it, is both too real and too mundane to inspire the imagination. Ultimately, "The Mark on the Wall" dramatizes a pacifist's wartime desire to obliterate memory, to reject a world in which memorials are necessary. The story is an antimemorial, and the mark, a sign of interpretive possibility, is an image for the impossibility of fixing meaning.

The culmination of Woolf's thinking on memory and the imagination in this period comes in "The Elizabethan Lumber Room," an essay first collected in *The Common Reader* that borrows liberally from her reviews and from the posthumously published 1919 essay "Reading." Where the "The Elizabethan Lumber Room" begins with Hakluyt, "Reading" opens with a meditation on country house libraries—the pleasures they promise and how they coexist with the larger world of tennis and farming. One dependable pleasure, the narrator asserts, is the presence of Elizabethan travel narratives, and the essay opens with an account of what it is like to read about Queen Elizabeth on a summer's day while others play and work outside. Suddenly it is dusk and the scene changes to one of moth hunting. This small essay within the essay revisits, in miniature, the pleasure of conquest and the insatiable enthusiasm for ephemera. The story of moth hunting helps fill in the story of how Woolf understands adventure, how she values these small, domestic excursions and their expansive influence on the imagination as much or more than the voyages themselves. In "Reading," the scene next shifts to morning, when one does not want to read Hakluyt but turns instead to Browne.

"The Elizabethan Lumber Room" opens with the essay's central analogy: a comparison of *Trafficks and Discoveries* to a lumber room:

> These magnificent volumes are not often, perhaps, read through. Part of their charm consists in the fact that Hakluyt is not so much a book as a great bundle of commodities loosely tied together, an emporium, a lumber room strewn with ancient sacks, obsolete nautical instruments, huge bales of wool, and little bags of rubies and emeralds. One is for ever untying this packet here, sampling that heap over there, wiping the dust off some vast map of the world, and sitting down in semi-darkness to snuff the strange smells of silks and leathers and ambergris, while outside tumble the huge waves of the uncharted Elizabethan sea. (CR1, 39)

In comparing the book to a lumber room, Woolf makes a strong claim for reading as a physical pleasure. Reading Hakluyt has an almost hallucinatory intensity: these pages have the power to make one feel one is tasting exotic foods, smelling "silks and leathers and ambergris" while hearing the waves crash outside. The variety that *Trafficks and Discoveries* offers is so vast, so palpable, that it is greater than the variety offered by a library, which houses only one kind of thing: books. As with the opening of the essay, "Lives of the Obscure" in which she dares to disturb the slumber of long unread books, Woolf transforms reading itself into an adventure. Unlike Professor Raleigh's praise of Hakluyt the intrepid researcher, for Woolf reading Hakluyt qualifies as exciting not because of the physical exertion of traveling to acquire the text, but because of the anticipated imaginative treat of reading something exciting, enormous, and long unread.

Woolf proceeds to describe the abundance of stories to be found in Hakluyt and how they helped to recruit young men: "All this, the new words, the new ideas, the waves, the savages, the adventures, found their way naturally into the plays which were being acted on the Thames" (CR1, 42). This leads to an allusion to Montaigne's "Of Cannibals" which, in turn, leads her to wonder why, when English poetry and French prose flourished, English prose languished, remaining turgid and "unable to grasp a thought closely and firmly or to adapt itself flexibly to the chops and changes of the mind" (CR1, 44).

Criticism of Sidney in particular leads to praise for the theater and then, finally, to Browne: "He it was who first turned from the contacts of men to their lonely life within" (CR1, 45).

At the end of the essay, Woolf extends the analogy between the lumber room itself and *Trafficks and Discoveries* to include the work of Browne. She attributes to Browne's work all the wonder and abundance that she initially attributed to Hakluyt. This turn from journeys to their narratives to essays, which are as rich as the narrative of a journey, is increasingly inward: it is also and more importantly a celebration of the imagination and how the imagination is nourished by the world: "Now we are in the presence of sublime imagination; now rambling through one of the finest lumber rooms in the world—a chamber stuffed from floor to ceiling with ivory, old iron, broken pots, urns, unicorns' horns, and magic glasses full of emerald lights and blue mystery" (CR1, 47). Woolf is moved by Browne's ability to be inspired by what he learns of the world: his capacity for wonder, his quickness, and his honesty all contribute to his writing's continuing power. For him stories like the ones in Hakluyt do not represent a siren's song, luring him to travel in search of riches, but an opportunity for reflection. He turns inward and finds equivalent wonders in his own soil, his own soul, and the oddities of his own body.

The inward turn, the increasing confidence in the power of imagination, is matched by a transformation in Woolf's outlook. In the 1925 novel *Mrs. Dalloway*, she changes the scale of the journey from the transatlantic voyaging of *The Voyage Out* to a bus ride across town. This comic diminution has serious implications: it participates in a larger modernist turn to the details of ordinary life and, in so doing, permits women to participate. At first, in the case of poor Miss Kilman, Elizabeth Dalloway's tutor and friend, the application of nautical imagery still works to the disadvantage of women. Miss Kilman is abandoned in a department store, clumsily listing amidst goods that remind her of the opportunities she has lost: "hemmed in by trunks specially prepared for taking to India; next got among the accouchement sets and baby linen; through all the commodities of the world, perishable and permanent, hams, drugs, flowers, stationery, variously smelling, now sweet, now sour, she lurched" (MD, 133). Unlike the celebratory and wondrous catalogs in "The Elizabethan Lumber Room," this list taunts Miss Kilman with what she lacks: funds for travel, children, and food.

Elizabeth Dalloway, by contrast, voyages out as the Queen Elizabeth, with whom she shares a name could only do by proxy. She rides the bus east, out of haute-bourgeois Kensington toward the City, commerce, poverty, and immigration. Although Elizabeth herself "inclined to be passive," the bus is "a pirate" (MD, 135). Invigorated by its "reckless, unscrupulous" passage through London, Elizabeth first feels herself to be "like the figure-head of a ship" then, increasingly emboldened, she becomes "quite determined . . . to become either a farmer or a doctor" (MD, 137). Elizabeth Dalloway fulfills the promise of Evelyn Murgatroyd. Inspired by travel to imagine new possibilities for her life, Elizabeth dreams not of possessing something but of breaking free of being possessed. (She shudders at the admiration of men who would compare her "to poplars—which was rather exciting, of course, but very silly" [MD, 137].) Piracy here is a metaphor for the single-minded ability of a bus to cut through traffic while controlling a complex flow of boarding and disembarking travelers. With the pirate ship metaphor, Woolf retains what is bold, exciting, and adventurous about travel without any of the exploitative violence of real piracy. Woolf, like Clarissa Dalloway, may not have known what the equator was, but in knowing how to navigate London, Woolf and *Elizabeth* Dalloway eliminate some of the limitations that faced women of earlier generations.[56] Thus, in 1925, Woolf began, through the young, passive, hopeful Elizabeth Dalloway, and the eccentricities of Browne, to show the centrality of diverse and broad experience for the imagination to thrive.

## Discovering London, 1926–32

If the beautiful but ultimately very normal Elizabeth Dalloway needs the hum of a London adventure for inspiration, then a writer, whose work depends on taking memories and transforming them into art by way of the imagination, must need London adventure all the more. What began with an Elizabethan lumber room and young Elizabeth Dalloway in 1925 intensified in the next phase of Woolf's writing on memory and the imagination: from 1926 to 1932, Woolf celebrated the freedom to wander London while condemning patriarchal efforts to control wandering feet and wandering minds. This period of Woolf's writing begins and ends with celebrations of rambling through modern London. The first, "Street-Haunting: A London Adventure" (1926), compares a walk to an Elizabethan voyage, and the second, "Docks of London" (1932), compares a modern warehouse to an Elizabethan lumber room. In between, I discuss Woolf's critique of the drive to systematize in her discussion of the British Library in *A Room of One's Own* (1929).

Where Elizabeth Dalloway is initially a passive voyager, the unnamed walker in Woolf's 1926 essay "Street-Haunting" sets off with confidence. The conceit of the essay—that the pleasure of a winter's evening walk in the city needs to be justified by an errand, in this case, shopping for a pencil—triumphantly celebrates wandering over discovery and possession. Even the purchase of the pencil itself, from a man who "would not have disgraced Ben Jonson's title-page" (DM, 35), participates in a small drama—first rousing then easing tensions between the husband and wife stationers. Upon her return, she reminds herself of the scenes she had witnessed: "walking home through the desolation one could tell oneself the story of the dwarf, of the blind men, of the party" (DM, 35). That she has come home with so much imaginative wealth and yet so few things is part of the walk's success: "And here—let us examine it tenderly, let us touch it with reverence—is the only spoil we have retrieved from all the treasures of the city, a lead pencil" (DM, 36). Window shopping takes precedence over actual exchange: "having built and furnished the house, one is happily under no obligation to possess" (DM, 27). But to be "happily under no obligation to possess" is by no means the same as not needing to ramble. Seeing beauty, diversity, strangeness is everything; she need not possess it, but her imagination feeds on its presence. "Street-Haunting" is as fully under the spell of Hakluyt as the descriptions of the South American coast in *The Voyage Out*. The catalogues of diversity—of people and goods—owe their energy to similar passages in Hakluyt, such as this one:

> With this people linen cloth is good merchandise, whereof they make rolls for their heads and girdles to wear about them. Their island is both rich and beautiful: rich in gold, silver, copper, and sulphur, wherein they seem skilful and expert. Their fruits be diverse and plentiful, as nutmegs, ginger, long pepper, lemons, cucumbers, cocos, sago, with divers other sorts: since the time that we first set out of our own country of England, we happened on no place, wherein we found more comforts and better means of refreshing.[57]

For Woolf, adventure is Elizabethan.

Woolf's debt to Hakluyt manifests itself through analogies: walks and bus rides through London are like voyages of exploration, and reading Browne or Hakluyt is like wandering through a great lumber room. For all the time that Woolf spent reading and writing and for all the satisfaction she expresses for these physical spaces of display and storage, one might think she would harbor special affection for the library. In fact, and in spite of analogies others make between libraries and lumber rooms, Woolf's view on libraries was equivocal. In

"Street-Haunting" she openly prefers the used bookstore to the library: "Second-hand books are wild books, homeless books; they have come together in vast flocks of variegated feather, and have a charm which the domesticated volumes of the library lack" (DM, 29). Unlike a library, whose collection accumulates under the regulations of a librarian and whose catalogue is systematically organized, used book stores consist entirely of discards: random and unwanted, the books only share the fact of their having been cast aside. But other libraries, especially private ones, are remembered fondly, as in *Between the Acts* (1941), as well as in the essays "Reading" (1919), "How Should One Read a Book?" (1926), and "Leslie Stephen" (1932). In "The Lives of the Obscure" (1925), the prospect of "rescuing" neglected books from the closed stacks of a library is imbued with romance. In "The Leaning Tower" (1940) a librarian's request to be notified of defective books gets transformed into a credo of the common reader's responsibility: "England's way of saying: 'If I lend you books, I expect you to make yourselves critics' " (M, 153). Woolf consistently preferred the local, personal, and idiosyncratic, while reserving her most powerful feminist critique for the British Library. There, Woolf sees not an impressively large collection but an oppressively regulatory attempt to control memory and rein in the imagination.

Libraries and lumber rooms: these two Elizabethan spaces correspond to two Elizabethan styles of thinking—systematizing and accumulative, and hierarchical and diverse. These styles of thinking have parallels in common metaphors for the mind: the memory palace (systematic) and the cabinet of curiosities (idiosyncratic). We may better understand the notion of the lumber room by contrasting it with this competing model of how the mind stores memory—the memory palace. The Renaissance art of memory involves creating a memory palace, an imaginary architectural organization of thoughts and knowledge whereas the lumber room, like the commonplace book or *Trafficks and Discoveries* itself, rests content with accumulation. Giordano Bruno (1548–1600) and others who prefer the metaphor of the memory-as-library seek to avoid the frustration of Augustine, who finds that "When I am in this storehouse . . . some things require a longer search, and have to be drawn out as it were from recondite receptacles. Some memories pour out to crowd the mind and, when one is searching and asking for something quite different, leap forward into the centre as if saying 'Surely we are what you want?' "[58]

Just as the dominant model of voyaging in the Renaissance came to be possession, so, too, the preferred model of the mind came to be the memory palace, promising, as it does, organization and ease of retrieval. And just as readers and scholars such as Woolf and Stephen Greenblatt must now labor to find instances of mutually beneficial wandering, so, too, must they work against the systematizing impulse in order to find models of memory and imagination that celebrate the individual, the eccentric, and the serendipitous over the national and the standard.

Woolf's serendipitous small objects (the wart, the mark on the wall, and the lead pencil) act as mnemonic devices, reminding Woolf of imaginative possibility. As such, they contrast sharply with another Renaissance art: the art of memory. This art, notably practiced by James Joyce's hero, Giordano Bruno, originated in the classical world but expanded in the Renaissance to promise a master key to all knowledge. Those who practiced the art of memory memorized not by rote, but by constructing elaborate and personal imaginary architectures. These mnemonists profited from the observation that, in passing a familiar landmark, we often remember what we were thinking the last time we passed it. Thus, they memorize a spacious room, a cathedral, or a street scene, and then deliberately "place," in order, the elements of a speech, text, or list they need to remember.[59] This way a person can retrieve his or her speech in its correct order by taking an imaginary walk through his or her "memory palace." But whereas medieval mnemonists are eager to remember the Bible and Cicero and Renaissance mnemonists conjure up "all that the mind can conceive and all that is hidden in the soul,"[60] Woolf creates anti-images that aim to liberate women's imaginations from official memory without constructing an equally imposing replacement. Once we understand why she resists remembering and memorializing on a national scale, we may be better able to see what, if anything, she proposes as a replacement.

Whereas the Renaissance art of memory depends on an individual's ability to build a memory palace in one's mind, Woolf shows us how the British Library presents itself *as* a mind. In turning the metaphor of memory-as-palace inside out, Woolf displays the contents of the mind for our admiration as well as our scrutiny. The elaborate memory images of Renaissance mnemonists find their parallel in Woolf's emblematic figures such as Judith Shakespeare and Mrs. Brown. Her criticism of the art of memory emerges with the turn to architecture, especially with her observation that the British Library operates as a culture-wide memory image, not an individual one.[61] Juxtaposing Woolf—whose ambivalence to Freud's totalizing metaphors is well documented—with the Renaissance mnemonists sharpens the distinction between her ability to create new images and her consistent commitment to questioning cultural myths, totalizing schemes, and the way that memory images reinforce them.[62] The history of the art of memory demonstrates the human impulse toward system and may even suggest something about the deep structure of our minds. Woolf rejects the systematizing obsession that was part of the Renaissance art while reviving the arts' personal elements. Where the Renaissance mnemonists would have understood the memory image as a tool to assist the higher faculty of memory, Woolf understands the image as an end in itself, the amazing product of an individual imagination.

In *A Room of One's Own*, Woolf sought to destroy officially endorsed "collective" memories and their cues that interfere with women's ability to think for themselves.[63] In creating her own memory images, she profits from the tension between the official and the individual, and, in doing so, she attempts to create, if not recapture, a social memory of and for women. In figuring the British Library as a mind, Woolf articulates one of the great ambitions of a library: to store knowledge beyond any individual mind's ability. The library is a vexed site for Virginia Woolf. There is nothing ambiguous in her narrator's anger at being kept out of the library at "Oxbridge" in *A Room of One's Own*: she curses it (ARO, 8). Nor is she indefinite in *Three Guineas* (1938): "Do not have museums and libraries with chained books and first editions under glass cases" (3G, 33).

In *A Room of One's Own*, much of the narrator's anger at being kept out of one library, or the frustration during research at another, stems from the suspicion that the library may contain the "truth," that after a morning's reading she shall have "transferred the truth to my notebook" (ARO, 26). But in her second feminist pamphlet, *Three Guineas*, the object of Woolf's satire has shifted from an amused and gentle look at the predicament of the intimidated female student, still hoping for enlightenment, to a straightforward attack on the guardians of knowledge who treat books as treasured captives. As central as books are to Virginia Woolf, she finds something obnoxious in the institution of the library. In 1857, the round Reading Room of the British Library opened to great public acclaim, chiefly, it seems, expressed as national pride at the vast size of the dome itself—a feat of industrial age ironwork. The schematic diagram of the contents of the room reprinted in the 1924 *A Guide to the Use of the Reading Room* resembles the spoked-wheel structure of Frances Yates's reconstruction of Giordano Bruno's memory system. And for a moment it would seem that Victorian engineering and bibliography combine to fulfill the dreams of these late-sixteenth-century mnemonists. If Renaissance thinkers dreamt of a system for organizing and remembering human thought, what better culmination of that dream than its embodiment in the very architecture of a great national library?

In her descriptions of Bruno's ambitions and his sense that these magic images comprised a worthy store of "secret" knowledge, Yates continually admits that Bruno's project is "extremely difficult for a modern to recapture."[64] The design of the Reading Room offers a less distant example of a related impulse. The appeal of the circular room, like that of Bruno's wheels, is not mysterious: the circle is both ordered and without a beginning or an end. The reader enters the room flanked by atlases on the right and maps of the British Isles on the left, implicitly equating orientation in the library with the work of surveyors and explorers. At the center sits the superintendent at a raised desk: the library as panopticon. The "History" section presents a transparent narrative of the official history of Britain: from "Ancient History," the reference works progress to Scotland, Ireland, and Wales to culminate in "State Papers" and "British History," finally winding down with two sections of "Foreign History" surrounding (to avoid contamination?) a section on France. Theological works stand at the far end of the room as if to guard the entrance to the North Library, where the library's most rare and valuable books are kept. In spite of the logic of this arrangement, the designers of the library plainly had no intention for us to seek knowledge from imagined combinations derived from revolving the general catalogue clockwise; it is of no significance that the topography catalogue rotated 90 degrees would be opposite heraldry. This kind of fancy comes from spending too much time with the Renaissance mnemonists. Yet a faith in the potential significance of this sort of correspondence is precisely what inspires Bruno to pass his time in the design of memory systems. For Woolf, by contrast, the unsystematic Hakluyt promises more.

The designers of the round Reading Room failed to appreciate what Woolf continually emphasizes: that in fastening onto the systematic principle of the architectural mnemonic, the Victorians lost sight of the importance of the personal. The reader at the British Library does not walk through her own memory palace, but through someone else's. Just by its existence, the Reading Room influences the imagination of its readers: an influence that is precisely the ambition of a national library. Nonetheless the difficulties of settling on a scheme to decorate it revealed vulnerabilities in the Victorian plan for the British Library as an embodiment of the Renaissance memory palace. Although several artists proposed schemes for decorating the dome with allegorical statues and paintings, the dome was left plain for decades. Finally, in 1907, a more modest scheme was adopted and "the names of nineteen British writers were painted on the panels"[65] only to be left to fade and disappear. The names, which, according to J. Mordaunt Crook, "evoked some controversy at the time,"[66] were Chaucer, Caxton, Tindale, Spenser, Shakespeare, Bacon, Milton, Locke, Addison, Swift, Pope, Gibbon, Wordsworth, Scott, Byron, Carlyle, Macaulay, Tennyson, and Browning.[67]

When Sir John Burnet oversaw the 1907 redecoration, he may have struggled over the choice of some of these 19 names, but it is unlikely that he foresaw the attitude Woolf would take to his choices just 16 years later:

> Miss Julia Hedge, the feminist, waited for her books. They did not come. She wetted her pen. She looked about her. Her eye was caught by the final letters in Lord Macaulay's name. And she read them all round the dome—the names of great men which remind us—"Oh damn," said Julia Hedge, "why didn't they leave room for an Eliot or a Brontë?" (JR, 106)

This is more than just a moment of distracted study; it is more, even, than a moment of criticism of the canon, though it is both of those things. Sitting in the Reading Room, waiting for her books, Julia Hedge falls into the automatic thoughts that are precisely what such rooms mean to inspire: "the names of great men which remind us—." But Woolf's character interrupts this involuntary thought with a private one: those men's names remind Miss Hedge not of the greatness of English literature but of the immensity of the feminist project before her. How long must she work and wait until a woman's name joins that uninterrupted band?

In contrast to the vivid and idiosyncratic images recommended by Bruno and other Renaissance mnemonists, the band of names in the Reading Room is distinctly classical. In decorating the Reading Room, in selecting authors who will be honored, the Victorians significantly distorted one of the purposes of the Renaissance art. A band of names does nothing to help the patron distinguish a Chaucer from a Caxton, an Addison from a Shakespeare. Thus, in her refusal to succumb to the automatic prompts for memory of the Reading Room's band of names, Woolf's Julia Hedge is closer than the room's designers to the Renaissance spirit of transforming a familiar room into a personal memory palace. She knows she is meant to be reminded of the institutionally endorsed English writers, but the band of names reminds her not of the canon but of her desire to resist the power of collective memory and continue her feminist work.

The pompous language of the library catalogue that would surface in *A Room of One's Own*, where women are subdivided according to "Condition in the Middle Ages of, / Habits in the Fiji Islands of, / Worshipped as goddesses by" (ARO, 28), differs sharply from the scene in *Jacob's Room* (1922). Here, Woolf imagines only poetry. She imaginatively redecorates the room more to her liking. In her fantasia of the library at night, it takes a moment for the letters to resolve themselves into names, and when they do, only one among them—Shakespeare—was really painted around the dome. Instead of depicting the library as a national treasure, Woolf makes it a global one, combining "the literatures of Rome, Greece, China, India, Persia. One leaf of poetry was pressed flat against another leaf, one burnished letter laid smooth against another in a density of meaning, a conglomeration of loveliness" (JR, 107–08). What is beautiful here, as with the mark on the wall, is the moment just before things make sense. Fixing meaning to name the great authors of the English tradition, or the stars themselves, spoils the moment and restricts the imagination. In *Mrs. Dalloway* (1925), old Joseph and Peter Walsh interrupt Clarissa and Sally's kiss by naming the stars, for which Clarissa hates them: "She heard the names of the stars. 'Oh this horror!' she said to herself" (MD, 36).

The scenes of the British Library in *Jacob's Room* and *A Room of One's Own* resist the institutional power of the library while confessing a reluctant attraction for the vast dome full of books. For Woolf the domed room symbolizes the false promise of patriarchal education. As one critic puts it, "the androgyny, ambiguity, and activity possible in a domed structure does not belong to women."[68] Thus, in these works, the Reading Room becomes a memory image dedicated to destroying the complacent acceptance of the all-male canon of English literature. Woolf accomplishes the dream of the Renaissance mnemonists, but through imagination, not system. The silence of nightfall rids the library of its human actors, who bring with them the "little grunts of satisfaction" (ARO, 28). We are left with "a conglomeration of loveliness" (JR, 108).

Leaving the library behind and returning to the streets of London, Woolf again celebrates spatial and imaginative freedom in terms of the Elizabethan age. In her ambition to unseat public memory images, Woolf succeeded; readers of Woolf learn to be suspicious of individual buildings and the messages they intend to impart: "Walk through the Admiralty Arch . . . or any other avenue given up to trophies and cannon, and reflect upon the kind of glory celebrated there" (ARO, 38). Instead of succumbing to automatic thoughts of glory, Woolf forces us to think about what "kind of glory" is being put forward for our admiration. Woolf has transformed London for her readers. The chimes of Big Ben are "first a warning, musical; then the hour, irrevocable" (MD, 4); the Elephant and Castle is the site of Judith Shakespeare's unmarked grave (ARO, 48); the statue of Nurse Edith Cavell "always reminds me of an advertisement of sanitary towels" (Y, 336); and Whitehall is the place where "if one is a woman one is often surprised by a sudden splitting off of consciousness . . . when from being the natural inheritor of civilisation, she becomes, on the contrary, outside of it, alien and critical" (ARO, 97). Without destroying London, Woolf has succeeded in changing our memory of it.

In *The London Scene* essays (1931–32), five essays published serially in *Good Housekeeping*, Woolf updates Hakluyt, seeing London as he might have seen it, privileging capital, adventure, and memory by beginning with the docks ("Docks of London") and moving on to shopping in "Oxford Street Tide," before treating culture ("Great Men's Houses"), religion ("Abbeys and Cathedrals"), and politics ("This is the House of Commons"). In "Docks of London," she describes a visit to the London warehouses. The passage that follows connects the order of the warehouse (mimetically represented in this passage uncharacteristically full of alliteration, internal rhyme, and repetitive parallel constructions) and the marvelous impact of the goods on the imagination:

> Rhythmically, dexterously, with an order that has some aesthetic delight in it, barrel is laid by barrel, case by case, cask by cask, one behind another, one on top of another, one beside another in endless array down the aisles and arcades of the immense low-ceiled, entirely plain and unornamented warehouses. Timber, iron, grain, wine, sugar, paper, tallow, fruit—whatever the ship has gathered from the plains, from the forests, from the pastures of the whole world is here lifted from its hold and set in its right place. A thousand ships with a thousand cargoes are being unladen every week. And not only is each package of this vast and varied merchandise picked up and set down accurately, but each is weighted and opened, sampled and recorded, and again stitched up and laid in its place, without haste, or waste, or hurry, or confusion by a very few men in shirt-sleeves, who, working with the utmost organization in the common interest—for buyers will take their word and abide by their decision—are yet able to pause in their work and say to the casual visitor, "Would you like to see what sort of thing we sometimes find in sacks of cinnamon? Look at this snake!"
>
> A snake, a scorpion, a beetle, a lump of amber, the diseased tooth of an elephant, a basin of quicksilver—these are some of the rarities and

oddities that have been picked out of this vast merchandise and stood on a table. But with this one concession to curiosity, the temper of the Docks is severely utilitarian. (LS, 11)

Woolf's description here concedes only *some* delight in order: the immediate impulse is aesthetic. The "rarities and oddities" and the "one concession to curiosity" interest Woolf most. Still, she gives the sense that a visit to a "severely utilitarian" place is so unusual for her that utility itself comes to have a kind of poetry. At one point, the essay indulges in a moment of Woolfian futurism, linking beauty, utility, and technology. Woolf celebrates how "the warehouse is perfectly fit to be a warehouse; the crane to be a crane. Hence beauty begins to steal in" (LS, 12–13). The objects are stored in "aisles *and* arcades," an alliteration that continues to undermine the unsmiling order of the scene; for Woolf—as for Walter Benjamin—the word *arcades* connotes urban shopping streets, precursors to malls, and thus, the eventual destination of these commodities. But before these items can arrive in the shops of Oxford Street, they must be inventoried and Woolf indicates the complexity of the task in the length of the list of what must be done to the things ("weighted, opened, sampled, and recorded"). Her description continues extravagantly, but the workers themselves act without "haste or waste." This neat rhyme seems to close the subject, but, as if to register her own distance from this mercantile world, she adds—unable to help herself—two more: "or hurry, or confusion."

Instead of the abundantly varied lists of Hakluyt, the list of containers strives to create the impression of order while eschewing monotony. Though everything in the warehouse is orderly, the warehouse itself contains an abundant variety of containers—barrels, casks, and cases. Later, in the expected list of imported commodities, timber comes first, so that the modern warehouse immediately alludes to the Elizabethan lumber room and may allude to Ben Jonson's *Timber* (1640). The abundance and order depicted here contrasts sharply with the passage's climactic list: "A snake, a scorpion, a beetle, a lump of amber, the diseased tooth of an elephant, a basin of quicksilver." Here, amidst all the curiosities, she finds not an ivory tusk, but a diseased tooth—something odder, cooler, and more difficult to price. The workers are benevolently accommodating to their visitor, not too sensational, and genuinely curious when they offer to show her the snake in the bag of cinnamon. Of course, it is a snake and nothing else, for the snake symbolizes the temptation in the midst of order. The snake's appearance marks the moment when the story of paradise gets interesting.

## AN END TO VOYAGING, 1933–41

Long as the memory of reading Hakluyt persisted, it began to fade in the final stage of Woolf's career (1933–41). True, we hear echoes of Hakluyt in the Elizabethan scene in *Between the Acts*, but the predominant move of this period is a relocation of the source of English poetry from the international to the domestic. Woolf's last novel and her posthumously published essay "Anon" have been celebrated for their continuation of her pacifism and her embrace of community. At the same time, others have noticed the disturbing role of scapegoating and the continued admiration for individual power. Coming at *Between the Acts* through Woolf's reading of Hakluyt reveals a surprising missed opportunity and, perhaps, the intensity of her sense of the threat of war. While persisting in her pacifism and her valuation of wandering, Woolf retreats from both internationalism and female traveling in these works: the minstrel, the commuter, and even the poet, Anon, all seem to be male. By letting her earlier admiration for Hakluyt lapse, by moving from heterogeneous London to the countryside, Woolf participates in the narrow localism of the 1930s' celebrations of community.

In 1917, Woolf reviewed an edition of Sir Walter Raleigh's writings. She opens her review with the editor's assertion that " 'the Elizabethan Age stands for one of two things: it is the age of jeweled magnificence . . . ; or it is the age of enterprise and exploration' " (E, 2.91). Woolf worked to dismantle this perception, substituting instead a more liberal vision in which actual and imaginative travel mutually benefit each other, in which the national imagination is stocked by vast experience of life elsewhere. In "Anon," however, she accedes to the earlier editor's judgment. There, the Elizabethan age comes to be dominated by the stiff courtly prose—prose she had never admired but had, in earlier essays, tossed aside much sooner. She mourns the codification of the old songs and lays of simple, sheep-herding people into stiff courtly language. It is a subtle but significant shift: she still thirsts for ordinary language, unadorned by ceremony, but now she finds it locally rather than abroad.

This more domestic impulse can be seen at work in *Between the Acts'* single allusion to Hakluyt:

> *Mistress of ships and bearded men* (she bawled)
> Hawkins, Frobisher, Drake,
> *Tumbling their oranges, ingots of silver,*
> *Cargoes of diamonds, ducats of gold,*

*Down on the jetty, there in the west land—*
(she pointed her fist at the blazing blue sky)
*Mistress of pinnacles, spires and palaces—*
(her arm swept toward the house)
*For me Shakespeare sang—*
(a cow mooed. A bird twittered). (BTA 84)

The miscellaneous catalogue of exotic goods, the names of the great captains (Hawkins, Frobisher, and Drake), these details from *Trafficks and Discoveries* persist, but they are no longer the prime source of Shakespeare's poetry. Instead, Woolf locates Shakespeare between the palace and the farm, firmly domestic, and separated by lines, stage directions, and external interruptions, from the oranges and gold of the New World. Even the abundance, heretofore so inspiring becomes suspect. Instead of imagining the sailor with an ingot in his pocket, Woolf turns her attention to Elizabethan clothes themselves, the commodities refined, purchased, and in use:

> Elizabethan clothes have had too much attention from the historical novelist, and too little from the psychologist. What desire was it that prompted this extraordinary display? There must have been some protest, some desire to affirm something, behind the slashed cloaks; the stiff ruffs; the wrought chains and the loops of pearls. The cost was great; the discomfort appalling; yet the fashion prevailed. ("Anon," 684–85)

Here, instead of Queen Elizabeth "rough with rubies" (CDB, 158) and tossing back mugs of beer as Woolf imagined her in the 1919 essay "Reading," Woolf imagines a court both remote and pretty. By forgetting about Hakluyt at the end of her life and turning inward to England alone, she makes the authentic voice of the ordinary Englishman into an anonymous and national voice instead of a humble but named, traveling one. The commodities that thrill and inspire when they are on a distant shore, in a sailor's pocket, in a warehouse, or in a shop window have stiffened into impractical (and immoral) display at court.

"Docks of London" (1931) ends with a paean to trade, an expression of faith in the power of ordinary consumers to shape the machinery of capital: "It is we—our tastes, our fashions, our needs— that make the cranes dip and swing, that call the ships from the sea. Our body is their master. We demand shoes, furs, bags, stoves, oil, rice puddings, candles; and they are brought to us. Trade watches us anxiously to see what new desires are beginning to grow in us, what new dislikes" (LS, 14). This turns out to be Woolf's most hopeful expression of the possibility of bringing together actual and imaginative travel in such a way so as to benefit and empower women artists.

The voyages of the Renaissance changed every aspect of the English society. We cannot separate the imaginative gains, embodied by Shakespeare, from the human costs in the violence Woolf abhors or the slavery she fails to comment upon. Woolf's retreat from Hakluyt in the last decade of her life suggests a waning faith in internationalism. It creates a distinction between her pacifism around World War I and her continued pacifism during World War II. It also suggests that her anti-imperialism was, at the end of her life, more isolationist than cosmopolitan. In *Between the Acts*, actual travel is neither a transatlantic voyage nor a ramble across London but a wearing commute to a country house. Imaginative travel is not through space but across time: it is not Hakluyt who inspires, but the mastodon.

# CHAPTER 3

# A Feminist Public Sphere?
# Virginia Woolf's Revisions
# of the Eighteenth Century

Since the historicist turn in scholarship on modernism, critics have focused on the ways modernist writers have marketed themselves. The modernist writers who expressed disdain for mass culture have been shown to have used and depended on the tools of advertising, marketing, professionalization, and self-promotion that was provided by mass culture. Thus, Peter McDonald argues that "the cultural divisions between the high-class reviews and the illustrated monthlies were not always as rigid as might be supposed," and Lawrence Rainey asserts that modernist publishing depended upon an intermediate economic stage, such as an early limited or subscription-based edition, during which a text's cultural value rose, potentially helping create demand for broader sales.[1] When this sociohistorical approach focuses on a single writer's career, it shows how he or she fits into, or, more often, attempts to subvert or challenge the cultural categories of high, low, and middlebrow. Virginia Woolf was, of course, a woman, and thus something of an outsider in the London literary scene; she was also the daughter of Victorian man-of-letters and editor Leslie Stephen, and thus, the ultimate insider. This combination makes her career an ideal case for further study. As one recent critic puts it, "Woolf entered public discourse by the side door."[2] For Woolf, the political and financial advantages of gaining status as a person of letters outweighed any modernist disdain for journalism. Though most modernists published short pieces—often nonfiction and reviews—in periodicals, they did so amidst a continuing distinction between art and journalism; each writer negotiated a separate peace with this tension. For her part, Woolf drew upon her knowledge of the literary world of the eighteenth century to justify her decision to pursue journalism alongside her novel writing.

Woolf's understanding of the aesthetic practices of eighteenth-century culture shaped her understanding of going public and her beliefs in the value of journalism as a source of income and as a worthy practice for a serious writer. This chapter traces three distinct phases of Woolf's engagement with the public sphere. From the beginning of her career to 1919, Woolf was still, to a certain extent, respectful of an eighteenth-century notion of a public sphere, accepting anonymous publication (as was then the practice at the *TLS* [*Times Literary Supplement*]) and analogizing eighteenth-century coffeehouses and salons to her experience in Bloomsbury (depicted in her memoirs and *Night and Day*). The year 1919 marked a turning point. *Night and Day* (1919) contains Woolf's most optimistic depiction of a mixed-sex public sphere dependent on talk. It also brings this phase of Woolf's thinking to a close. In its place, a growing frustration with anonymity and the elusiveness of talk emerges. The essay "Eccentrics" and the story "A Society," both published in 1919, each contributed a new, nascently feminist, skepticism about women's participation in the public sphere whereas the essay "Addison," also published in 1919, turns a slightly more hopeful gaze to print. In the 1920s, Woolf recasts the rise of the public sphere more critically, mercilessly satirizing its masculinism in *Mrs. Dalloway* (1925) while, in *Orlando* (1928), lamenting the impotence of an all-female counterpublic sphere. Finally, her *Three Guineas* (1938) represents the third phase of extreme skepticism as to the public sphere's capacity to represent or include women.

## APPRENTICE IN THE PUBLIC SPHERE, TO 1919

Woolf sought to participate in public debate and make a living as a respected mainstream cultural authority without giving up her feminism or her independence of mind. To do so, she had to begin by negotiating the literary marketplace as it was then structured. First, to establish herself in the mainstream public sphere of her time, to avoid the label of a "lady writer," and, more ambitiously, to advance her feminist literary-historical project of educating women in the history of women writers, she needed to be recognized by London's literary elite. Consequently, she quickly stopped writing for the prim *Guardian* and began to publish her works in the recently founded (1902), but already dominant, *Times Literary Supplement* although this meant initially giving up the chance at longer reviews of better books. The tenth publication of her career, in March 1905, was her first appearance in the *TLS*.[3]

For the sheer number of her contributions, no other periodical approaches the *TLS*: about 240 of her nearly 600 essays, or around 40 percent, appeared there first. Nearly every essay that Woolf published between 1912 and 1918—with one lone exception and that published in the *Times* itself—appeared in the *TLS*.[4] Most of these were short reviews; all were unsigned. Thus, Andrew McNeillie notes that, at the beginning of 1919, outside of her intimate friends, the London literati would likely know Virginia Woolf only as the author of *The Voyage Out* (1915) even though "since 1904 she had published anonymously a vast quantity—more than a quarter of a million words—of journalism."[5]

One of Woolf's last essays, "Anon," argues that many works whose authorship is unknown to us must have been written by women and further argues for the importance of this swelling of voices in literature. The practice of anonymous publishing, which has all but died out today, has a predictably mixed effect. For unknown writers hoping to build a reputation, such as the young Arthur Conan Doyle, it meant that years of publishing led to no recognition:

> given the policy of authorial anonymity . . . Conan Doyle's early successes were largely private rather than public. For someone with aspirations, this inevitably became a source of frustration, and, after seven years as an anonymous magazine author, he realized that "a man may put the very best that is in him into magazine work for years and years, and reap no benefit from it, save, of course, the inherent benefits of literary practice."[6]

In contrast, centuries earlier, "Thomas Traherne, Henry Kind, and the Earl of Rochester . . . followed patterns of literary creation identical to that of Lady Mary Wortley Montagu, circulating their works in manuscript and occasionally publishing an anonymous piece that was usually attributable to them given their wide readership in manuscript."[7] As significant as the difference of 200 years is the difference between Montagu's insider status in her coterie of readers versus Conan Doyle's outsider status. As we have seen, because Bloomsbury was at the epicenter of literary London in the 1920s, Woolf's position as an "anonymous" reviewer was closer to that of Montagu's and Rochester's, in spite of her political sympathy for, and affiliation with, outsiders.

Why was publishing in the *TLS* so important to Woolf during the very years when she broke from convention in fiction? The centrality of the *TLS* itself has never been in doubt. Almost from the beginning it was "the major journal" with all the respect and reputation for conventionality such a title suggests (D, 5.145). When, in 1919, T. S. Eliot began reviewing for the *TLS*, he boasted to his mother, "[T]his is the highest honour possible in the critical world of litera-ture."[8] Though Woolf laments the "tea-table training" of her *TLS* prose in later life, she was clearly excited by the deluge of books to review during her peak years as a reviewer and she took reviewing seriously as part of a writer's apprenticeship (MB, 150).[9] Later, many *TLS* contributions became the backbone for longer essays such as those in both the *Common Readers*, the two essay collections that Woolf published in her lifetime.[10] Both Woolf and the *TLS* benefited from this close association. Woolf's role in the history of the paper is unique. Recognized from the beginning as a key contributor, com-memorated as such in the fiftieth and hundredth anniversary issues, she remains the only woman so celebrated by the paper (although now it has many prominent women reviewers). As the number of her contributions diminished, their length and importance increased: she wrote the obituaries for both Thomas Hardy and Joseph Conrad and "*as a privilege exclusive to her*, £15 was added" to the standard fee of about £13 for a lead review or essay.[11] The cultural capital that Woolf amassed during her years writing for the *TLS* is both hard and easy to measure: though no one learned her name from her contributions, her voice—and her opinion—were part of the center of London's literary world. For a woman who wrote frequently about the chal-lenges of a woman expressing herself in a man's world, this accession to an authoritative voice under the cover of anonymity was crucial. Publishing in the *TLS* was thus central to her understanding of how to achieve her ambitions.[12]

The importance of *TLS* can be judged in part by the pains critics have taken to explain why an author did or did not review for it. T. S. Eliot's contributions were once mocked "as a parody of official British literary discussion"[13] and have been more recently seen in terms of his intense effort to "inch his way to the hallowed circle of [Bruce] Richmond," the supplement's influential editor.[14] Although Eliot's contributions were once explained as brilliant parody and are now understood as professionalism, Woolf's contributions have under-gone an opposite interpretation. As recently as 1997, a critic notes, "Woolf speaks in the voice required and often demanded by the editorial policy of the relevant journal."[15] Here, as in earlier studies, Woolf's ability to mimic the voice of her editors is read as the submis-sion of a literary angel in the house. Ironically, feminist critics have been slow in identifying either self-consciousness or professionalism. Leila Brosnan, however, does concede that, after a few years of reviewing, Woolf "of necessity taught herself a language of duplicity" that she detects, for example, in a 1921 review where Woolf's play on "exceptional" and "standard" from the publisher's puff combine to dismiss a pulpy popular novel.[16] To complicate matters even further, both Woolf and Eliot wrote regretfully of the tone of their contributions. Woolf likens the "suavity" of her tone to her "tea-table manners," whereas Eliot casts his failings in grander imagery: "There are, it is true, faults of style which I regret and especially I detect a stiffness and an attempt of pontifical solemnity which may be tiresome to many readers."[17]

The *TLS* had been concerned from the beginning with establishing itself as a guide for what the common reader should read, a project that has its roots in the criticism of Joseph Addison and Samuel Johnson. At the same time as she was securing her place in this world, Woolf also wanted to establish herself as an avant-garde writer, which, for her, meant leaving her stepbrother's commercial publishing firm, Duckworth's, for her own press in 1917.[18] The press took as its name the backward-looking "Hogarth."[19] The name not only came from their house in the London suburb of Richmond, but it also inevitably evokes the eighteenth-century artist William Hogarth (1697–1764), best known for his satiric narrative paintings such as "The Rake's Progress." Hogarth's art comes from the world that gave simultaneous rise to the novel and the mainstream public sphere; it satirizes the follies and vices of individuals in the new urban bourgeoisie. For Jürgen Habermas, the emergence of satire like Hogarth's indicates that "critical public debate" had risen "to the status of an institution."[20] Thus, in naming the Hogarth Press, Woolf allied herself with the mainstream public sphere, the literary inheritance of satire, the emergence of writing as a profession, and her father (who wrote a still-influential social history of the century), rather than either her fellow modernists or a feminist counterpublic sphere. Early in her career, Woolf's concern was as much with making her voice heard in the male-dominated mainstream as it was with the recovery of the lost voices of women. To make the obvious point, Woolf recognized that those "lost voices" cannot be said to be recovered until they are heard in the mainstream.

The eighteenth century was not an unproblematic model, however. Habermas argues that the classical public sphere emerged in England in the eighteenth century as the rise of newspapers and coffeehouses, in which newspapers were read and discussed, led bourgeois men to a habit of criticism, which in turn became a powerful political force. From the beginning, however, as feminist critics of Habermas have shown, the rhetorical openness of the public sphere that Habermas champions as a liberal democratic ideal was premised on practices of exclusion.[21] When Habermas's feminist readers point out how the relation between public and private affects a person's ability and power to communicate and, by extension, to be a full-fledged citizen, they unwittingly echo Woolf's criticism of her father: "Feminists have long complained that Habermas' notion of a 'public sphere' conflates the middle-class man with citizenship much as—according to Woolf— the reading room dome merges masculinity with cultural achievement."[22] This similarity is no accident; it is an overlooked part of feminist intellectual genealogy. Woolf anticipates subsequent feminists because, in revising her father's eighteenth century, she was revising material upon which Habermas uncritically relied.

For Habermas in 1962, when his work first appeared in German, such restrictions were simply part of a gradualist process. Even "restriction of the franchise . . . did not necessarily have to be viewed as a restriction of the public sphere itself as long as it could be interpreted as the mere legal ratification of . . . the status of the private person who both was educated and owned property"—two qualifications that automatically exclude almost all women. Habermas confirms his masculinist bias two pages later, writing, "For the private person, there was no break between *homme* and *citoyen*, as long as the *homme* was simultaneously an owner of private property who as *citoyen* was to protect the stability of the property order as a private one. Class interest was the basis of public opinion."[23]

Habermas had a model for linking the exclusion of women to the rise of the public sphere's power in Leslie Stephen. Stephen's 1903 lectures on the eighteenth century are a primary source for Habermas's description of the London coffeehouses; he cites Stephen twice in his discussion. Both Habermas and Stephen concur on what the latter calls "the critical point": that "the vehicle of public opinion put the state in touch with the needs of society."[24] For Stephen, the extension of "the reading part of the nation" is a crucial element in "the changes of belief which have been the cause and effect of the most conspicuous political changes."[25] Habermas's public is more political still: he argues that the bourgeoisie "soon claimed the public sphere regulated from above against the public authorities themselves."[26] Stephen writes with mounting national pride that "England had become a land of free speech" only a page earlier having admitted that "the Clubs meant essentially a society of bachelors, and the conversation, one infers, was not especially suited for ladies."[27] Thus, for both Stephen and Habermas, the emergence of the public sphere as the crucial organ of democratic participation corresponded exactly with the exclusion of women. This patriarchal blindness lies behind Woolf's move in *Three Guineas* (1938), where she insisted that her social class was that of one of the "daughters of educated men": that is, because she was not a *homme*, she could not be a *citoyen*.

Contemporary feminists have been quick to note this focus on the all-male political world. But neither Habermas nor his feminist inter-locutors have, until now, been conscious of Woolf's contribution to eighteenth-century cultural history. As we will see, her essays and the eighteenth-century chapter of *Orlando* are overlooked instances of feminist consideration of the Habermasian public sphere *avant la lettre*. In fact, *Orlando* presents the rise of the public sphere as the defin-ing event of the eighteenth century while dramatizing the significant and detrimental exclusion of women.

Leslie Stephen's influence on Virginia Woolf was profound, partic-ularly when it comes to judgments of the eighteenth century.[28] Both write literary criticism emphasizing social and historical context, and both value the common reader's judgment. Stephen begins his study, "We must start from experience. We must begin by asking impartially what pleased men, and then inquire why it pleased them"; Woolf, similarly interested in following the reading habits of the English public, names her two collections of essays—largely expanded pieces from the *TLS*—*The Common Readers* after a phrase in Samuel Johnson's *Life of Gray*. There are even strong parallels in their partic-ular taste: for example, both are highbrows who admire Defoe, whose origins were firmly rooted in Grub Street journalism.[29]

There are, of course, significant differences of opinion, too, and Woolf frequently writes back to her father. Anticipating Carole Pateman and Nancy Fraser, who pay special attention to the way that public and private are gendered to the disadvantage of women, Woolf insists upon both the obvious fact of women's exclusion from and limitations in the public sphere and their less obvious but still damaging subordi-nation in private. Her rebuttals of her father are almost never explicit: what we find instead are parallel passages. Thus, wherever Stephen mentions the role (or exclusion) of women in eighteenth-century English culture, we find in Woolf a corresponding expression of the price women paid for their disadvantages. For example, Stephen notes, "the *Spectator* was the most indispensable set of volumes upon the shelves of every library where the young ladies described by Miss Burney and Miss Austen were permitted to indulge a growing taste for literature."[30] What is a mark of Addison's influence for Stephen became an occasion for comment on the circumscribed life of women for Woolf: in *A Room of One's Own*, she writes of the small miracle that, in spite of Jane Austen's limited experience, she was able to produce masterpieces (ARO, 68). Stephen replicated his happy view of the role of the private library in educating his daughter, Virginia: she was not to be sent to school, but rather to have the run of his library, a fact that remained both a blessing and a curse. (Few private libraries could match his, but that advantage could not erase the insult and isolation of not being allowed a proper "paid-for education" [3G, 4].) Woolf refused to accept reading the *Spectator* as an adequate substitute for *being* a spectator.

Early in her career, however, Woolf seemed to hope that the exclusion of women was coming to an end. *Night and Day* (1919) contains Woolf's most optimistic fictional depiction of a mixed-sex public sphere. In chapter 4, 20 young people, mostly aspiring artists, gather in the apartment of suffrage worker Mary Datchet to listen to a young man read a paper on "the Elizabethan use of metaphor in poetry" (ND, 52). In spite of his extraordinary nervousness and poor delivery, the paper excites animated discussion. Woolf emphasizes the frustration of the questioners, whose competing "conceptions" are as if "hewn" "with an ill-balanced axe" (ND, 54). Nonetheless, the men's inarticulate responses become an unexpected source of optimism, for the failure to make pronouncements leads to more intimate talk, which begins to include women. Frustration inspires the talkers (all men here) to continue talking in private, and soon, instead of public speaking, we have "communication," between men and women, amateurs and experts, friends and new acquaintances.

In short, this is the public sphere in action; when the topic of conversation turns from metaphor to politics, Mary pointedly wonders aloud to Katherine, "I wonder why men always talk about politics? . . . I suppose, if we had votes, we should too" (ND, 58). Woolf depicts the natural evolution of talk about art into talk about politics just as Habermas describes it: "critical debate ignited by works of literature and art was soon extended to include economic and political disputes" (ND, 33). Woolf's female characters are initially distant from political talk, but she makes them self-consciously disengaged. Mary's observation introduces politics into her conversation with Katherine, and they go on to discuss Mary's suffrage work. Woolf thus ensures that their budding friendship includes both shared convictions and a common interest in discussing them. Of all of Woolf's characters, Mary Datchet is the hostess who best inspires substantial and exciting talk of poetry and politics. Mary's success at generating talk is Woolf's refutation of the prejudice against women that long excluded them from coffeehouses and debating societies. In creating Mary Datchet, Woolf makes a claim for the contribution that women can make to the public sphere.[31]

## SKEPTICAL OF TALK, 1919–28

From her experiences of good talk in Bloomsbury, Woolf knew its thrill and its intellectual potential. But, as Woolf writes in the posthumously published memoir "Old Bloomsbury" (1921 or 1922): "Talk—even the talk which had such tremendous results upon the lives and characters of the two Miss Stephens—even talk of this interest and importance is as elusive as smoke" (MB, 165).[32] How to capture this elusiveness became one of Woolf's goals. When she emphasizes Bloomsbury's effect on "the two Miss Stephens" (Virginia and her sister, the painter Vanessa Bell, both née Stephen) in particular, she is noting the seismic impact of the inclusion of women in this free-floating undergraduate talk about "the nature of beauty" (MB, 170). The ironic formality of the phrase "the two Miss Stephens" and her comment that "we were not wearing white satin or seed-pearls" (MB, 167), however, reminds us of the persistent sexism of English society at the time, all of which made Bloomsbury's inclusion of Virginia and Vanessa remarkable. Thus, more than any other English writer of her era, Woolf was well placed to appreciate the importance of rational critical debate. And, from the beginning, she understood and articulated the criticism of conversation that forms the basis of any feminist criticism of the public sphere.

Easy and frank talk between men and women, such as that depicted in *Night and Day* or "Old Bloomsbury," is a persistent Utopian strain in Woolf's writing. She experimented with the dialogue form in several essays (most notably "Mr. Conrad: A Conversation" [1923]) and even, at one point, planned to link the essays of *The Common Reader* through dialogue. Her letters and diaries as well as the reminiscences of her friends show Woolf to have been a brilliant, imaginative, fearless talker. In spite of all this, the experiments at essays in dialogue never blossomed into a book; the hopeful moment of *Night and Day* gave way to a darker, more ironic feminism. Furthermore, unlike Mary Datchet's self-consciously contemporary Bloomsbury gathering, Woolf's subsequent depictions link society's compromises and exclusions of women's talk directly to an eighteenth-century legacy of exclusion.

By 1920 Woolf had become impatient with anonymity. As Woolf accepted and pursued the opportunity to express her opinions and, increasingly, sign her name on her writing, she had to find a way to overcome the taboos against women entering debate in the public sphere. When she responded to Desmond MacCarthy's gentlemanly misogyny with two letters published in the *New Statesman* in 1920 (reprinted as "The Intellectual Status of Women"), she did something many of her characters and the many women writers whom she admired could not imagine themselves doing: she signed her own name. In "The Intellectual Status of Women," Woolf participates in the marketplace of ideas not as a Victorian woman would, but as an eighteenth-century man. She does not insinuate, flatter, or suggest; she signs her name and she answers MacCarthy's arguments directly with arguments of her own.

As Woolf looked for outlets for longer, signed reviews, she had many options. "The inherent benefits of literary practice" that Arthur Conan Doyle noted impatiently as central to any apprenticeship had clearly paid off.[33] Furthermore, she was now very well connected. Her friends dominated the highbrow publishing world and Bloomsbury's editorial power in the 1920s was unmatched:

> T. S. Eliot was editor of the *Criterion* from 1922–39; Desmond MacCarthy was literary editor of the *New Statesman* from 1920–27, editor of *Life and Letters* from 1928–33 and senior literary critic on the *Sunday Times* from 1928 until his death in 1952; the *Athenaeum* was edited by John Middleton Murry from 1919–23, when it was purchased, in conjunction with the *Nation*, by Maynard Keynes, and from 1923–30, Leonard Woolf was its literary editor; David Garnett was the literary editor of the *New Statesman and Nation* from 1932–35 and Raymond Mortimer from 1935–47.[34]

At the time that Bloomsbury modernists occupied themselves with "high-class reviews," other modernists (notably Rebecca West and Wyndham Lewis) focused on the little magazines.[35] At the same time, the mass market for glossy monthlies like *Vogue* and *Vanity Fair* was growing. Critical attention has clustered around the poles of avant garde and mass market; however, as important and fascinating as were Woolf's five essays for *Vogue*, all contributed during the dynamic editorship of Dorothy Todd (1922–26), they do not approach the volume of essays she wrote for the *TLS*.[36] Jane Garrity and Nicola Luckhurst have shown how the *Vogue* essays mark a shift in Woolf's conception of herself as a woman writing to an audience of women, as a celebrity, as fashionable, and as prosperous (for *Vogue* paid well). Complementary to their analyses, my aim here is to write the story of the center: what drew Woolf to cultivate an active, if anonymous, voice in the mainstream and predominantly male world of high-class reviews.

From 1919 through the 1920s, Woolf played with the different aspects of the public sphere's rise. Again and again, Woolf tried to see whether writing might be able to do what talk still could not: allow women a chance to participate in rational critical debate. As her success in so doing increased, so too did her awareness of the obstacles faced by the women writers who preceded her. In *A Room of One's Own* (1929), with the exhortation for women to lay flowers on the grave of Aphra Behn in gratitude for her pioneering work as a professional writer and the assertion that "we think back through our mothers if we are women," Woolf initiated the historical work that taught feminists to seek and take interest in women writers of the past. Even so, she was by no means always a promoter for her precursors; Woolf's references to Behn are consistently ambivalent, celebrating her as a foremother without engaging with her writing. Feminists since Woolf, writing after her exhortation to recover the forgotten lives of women, see clearly what Woolf herself could not see: that Eliza Haywood—a pioneering woman journalist, the editor of *The Female Spectator* and *The Parrot*—warrants recognition. *The Female Spectator* was the "first periodical for women actually written by a woman."[37] When, in 1916, Woolf reviewed a biography of Haywood, she was dismissive of Haywood's place in literary history: "It does not matter, presumably, that she was a writer of no importance, that no one reads her for pleasure, and that nothing is known of her life. She is dead, she is old, she wrote books, and nobody has yet written a book about her" (E, 2.22). Woolf notes, "she turned publisher, edited a newspaper called *The Parrot* . . . In none of these departments was she a pioneer, or even a very distinguished disciple" (E, 2.24).[38] Most damning of all, she opens her essay with the very kind of miniaturization she would later use to characterize Addison: "There are in the Natural History Museum certain little insects so small that they have to be gummed to the cardboard with the lightest of fingers, but each of them, as one observes with constant surprise, has its fine Latin name spreading far to the right and left of the miniature body" (E, 2.22).

In contrast to her dismissal of Haywood, Woolf clearly admires women who treat their writing as a profession and have the courage to dignify it by calling it "writing." For example, in "Jane Austen" (1925), Woolf describes Austen's juvenilia as "writing," a privileged term, distinct from "scribbling" or "dabbling": "And yet, nothing is more obvious than that this girl of fifteen . . . was writing . . . not for home consumption. She was writing for everybody, for nobody, for our age, for her own; in other words, even at that early age Jane Austen was writing" (CR1, 136). Woolf's ambition, her commitment to being a great writer, and her struggles to be ambitious in a family that reserved its highest ambitions for its sons made her especially alert to any signs of conciliation in the writing of her female precursors. She called such women "scribblers," using the word of Fanny Burney in "Dr. Burney's Evening Party" (1929) and of Dorothy Osborne in her essay on the letters (1928). Her own intense desire was to avoid the pattern of Laetitia Pilkington (1712–50), who Woolf writes, "is in the great tradition of *English women of letters*. It is her duty to entertain; it is her instinct to conceal" (CR1, 118; emphasis added). Instead, Woolf wanted to join the great tradition of *English letters*. In her 1936 memoir, "Am I a Snob?" Woolf asks, "Who am I that I should be asked to read a memoir? A mere scribbler" (MB, 204). As she well knew, her ironic description of her career as a writer—a "scribbler"—accords with some serious dismissals of her. When John Maynard Keynes singled out another memoir for praise, she worried "if [that] is my climax I'm a mere scribbler" (D, 2.121).

For Woolf, serious writing involves a refusal of "scribbling," the kind of disposable writing that only serves one's own immediate milieu, though writing for everyone is not by any means synonymous with writing *about* everyone. Austen's novels are composed of minute social observations of very few upper class English families, the same material of the women's diaries that Woolf dismissed. But Woolf stresses the difference between scribbling in a diary and taking care of making one's world intelligible, moving, and significant to readers outside of it. In her journalism, Woolf continually strove to balance the need to make money against her dislike of disposable writing. Woolf's essays address political and social questions of the age in the knowledge that such questions will be asked again by a new generation and in the hope that her thoughts may once again be of use and interest. Furthermore, the genesis of these longer essays, frequently traceable from letters and diaries, through short reviews, to longer, more meditative essays indicates how she used even her most apparently ephemeral assignments as opportunities to test ideas, occasions for *writing* in her special, serious sense of the word. But, because she is Virginia Woolf and not, for example, George Orwell, her political essays are still written in the Woolfian language of unflinching yet free-floating intelligence. Politics is accustomed to a brisker style.

The 1919 essay "Addison" investigates the *Spectator* and finds in it many of the qualities Woolf praises in Austen's works. Moreover, she finds in the example of Addison an acute social observer who, because male, did not have to hide his manuscripts when interrupted. Woolf, through reconsidering Addison, revolutionizes and then inhabits a sense of authorship as public participation that has its roots in eighteenth-century public sphere. It is not, then, the talk at the coffeehouse but the writing in the *Spectator* that inspires Woolf's most profound engagement with the eighteenth century. For Woolf, talk is cheap, regardless of the particular bourgeois social institution through which the talk occurs. By contrast, the essay of Addisonian judgment is superior to its counterparts (the salon, the letter, the coffeehouse) because, to Woolf, it seems bolder, more individualistic, and less porous to corrupting influences.

Woolf's essay, written to commemorate the bicentennial of Addison's death, is governed by an extended metaphor comparing the latter to an archaeological find: is he "a head of the best period" or "only the chips of an old pot"? (CR1, 97). The essay opens by quoting the extravagant praise of Macaulay's 1843 essay on Addison; indeed, the entire first half of Woolf's essay works to separate Addison—the man and his works—from "incrustations," be they "the corrosion of Pope's wit or the deposit of mid-Victorian lachyrmosity" (CR1, 100). The second half of the essay works to establish a new Addison: not monumental (as Macaulay would have it) but small, not Shakespeare's equal or a potential novelist (as, again, in Macaulay's estimate), but a perfect essayist, a second-tier writer in tune with his time, small yet valuable, a skilled miniaturist. Woolf concludes, "Two hundred years have passed; the plate is worn smooth; the pattern has almost rubbed out; but the metal is pure silver" (CR1, 105). This conclusion is more resounding than justified by the body of the essay; it risks, on a smaller scale, the monumentality she criticizes in Macaulay. But two wayside judgments offer insight into Woolf's opinion of Addison. On the one hand, she suspects that the essays are "nothing but talk" (CR1, 99). Nonetheless, his essays have merit "in the fact that they do not adumbrate, or initiate, or anticipate anything" (CR1, 100). For all this, they are not for Woolf early examples of modernist fragmentation and experiment: they are each "very highly finished" (CR1, 103).

On March 1, 1711 in the first number of the *Spectator*, Joseph Addison wrote, "I live in the world rather as a spectator of mankind, than as one of the species."[39] As the title declares, the stance of spectator defines the position from which Addison and Steele write. As the *Spectator* itself attests, however, spectators are only temporarily silent; participation is not withheld but deferred. Addison writes, "where-ever I see a cluster of people I always mix with them though I never open my lips but in my own club."[40] Woolf adopts Addison's word in her 1919 essay, characterizing his essays as "studies done from the outside by a quiet spectator" (CR1, 103).

Though eighteenth-century men enjoyed talk in one of over three thousand coffeehouses, Addison wrote up samples of that talk for the consumption of eighteenth-century women. Woolf portrays Addison as "a lutanist," a transparent, benignly timid man whose misogyny stemmed from fear (CR1, 102; O, 210). His essays survive as "collector's literature": "Neither lusty nor lively is the adjective we should apply to the present condition of the *Tatler* and the *Spectator*" (CR1, 99, 96). Throughout her 1919 essay, Woolf's estimate of Addison's stature in English literature emphasizes smallness and privacy: "if Addison lives at all, it is not in the public libraries. It is in libraries that are markedly private, secluded, shaded by lilac trees and brown with folios, that he still draws his faint, regular breath" (CR1, 96–97). This is perhaps the ultimate insult to a writer who was once admired for his timeliness and use. In diminishing Addison, Woolf diminishes his dominance over her. But Woolf has more in common with the spectator than her writings on him suggest. In suggesting how much of Addison's popularity depended upon his ability to draw upon and build consensus, she explores her own ambivalent role as a lead reviewer for the *TLS* and anticipates our current difficulty in disentangling that organ's official voice from her own.

The Addisonian spectator, for all his class-bound, male-centered exclusivity, helped create the principles of the critical judgment that still shape our discourse. Although Woolf's treatment of Addison is not a case of the anxiety of influence, Addison's symbolic position as a foundational figure of the periodical essay gives him a claim on our attention. The periodical essay was central to the development of, and now forms our chief evidence for, the emergence of the public sphere. Woolf and Addison were skillful professionals, who were adept at folding their opinions into those of their core audience, skilled at writing in the voice of the intelligent "we," and who engaged in the life of the city without succumbing to its fads. Both writers defined newsworthy topics broadly with a large female readership in mind, although Addison's motives for doing so were more patriarchally preceptorial than feminist. Moreover, the line from the *Spectator* to the *TLS* may be straighter than at first appears. Both periodicals addressed issues at greater length than the newspapers, both attracted a broad urban audience, and both consisted of unsigned contributions. Thus, although Woolf mocks Addison's place and status in literary history, the stance of the spectator nonetheless offers her a kind of resolution to the tension between public and private, not least for women.

Woolf's story, "A Society" (1919), makes the stance of the spectator the natural goal of the women's group: "So we made ourselves into a society for asking questions" (CSF, 125). The situation promises to fulfill Katherine's and Mary's serious, feminist friendship begun in *Night and Day*; however, this story, published in the same year, shows Woolf's dawning skepticism about the possibility of truly open, rational, critical debate. Following the model of Joseph Addison's Spectator's Club, in which "there is no rank or degree among [my readers] who have not their representative in this club,"[41] Woolf's young women (as homogenous a grouping as Addison's middle-aged men) disperse themselves into the various professions, claiming, like Addison's cohort, their right to represent large segments of society. Nevertheless, while these women write and present papers, which "had been framed after much consideration," their collective efforts never reach an audience beyond the confines of that society (CSF, 131). Indeed, their frequent lament that they themselves ever learned to read indicates their frustration at their own disempowerment. Embarked on a similarly collective project, Clarissa Dalloway and Sally Seton (in *Mrs. Dalloway* [1925]) get no further: "They meant to found a society to abolish private property, and actually had a letter written, though not sent out" (MD, 49). The young women in "A Society" promise the kind of unguarded conversation that attracts people to clubs, compensation, albeit meager, for the losses that women's minds sustain under patriarchy. Because the talkers are all women, female and feminist subjects have a primacy that they could not have with men present. Still, the society of "A Society" breaks into chaos when one of its members returns from her research pregnant, unmarried, and delighted at the prospect of motherhood; the other women, scandalized, cannot continue to meet.

If concerns about chastity still lead most women to self-censorship, then perhaps eccentrics offer a better model of public participation. The essay "Eccentrics," also published in 1919, opens with a meditation on what it might mean to have one's life summed up by the *Dictionary of National Biography* with the single word "eccentric." Woolf consistently expressed her admiration for eccentrics and aristocrats (and, best of all, eccentric aristocrats) who seem to live outside the pressure to conform: women like Lady Bath, "whose indifference to public opinion intrigued and delighted me" (MB, 207). The figures she discusses in "Eccentrics"—Lady Hester Stanhope; Margaret Fuller; Elizabeth Hitchener; Harriet Grote, née Lewin; Margaret Cavendish, the duchess of Newcastle—are all women. None of these women, Woolf writes, would not "have seen any force in the word *eccentric* as applied to herself, though it would not have surprised them in the least, could they have woke a century later, to find Temples dedicated to them," for a hallmark of eccentricity is complete belief in oneself against all pressures to conform (E, 3.40). Woolf admires these women because they seem to stand outside material society. Dependent upon no one, they are free to pursue their dreams. These women possess the imaginative freedom that Woolf deemed essential for creativity. "Eccentrics" is not a feminist essay, and, in fact, seems rather to enjoy mocking these women until the end, when it asks us whether the values of conventional history are right: "Do you never pause for a moment to wonder where all those nimble lives have gone to and what pranks they are playing beyond your sight, and whether, after all, the solid and the serviceable fulfill every need of the soul?" (E, 3.41). But, poised between the two alternatives of the Addisonian spectator and the female eccentric, Woolf always, in the end, chose the spectator's position.

Although Woolf may have successfully transformed aspects of Addisonian authorship to her own ends, modernism's ambivalent relationship to the public—as public sphere and, increasingly, mass market—meant that her success also involved her in the denial of any connection to Addison and his contemporaries. On May 25, 1919, Woolf recorded in her diary one of her many conversations with Lytton Strachey about writing and reviewing, this one coinciding with a conversation about her *TLS* lead article on Addison:

> Lytton came to tea on Friday & half maliciously assured me that my industry amazed him. My industry & my competence, for he thinks me the best reviewer alive, & the inventor of a new prose style, & the creator of a new version of the sentence. . . . But then money—he must make money—he cant write reviews—& I've to do Addison, & other books, & protested that all the same I'm not a hack, & he runs the risk of becoming . . . a superior dilettante. To which he agreed, & then we talked about Addison, & read scraps of Johnson's lives. (D, 1.277–78)

Strachey's "half-malicious" compliment reveals the competitive atmosphere of Bloomsbury. Its substance also captures the persistence of antiprofessional bias against which Woolf had to defend herself: to be "the best reviewer alive" is not to be the best writer; to be competent and industrious is not to be gifted. Nonetheless, this diary entry also records her sense that one can have a range of writing assignments to complete for pay and not be "a hack"; that to be "the inventor of a new prose style" and "the creator of a new version of the sentence" ranks as the highest compliment. Woolf's suggestion that there might be such a thing as a woman's sentence in *A Room of One's Own* indicates her sense of the importance of this endeavor.

For both Woolf and Strachey, the course of an artist stood between industry and dilettantism. As Peter McDonald explains, "These rival extremes, which give the field its hierarchical structure, set what I shall call the 'purists' against the 'profiteers.' For the former, the literary field exists in and for itself; for the latter, it is an instrument for achiev-ing other purposes."[42] While Strachey preferred the risk of becoming a "purist" dilettante, Woolf withstood the ambiguous judgments of her friends in favor of the artistic freedom that money brought her and the legitimate influence to intervene in public discourse that recognition carried with it. In the context of Bloomsbury—or of other modernists—Woolf was something of a profiteer. However, whereas class motives animated Arthur Conan Doyle and Arnold Bennett's ambition to earn money from art, and a foreigner's ambi-tion to assimilate drove Joseph Conrad to place his stories in the "right" magazines, Woolf strove to prove that a woman and a feminist could make a living, claim mainstream cultural authority, and reshape public discourse.

Significantly, although Woolf takes some anxious pride in her reviewing, she avoids the obvious parallel between her writing and Addison's. In fact, she goes out of her way to distance herself from him and emphasizes his aesthetic mediocrity while remaining silent on his sociocultural centrality. In a letter to Strachey, she continues their conversation, writing with a condescension that survives in the published essay: "Addison improves a little—if one likes that sort of thing" (L, 2.361). A few days later, Woolf continues in the same vein, calling the review "the problem of my life," her reading of Addison as conducted "in a sort of coma," abandoned in favor of the "great task of weeding the terrace . . . Can I say, on your authority, that he's a complete humbug? The worst of it is that he's not" (L, 2.363). Years later, when Max Beerbohm offered high praise for the piece, Woolf again records ambivalence at his flattery: does she want her reputation to be linked to the tradition that Addison and Beerbohm represent? "He told me how he had read an article on Addison at Bognor during the war; when literature seemed extinct; & there was his own name" (D, 3.213), she writes. Woolf's aversion to the reputation of journalist rather than writer shows up in a slip: in several diary entries shortly after the Addison piece, she refers to Mr. Allison, the Rodmell landowner and editor of *The Field*, whom she disliked, as "Addison," as if the name itself signifies professional writing divorced from art (D, 2.66, 128).

This ambivalence emerges in her writing in the 1920s as biting satire of the public sphere, especially in *Mrs. Dalloway* (1925) and *Orlando* (1928). *Mrs. Dalloway* investigates the significance of women's influence on the male-dominated world of politics with a jaded eye. Although the young women in the prewar world of *Night and Day* are enthusiastic about the possibilities of social and civic inclusion that the vote might bring, the emphatically postwar and middle-aged *Mrs. Dalloway* offers no such hope. The novel satirizes the public sphere as a still-functioning reality, conservative, and more exclusive than the democratic fantasy of Habermas. Newspapers and talk are essential: Septimus Smith's suicide reminds Dr. Bradshaw to lobby Richard Dalloway for a provision for "the deferred effects of shell shock . . . in the Bill"; Peter Walsh scoffs that he knew "to a tittle what Richard thought by reading the *Morning Post*"; and, while he is in India, he follows Hugh Whitbread's career at the Palace by reading "those admirable letters . . . in the *Times*" (MD, 279, 116, 263).

Clarissa Dalloway imagines her parties as "an offering" to the social world and figures her connection to others in a spidery metaphor: "the unseen part of us, which spreads wide, the unseen might survive, be recovered somehow attached to this person or that" (MD, 185, 232). Woolf's interests in the ephemeral and in women's role in creating it make parties of special interest to her. The party—be it a small luncheon or a lavish evening—is one of the few social structures in which the classical public sphere permits some female participation. Still, by Clarissa's own admission, the idea of a party as an offering "sounded horribly vague" (MD, 185). Increasing her ironic distance from her protagonist, Woolf lets Clarissa fumble for words, but her ambition "to combine, to create," her sense of her parties as "her gift" to the world and to life, as her stand against death, all speak to the idea of creating community by bringing people together (MD, 185). At its best, Clarissa's hospitality is symbolized by the act of taking the doors off their hinges to make room for the expected guests; her party will, for a few hours, erase the borders between rooms, between public and private, between the subclasses of the London elite. Her thoughts about parties and her judgment of her own party as successful have led some critics to elevate hostessing to an art form. However, Woolf's diminishment of the party's significance elsewhere in the novel must temper that judgment at least in the context of its role in the public sphere—a role to which it certainly aspires. Unlike Stephen and

Habermas who express nostalgic wonder at the thriving informal social institutions at the height of the public sphere of the eighteenth century and find the origins of these institutions mysterious, Woolf recognizes that women's work created these hospitable conditions. However, Woolf's feminist perspective prohibits unqualified admiration for Clarissa Dalloway—a woman who does not know what the equator is and who confuses Turks and Armenians; a woman, in short, unqualified to talk at her own parties—nor does Woolf silently condone the social conditions that create Mrs. Dalloways.

Throughout Woolf's writing, the hope for what a party might achieve gets checked by the reality of triviality, boredom, and personality clashes. While Clarissa herself only hesitantly ascribes to her parties the status of "an offering," others judge their ephemerality more harshly. Clarissa's self-damning admission that "she cared much more for her roses than for the Armenians" insures that she will neither be given nor take credit for the role her party has in the public sphere (MD, 182).[43] In *The Years* (1937), Woolf takes her satire further, targeting the very goal of bringing people together. While Delia surveys her own party with pride in achieving her aim "to mix people," her nephew thinks, "For all Delia's pride in her promiscuity . . . there were only Dons and Duchesses" (Y, 398, 404). Furthermore, the talk, though animated, only diminishes each subject it touches. The men reduce politics to a childish contest: "It was like hearing small boys at a private school, hearing these young men talk politics. 'I'm right . . . you're wrong' " (Y, 404). And the women are not much better (though, notably, they, too are talking politics): "It was . . . shuttlecock talk, to be kept going until the door opened and the gentlemen came in. Then it would stop. They were talking about a by-election. She could hear Lady Margaret telling some story that was rather coarse presumably, in the eighteenth-century way, since she dropped her voice" (Y, 258–59). Woolf associates insubstantial political talk and vulgarity with the eighteenth century and the aristocracy, recalling the century of Hogarth and Swift rather than Addison and Johnson. In both *Mrs. Dalloway* and *The Years*, people merely gossip; talking is a game.

Clues to Woolf's reasons for resisting the pull of the salon, in spite of Bloomsbury's resemblance to one, can be found in the way Lytton Strachey characterizes the salon of Madame du Deffand, which Woolf drew on for the salon scenes in *Orlando*.[44] Deffand's world, Strachey writes, exerted a pull on Napoleon (who read an edition of her letters in proof on his way to Russia) precisely because after 1789, it had already "vanished for ever."[45] Strachey characterizes Deffand's circle

as one of "innate skepticism, a profound levity, an antipathy to enthusiasm that wavered between laughter and disgust, combined with an
unswerving devotion to the exacting and arduous ideals of social
intercourse."[46] Furthermore, "literature and art," the staples of
Bloomsbury drawing room talk, were treated as "trifles" without "a
value of their own."[47] In short, the salon belongs to the *ancien
regime*, politically blind to the revolution around it (the revolution
that free talk helped to spark) and more skeptical than idealistic. What
attracted Woolf's imagination more vividly was the talk "here in
Somers Town" where "a party of ill-dressed, excited young men, one
with a head too big for his body and a nose too long for his face,
hold[s] forth day by day over the tea-cups upon human perfectibility,
ideal unity, and the rights of man" (CR2, 156). Her praise for William
Godwin's circle of radical Londoners, and for Mary Wollstonecraft's
easy admission into it, shows Woolf's love for conversation of
substance.

Habermas argues that the female-dominated salons were the closest
French equivalent to the coffeehouses of London, even though he
also suggests that the aristocratic, aesthetic, and heterosexual atmosphere of the salon discouraged political discussion.[48] Citing a rare
agreement between Habermas and Hannah Arendt, Seyla Benhabib
explains how it can be that a living room becomes part of public life:
"public space is the space 'where freedom can appear' [Arendt]. It is
not a space in any topographical or institutional sense: a town hall or
a city square where people do not act in concert is not a public space
in this Arendtian sense. But a private dining room in which people
gather to hear a *samizdat* or in which dissidents meet with foreigners
become public spaces."[49] While evenings at Clarissa Dalloway's or
with "some of the greatest ladies in the land" (O, 192) in *Orlando* can
scarcely be said to rise to the crackling political significance Benhabib
imagines, such parties do comprise a public space. In fact, the gap
between the public sphere's potential to "let freedom appear" and a
boring evening animates Woolf's interest in society.

In this world of parties, Woolf imagines women with greater
influence than Habermas or his feminist critics might have predicted.
At the same time, Woolf shows that influence is a weak form of power
and a secondary form of participation. Lady Bruton, who "derived
from the eighteenth century" (MD, 173), exemplifies the limits of a
woman's influence on the workings of the classical public sphere: she
brings Richard Dalloway and Hugh Whitbread to her house where
they write a letter to the *Times*; Richard's experience and Hugh's connections will help ensure its publication; Richard's kindness then

deepens Lady Bruton's obligation to attend Clarissa's party that evening where she discusses her plan with the prime minister. Lady Bruton's plan, to combat British overpopulation by encouraging emigration to Canada, is reactionary enough to make even Richard Dalloway disapprove, but that is part of Woolf's point about the complex and compromised workings of power and influence (MD, 264). These characters—linked by Lady Bruton's luncheons, Clarissa's parties, and the newspapers they all read—range from the charming to the silly to the contemptible; none of them is taken too seriously, but their influence on public debate is real.[50] Where Habermas describes talk as "rational critical debate," Woolf depicts influence and obligation.

Woolf relentlessly exposes the eighteenth century's reputation for intellectually stimulating and politically influential conversation as myth in *Orlando* (1928). There her comparison of the Lady R's parties to a salon diminishes both. Even her narrator conspires against any fantasy of abundant wit. With characteristic axiomatic pomp, he asserts that a hostess is allowed only three witty sayings; any more, and congeniality is destroyed (O, 199–200). Nonetheless, the ever-optimistic Orlando leaps at her invitation, then quickly experiences the gulf between public report and reality when she first spends the evening at Lady R's where, "nothing (so the report ran) was said inside that was not witty": "In three hours, such a company must have said the wittiest, the profoundest, the most interesting things in the world. So it would seem indeed. But the fact appears that they said nothing" (O, 198–99). Woolf doubts that honest conversation could occur in such a brittle social setting.[51]

Orlando swears off society, but is lured to Lady R's with the promise of meeting genius. Eventually genius appears in the shape of Alexander Pope, whose wit fills Lady R with "sarcastic fury" and breaks up her salon ("that they would ever come back after such an experience was doubtful") and whom Orlando rashly escorts home (O, 202). Eager to trade society conversation for the imagined superior conversation of the coffeehouse wits, Orlando enters into a friendship with Pope, and, soon thereafter, Swift and Addison, only to find them more interested in being pampered than witty. While Orlando spends time with wits, she quickly recognizes that they do not talk openly to her: "A woman knows very well that, though a wit sends her his poems, praises her judgment, solicits her criticism, and drinks her tea, this by no means signifies that he respects her opinions" (O, 214). Woolf's point here is not subtle: the eighteenth century is, for her, fundamentally misogynist and nothing can erase the discomfort Woolf imagines as the eighteenth-century woman's lot: " 'Lord,' [Orlando] thought, as she raised the sugar tongs, 'how women in ages to come will envy me! And yet—' she paused; for Mr. Pope needed her attention. And yet—let us finish her thought for her—when anybody says 'How future ages will envy me,' it is safe to say that they are extremely uneasy in the present moment" (O, 212–13). Here, as hostessing duties prevent Orlando from completing a thought, the narrator intervenes. Within the double filter of Orlando's incomplete, interrupted thought and the narrator's mock-scholarly euphemism "extremely uneasy," Woolf embeds a more fundamental critique than either character or narrator yet dares.

In the end, Orlando's two most satisfying experiences of the coffeehouse are as a spectator: watching Addison from the prow of a ship and spying on Dr. Johnson (while she is in drag) from outside a coffeehouse. Musing on the superiority of distance over participation, Orlando thinks, "One can only believe entirely, perhaps, in what one cannot see. The little glimpse she had of the poets from the deck of the ship was of the nature of a vision" (O, 198). Orlando's delight reminds us of how new such leisure and open conversation was in the first decades of the eighteenth century. For writers, politicians, and sociologists of community, there is something intoxicatingly attractive about this culture in which "the reading part of the nation" inspired the discussion that led to class solidarity and, eventually, democratic reforms (including the extension of the franchise and educational reforms), in which it is reasonable to guess that as many as 20 readers saw every copy of the *Spectator*.[52] From a distance, the activities at a coffeehouse seem to matter so much and the exclusion of women seems, briefly, an oversight. Woolf's flat, heavily ironic presentation of familiar scenes prevents her from falling into the historian's enthusiasm for the past (a fault that Stephen and Habermas do not entirely escape) and creates the critical distance necessary for her feminist critique. She thematizes nostalgia while emphasizing the past's limitations. Talk is ultimately as suspect in the coffeehouse as it is at the society party. The pressure to conform that Habermas warned of is crippling in Woolf's account. Dissent is impossible in both settings; in both settings, the price of inclusion in the conversation is consenting to be an agreeable listener. In Woolf's revisionist version of the eighteenth-century public sphere, both heterosocial and male homosocial conversation are not triumphantly democratic but exclusionary and problematic. In dismantling the reputation of eighteenth-century conversation that was popularized by her father, Woolf not only criticized the century, but she also criticized the possibility of meaningful conversation even in the present.

*Orlando* eventually turns away from the mainstream. When it does, it depicts not bluestockings—eighteenth-century women intellectuals—but a group of prostitutes whose class background (many are the natural daughters of aristocrats) better suits Orlando's anti–middle-class bias (as well as Woolf's) and, more importantly, whose comfort with their bodies and their sexuality provides an opportunity for Woolf to imagine a crucial advantage of free discourse, one quite different from any imagined by Stephen or Habermas. Disgusted with high society as well as with the company of writers, yet still lonely, Orlando disguises herself as a man, picks up a prostitute and, in befriending her, discovers she and her friends have "a society of their own" in which Orlando is welcomed; in fact, "Orlando had never known the hours speed faster or more merrily" than in the company of Nell and her friends (O, 219, 218). Nell and her friends, in sharing their life stories and "amusing observations" parallel the consensus of the men's club (O, 219). Nell's crowded rooms (she undresses behind a screen) inspire intimate talk about bodies, desire, and sex whereas the newspapers of clubs and coffeehouses inspire political talk. The women's shared talk demonstrates how fully they, like men in a club, construct themselves as spectators in the street, commentators within their society, rather than merely being the objects of talk.

Orlando's conversations with Nell and her friends are a reminder of the topics that remain taboo, and a glimpse of what society might be like if women were accepted as full participants in discourse. The prostitutes possess an unselfconscious comfort with their bodies. Nell and her friends represent a thought experiment: what might it be like to speak frankly about being a woman with women who think freely and frankly? In projecting herself into a better future for women, Woolf imagines a world in which Nell's mental freedom might coexist with the material freedom of the twentieth century. In Woolf's fictional eighteenth century, Nell's circle can never make the transition to the public. It remains a kind of Sapphic *hortus conclusus*, one we only know about, according to the conceit of the novel, thanks to the presence of the androgynous main character. However attractive women's conversation may be, even in the fantastic world of *Orlando*, Woolf depicts it as circumscribed and almost wholly shaped by social expectations, at the same time, without any outside influence.

The historian in Woolf laments Nell's exclusion from the political imaginary as a symbol of lost women's history; Orlando's pleasure in Nell's company adds poignancy to the loss. As in *A Room of One's Own*, where Woolf interrupts her "I often like women" with the worry that a man might be hiding in the linen cupboard, a man interrupts Orlando's conversation with Nell and her friends just as the narrator gestures at substance, at an answer: "All they desire is—but hist again—is that not a man's step on the stair?" (ARO, 111; O, 219). Woolf continues the joke, having the prostitute's client enter and announce, "Women have no desires" before he disappears with Nell to gratify his own animal desires (O, 219). Orlando's narrator may satirize the man's pomposity, but his interruption ends the conversation; Orlando may delight in the company of these women, but she gains entry only by dressing as a man. In both cases, the person dressed as a man controls the flow of talk. Woolf indicts the men who interrupt rather than the women who silence themselves, but this "society of their own" does not and cannot influence the mainstream public sphere or, to Woolf, represent a counterpublic sphere.

The prostitutes present a harmonious conversation, but as enthralling as it apparently is, Woolf depicts it as unable to influence the mainstream public sphere, irrecoverable, and withheld from circulation. In *Orlando*, Woolf satirizes the misogyny that was based on a refusal to distinguish among working women, be they sex-workers, actresses, or writers. Woolf profited from these ambiguities in her social critique, using the comic tone of *Orlando* to bend convention without breaking it. In drag, Orlando wanders the London streets of the 1710s and mixes with prostitutes. The prostitutes in *Orlando* are social critics whose marginal status grants them freedom to move about the city, observing its customs and structures of power. Woolf gives voice to these observations, recognizing these potential writers in her own writing. To borrow Barbara Green's formulation, Woolf's political awakening led not to "the spectacle of woman (feminist activism)" but to "the woman who looks (feminist critique)," not to collectivity, but to independent commentary.[53] Crucially, Woolf celebrates not her prostitutes' access to the streets but their interiority— precisely where social historians (less biased against the bourgeoisie) give the advantage to bourgeois women. In so doing, Woolf makes full subjects, and, by extension, potential writers of them.

Woolf emphasizes the way that prohibitions against public notice for women tended to equate writing with unchastity. The client's interruption proves fatal to this conversation because the women are eager to keep their talk secret, an eagerness that Woolf attributes to the whole sex: "when women get together . . . they are always careful to see that the doors are shut and that not a word of it gets into print" (O, 219). Although, as Woolf herself notes elsewhere, publishing was then opening up to women, a residual sense of it being "ridiculous," as letter-writer Dorothy Osborne feared, persisted long after women writers gained acceptance (CR2, 60). Woolf highlights the intensity of women's shame at being writers by having even her prostitutes avoid the shame of authorship. Trading on these deep prejudices in 1929, Woolf imagines the young woman writer of the eighteenth century trying to persuade her father that she could make a living by her pen, and his reply: "Yes! by living the life of Aphra Behn! Death would be better!" (ARO, 64).

The negative facts of women's lives—not sending letters, not publishing papers, not recording conversations—and the overwhelming desire to avoid publicity make them fascinating subjects for a novelist's speculation but do not make them models for Woolf's own public participation. Also inadequate, for different reasons, is the sad history of misogyny toward eccentric women. Their lives provide models of resistance to conformity but not of the active role in mainstream debate that Woolf sought.

## A Radical Intervention, 1938

Habermas would have it that consensus gets built in the coffeehouses through "rational critical debate." However, the *Tatler* and the *Spectator* tell a different story. Their mild satire and "capacious blandly homogenizing language" performs in prose what the French denizens of the salon perfected orally: consolidation of their audience's opinion and thus, their class identity. As one critic puts it, "modern criticism in England was born ironically of political consensus."[54] An essay by Addison may have been "animated by moral correction and satiric ridicule . . . but its major impulse is one of class-consolidation . . . whereby the English bourgeoisie may negotiate an historic alliance with its social superiors."[55] Addison and Steele succeeded where Pope failed for the same reasons that Madame du Deffand and Mrs. Dalloway succeeded: they do not act with "sectarian truculence."[56] As Woolf writes, Addison's "essays at their best preserve the very cadence of easy yet exquisitely modulated conversation—the smile checked before it has broadened into laughter, the thought lightly turned from frivolity or abstraction, the ideas springing, bright, new, various, with the utmost spontaneity" (CR1, 102). For all her faith in the power of words to change people's minds, Woolf saw the difficulties of using a discourse arising out of consensus-building for the purpose of advocating revolutionary change.

Spectatorship may have begun for Addison as a means to maintain some privacy and still participate in the larger world, a way to eavesdrop in the streets and share a distillation of one's observations only in the safety of the club. Spectatorship evolves, however, into the ability to build consensus, for in the pause between observing and recounting, the spectator forms a judgment. For Addison this judgment was the judgment of his class and, in expressing it, he captured and consolidated fellow-feeling, building consensus. The dangers of institutionalizing this paradigm are easy to see: it can be difficult to discriminate between the public opinion formed in the crucible of the public exercise of reason and public opinion based in conformity. As Woolf notes more damningly of Madame de Sévigné: "She is by no means a simple spectator. Maxims fall from her pen. She sums up; she judges. But it is done effortlessly. She has inherited the standard and accepts it without effort" (DM, 55). As Habermas discusses at length, once the bourgeoisie gained power, strategies developed to protest authoritarianism developed an authority of their own. Woolf's accounts of the eighteenth century anticipate Terry Eagleton's cautious account of consensus. Nonetheless, the essay emerges as a privileged form of conversation and participation. An essay combines the authority of male talk with the possibilities of female participation. What an essay may lose in immediacy, it gains in substance and, potentially, longevity.

When Woolf next takes up the idea of a counterpublic sphere, she imagines one constructed for the purpose of intervening in the mainstream. The occasion of *Three Guineas* (1938) is a barrister's letter requesting a donation for a society for the prevention of war. There, "the rejection of professional or military spectacle is uncompromising."[57] Woolf's oblique response is a proposal: rather than join his organization, she and all women would do better to form an Outsider's Society, untainted by patriarchy and capable of challenging it. The imagined Outsider's Society is constructed as explicitly and unabashedly pacifist and feminist, changing society by refusing institutional connections with it. The idea of an Outsider's Society builds on and marks a significant intellectual departure from Woolf's explorations of a counterpublic sphere in the 1920s. In *Three Guineas*, the stance of the spectator becomes a stance of feminist resistance, a resistance that, as Barbara Green has argued, engages in intellectual activism through "critical modes of viewing and through spectacular forms of writing."[58] Part of the interest of the prostitutes' conversation in *Orlando* derives from the fact that, in the 1930s, Woolf found a way to convert women's private talk into print.

Woolf and Habermas are largely in accord on the role of letter writing in the formation of the public sphere. For Habermas, the rise of letter writing played a key role in creating the bourgeois individual's sense of self: receiving a letter so patently confirms individuality. The rise of letters meant that "the relations between author, work, and public . . . became intimate mutual relations between privatized individuals who were psychologically interested in what was 'human,' in self-knowledge, and in empathy."[59] Woolf praises Madame de Sévigné's letters for their ability to convey, across centuries, this very sense of "a living person, inexhaustible" (DM, 51). Woolf goes on to generalize: "This of course is one of the qualities that all letter writers possess" (DM, 51). Woolf's six volumes of personal correspondence confirm her status as a letter writer. Moreover, her many public letters participate directly in the public sphere. In her letters to Desmond MacCarthy (reprinted as "The Intellectual Status of Women" [1920]), in "Letter to a Young Poet" (1932), the pamphlet that inaugurated the Hogarth Press's "Letters" series, and, most radically, in *Three Guineas* (1938), Woolf continues the eighteenth-century tradition of the political letter. The letters that frame her argument in *Three Guineas* revive, for pacifist feminist purposes, letter writing as a way for women to enter politics.

In making the respectability of women's letter writing a subject of analysis, however, Woolf surpasses Habermas. Precisely because female letter writing is patriarchally sanctioned, writing letters does not help women achieve a greater public role. In her writing on letters, Woolf seems to accept the notion of letters as transparent and transient communication, addressed to "a public of one" (CR2, 61). Woolf writes, "the fourteen volumes of [Madame de Sévigné's] letters enclose a vast open space, like one of her great woods" (DM, 51), but at the end of her essay she asks, "What was happening outside?" (DM, 57), referring at once to the world outside de Sévigné's enclosed parks, her small social circle, and her texts. Letters have long been recognized as possessing an "ontological ambiguity."[60] Especially in the seventeenth and eighteenth centuries, women took advantage of the "quasi public"[61] space of letters, the fiction of letters being addressed to a (suitably modest) "public of one," in order to maneuver their way into the public sphere. Woolf, recognizing this (and, in *Three Guineas*, ironically deploying it), nevertheless sought to expose the indirection of letter writing as public discourse. As we have seen, in *Mrs. Dalloway*, she associates letter writing with the highly compromised Lady Bruton. For all Lady Bruton's manliness ("if ever a woman could have worn the helmet and shot the arrow" [MD, 274]), she spends the novel inside; she walks London only metaphorically, as a "thin thread" and with her letter. The letter she writes with Hugh Whitbread and Richard Dalloway represents the safest possibility for women to enter the public sphere: a symbol of patriarchy's difficulty with women's bodies. Lady Bruton's sense that she needs male assistance to effectively participate sheds light on how gendered assumptions about public discourse undermine and limit women. Woolf's strategy enables her to recover a history of women's writing at the same time condemning social conditions that made direct literary channels (pamphlets, broadsheets, books) closed to women. *Three Guineas* is not, after all, a letter but a pamphlet employing the conventions of epistolary discourse as but one of several tools of persuasion. As for employing the old methods of indirect influence, "many of us would prefer to call ourselves prostitutes simply and to take our stand openly under the lamps of Piccadilly Circus rather than use it" (3G, 15). Ultimately, the quasipublic of letters is too limited and conventional to offer a truly free voice to an individual woman; like a woman wandering the park of a great estate and suddenly coming to the fence she must not cross, Woolf explores these roles and finds them confining. She seeks a way to reach the vaster public outside, to follow her father's advice and "trespass at once" (M, 54).

In making use of the stance of the spectator, Woolf explores the moral ambiguity of detachment. Woolf's characters watch the world intently, through windows at the street or countryside below, through a spyglass at a coffeehouse, in third-class train carriages, from the top of omnibuses, from an airplane, at the movies, in art galleries, and in newspaper photographs. In many essays, the personified eye, often likened to a fish, swims through the world trying to navigate its way clear of obstacles. In these examples, Woolf celebrates new technologies—the emerging mass media, communication and transportation networks, film and photography—for offering expanded access to the world, especially for the middle-class women with whom Woolf often allied herself, who now witness war without setting foot on a battlefield and travel unescorted and unmolested across London. Regardless of the technology, however, Woolf depicts the act of looking as crucial and crucially prior to judgment. Looking is what one does to gather information. Woolf is much less concerned than Walter Benjamin, the Frankfurt School more broadly, and the social critics and historians who have followed in their wake, with how new technologies of seeing will evacuate aura from the public sphere and diminish the individual's influence over and within culture. Being a spectator, with its theatrical and passive connotations and its Addisonian connection, is an ambiguous role. For Woolf, spectators are outsiders, sometimes with great powers of impartial observation, sometimes vaguely irrelevant. Woolf calls Henry James "a spectator, alert, aloof, endlessly interested, endlessly observant" and she writes of William Cowper, "a quiet and solitary life that must have been . . . in which the sight of an attractive face was an event" (DM, 147; CR2, 140).[62] James, Cowper, and Addison are spectators in defiance of their era's gender norms. In *Three Guineas*, by contrast, female spectators put to use the "understanding of human beings and their motives" that women have developed in their pursuit of "the one great profession open to our class" (i.e., marriage) in order to understand how to prevent war.

In short, *Three Guineas* transforms the limitations of spectatorship into a source of power. In Woolf, Addison's strategy of spectatorship finds a substantial and modern object. Woolf, by understanding the position of the spectator as feminized, uses it to criticize patriarchy. Addressing an anonymous gentleman—perhaps a descendant of one of Addison's readers—Woolf invites him inside, to view the world from the female perspective: "Let us then . . . lay before you a photograph . . . of your world as it appears to us who see it from the threshold of the private house; . . . from the bridge which connects the private house with the world of public life" (3G, 18). By inviting the man into the sheltered, female space from which women observe and form judgments about "public life," Woolf transforms the stance of the spectator from a vaguely irrelevant, aesthetic pose to a strategy, not only of resistance to but also of communication with patriarchy. Her invitation to the male reader seeks to empower the female spectator, making her the viewing subject who understands the connection between private life and the public spectacle of men, who are demoted merely to the objects of the observant gaze. She also asserts her right to move from being a spectator on "the threshold of the private house" into being a participant in public life when she claims that her outsider's position has given her an important vantage point from which to contribute to public debate. Later in the book, her dream of what women might do if "rich women were as common as rich men" takes a distinctly eighteenth-century cast: "You could finance a woman's party in the House of Commons. You could run a daily newspaper committed to a conspiracy, not of silence, but of speech" (3G, 68). This transformation of spectatorship performs what Habermas sees as a citizen's ideal function: "If you shift from an observer's role to a participant's role and carry over your insight into it, at least you would be in . . . the position that is desirable as a model position. I mean not a position that we in fact take but a position that everybody should take and is supposed to take in a public discourse that would live up to its own standard."[63] In the process of Woolf's move from observer to participant, she worked assiduously to demonstrate that a woman observing the world possesses insight worthy of male attention. That she felt the need to prove her intelligence to a patriarchal and prejudiced implied audience reminds us of our distance from her world; that she succeeded in doing so is its own tribute.

From the beginning, Habermas acknowledged that social pressure to conform hinders intellectual freedom.[64] For rational critical debate to survive the homogenizing pressure of public discourse, a strong sense of individual subjectivity—and thus, the access to solitary space—becomes necessary. As she developed her own strong sense of individual subjectivity, Woolf emphasized the extra pressures on women to conform. For Woolf, as for Habermas, a thriving public sphere in which ideas are exchanged depends on an individual's ability to move between the public sphere and solitude. In fact, for Habermas, these two spaces—the family home with its potential for solitude and the world of the coffeehouses and clubs—together constitute the private realm.[65]

Distinguishing the private realm from public authority (the state and the court), Habermas explains that "included in the private realm was the authentic 'public sphere,' for it was a public sphere constituted by private people."[66] Ideas become public—that is, they enter the realm of the state and the police—only after being formulated, debated, and recast in the private realm. In her explorations of the public and private spheres, Woolf dramatizes the difficulties of women, whether seeking solitude or seeking to participate. As a man and as a woman, Orlando spends vast stretches of time alone on the family estate, but it is only as a woman that "Orlando hid her manuscripts when interrupted" (O, 187). By contrast, in the 1930s, the privacy to which women have been confined becomes an advantage: affording the critical perspective on the spectacle below that helps them see the link between patriarchal pomp and war and, by extension, teaching them how to work for peace.

In *Three Guineas*, Woolf would argue that "freedom from unreal loyalties" was one of the great teachers of the "daughters of educated men" like herself, but early on, Virginia Stephen worked hard to capitalize on the real influences and acquaintances that established her as a regular reviewer and essayist (3G, 79). These texts from the last days of World War I, the guardedly hopeful *Night and Day*, the cautiously feminist "Eccentrics," and the defensively dismissive "Addison" set up a problem that, a decade later, *A Room of One's Own* and *Orlando* were still addressing: how can one be a feminist and still be heard in the public sphere? Woolf never turned her back on the mainstream public sphere and her success there continues to pose a problem for those critics attempting to place her in the otherwise anti-mainstream world of high modernism. I have tried to address this puzzle here by taking seriously Woolf's ambition—perhaps already old-fashioned in the 1920s but powerful nevertheless—to be a woman of letters. It was only after she had achieved that ambition that she began to distance herself from that old-fashioned title in favor of the greater and simpler one of writer.

# CHAPTER 4

# A Very Sincere Performance:
# Woolf, Byron, and Fame

*When he is serious, he is sincere.*

Virginia Woolf

*Yet, suddenly, between the acts, the figure of Byron appears, how tawdry, insincere and theatrical!*

Virginia Woolf

As the above epigraphs show, Byron represented not just one thing to Virginia Woolf. She read him critically and carefully, ready to detect either greatness or cant. But the very contradiction we find in her judgment of Byron—he was alternately sincere and insincere—speaks to something central to Woolf's aesthetic. She had a long-standing interest in the attraction of opposites, in friendships and within one's own personality. Her interest in androgyny itself represents an attempt to reconcile the apparently incompatible. Here is how she describes one such unlikely pairing:

> As they gazed at each other each felt: Here am I—and then each felt: But how different! Hers was the pale worn face of an invalid, cut off from air, light, freedom. His was the warm ruddy face of a young animal; instinct with health and energy. Broken asunder, yet made in the same mould, could it be that each completed what was dormant in the other? She might have been—all that; and he—But no. (F, 23)

The vast differences between Elizabeth Barrett (later Browning) and her dog Flush only increase their intimacy and mutual admiration. Eventually, in Woolf's retelling of the story—based heavily on Browning's correspondence—Browning teaches Flush patience and, by living with her, he becomes less of a snob. More important, however, is the lesson in courage: for through her love for Flush, the poet leaves her house when Flush is kidnapped, an adventure that prepares her for the greater one of her elopement. Though these lessons take time, the sympathy between the two is immediate and intense: they look at each other and feel "here am I!" At the same time, their unlikely attachment is amusing, even to Browning herself: "Flush always makes the most of his misfortunes—he is of the Byronic school—*il se pose en victime*" (qtd. in F, 65).

Virginia Woolf could no more become Lord Byron than Elizabeth Barrett Browning could become a spaniel. Still, canine allusions notwithstanding, Woolf's engagement with Byron, much like Browning's earlier passion for both Byron and her dog Flush, was deep, lasting, and profound. The hesitations, elisions, questions, and unfinished thoughts that conclude the passage from *Flush* dramatize the complexities of such a relationship: the intimacy of two so different creatures occurs somewhere on the far side of language. Woolf's admiration for Byron's vivacity, wit, and sense of adventure is not wholly unlike what Browning loves in her dog. And certainly the "pale worn . . . invalid, cut off from air" and the "ruddy . . . young animal" could be caricatures of Woolf and Byron. Looked at from this slightly different angle, it becomes surprising that it has taken so long to recognize the likeness between these two satiric sentimentalists who combined aristocratic temperaments with liberal politics.

Of the major romantic figures that Woolf admired, alluded to, and discussed, her most puzzling and most revealing fascination is with George Gordon, Lord Byron (1788–1824). In Byron, she had a precursor who was both sincere and insincere, one who spoke for himself and punctured the hypocrisy of others from behind multiple, elaborate personae. Thus, in looking at Woolf's debt to Romanticism, we can see the tensions in her democratic aspirations more clearly in her ambivalent response to the imperious, aristocratic Lord Byron than in her fondness for Coleridge and Shelley. We learn as much about her attitude to fame, its trappings and consequences, from her interest in Byron as from her far-less complicated sympathy for Keats. And we learn more surprising lessons about her feminism from her admiration for Byron than from her admiration for Mary Wollstonecraft. Though Wollstonecraft argued a powerful case, the ease of Byron's writing shows the prize for which Woolf fought: the freedom to imagine without restraint.

Woolf did not read Byron until she was in her twenties, but from then on, she turned to him with pleasure, always distinguishing between the Byron she admired and the one she found silly and "insincere and theatrical." Woolf occasionally enjoyed gossip about Byron; she also learned lessons about the perils of fame from that gossip. Byron provided a model—nearly impossible for a woman to follow, but instructive nonetheless—of what it might mean to scoff at conventions and still meet with success. Most of all, however, she admired his formal experiments. Immediately upon reading him, she saw that his mastery of both satire and romance permitted him to discuss a wide range of subjects, providing personae separate from his fame. More than any other romantic, Byron combined a heroic imagination with a playful cynicism that constantly called his sincerity into question. His persona was all performance, but within that performance he found room for expressions of genuine conviction. Furthermore, Byron's life dramatically embodies the twin romantic desires of poetic retreat and revolutionary action. For he was both an exile and a martyr to revolution.

A common reader today is likely to know more about the lives of Woolf and Byron than about their works. In the years following his death, Byron's fame grew, as Woolf's has in the years following hers.[1] Both Woolf and Byron saw this coming. They were famous in their own lifetimes and they worried about how to control the dissemination and commodification of their image, works, and ideas. Byron's fame, according to more than one critic, was so unprecedented that it called up a new critical vocabulary aimed at describing "not simply a new structure of poetic identity, the Byronic, but also a new cultural phenomenon, celebrity."[2] As such, his person and his reputation acted as a cautionary tale for Woolf, who worked to maintain her privacy not by being reclusive but through carefully managed publicity.

Byron became a celebrity when he was a young man, and, as a young man, worked—often self-destructively—to maintain his fame. Byron's poetic response to celebrity was to satirize it. *The Giaour* (1814) "creates a Byronic hero who satirically replicates his critics' view of him."[3] Woolf, on the other hand, did not become famous until she was in her forties. *Orlando* (1928), a mock biography based loosely on Woolf's friend and lover, Vita Sackville-West, begins with the title character as a young Elizabethan lord, and ends, centuries later, with Orlando as a modern young woman. This androgynous jest propelled her to fame. She followed *Orlando* with *A Room of One's Own* (1929): that is, in stark contrast to Byron, she turned her fame into an opportunity to make a serious feminist point about the importance of both androgyny and material independence. Though Woolf read *Childe Harold* in 1930 alongside Maurois's biography, the text of Byron's that she and her characters turned to most often was *Don Juan*, written in Italy after his fame and the scandal of his separation. In this poem, probably Byron's greatest, he found a way not only to keep writing in spite of the external strictures imposed by fame, but also to turn the mask of fame to his advantage, creating his most attractive Byronic hero and narrator combination: one, handsome, passive, and sincere; the other, a wit.

In this chapter, I discuss four phases of Woolf's interest in Byron. Since Woolf did not read Byron until 1918, I open with a discussion of literary gossip and what it means to be Byronic—and Woolfian. This section reviews what Woolf seems to have known about Byron before reading him and what Byron's celebrity taught Woolf about the perils of biographical criticism for readers *and* writers. Woolf wrote two extensive diary entries on Byron: one in 1918, when she read him for the first time while writing *Jacob's Room* (1922), and another in 1930, while writing *The Waves* (1931). Each of the next two sections analyzes how the diary entry is reflected in the novel she was then writing. In *Jacob's Room*, Byron inspires Woolf to experiment, but she has not yet found a way to combine a blank protagonist with a narrator who can compensate for the vacuum he leaves. When she returns to Byron in 1930 while writing *The Waves*, she uses Bernard's impersonation of Byron as a vehicle through which to explore the linked themes of promise, fame, death, and writing. Finally, I examine Woolf's last years, in which the Spanish Civil War—and especially the death of her nephew Julian Bell in Spain—causes her to intensify her opposition to political martyrdom and, thus, her suspicion of what Byron, a martyr himself, signifies for his admirers. As the Byronic figure crosses gender, age, and even, in the case of Flush, species, we can trace Woolf's shifting attitudes to fame and its consequences: its effect on one's financial and intellectual independence, its intrusions into one's privacy, and the political clout and responsibility that come with cultural capital.

## Being Byron, Being Woolf

Virginia Woolf associated Byron, who began his quest for fame as a prankster at public school and later at Cambridge, with subsequent generations of undergraduate men, beginning with her brother Thoby. In 1902, when she was 20, she wrote to her older brother, then at Cambridge: "Has Byron come to a decent end? Lord preserve me from spending my fine brains over other peoples bones! and for goodness sake, dont you either. You are an Original Genius, my Lord" (L, 1.59). Thoby has clearly been reading Byron, a poet whom Woolf was not to read for another six years. But, though she has not read

Byron, she knows enough literary lore to tease Thoby. There is nothing "decent" about Byron; the phrase "Original Genius" is high Romantic; the final tease, "my Lord," replaces Byronic aristocracy with the Stephen family's belief in an aristocracy of intellect.

This gentle teasing of her brother is more pointed when Woolf turns her gaze on others. We learn more about the range of meanings included in the term "Byronic" in her description of her friend and rival Katherine Mansfield's partner, John Middleton Murry: "a posturing Byronic little man; pale; penetrating; with bad teeth; histrionic; an egoist" (L, 2.515). At other times, her friend Rupert Brooke, her brother-in-law Clive Bell, and his son Julian get called Byronic.[4] And she calls Vita Sackville-West's friend, Dorothy Wellesley, Byronic: "We motored to the Long Barn &. . . . found Vita & Dotty sitting over a log fire. . . . Dotty byronic in her dress, but much improved over the London Dotty" (D, 3.157).[5] These people are all physically confident in spite of obvious flaws (bad teeth, baldness): unlike the beautiful and self-conscious Woolf, these uglier, more charismatic people present themselves as natural centers of attention. Byron himself did so, finding ways to compensate for his clubfoot. Woolf attributes this to his having a wife who "instead of laughing . . . merely disapproved. And so he became Byronic" (D, 1.180). For Woolf, self-important people, unchecked, become Byronic, and she has as little patience for self-importance as Byron did for hypocrisy. Throughout her life, when she calls someone "Byronic" she expresses bemused admiration. She treats Byronic people as one treats clever undergraduates—indulgently but lightly, bemusedly but skeptically. The adjective Byronic refers almost exclusively to the Byron she mocked; this, too, was the Byron she first wrote about publicly, and it is a Byron whose contours do not depend on having read Byron.

Woolf's sense of what it means to be Byronic emphasizes the confidence to present oneself boldly. When she calls Dorothy Wellesley "Byronic . . . much better than the London Dotty," the implication is that the country Dotty, while still putting on a show, is easier to take.[6] Dotty embodies the paradox at the heart of readers' fascination with Byron and his poetic personae: she is not ever natural, but some of her poses seem less forced. Woolf's frequent expressions of anxiety about clothes and shopping vividly demonstrate her own struggles with self-confidence, specifically the performative (or quasiperformative) aspects of public appearances (as opposed to the publication of her writing). While she poked fun at her Byronic friends, she also gathered them around her. She struggled mightily to overcome her feelings of social discomfort because she did not want the life of a recluse. She aimed, at some cost, to achieve the kind of ease depicted in a late 1920s photograph of her in a fur collar: beautiful, intelligent, independent, and uncompromising.

As we have seen, even before Woolf had read Byron, she had an idea of what it meant to be Byronic. In itself, this is not surprising. "Byronism," a word used "to name a phenomenon both self-fashioned and created by the age," was established in Byron's lifetime.[7] Admirers and detractors alike define the Byronic as deliberately heterodox and self-dramatizing. Byron himself defined his character, somewhat boastingly, thus: "There are but two sentiments to which I am constant, a strong love of liberty, and a detestation of cant, and neither is calculated to gain me friends."[8] But calculating is just what some of his contemporaries found him. William Hazlitt found Byron full of "self-will, passion, the love of singularity (with a conscious sense that this is among the ways and means of procuring admiration)."[9] Whereas Byron casts his changeability as part of his commitment to fight hypocrisy, Hazlitt sees it as opportunism and change for its own sake.

Just as the meaning of *Byronic* was complex and contested from the start, to be Woolfian today is freighted with contradictions. A taste for Virginia Woolf is certainly easy to caricature. Woolf has a reputation as a difficult intellectual woman, smoking in a cardigan (a type of sweater Woolf seldom wore, but never mind the facts),[10] snobby, anorexic, lesbian, mad, and delicate. Like other women writers who committed suicide, she has become a heroine to a certain type of earnest, middle-class, mainly white, American woman and, for that reason, many others may choose to avoid reading her. As for scandal, to continue this review of biographical gossip, her survival of sexual abuse and her suicide rival Byron's commission of incest and his martyrdom. Gender creates contrasts, however, and their fame and reputation do divide along gender lines. Today, a rock star or a politician may gain panache from the epithet Byronic; the glamour of being called Woolfian is more obscure. Still, just as the image of Byron changes with the times (witness the recent review entitled "Lord Byron Just Keeps Getting Gayer"[11]), so does that of Woolf. The change from the Woolf in the title of Edward Albee's *Who's Afraid of Virginia Woolf?* to the one depicted by Michael Cunningham in *The Hours* may somewhat tone down (without entirely eliminating) the impression of Woolf as a high-strung, childless hysteric. In either case, as Byron and Woolf observed with some regret, Woolf and Byron are figures of enough cultural familiarity that their names have meaning even to those who have not read their works.[12]

Whereas Woolf's fame continues to grow, Byron's may be on the wane. In his lifetime, however, his fame was immense. Byron is reported to have said that, when *Childe Harold's Pilgrimage* was published in March 1812, he awoke to find himself famous.[13] *Childe Harold* broke "every past sales record in poetry"; *The Corsair* (1814) reached an estimated 36 percent of the British reading public.[14] With this literary success came celebrity so great that "a woman was said to have actually fainted upon being introduced to" him.[15] This fame was at its height from 1812 to 1816. In 1816, Byron left England never to return. From his exile in Italy, he continued to publish. Upon achieving fame, Byron experienced it as polluted by the modern marketplace even as he sought to use it for both narrowly personal and broadly political gain.

Byron's posthumous reputation has been indelibly affected by critics who read his literature through his life. Late Victorian and Georgian critics emphasized his aristocracy, his love of liberty, and his outsize personality. John Addington Symonds, for example, thought the man "well-born but ill-bred."[16] He judged Byron's mind less harshly: "His mental powers were acute and vigorous; his emotions were sincere and direct."[17] Symonds's attribution of sincerity to Byron stands in counterpoint to those who emphasize his poses, the staginess of his verse, and the scenes he made of his life. Thus, for George Saintsbury, Byron's "appeal consists very mainly" in "the installation, as principal character, of a personage who was specially recognised as a sort of fancy portrait . . . of Byron himself as he would like to be thought."[18] Woolf may have been drawn to Byron as a kind of opposite, but one need not read very deeply into Byron before finding that Byron's own character contains multiple contradictions.

Woolf's father, Leslie Stephen, wrote the entry on Byron for the *Dictionary of National Biography*. There, Stephen singles out Byron's "aristocratic vanity" and "his genuine hatred of war": "Though no democrat . . . He was ready to be a leader in the democratic movements of his time."[19] In emphasizing the tension between aristocracy and democracy, Stephen unwittingly draws our attention to another link between Byron and his daughter. Byron took his title seriously believing that his status as the sixth Lord Byron meant something noteworthy and impressive—even though it was his uncle, not his father (who was the younger brother), from whom he inherited the title, and even though his wife did not bear him a son on whom to confer it. Woolf was enough of a democrat to find this self-importance ridiculous (in spite of her love of occasional forays into aristocratic society). Still, Woolf not only cultivated friendships with aristocrats (Vita Sackville-West preeminent among them, also Lady Sybil Colefax), but she also took her own status as part of the intellectual aristocracy seriously. For example, in a 1918 diary entry on Byron, Woolf refers to "my father

Sir Leslie": Woolf insists on her having been born into the world of writing, to being the daughter of a man who "earned" an honorary title. In her diary, she boasts. The phrase "my father Sir Leslie" is not only a joke on pretensions, but it is also a prop to her ego and a signal to future editors: insert a footnote here remarking on my distinguished literary lineage. In the end, Woolf and Byron both insist on fame and professional success as a kind of birthright, not because of their vocation, but because of their aristocratic (real, honorary, or metaphorical) backgrounds. In trying to shape their careers, they make willing and generous use of their social capital to build their cultural capital.

In addition to Byron's flamboyance, fame, commitment to liberty, individualism, and snobbery, there is also, as Woolf's 1902 letter to her brother hints, knowledge of scandal attached to his name. Even more than his tempestuous affair with Caroline Lamb, the prime scandal of Byron's life was his incestuous affair with his half-sister, Augusta Leigh. Unexpurgated editions of his letters, now widely available, confirm what was long and widely rumored: Byron admitted the affair to several confidantes and corroboration by other intimates (including his half-sister and wife) leaves little room for doubt that he carried on an affair with Augusta during 1813. Leslie Stephen treats the scandal with a combination of a historian's precision and Victorian delicacy: "According to Mrs. Stowe, Lady Byron accused her husband . . . of an incestuous intrigue . . . letters since published, prove this hideous story to be absolutely incredible."[20] To revise Stephen, we might now say that, in fact, letters since published show Lady Byron's accusations were founded. Stephen's *pudeur*, however, still admits mention of the substance of the scandal, confirming that even a sheltered young reader like his daughter could well know the substance of the gossip.

Byron's breaking sexual taboos in life bled into critical assessments of his poetry. In the early nineteenth century, writers resented Byron's fame, linking it to his cultivation of a rakish image, and feared that it polluted his talent, tempting him to write with a market in mind.[21] Vivid metaphors of monstrosity and prostitution indicate the intensity of the reaction: "For Coleridge and many like him, poet-magicians such as Byron had created a monster . . . pandering to the reading public and its low tastes."[22] Seeing how bruised a lord's literary reputation might be by sexual intrigue must only have increased Woolf's consciousness of the gender imbalance in public perceptions of male and female writers. As Woolf often notes, in the public eye, a woman writing in itself was once scandalous, a sign of an improper quest for attention—a shame. While Byron's contemporaries accused him of pandering, Woolf wondered when writing crossed the line into whoring. Woolf depicts prostitutes who are reluctant to stoop to writing in *Orlando*, compares feminine influence to prostitution in *Three Guineas*, and refers to her contributions to *Vogue* as whoring (L, 3, 200). Woolf was uncomfortable with popularity and celebrity in spite of her ambitions for success as a writer. She is even reported to have remarked, "This celebrity business is quite chronic."[23] And yet, as Brenda Silver notes, "As Woolf became a public figure in her own right, she allowed herself, however grudgingly, to be photographed."[24] And those photographs, such as the studio photograph, c. 1927, of Woolf in a fur-collared coat, were used in "ads and articles about Woolf and/or her works in the States during the late 1920s and 1930s."[25]

This Byron, the silly and famous poet, shows up in Woolf's 1919 novel *Night and Day*, where a fondness for Byron is parodied as a rather silly Victorian weakness. Mrs. Hilbery, a former beauty, hopes her daughter's suitor has "found something nice to read . . . Byron—ah, Byron. I've known people who knew Lord Byron" (ND, 425). Her rather prosaic daughter cannot "help smiling at the thought that her mother found it perfectly natural and desirable that her daughter should be reading Byron in the dining-room late at night alone with a strange young man" (ND, 425). Here, it is the flighty and enthusiastic mother who approves of Byron as reading material to move a courtship along. The stiff young people feel a mother ought, perhaps, to disapprove. Katharine and Ralph are hardly in danger of acting out the passions inflamed by their reading, but it amuses Woolf to create this ironic scene in which the discovering mother *hopes* rather than fears her daughter will be excited into passion. Helping things along, Mrs. Hilbery adds, "I'm sure I should like your poetry better than I like Lord Byron's." But, upon being informed that the suitor is not a poet but a critic, an occupation she pronounces "dull," she recovers, saying, " 'But I'm sure you read poetry at night. I always judge by the expression of the eyes.' . . . ('The windows of the soul,' she added parenthetically.)" (ND, 425). Mrs. Hilbery is delightfully goofy, and Byron is diminished by association with her; he becomes a comic prop in Woolf's satire on Victorian mothers.

## VENTRILOQUIZING BYRON, 1918–28

Byron's appearance in *Night and Day* does not depend on having read Byron, but, in fact, by 1919 when the novel appeared, Woolf had read him and was beginning to develop a more favorable view than she was yet willing to publish. Her growing appreciation shows up first in her diary and then in her third novel, *Jacob's Room* (1922). As we have already seen, it was Woolf's brother, Thoby, who first introduced her to Byron. Thoby died in Greece of typhus in 1906 at the age of 26. Two years later, Woolf's brother-in-law, Clive Bell, gave her Byron, "a poet I have never read" (L, 1.376). A personal copy of Byron might have stimulated reading, but she does not seem to have read Byron until 1918. When she did, however, she found much to interest her.

Woolf wrote about Byron, his life, his posthumous reputation, and his writing in diary entries from August 1918 as well as in the essay "Byron and Mr. Briggs" (c. 1922).[26] In both, Woolf focused on what it is like to *read* Byron, but both also share a fainter set of speculations, too, on what it was like to *be* Byron. After a discussion of these two explicit considerations of Byron, I turn to two instances of her working through ideas she encountered there. First, *Jacob's Room*: there, Woolf explores Byronic narration within a text that, like *Don Juan*, is digressive, capable of treating all manner of scenes from every genre, from serious to comic, from romance to tragedy, and combining a sophisticated narrator with a somewhat blank protagonist. Second, Woolf, like Byron, used her emergence into fame to lend support to political causes.

During the summer of 1918, as she was completing the manuscript of *Night and Day*, Woolf was reading Byron, and, over a few days in August, Woolf wrote about Byron in her diary. Several themes emerge: the pleasure of reading him, her sense of him as a masculine writer, and speculations as to whether or not he is a born writer. Her rivalry with Katherine Mansfield seems to have been the catalyst for turning to Byron. In an openly jealous diary entry in which Woolf calls "the whole conception [of Mansfield's *Bliss*] poor, cheap, not the vision, however imperfect, of an interesting mind. She writes badly too" (D, 1.179). There is much to say about this conflicted and competitive comment, but the salient point is that Woolf piles on criticism (poor, cheap, imperfect, dull, badly written), overeager to dismiss her rival. Woolf finds relief from Mansfield by turning to Byron: "He has at least the male virtues" (D, 1.179). Almost as strange as Woolf's interest in Byron itself is her expression of that interest in terms of "male virtues." "In fact," Woolf continues, "I'm amused to find how easily I can imagine the effect he had on women—especially upon rather stupid or uneducated women unable to stand up to him" (D, 1.179–80). Little elsewhere in her art or life would predict such a taste; after all, Woolf famously championed both androgynous artists and the recovery of the forgotten history of women, *not* manliness in life or art.

The turn away from Mansfield is, in itself, an important clue to Woolf's literary crush on Byron. The lushness of Mansfield's prose shares much with the poetic sensibilities of Woolf. However, Mansfield's style can seem an unrelieved lushness and Woolf sought an art that offered contrasts, an art as rich in variety as life itself. The relief of Byron is not that he writes well where Mansfield writes badly (in fact, here and again in 1930, Woolf concedes that much of Byron's writing is bad), nor that his writing is less inward than Mansfield's, but that his prose is multivocal. Where Mansfield's prose can feel claustrophobic (as Woolf's sometimes can), Byron seldom takes the time to develop ideas, scenes, or characters (using, e.g., the ready-made character of Don Juan). The language is not intricately constructed but has flashes of brilliant intelligence. Byron can do the thing Woolf wished to learn: create action. Nothing develops in Byron, but everything moves.

Woolf continued to contemplate Byron's maleness and his attractiveness in an extended account of the experience of reading *Don Juan*. I will quote at length for this diary entry is full of praise: the praise is high and enthusiastic and also profoundly attentive to the technical details of writing, details she was then refining in her fiction. In analyzing this entry, I want to consider what it might mean to take Woolf's praise seriously:

> Having indicated that I am ready, after a century, to fall in love with him, I suppose my judgment of Don Juan may be partial. It is the most readable poem of its length ever written, I suppose; a quality which it owes in part to the springy random haphazard galloping nature of its method. This method is a discovery by itself. Its what one has looked for in vain—a[n] elastic shape which will hold whatever you choose to put into it. Thus he could write out his mood as it came to him. . . . When he is serious he is sincere; & he can impinge upon any subject he likes. He writes 16 canto's without once flogging his flanks. He had, evidently, the able witty mind of what my father Sir Leslie would have called a thoroughly masculine nature. I maintain that these illicit kind of books are far more interesting than the proper books which respect illusions devoutly all the time. Still, it doesn't seem an easy example to follow; & indeed like all free & easy things, only the skilled & mature really bring them off successfully. But Byron was full of ideas—a quality that gives his verse a toughness, & drives me to little excursions over the surrounding landscape or room in the middle of my reading. (D, 1.180–81)

Where, in the prior entry, she distances herself from Byron's attractions by imagining "rather stupid" women falling in love with him, the next day she admits that she herself is falling under his spell. The entry opens with her readiness "to fall in love" and, throughout the entry, Byron is portrayed as possessing "masculine" "toughness." We would seem, in short, to be in fairly conventional territory of divided roles, territory, in short, that is wholly *un*characteristic of Woolf. The metaphors of horsemanship—"haphazard galloping," "flogging his flanks"—make Byron both animalistic and aristocratic: he is both the horse and the rider. This Byron is emphatically male: his verse is tough, he is athletic, and has a "thoroughly masculine nature," a judgment she displaces onto her father, all of which conspire to encourage us to think that Woolf, so unmasculine in her sensibilities, was reading Byron as a brief foray into alien territory. After all, she begins, flirtatiously enough, being "ready . . . to fall in love." However, the comparisons here, to horsemanship and infidelity, are not connected to fantasies of Byron as a lover but to a sense of Byron's mind. It is his prose that gallops, his mind that canters through the cantos (to revive Woolf's embedded pun) without need of urging from a whip. Moreover, she admires his galloping as much for the speed as for the amount of territory it covers.

Reading Byron is an "illicit" pleasure. Here, once again, Woolf tempts us with a biographical allusion only to redirect our attention to his writing. Her metaphors resonate with things we know of his life—his womanizing, his love of riding, his life as a Regency playboy, and then a *cavalier servente* (the acknowledged and subservient lover of a married woman) in Italy—but she does not refer to biography here. The word "illicit" turns out to refer to his formal play, his lack of respect for the rules and conventions of genre, different from those "proper books which respect illusions devoutly." His illicitness, too, links him to the bohemian world with which Woolf affiliated herself against the propriety for her Victorian forbears. *Don Juan* is not only "free & easy" and "readable," but it is also "full of ideas," so the poem, for all its illicit fun, has, in the end, enough substance to make the pleasure more than fleeting. Byron has found a way to keep his audience while expressing his ideas, something Woolf knew to be vital to her success as a feminist artist. Its method, "a discovery by itself," consists in "a[n] elastic shape which will hold whatever you choose to put into it." Reading such a varied poem inspires its own interruptions, inspiring in Woolf "little excursions . . . in the middle of my reading."

Byron's letters, which Woolf may have been reading alongside *Don Juan*,[27] manifest his charisma. One of the chief outward signs of Byronic energy in his writing is his neglect of grammar, particularly in the letters. The abundant dashes, which he uses in an utterly modern way, indicate any small diversion from his original tack (a digression, a parenthetical remark, a *non sequitur*). There are so many dashes that some sentences could never be put aright. Furthermore, Byron peppers his letters with accounts of how the outside world interrupts his correspondence: letters frequently note not only the time and place of composition, but also the presence of a lover in his bed, or, notably, the interruption by a lover's husband. Although the types of interruption in Woolf differ greatly, she too records the ways in which her writing starts and stops as guests come to tea or Nelly the cook quits, again. Seduced by these formal indicators of immediacy, editors of the private writings of both Woolf and Byron consistently preserve the quirks of their punctuation, the dashes, misspellings, and ampersands, as a way of communicating in a bound volume the speed of composition. Part, then, of the eros of reading both Byron and Woolf is the illusion of speed.

These excursions around the room that reading Byron inspires in Woolf mark not only a pleasure of reading, but they also lie at the heart of Woolf's aesthetic. As much as she argued for the privileges of privacy afforded by a room of one's own (and against the incessant interruptions of domestic life), her art proceeds by digression and interruption.[28] This interruptive method, Woolf's special version of the stream of consciousness, can be far more jaunty, idiosyncratic, and alive to outside forces than that phrase usually indicates. Byron is, of course, not the only source for Woolf's stylistic innovations, but he seems an important—and heretofore unacknowledged—one. Woolf praises his method and seems to set herself up to the challenge of coming up with a similarly illicit, capacious method, reminding herself that apparent ease is the domain of the "skilled and mature," that the unconventional, wide-ranging genre-bending poetry of *Don Juan* is not "an easy example to follow." Her assessment that it is not an easy model does not necessarily indicate that Woolf did not try. In fact, she took this model so seriously that she repeated the sentiment in a 1927 essay: "Byron in *Don Juan* pointed the way; he showed how flexible an instrument poetry might become, but none has followed his example and put his tool to further use" (GR, 17).

For all she finds to admire, Woolf wonders at Byron's lack of faith in himself as a writer: "But he never as a young man, believed in his poetry: a proof, in such a confident dogmatic person, that he hadn't the gift. The Wordsworths and Keats' believe in that as much as they believe in anything" (D, 1.180). A similar comparison appears in the diary a few days prior: here Woolf compares Byron to Christina Rosetti, who "has the great distinction of being a born writer" (D, 1.178).[29]

In contrasting Byron with Rosetti, Wordsworth, and Keats, Woolf circles around a set of questions about belief in oneself, vocation, and careerism that Byron seems to excite in his readers: Is he a born writer? Does his strength derive from his genius, his name, or something else?

Judging from the born writers on Woolf's list, we know that born writers do not have long, public periods of derivative juvenilia. A born writer is not necessarily from a literary family. A born writer has a feeling for language and a passionate and idiosyncratic way of using it. Born writers stand outside and, occasionally, at the forefront of literary fashion. Byron was not a born writer partly because of his lack of belief in his talent and partly for the reason articulated by Eliot in his 1937 essay on Byron: Byron did not add anything to the language.[30] But Eliot's conclusion is self-serving. He seems to be judging Byron on the level of words or the poetic line—where Eliot's contribution has been most deeply felt. Byron did add something to English literature at the level of genre: without Byron, there would be no Brownings, no Wilde and, perhaps, no Virginia Woolf.

Since Woolf set up this category of the born writer, it is natural to ask whether she herself was one, whether she considered herself one. But, though the rough appellation seems to call for a yes or no answer, the answer in Woolf's case seems considerably more complicated. She is certainly not a born writer in the sense of having a rigid devotion to a reclusive life dedicated to art. From the beginning, Woolf forged a career for herself as a professional writer. In so doing, she began not with derivative juvenilia, as Byron did, but by following conventions nonetheless. She, like Byron, grew into her talent. She did not starve "into austere emaciation a very fine original gift" (D, 1.179) as Christina Rosetti did. She was, however, a born reader, happily insisting on reading widely, eccentrically, and without regard to fashion.

From the beginning, Woolf approached her writing life as a profession and saw reviewing as a necessary evil. In spite of her protestations to the contrary, it is fitting that Woolf was invited to speak on the subject of "Professions for Women." She was a professional writer. Much as she sympathized with Keats's longing for inherited or bestowed financial independence, Woolf felt that women had better earn their financial freedom: the price of being dependent on fathers and husbands was too high. In her hard-nosed attitude to earning money from her writing, she bears surprising resemblance to Byron, whose private papers, like Woolf's, are full of detailed negotiations on price for his work. For Jerome Christensen, Byron's pursuit of writing as a career and his lack of vocation are central facts: "Byron's poetry, unrepentantly renegade, neither imitates a progress nor heeds any call.

He has no poetic vocation."[31] Distinguishing between vocation and career, Christensen emphasizes the religious and nonmonetary focus of the former: "the teleology of the vocation is the promise, if not of worldly success, then of spiritual fulfillment" whereas a career, by contrast, "can be planned but not fully controlled" since it is subject to market forces.[32]

If, as Woolf notes several times, Byron might have been a novelist, then Woolf might have been a poet. Both writers have been subject to praise—and criticism—for the way that their styles do not seem to quite match with their form. Depending on the reader, her poetic prose and his satiric stanzas can be a source of admiration or frustration. What is undoubtedly the case about both is that, though neither invented a new genre, each stretched the boundaries of their chosen form so completely as to make it new. By writing in the genre expected for writers of their time, sex, and class, and by using this genre to express their unorthodox sentiments—political, sexual, and otherwise— Byron and Woolf broke the rules of their day.

Fittingly, Byron's first speech to Parliament was in support of frame-breakers. On February 27, 1812, the 24 year old spoke to the House of Lords in opposition to the Frame Work Bill. This bill, if passed, would have made the destruction of machinery by weavers punishable by death. Byron supported the weavers' right to protest. Two weeks later, *Childe Harold* was published and his successful (if apparently stilted and strangely antique) speech contributed to the poem's stunning success.[33] As Byron turned from the political career he originally envisioned toward poetry, his frame-breaking became metaphoric. Nonetheless, it was not mere formal play; it made room for his ideas. For example, in the third canto of *Don Juan*, where Juan is shipwrecked with the lovely Haidee, the lovers employ the services of a wandering poet. His interruption breaks the rhythm of the tale while his song, framed by their love story, offers an impassioned plea for Greek independence, Byron's favorite subject and the cause for which he ultimately died. This bard, an "eastern antijacobin"[34] does not hesitate to sing whatever he thinks his employers might want to hear:

> when he was ask'd to sing,
> He gave the different nations something national;
> 'Twas all the same to him—"God save the king,"
> Or "Ça ira", according to the fashion all.
>
> . . .
>
> In Italy, he'd aped the "Trecentisti";
> In Greece, he'd sing some sort of hymn like this t'ye:[35]

The frame here mocks poets who will sing for whomever pays them best.[36] Furthermore, he makes revolution into a fashion and poetry, its accessory. But we also learn that "He deem'd, being in a lone isle, among friends, / That without any danger of riot, he / Might for long lying make himself amends."[37] With his mercenary past and his desire to atone for it in mind, then, Byron offers a hymn, such as the itinerant poet (and, by association, Byron himself) might have sung in Greece, were he in Greece.

The 16 stanzas that follow contain unambiguous national sentiment, drawing on the classical past to argue for a renewed future greatness: "I dream'd that Greece might still be free; / For standing on the Persian's grave, / I could not deem myself a slave" (3.704–06)[38]. This hymn, which ends as heroically as it begins, interrupts Juan's and Haidee's lovemaking and calls attention to the plight of the Greeks, whose cause Byron had supported since his first trip to the continent. The mood changes again after the ballad, returning to the theme of the untrustworthy poet: poets "are such liars, / And take all colors—like the hands of dyers."[39] But, for all of that uncertainty, poetry itself endures. Byron writes, "But words are things, and a small drop of ink, / Falling like dew, upon a thought, produces / That which makes thousands, perhaps millions, think."[40] The trope of the immortality of language is an old one, and it is not the last turn of perspective in this episode, but its placement here suggests something important. Typically, the trope of the endurance of poetry undercuts the poet's praise of his beloved (as in Shakespeare's sonnets); Byron invokes it to suggest that this interpolated hymn, sung to young lovers by a traveling bard of dubious ethics, should be attended to on its merits. And, by extension, we should read his poems with more attention to the potential *immortality* of his words than the putative *immorality* of the poet.

Byron's reputation for immorality distracts even his most sympathetic readers. In the essay "Byron and Mr. Briggs" (c. 1922) Woolf returns to the question of the fascination of a writer's personality, which, in the case of Byron, means charisma and scandal. This essay, unpublished in Woolf's lifetime, parodies literary gossip as it tries to move beyond it. Byron may be the ostensible subject of "Byron and Mr. Briggs" but there is only a page or so of direct Byron criticism there. That page sketches Byron as a common reader first encounters him, repeating many of the old saws Woolf herself knew before reading Byron: He "wrote far better letters from abroad than his people had a right to expect"; "He should have stayed an undergraduate forever"; "Caroline Lamb, insane but generous, would have made a better wife than the mathematical Miss Milbanke" (B&B, 331). Woolf concludes this thumbnail sketch with a jab at Byron's lameness: "And up fly our caps as he limps off the field in a rage" (B&B, 331). Then, moments later, she turns her critical eye back on itself, to demonstrate why the remark "is not literary criticism."[41] She quickly sketches an ironic overview of the received opinion of a writer like Byron, implicitly assenting to such opinions, while acknowledging the difference between gossip and biography.[42] As she writes of the overview, "Some reading is implied" (B&B, 332). For one has to be relatively well read to compare Byron's letters to "the stiff and stilted compositions by Shelley" (B&B, 332) or to observe: "He goes to Venice, and is there a single phrase to show that he saw it?" (B&B, 331–32).

For Woolf, getting some perspective on one's reading is one of the biggest challenges facing a common reader. Woolf names the process of linking, judging, and comparing books "making a whole" and deems it extraordinarily difficult. She writes, "In what sense can we talk, even lazily over the fire, of making a whole? To make a whole even of one man, Lord Byron, must we not have read some three hundred volumes, and a good many papers still waiting to be published?" (B&B, 335). The parenthetical addition of Byron as an example adds weight to Woolf's claim—so central to her art that it might be a credo—of the immense complexity of every individual life. One feels the truth of this complexity more intensely with regard to Byron than one does of his more solid contemporaries, William Wordsworth and Walter Scott. In writing about making a whole, Woolf writes of the desire for mastery and the way that literature thwarts this desire even as, with the promise of more and more new books, literature constantly feeds desire. The embedded pun on *whole* and *hole* only reinforces Woolf's point: reading is never done; the whole is never complete.

Everyone, Woolf thinks, plays this game of making a whole—for Woolf, it is the game one plays on a train journey, and there is a train journey in "Byron and Mr. Briggs," as in *Jacob's Room*, "An Unwritten Novel," "Mr. Bennett and Mrs. Brown," and *The Waves*. In each case, an observer tries to make up a life story for the person in the opposite compartment. In the most polemical of these scenes, "Mr. Bennett and Mrs. Brown," Woolf distinguishes her style of play from that of the Georgian or realist novelist, rather than correlate every observable detail to a sociological likelihood, she selects a few telling details to concoct a satisfying narrative hypothesis. The game works as long as we recognize that "such wholes as these are extremely imperfect, & probably highly inaccurate" (B&B, 334). What interests me here is the link that Woolf makes between what the observer does in the railway carriage and making a whole of Byron's life. The conflation of the common reader's judgment of Byron and the game of making a whole on the train is both telling and puzzling. Are both activities really the same? Woolf emphasizes the inaccuracy of the game and strengthens the link between making a whole of a writer and a stranger by returning to her own essay, as if it is a rough draft, writing: "Certainly if we examine the fragment on Byrons letters we shall find slips enough in five hundred words to infuriate a scholar" (B&B, 334–35).

Byron and Mrs. Brown, fame and anonymity: both provide pleasure for the viewer. The subject of a biography, like the stranger in the railway carriage, seems to offer up a life for outside consumption. Where the stranger is one's contemporary, one can speculate based on context. (We think we know what certain clothing or choice of reading material indicates about a person.) The subject of a biography offers a different type of narrative pleasure. A biographer (or a memoirist), looking back over life, appears to offer a whole, spanning years and often offering us an entrée into a world otherwise closed to us. In spite of these differences of time and space, both the subject of a biography and the stranger on the train offer the intense narrative pleasures of apparent reality and coherence. The wholes that we consume in reading a biography or constructing one of a stranger please us in part because they suggest that the right narrative frame can make a life whole.

The link Woolf makes between fame and anonymity suggests a parallel link, one that was a source more of anxiety than pleasure. Woolf's anxiety about her appearance and her ambivalence about the more public aspects of fame stem from the voraciousness of her own appetite for the lives of others: she suspected that others sought to consume her as hungrily as she did them. In Woolf's passages about the pleasures of making a whole, and especially in those about the longing to connect biography to art, another theme emerges: the writer's resistance to being caught. Although her reading was ravenous and her writing truth-seeking and unafraid, Woolf fought to hold something back in her construction of herself as a writer in the world.

In the essay "How It Strikes a Contemporary" (1923), Woolf discusses the difficulty of judging contemporary writing with a different metaphor for how hard it is to make a whole. She advises critics, "Beware . . . of putting under the microscope one inch of a ribbon which runs many miles: things sort themselves out if you wait" (CR1, 239). Once again, Byron is the synecdoche for impossible complexity, the irreducible. She continues, "Moreover, life is short; the Byron centenary is at hand; and the burning question of the moment is, did he, or did he not, marry his sister?" (CR1, 239–40). This same salacious gossip returns in the next paragraph of the essay where Byron becomes an antimodel—the writer whose personality was so big that gossiping about him eclipses other concerns. Meanwhile, in the background, perhaps, masterpieces are being created anonymously. So, she urges critics to "take a wider, a less personal view . . . and look indeed upon the writers as if they were engaged upon some vast building, which being built by common effort, the separate workmen may well remain anonymous" (CR1, 240). All this gossip, delightful as it may be for the reader, tends to distract writers from their writing.[43] In another essay she makes a similar point, that it is anonymity, not celebrity, where "writers write most happily," and anonymity "is the prerogative of the middle class alone" (CR2, 218). This leads to the rather odd speculation that "it must have been harder for Byron to be a poet than Keats" (CR2, 218). Her yearning for a respite from the pressures of fame only increased as her fame grew. So, in 1932 she wrote definite advice against the pursuit of fame: "As for fame, look I implore you at famous people; see how the waters of dullness spread around them as they enter" (DM, 225).

If dullness is one peril of fame, insincerity is another. In the diary entry of 1918 quoted above, Woolf writes, "when he is serious he is sincere," but four years later she writes, "the figure of Byron appears, how tawdry, insincere and theatrical!" (B&B, 346). Which is it? And why does Byron excite this question of sincerity? The question, an old and continuing one in the criticism of Byron, derives from his ability to rapidly shift tones, to move swiftly among registers, and his penchant for constructing personae temptingly "like" Byron himself. Amidst the changes of tone in Byron's writing, however, some consistencies begin to emerge. In a similar vein, many critics have noted how, in reading Shakespeare, we see his faith in romantic love[44]; in reading Byron, we see, again and again, a love of freedom. Byron's style, however, is the opposite of a Shakespearean negative capability: we know far too much about Byron. Strangely, though, knowing too much about someone as mercurial, complex, and self-involved as Byron, comes to look a lot like knowing little.

In "Byron and Mr. Briggs," Woolf touches on the complex relationship between fame and reading through a literary conversation on sincerity. It opens with Hewet's and Rose Shaw's differing attitudes toward Byron's power over women as the source of his fame (he disapproves; she, like Woolf, understands). From Byron, the conversation shifts, as it is wont to do when Byron comes up, to the question of sincerity.[45] Rose Shaw comments that she finds Sterne insincere,

Hardy sincere. Hewet, eager to impress, calls Tolstoy sincere. Through it all, one thing emerges clearly: Rose may be inarticulate, but she has a notion worth pausing over. She gets a sense from reading certain books of emotional directness, of clarity of intent, that makes her feel connected to her reading—perhaps to the author, perhaps to the situation, but she is not reading biographically: she is responding to the language, not gossip about the life. Even Hewet pauses over her ideas: "So far life and literature seem to help each other out. Rose Shaw and Hewet are using literature partly in order to make them understand each other" (B&B, 345). This is clumsy prose, and far more explicit than Woolf's more polished work; for that, her comments here reveal underlying attitudes. Woolf here confirms that we are right to attach significance to what her characters read, remember, and pass on to their friends.[46]

In 1922, the year Woolf wrote "Byron and Mr. Briggs," she also oversaw the publication of *Jacob's Room*, her first experimental novel. Where the essay considers the difficulty of making a whole of a great author, the novel partakes in her lifelong interest in making a whole of an ordinary person. In this case, the subject is Jacob Flanders, who grows up with a widowed mother, graduates from Cambridge, travels to Greece, and works in London only to be killed—as his surname has prophesied all along—in the trenches during World War I. The character of Jacob is based partly on her brother Thoby, with whom she once gossiped about Byron and who had died in 1906 and there are some intriguing passing allusions to Byron in the novel.[47] However, as the preceding discussion of Woolf on Byron prepares us to see, Byron's influence on *Jacob's Room* is greater than mere passing allusions suggest. In fact, the two critical commonplaces about *Jacob's Room*—that the narrator's detached wit derives from the eighteenth century and that the protagonist is a somewhat empty and conventional figure—are the mainstays of Byron's poetic narratives. Like Don Juan's, Jacob's inner life remains closed to us while we are privy to speculative gossip about him from his many admirers; Woolf's narrator, like Byron's, satirizes both her blank hero and those who invest so much meaning in him. Both Woolf and Byron clearly owe a large debt to *Tom Jones* (1749) and *Tristram Shandy* (1760–67), but, as Woolf saw, it was Byron who shifted the balance most decisively away from the character to the narrator. Woolf's transformation of Byronic devices in a novel that questions the Byronic values of womanizing and self-sacrifice throws her transformational reading, her insistence on carefully separating the Byron she admires to the one she does not, into sharp relief.

Byron's major innovation in *Childe Harold* was to enliven the travel narrative with novelistic plot details and an ironic narrator. His major innovation in *Don Juan* was to turn the myth of the seducer on its head, inverting power relations between the sexes to present a Don Juan who is objectified, seduced, and passive in the face of powerful women. In both, he injected the travelogue with elements of romance and irony. Woolf adapts each of these devices to her use in *Jacob's Room*. Jacob's first sexual experiences are with women of lower social class who pursue him. Like Byron (and Childe Harold), Jacob has a meaningful affair with a married woman. There, too, as in Byron, the women orchestrate the liaison under a husband's tolerant gaze. And, as Byron's heroes are occasionally overwhelmed by their surroundings, in Greece, Jacob fails to sort his observations into a meaningful experience.

Jacob's experience of Greece is all out of proportion to official expectations but in line with novelistic ones. He cannot seem to feel or see what his education led him to expect, and he gets distracted by contemporary street life and his own affairs. As Woolf observed, Byron's private writings seem more concerned with social intrigue than history or contemporary politics. The humor in his poetry often depends on the contrast between sightseeing and carousing: "In Seville was he born, a pleasant city, / Famous for oranges and women."[48] Woolf has fun with her protagonist's perplexity:

> It is highly exasperating that twenty-five people of your acquaintance should be able to say straight off something very much to the point about being in Greece, while for yourself there is a stopper upon all emotions whatsoever . . . he had met several droves of turkeys; . . . had read advertisements of corsets and of Maggi's consommé; . . . the place smelt of bad cheese; and he was glad to find himself suddenly come out opposite his hotel. (JR, 137)

Jacob cannot make a scene because he expects to see his reading brought to life. The narrator's list, by contrast, makes a coherent scene of a very different sort from the one Jacob hoped to compose. Ads for corsets and consommé suggest a nation of dieting women; strong smells and droves of turkeys test Jacob's English fussiness and anxiety about foreign dirt. In the tradition of Sterne and Byron, Woolf's anticlimactic juxtapositions bring to life for us a Greece that is lively, comic, and modern: full of bad cheese and an earthy sexuality. However, where Byron might have found this combination amusing (although his comments would surely have had a misogynistic ring),

Jacob is unnerved, as lost as Freud in a red-light district, but without the intellectual resources to turn the experience into a theory of the uncanny. Through Jacob's disorientation, Woolf offers a dig at the priggishness of the young Cambridge graduate and exposes a result of a society where the sexes are segregated from a very early age.

The comedy of *Childe Harold* and *Don Juan* depend on their heroes being somewhat blank. When Byron's publisher complained of this to him, he replied "anything is better than *I I I I* always *I*."[49] Perhaps Byron did not then possess the self-awareness (or the fame) to anticipate that subsequent readers would fill that empty center with the great, assertive *I* of Byron himself. Still, it is amusing to find Byron, one of Woolf's primary examples of the manly assertive *I* in whose shade nothing can grow (ARO, 100) backing away from assertions of self. Like Childe Harold and Don Juan, Jacob is a cipher.[50] At one point, the narrator stops to ask, "But how far was he a mere bumpkin? How far was Jacob Flanders at the age of twenty-six a stupid fellow? It is no use trying to sum people up" (JR, 154). The clear implication is that Jacob is indeed a bumpkin, that the narrator's suspicions are founded. The conclusion that "it is no use trying to sum people up," reiterates Woolf's idea of the impossibility of making a whole and anticipates the ironic, overconfident opening of Bernard's soliloquy in *The Waves*: "Now to sum up" (W, 238).

Unlike Childe Harold and Don Juan, however, we do not fill in the blank of Jacob with Virginia Woolf. Woolf insulates herself from such identification (and the scrutiny that might ensue) simply by making her protagonist a man. Still, Jacob is not yet a person, and the novel shows us how others create a person, how conventions, books, and expectations put pressure on an individual. Ultimately, as Christine Froula argues, "the novel's vitality lies less in what its characters say than in the essayist-narrator's angle of vision."[51] I am arguing that the essayist-narrator is Byronic; furthermore, understanding her as such gives a literary precursor for her essayist-narrator and helps explain the variety in her voice, the ways in which "essayist-narrator is at moments explicitly embodied. At times she seems simply a human presence. . . . At other moments she seems female."[52] Reading the essayist-narrator's shifts as an outgrowth of Woolf's reading of Byron provides a literary history for Froula's point. We can see, through comparing Byron's use of a similar device in *Don Juan* to Woolf's, the emergence of a feminist point to the contrast between blank protagonist and knowing, satiric narrator. What was, for Byron, a method of comic social observation, becomes, for Woolf, a technique through which to explore and expose the idea of the young Englishman, to treat his sacrifice during the war with both sympathy and outrage, and, through it all, to highlight the price of women's complicity with a society that turns its women into sex objects and its men into cannon fodder.[53]

A look at how the essayist-narrator shapes chapter 8, on the dissolution of the romance between Florinda and Jacob, helps explain the Byronic link. The eight-page chapter consists of nine short sections, separated from each other by a blank line. This method, new to *Jacob's Room* but soon to be a staple of Woolf's novels, permits Woolf to range widely: a report on Jacob's bachelor activities stands in counterpoint to the arrival of a letter from his mother, full of the ardent hopes and fears that she can "never, never say, whatever it may be—probably this—Don't go with bad women, do be a good boy; wear your thick shirts; and come back, come back, come back to me" (JR 90). Jacob and Florinda ignore the letter and disappear into his bedroom; meanwhile, Woolf writes, "if the pale blue envelope . . . had the feelings of a mother, the heart was torn" (JR, 92). When Jacob turns to read the letter, a section break announces a short essay, begun in the arch eighteenth-century voice that both Byron and Woolf enjoyed affecting: "Let us consider letters—" (JR, 92); the miniessay continues, considering how "Byron wrote letters. So did Cowper. . . . Masters of language, poets of long ages, have turned from the sheet that endures to the sheet that perishes" (JR, 92). Byron's appearance here in one of the novel's most essayistic digressions ostensibly derives from his fame as a correspondent. It also announces Woolf's debt. The narrator's voice blends into Jacob's who thinks about letters from women, the sincerity of women, their (and especially Florinda's) inability to deceive, All of which leads to a punch line: Jacob sees Florinda "turning up Greek Street upon another man's arm" (JR, 93). It is wonderful that it can be Greek Street, a bit of Soho where one might find a prostitute to this day, but also echoing the love of Greece that inspired Byron and Jacob (who travels there later in the novel). In this springy, random, Byronic way, Woolf can tease Jacob's naïveté, expose Florinda's linked duplicity and vulnerability, and surprise us without having to set a scene.[54]

While Byron's formal innovations showed Woolf a way toward her own, his life offered a model of which she was more critical. Jacob never outgrows his enthusiasm for Byron but his boyhood love of Greece matures into admiration not for the cause of Greek independence but admiration for Latin words, hinting, via imperial Rome, at his growing support of empire (JR, 164–65). Jacob's admiration for Byron is shallow: he picks Byron as a memento, but we never see him reading it. The implication is that the Byron Jacob admires is the traditional hero, the womanizer, the adventuring aristocrat who willingly sacrificed his life. By contrast, Woolf, through her essayist-narrator, distinguishes between that Byron and Byron the poet who showed her how to give her own formal innovations a feminist point. In *Jacob's Room*, Woolf links Jacob's changing taste in reading—carrying, but not reading, Byron, moving from Greek to Latin—to his vulnerability to a soldier's death. As Septimus's reading of "Aeschylus (translated)" (MD, 88) bolstered his decision to enlist, so does Jacob's turn to Latin presage his. Ultimately, *Jacob's Room* is a meditation less on fame than on promise. The senseless and abrupt end of that promise indicts the hero-worshipping elements of English society.

*Jacob's Room* does not thematize fame, but it brought fame to its author. After it was published, Woolf began to attract serious attention not only in Bloomsbury but also in the more popular world of London sophisticates. One result was that Dorothy Todd invited her to contribute to *Vogue*. Another was that, when the General Strike came, Woolf cycled around the city collecting signatures of other writers in support of the striking workers.[55] A comparison between Woolf's activities from 1924 to 1926 and Byron's brief parliamentary career demonstrates the obstacles to both reputation and effectiveness still facing a politically active woman in the 1920s.

A few months after his parliamentary debut, Byron took up a second liberal (and controversial) cause. On April 21, 1812, Byron spoke passionately on behalf of rights for Catholics during a debate in the House of Lords. But when the issue came to a vote, "the strength on the two sides of the House was so equal (the motion was finally defeated by one vote) that Byron was 'sent for in great haste to a Ball, which I quitted, I confess, somewhat reluctantly, to emancipate five Millions of people.' "[56] Virginia Woolf's involvement with the 1926 General Strike and subsequent assessments of the significance of that involvement offers an instructive parallel. Her complex reaction to the strike reveals how much, in spite of her socialism, her "real affiliation" was with members of her own class.[57] This personal alliance does not detract from her support for the strike. She worked with Leonard to gather signatures on a petition "requesting that there should be no victimization of the miners when the strike was over."[58] Still, her happy announcement, in a letter to Vanessa, that "we're going to have a strike dinner and drink champagne" (L, 3.262), confirms her relief at the chance to return to her normal world of intellectual socializing. Furthermore, it has become a sign, for some critics, of her lack of political seriousness.

In her discussion of the General Strike, Kate Flint argues that Woolf's "tendency, as always, was to stress simultaneity of thoughts and sensations. . . . Surrounded by political debate, beset with constant callers and telephone calls, dealing with requests to print the liberal journal, the *Nation*, on the Hogarth Press, she seized gratefully on a visit from Desmond MacCarthy" with whom she could "argue about psycho-analysis and Swinburne, which is some relief" (L, 3.261).[59] This "tendency" to combine political commitments with other pursuits—both social and aesthetic—links Woolf to Byron. However, Byron supports Catholic Emancipation and attends a ball and, in doing so, earns his readers' amused, indulgent admiration whereas, should Woolf drink champagne to celebrate the end of the General Strike, her sympathies are suspect.[60] To this day, as Woolf herself might have ruefully predicted, critics judge men and women writers by a double standard.

## Impersonating Byron, 1927–36

*The Waves* (1931) has the strongest echoes of Byron in this period.[61] *The Waves* took Woolf's formal and psychological experiments further than they had gone before. There, Bernard, the novel's author-figure, models himself explicitly on Byron. In this section, I argue that Woolf's experiments with gender and voice in these years—the androgyny of *Orlando*, the linked dramatic monologues of *The Waves*, and the ventriloquizing of Elizabeth Barrett Browning's spaniel Flush—emerge from Byron and find their fulfillment in Bernard's final soliloquy in *The Waves*. At the same time, Woolf found something Byron never found except in death: a way to use her talent and her fame in support of the cause that was most important to her, the intellectual freedom of women.

Woolf's diary always emphasized the writing life. During the period from 1927 to 1936, she took special care to chart the genesis of her books. Upon the completion of *To the Lighthouse* in September 1926 (D, 3.113), Woolf promises to keep track of the moment when an idea for a new one arises. Six months later, she conceives of "a fantasy" in which her "own lyric vein is to be satirised" (D, 3.131). This notion for a book, tentatively called "The Jessamy Brides" became, as Woolf's marginal comment from July 8, 1933 notes, "Orlando Leading to the Waves" (D, 3.131).[62] The desire to write something different and quick, the "need of an escapade" (D, 3.131), the hunger for a change, and the willingness to satirize herself are all recurrent topics in the diary of this period. For both Woolf and Byron, the satiric voice authorizes the "lyric vein" and, in Byron, Woolf found someone who "could write out his mood as it came to him" (D, 1.181). Her desire to write "books that relieve other books" (D, 3.203) has often been noted: the comedy of *Flush* follows the seriousness of *The Waves* as the historical sweep of *Orlando* follows the narrower domesticity of *To the Lighthouse*. This hunger for difference, for relief, forms the basis of the theory of reading she proposes in the long 1929 essay "Phases of Fiction."[63]

Woolf frequently expresses her longing for a book that would progress quickly with metaphors of physical movement—especially galloping or swimming. These particular athletic metaphors have strong Byronic resonance: a strong athlete hampered from dancing or playing tennis by his clubfoot, Byron was a good horseman and a remarkable swimmer (swimming home from Venetian parties through the canals, torch in hand, as well as swimming the Hellespont). Woolf writes that she is "eager to be off—to write without any boundary" (D, 3.223); recovering from the flu, she writes, "I must canter my wits if I can" (D, 3.289); in *A Room of One's Own*, thought is a fish, the thinker's job is "the cautious hauling of it in" (ARO, 5), and, re-reading *A Room of One's Own*, she notes how she feels the writing "arching its back & galloping on" (D, 3.242). A decade earlier, Woolf had characterized Byron's prose as "galloping," and, when she returned to Byron in 1930, she remarked on the movement, energy, and variety in his prose.

Woolf estimated that it took her 19 months to write *The Waves* (from September 1929 to July 1931) (D, 4.35). Fast as this composition was, her writing hit snags. Midway through, in February 1930, she notes a bout of mild influenza with a combination of anxiety and expectation: "If I could stay in bed another fortnight (but there is no chance of that) I believe I should see the whole of The Waves" (D, 3.286). At the same time, Woolf was reading André Maurois's *Byron*, "which sends me to Childe Harold." So, longing to regain her momentum on her novel, she returned to the writer she admired for his speed. As she wrote that same day to Clive Bell, with whom she could unabashedly share admiration for Byron, "I am reading Byron—well, there's a lot to be said about Byron—Maurois does not understand him, but has the merit of making me think that I do" (L, 4.139). After the entry of 1918, this 1930 diary entry, with over a page devoted to Byron, is her most extensive consideration of Byron. And, once again, Woolf marks him out as a writer worthy of consideration: when she read him, she wrote about him.

As with the 1918 entry, this entry bears quoting at length. "To lie on the sofa for a week," she begins, describing her convalescence and her desire for it to continue in strangely abstracted language, language that announces her distance from herself and from the everyday hub-bub of people who are not convalescing, turning at last, to a discussion of Byron:

> I am reading Byron: Maurois: which sends me to Childe Harold; makes me speculate. How odd a mixture: the weakest sentimental Mrs. Hemans combined with trenchant bare vigour. How did they combine? And sometimes the descriptions in C.H. are "beautiful"; like a great poet.
>
> There are the three elements in Byron:
>
> *1* The romantic dark haired lady singing drawing room melodies to the guitar.
>
> > "Tambourgi! Tambourgi! Thy 'larum afar
> > Gives hope to the valiant, & promise of war:
>
> > .   .   .   .   .
>
> > Oh! Who is more brave than a dark Suliote,
> > In his snowy camese & his shaggy Capote"
> —something manufactured: a pose; silliness.
>
> *2* Then there is the vigorous rhetorical, like his prose, & good as prose.
> > Hereditary Bondsmen! Know yet not
> > *Who* would be free *themselves* must strike the blow?
> > By their right arms the conquest must be wrought?
> > Will Gaul or Muscovite redress ye? No! . . .
>
> *3* Then what rings to me truer, & is almost poetry.
> > Dear Nature is the kindest mother still!
> > Though always changing, in her aspect mild;
>
> (all in canto   From her bare bosom let me take my fill,
> II of C H.)   Her never-weaned, though not her favoured child.
>
> > \*   \*   \*
>
> > To me by day or night she ever smiled,
> > Though I have marked her when none other hath,
> > And sought her more & more, & loved her best in wrath.
>
> *4* And then there is of course the pure satiric, as in the description of
> *5* a London Sunday; & finally (but this makes more than three) the inevitable half assumed half genuine tragic note, which comes as a refrain, about death & the loss of friends.
>
> > All thou could have of mine, stern Death! Thou hast;
> > The parent, Friend, & now the more than Friend:
> > Ne'er yet for one thine arrows flew so fast,

> And grief with grief continuing still to blend,
> Hath snatch the little joy that life had yet to lend.

These I think make him up; & make much that is spurious, vapid, yet very changeable, & then rich & with greater range than the other poets, could he have got the whole into order. A novelist, he might have been. It is odd however to read in his letters his prose an apparently genuine feeling about Athens: & to compare it with the convention he adopted in verse. (There is some sneer about the Acropolis). But then the sneer may have been a pose too. The truth may be that if you are charged at such high voltage you cant fit any of the ordinary human feelings; must post; must rhapsodise; don't fit in. He wrote in the Inn Album that his age was 100. And this is true, measuring life by feeling. (D, 3.287–88)

This discussion of Byron opens more critically than the discussion of 1918. Similar elements are present, but with less fully appreciative connotations: instead of being sincere, he is sentimental; instead of being manly, his writing has "trenchant bare vigour"; instead of an admirable variety, it is an "odd mixture."[64] This more nuanced opening leads into a series of quotations from *Childe Harold*, introduced with the stiff phrase, "There are the three elements in Byron." This sounds about as promising as the introduction to any dutiful exercise, but the list grows and changes, and pretty soon there are five "elements," each illustrated by a quotation from *Childe Harold*. They provide the relief and variety that Woolf seeks from her reading. The entry moves rapidly from criticism to praise, through many moods, never settling on a judgment. Byron is consistently interesting although alternately annoying, disappointing, and worthy of admiration.

Woolf puts "beautiful" quotation marks, noting that Byron sounds "like a great poet," questioning his hold on "greatness" and calling our attention to how his attempts at beauty come off as set pieces. Her first example continues in this vein, isolating the songs of the "romantic dark haired lady." Byron's exotic beauty rhymes the " 'larum afar" with "promise of war," sings in praise of the brave soldier dashing in his uniform, and parrots the automatic sentiments about bravery and patriotism that Woolf elsewhere worked to expose and undo. Still, Woolf keeps reading and she finds things to admire. In the second example, Byron does not romanticize violence but celebrates the struggle for freedom, in antique language ("Gaul or Muscovite") but without cant: "*Who* would be free *themselves* must strike the blow." The sentiment here—"strike the blow"—is by no means pacifist, but it emphasizes working for your own freedom, not waiting for someone else to free you. In these first two examples, while apparently distinguishing between good writing and bad, Woolf also distinguishes between the automatic praise of soldiers as romantic objects and more thoughtful praise of fighting—in words and perhaps also in deed—for freedom. Her aesthetic distinction is a political one. She goes on to praise some lovely lines on nature and then a celebrated bit of satire. This juxtaposition shows her inspired—rather than troubled—by the combination of a Wordsworthian aesthetic with Pope's sensibility. Then she writes with cautious admiration of "the inevitable half assumed half genuine tragic note," in Byron's response to the death of friends. This, Woolf's fifth element, found its way directly into *The Waves*. Here, in his poetry of regret, Byron achieves a truly admirable complexity where elsewhere he seems to Woolf to oscillate between conventionality and near-greatness, between eighteenth- and nineteenth-century styles. Woolf, who had lost so many loved ones to death in her youth, understood both grief and its strangely artificial companions. In *The Waves*, as we will see, she gives this observation that grief is both "genuine" and "assumed" to Bernard who notes with great precision the moment when grief for Percival calcifies into something formal, "half assumed."

After five, it no longer makes sense to keep counting, and the numbers in the margin cease as her discussion continues. As in 1918, Woolf admires Byron's writing for the variety it offers: Byron seems to offer the promise, in a single writer, of satisfying the many moods of a reader. This variety only increases when she turns to his prose: "it is odd however to read in his letters his prose [*sic*] an apparently genuine feeling about Athens: & to compare it with the convention he adopted in verse" (D, 3.288). At first she counts a letter's "sneer about the Acropolis" as a sign of candor; then, she rightly wonders whether "the sneer may have been a pose too." In doing so, she lets herself play with the fantasy of "making a whole" of Byron, of getting him right, of understanding him as his biographer does not. At the same time she does not make pronouncements or allow herself the satisfaction, even in a diary entry, of summing up. Furthermore, Woolf moves between public and private writing, among biography, letters, and poetry, but she does not dwell in gossip. The distinction here is an important one. Her willingness to draw a conclusion about a writer based on the contrast between life and work is a hallmark of her style of biographical criticism. She is happy to gossip and joke in other contexts, but when it comes to concluding about a writer's merits, she leaves gossip to the side.

In addition to trying to construct a whole of Byron, Woolf tries to imagine what poetry we might have had "could he have got the whole into order." Byron did not bring his gift "into order," and his poetry remains a glorious, abundant mess. But Woolf's speculations here show her imagining such a taming as a possibility to be desired. As such, this diary entry nominates Byron as an important model for her aesthetic of variety, the ability to speak to a purpose and to satisfy a reader's many moods—for political point and for pleasure, for satire and for sincerity, for story and for interruption. For all the turns and reversals in this entry, it is difficult to summarize this diary entry's assessment of Byron. Still, as she turns away from Byron, Woolf grants that "measuring by feeling," one might well count Byron as 100 years old. In doing so, she acknowledges the intensity of his feelings, a concluding acknowledgment of his worth to her.

In spite of the irritation with which she begins, she continues to write about him far longer than many of the literary diary entries. To praise Byron for his range but find his focus wanting hardly breaks new ground in Byron criticism. To wonder, as Woolf does, if "the sneer may have been a pose," while taking for granted that his was a life lived at "high voltage," is to think about Byron as others have. But all of these critical commonplaces add up to something that we should pause over with more care: Woolf was thinking about Byron—reading a biography, turning to *Childe Harold*, writing about him in her diary and to a friend—while writing *The Waves*. In saying Byron might have been a novelist, Woolf is not merely echoing a truism about his narrative gifts but also reiterating her praise for a writer who dwelt between genres, breaking their frames, as Woolf herself did in her poetic novels. Thus, Bernard's love of Byron is not only a prop or a parody, but also a reflection of Woolf's reading life at the time of composition. Reading Bernard's final soliloquy in that light offers a richer context in which to hear what is both moving and ridiculous there. In short, it teaches us that we cannot understand Bernard without seeing that he simultaneously is and is not a stand-in for his creator.

In *The Waves* (1931), Bernard, who wants to be a writer, models himself on Byron. From his shallow undergraduate days to his emotional final soliloquy, Woolf imbues Bernard with a thoroughgoing Byronism. The novel follows six friends, three men and three women, from childhood through middle age and is written in interlocking monologues; the reader moves seamlessly through the minds of Bernard, Neville, Louis, Jinny, Rhoda, and Susan. The boys' schoolmate, Percival, beloved of all, is the silent seventh character: we are never privy to his thoughts and he dies young in India. For Jane Marcus, the final chapter of *The Waves*, in which the six voices give way to Bernard's voice alone is "the swan song of the white Western male author with his Romantic notions of individual genius, and his Cartesian confidence in the unitary self. Byronic man . . . sings his last aria against death."[65] But Marcus's characterization needs refining. Reading the final chapter of *The Waves* is nothing like reading Byron: it is not funny, witty, exotic, or erotic. It is, however, full of the lessons Woolf learned from reading Byron. Bernard may want to continue a tradition that was already dead, Jane Marcus argues, but Woolf, through Bernard, transforms and gives new life to Byron.[66] This is why, in my view, reading Bernard dialectically, as Woolf herself read Byron, brings his full complexity to the fore and enables us to grasp how the final soliloquy operates simultaneously as critique and paean, as a farewell to patriarchal individuality and a celebration of the articulation of selfhood.

What are the gender politics of *The Waves*, especially of Bernard's final soliloquy? What, in the end, is the significance of Byron's prominence?[67] Much of the reception of *The Waves* hinges on how critics have read its final chapter. Where all preceding chapters establish shifting and organic links among the characters, Bernard alone speaks here, having the final say and the opportunity to define his friends. The character, who long wanted to be a writer but has not thus far succeeded, has the chance, in this long final soliloquy, to take artistic control of the book. Is this gesture sincere or ironic on Woolf's part? Is it a straightforward summary by the novel's artist-figure or an ironic adieu to the individual (male) author? To call Bernard an imperialist, or a even fascist, oversimplifies his character as much as those readings that see him as a spokesperson for Woolf, a simple author-figure. As Woolf was beginning to write *The Waves*, she recorded her desire "to break my rule & write about the soul for once" (D, 3.241). In March 1930, Woolf wrote, "The test of a book (to a writer) [is] if it makes a space in which . . . you can say what you want to say" (D, 3.297) and she records her satisfaction that *The Waves* is doing that. This victory suggests that *The Waves* did for Woolf what she once thought *Don Juan* did for Byron: it provided "an elastic shape which will hold whatever you choose to put into it" (D, 1.181). A few weeks later in the composition of *The Waves*, she notes with some pride that she "can give in a very few strokes the essentials of a person's character" (D, 3.300). Then, returning to the metaphors of swiftness, ease, and physical movement that attracted her, she noted that she had "got Bernard in the final stride" (D, 3.301). When the book was done, she noted that it was her "first work in my own style" (D, 4.53).[68] These entries, her evident pride in the speed and agility of composition and the fact that "few books have interested me more to write" (D, 4.4) all indicate the pleasure she took in writing the book, and especially in writing Bernard's final speech.

For Bernard, becoming an individual means first taking on the role of Byron, then shedding it. As an undergraduate, Bernard thinks, "I want her to say as she brushes her hair or puts out the candle, 'Where did I read that? Oh, in Bernard's letter.' It is the speed, the hot molten effect, the lava flow of sentence into sentence that I need. Who am I thinking of? Byron of course. I am, in some ways, like Byron" (W, 79). His utterly unselfconscious vanity is both familiar and staggering. But the desire for speed and ease is one Woolf herself possessed and one she associated with Byron. Thinking back on these days as a much older man, Bernard remembers how, at university, he "was Byron chiefly. For many weeks at a time it was my part to stride into rooms and fling gloves and coat on the back of chairs, scowling slightly" (W, 249). For the undergraduate Bernard, Byron is a character, a dandy, and a lover, someone to emulate, a pose to strike in order to impress and seduce. Thus, Byron appears in *The Waves* in his comic, negative guise. Nonetheless, Woolf, not Bernard, wrote *The Waves* and neither the final chapter itself nor the character of Bernard is Byronic in the simple sense implied by Marcus's judgment.

Bernard's treatment of Percival's death helps us gauge how *The Waves'* Byronism helped Woolf say what she wanted to say. Bernard compares the initial sincerity of his and his friends' grief to the more *pro forma* gestures of mourning that follow: "he was already covered over with the lilies. So the sincerity of the moment passed; so it became symbolical" (W, 265).[69] For Bernard, the shock of hearing about Percival's death becomes the standard of a sincere feeling. *The Waves* depends on our accepting the characters' love of Percival even as we do not know him, even as what we do know leads us to suspect him of being unworthy of intense admiration. In this, Percival shares much with Jacob and, through Percival, Woolf revisits the questions of promise that she explored in *Jacob's Room*. Thinking about his friend years later, Bernard reflects on unfulfilled promises: "He would have done justice. He would have protected. About the age of forty he would have shocked the authorities. No lullaby has ever occurred to me capable of singing him to rest" (W, 243).[70] The flat declarative sentences that begin this passage are central to Percival's status as the novel's vacant continuer of empire. The accomplishments Bernard imagines for him are incoherent: justice, protection, and antiauthoritarian action do not combine easily in one man. Bernard admires all three indiscriminately; Percival, who dies in India on a flea-bitten mare, achieves none of them. Elsewhere, Bernard pretends to assume the mantle of achievement, imagining that a phone call "might be (one has these fancies) to assume command of the British Empire" (W, 261).

Bernard's fantasy is not to his credit: claiming to admire justice, protection, and antiauthoritarian revolt, he fantasizes about power. Encouraged from youth to admire physical beauty, Bernard, like all the characters, is seduced into following that beauty, embodied by Percival. Percival loses his life while in India maintaining the empire, neither acting nobly within it nor working to dismantle it. Bernard's own achievements—marriage, fatherhood, steady work, continuing friendships—are ordinary and Woolf seems ready to accept that most of us are ordinary. She also believes that we all need illusions and that a culture that encourages its men to fantasize about war, power, and empire condemns itself to continued violence. Bernard may not be playing at Byron anymore, but he still plays a role. And, Woolf implies, imagining himself as the leader of the empire is alarmingly grandiose. Here, most anti-imperial critics of Woolf stop, praising her subtle but persistent cultural criticism. However, the final sentence quoted above, "No lullaby has ever occurred to me capable of singing him to rest," has a different tone from what precedes it: it comes out of an intense acquaintance with grief. With it, Woolf asks us to remember the genuine emotions that stand alongside Bernard's delusions. He may be a lazy writer—waiting for a lullaby to "occur to him"—but he knows what it is to live with a grief that cannot be put to rest. His soliloquy expresses the Byronic "inevitable half assumed half genuine tragic note," and, in giving that note to a character, Woolf, like Byron, recreates the puzzling and distressing gap between grief and writing about grief.

The calcification of authentic feeling into a pose, a ritual, is one of the themes of *The Waves*. The book begins (as does Bernard's soliloquy) with an image of beings coated with virginal wax that protects them from experience; later in the soliloquy, Bernard talks about a casing that develops in adulthood ("a shell forms" [W, 255]). As the nurse squeezes water from a sponge down their spines, each of the six characters emerges into individuality. Though the moments of his acting a role are easy to parody and are, indeed, the kind of passages that encourage Jane Marcus to read the whole final section ironically, the moment in which Bernard claims to have shed Byron claims closer attention:

> I rose and walked away—I, I, I; not Byron, Shelley, Dostoevsky, but I, Bernard. I even repeated my own name once or twice. I went, swinging my stick, into a shop, and bought—not that I love music—a picture of Beethoven in a silver frame. Not that I love music, but because the whole of life, its masters, its adventurers then appeared in long ranks of magnificent human beings behind me; and I was the inheritor. (W, 253)

This is both ridiculous and sincere. It may be pretentious of him to think he is "the inheritor" but the emotion—he has just been stabbing the ground with matches to mark his thoughts, and then walking off to solidify them—seems sincere and important. His efforts to fix his thought in his mind by means of a physical gesture are not that different from the ways that Woolf writes about the tug of thought or walking on the grass in *A Room of One's Own*. The "I, I, I" recalls "the dominance of the letter 'I'" (ARO, 100) against which she objects in *A Room of One's Own*, the very "I" Byron hoped to avoid in *Childe Harold*. It also partakes of a modernist game of personae. Woolf's character, like the characters in Pound, Yeats, Joyce, Orwell, and Eliot, narrates his own life as if he were the protagonist of a novel; he learns how to become a self by impersonating someone else. And, like the male modernists, Woolf treats the habit with gentle irony. The habit of personification is hard to break: Bernard walks away, feeling himself a newly independent *I*, but his first act appears (in spite of his denial) to be yet another gesture of hero-worship: he buys a picture of Beethoven. The appearance of the musician here seems to be a synecdoche for transcendence, for his sudden vision of "the whole." And, in fact, Woolf listened intently to Beethoven during the composition of the novel and later linked Beethoven's works with Shakespeare's: "*Hamlet* or a Beethoven quartet is the truth about this vast mass that we call the world" (MB, 72).[71] Elsewhere, Woolf celebrates the habit of impersonation as a key stage in a poet's development: "I do not believe in poets dying. . . . You were Byron, remember, you wrote *Don Juan*" (DM, 220). The essay "Letter to a Young Poet" (1932), from which these sentences are quoted, was inspired by John Lehman's admiration for *The Waves*. Thus, immediately after writing *The Waves*, Woolf treated "being Byron" tenderly and sincerely.[72]

Central to successful impersonation is transformation, a fact Bernard may never fully grasp. He does, however, in the course of his final soliloquy, grasp the related lesson about the impossible, fascinating complexity of each individual life. To understand the possibilities of transformation, we must turn briefly to *Flush*, which Woolf wrote after *The Waves*. As a Byronic hero, Flush's most important achievement is his transformation, in Italy, from aristocrat to democrat. The lesson of democratic acceptance that Woolf parodies in the conclusion of *Flush* mirrors her movement toward democracy in the early 1930s.[73] This transformation Byron himself never fully made: in preparation for his journey to Missolonghi, he designed and ordered a special officer's uniform, including an antique-style helmet "of Homeric proportions . . . on the lines of that which . . . had so dismayed the infant Astynax" in *The Iliad*.[74] Flush, by contrast, suffers the indignities of mange, in treatment for which he is shaved. Losing his precious topknot teaches him a lesson about the superficiality of pedigree and he becomes a better dog for it. The dog who spends his London life acutely aware of "the laws of the Kennel Club" (F, 116) and absurdly proud that "he was a dog of birth and breeding!" (F, 32) comes to believe that "All dogs were his brothers" (F, 117). Flush's transformation is a glorious and triumphant revision of what happens to both Byron and Jacob in their travels. As with characters in a Forster comedy, Italy brings out the best and warmest qualities in the dog.[75]

In Elizabeth Barrett Browning Woolf found a feminist practitioner of literary impersonation, one who transformed and surpassed the inheritance she loved. Byron was Browning's first crush. In 1816, when she was ten, she wanted to run away and become Byron's page; to her father's dismay, she wrote verses on Byron's death and on Byronic subjects; her heroine Aurora Leigh's name combines the name of *Don Juan*'s Aurora Raby with the name of Byron's half-sister, Augusta Leigh.[76] But, in eloping to Italy and involving herself with the *risorgimento*, she enacted her own feminist transformation of Byron's story.[77] Woolf tacitly acknowledges the link between Byron and Barrett Browning: she read *Aurora Leigh* alongside *Don Juan* in 1931 (L, 4.294), and in the 1918 diary entries on being a born writer, Browning is the other writer who was not born to the role. *Flush* is, in itself, an opposite, the playful book that relieved the serious effort of *The Waves*.

Impersonation and transformation are difficult, but the difficulty of "making a whole" shadows Bernard's soliloquy. He begins confidently, "Now to sum up" (W, 238). However, the complexity of the topic soon overwhelms Bernard and the tension between Bernard's desire to "sum up" and the impossibility of achieving a summation animates the final pages. Throughout, Bernard compares his storytelling to that of a nurse reading to a child: "let us turn over these scenes as children turn over the pages of a picture-book and the nurse says, pointing: 'That's a cow. That's a boat.' Let us turn over the pages, and I will add, for your amusement, a comment in the margin" (W, 239). The whole he intends to make is not a personal scrapbook, but an impersonal and deliberately generic picture book designed to teach the rudiments of language. The picture book speaks to Woolf's early desire to write a mystical novel without traditional characters.[78] However, Bernard's promise to add "a comment in the margin" admits the pressure of individuality: this will not be just any cow or sailboat, but one seen from his unique perspective.

The conceit of the final soliloquy, that Bernard is telling a silent acquaintance the story of his life, breaks down quickly. In the beginning, he seems to take seriously his charge "to sum up" (W, 238). "Neville next" (W, 245), he writes, and what follows is a character-by-character sketch of the six characters, reviewing Bernard's opinion of their lives thus far: this is the most artificial part of the chapter. In contrast, when he describes what it is like to fall in love, "the being eviscerated— drawn out, spun like a spider's web and twisted in agony round a thorn" (W, 250), the language is not only intense and overdone but also sincere. Part of the sincerity comes from the way it echoes language Woolf uses elsewhere. Bernard moves between routine and an intense, individual response to life, between uninterrupted community and awareness of his difference from others. He also moves through many moods and knows that he does; he tells us of his flaws, counting on his self-awareness as a kind of charm (something Byron did, too, as Hazlitt noted). Throughout these shifts, Woolf lends him metaphors that she herself uses: the spider's web, the globe (W, 256), "a string of six little fish" (W, 256), and the fin breaking the waves (W, 273, 284). Of these, perhaps the most frequent is the linkage of Monday and Tuesday, a synecdoche for ordinary life, echoing the title of Woolf's 1921 short story collection. Bernard thinks, "Nevertheless, life is pleasant, life is tolerable. Tuesday follows Monday" (W, 257), brushing off "the torture" of selfhood to make a transition, back to nonbeing and routine.[79] The word "tolerable" and the repetition "life is . . ., life is . . ." sound bureaucratic and self-satisfied, but the phrase "Tuesday follows Monday," echoing Woolf's short story "Monday or Tuesday," prevents us from dismissing it as such.

Bernard speaks of himself in Adamic terms, as one walking "alone in a new world, never trodden; brushing new flowers, unable to speak save in a child's words of one syllable; without shelter from phrases" (W, 287). The language is both male *and* Woolfian. And when he says, "That man, the hairy, the ape-like, has contributed his part to my life" (W, 290), Woolf seems to be gesturing toward a male version of her efforts to tell the truth about women's bodies while presenting the male body as repulsive and alien. Thinking about personae is entangling: writers mean for it to be. In the end, Bernard is merely a linguistic figment of Virginia Woolf's imagination; in his final soliloquy, Woolf offers a performance of what it might be to sum up life. The moment we think we have caught Woolf speaking *in propria persona*, "the hairy, the ape-like" Bernard returns: in short, the soliloquy is the epitome of a Byronic performance, allowing Woolf to say everything she desires without getting "caught." In this case, Woolf desires to capture not only the full range of human emotion but also the capacity of a single individual to embody much of that range even as he remains stubbornly, brutishly an individual. Bernard is, finally, just Bernard: a sweet, annoying, self-satisfied middle-aged man who has a profound capacity to understand others.

In writing under the persona of Bernard, a straight man who is no feminist, Woolf granted herself freedom from anger and restrictive gender roles. The tension between moments when Bernard thinks something that "Woolf" also thinks and moments of divergence, when Bernard is priggish or sexist, work together to create a text in which Woolf can say what she wants to say, to adapt her judgment of Byron. Woolf uses moments of particularity, pomposity, and silliness to cut the intensity of passages elsewhere about what it feels like to grieve for a beloved friend or to enter the room where one's beloved awaits. If we take Woolf's desire for books that relieve other books (D, 3.203) seriously, then perhaps one of the pleasures of *The Waves* was the pleasure not only of variety but also of a less explicit feminism, of not being caught, of speaking in a different voice.

## Refusing Martyrdom, 1937–41

If readers locate Byron's greatness in his death, he may inspire promising young men to volunteer for war. If, however, we see him as a great poet who worked for democracy, he may inspire others to write masterpieces against tyranny. In writing about Byron, Woolf continually works to distinguish between these two Byrons. In the last years of her life, Woolf clarified her sense of the greatest kind of misreading of Byron—when promising young men fail to shed Byronic impersonations and become martyrs instead.

After 1816, Byron ceased to court fame. In 1823, after a decade of fame, he seems to have treated it as a slightly irritating fact: "the English visitors thronged the vestibule and passages [of the Genoese hotel] to stare at him as he went by. But he was on his best behavior: affable and engaging he ambled up the staircase."[80] The difficulty with this newer brand of fame, what we now call celebrity, is the "illusion of intimacy."[81] A famous person used to be distant from us: we knew of her achievement in life and learned of her private life only a decent interval after death. A celebrity, by contrast, offers her life up for consumption as she lives it: he passes through the lobby of our hotel, or the tabloids chart her cooling affections in photographs before the breakup is announced. To be consumed by a stranger on a train—hypothesized about, to have one's clothing judged—or to be read about, years hence, in a biography, is sufficiently alarming, but to be written about and photographed now is the worst of both worlds.

It is tempting to simply dismiss fame as bad, to say that our interest in personality is corrupt. But Woolf sees the impossibility and, ultimately, the undesirability of giving up our interest in other people's lives. People's lives are interesting, books lead to other books, and one of the most common ways into classic literature for a common reader is through a biography: "I'm reading Byron: Maurois which leads me to Childe Harold." As Bloomsbury's experiments with biography (e.g., Strachey's *Eminent Victorians*, Woolf's *Orlando* and "Lives of the Obscure") notably demonstrated, the way we tell a life story is a reading of that life. In *Jacob's Room, The Waves*, and *Flush*, Woolf explored the possibility of shifting Byron's reputation away from both ridiculous womanizing and, more importantly, a cult of martyrdom. That desire became more urgent with the death of her nephew Julian Bell.

The Spanish Civil War and Julian's death there in July 1937 crystallize the distinction between the martyr and the poet that was long latent in Woolf's admiration for Byron. For Woolf, Byron's death is not heroic, but merely the final episode in a dissolute and aimless life. She wrote in 1932 that highbrows "[u]ndoubtedly . . . come fearful croppers. . . . Byron, getting into bed with first one woman and then another and dying in the mud at Missolonghi" (DM, 177). The tone here is light, but the satiric linking of womanizing with a muddy death (not a martyrdom) prefigures an alternate reading of Byron's life. Had this more ridiculous version of Byron's life been the dominant one, it might have changed Julian's decision to go to Spain.

Still, there is a strong parallel between an Englishman fighting for Greece in the 1820s and one fighting for Spain in the 1930s; it is certainly stronger than that between an Englishman in 1820s Greece and an Englishman fighting for England during World War I. However, we can see the origins of Woolf's mistrust of martyrdom by looking back at *Jacob's Room*. Jacob's blankness contains within it a sharp attack on English culture's continuing admiration of war and heroic sacrifice and on the consequent understanding of Byron's life retrospectively through his death. The arc of Jacob's life is a pale imitation of Byron's. Both die young and senselessly at war, but only Byron achieves the dubious distinction of martyrdom, and only Byron dies having already achieved something in poetry. Unlike Byron, whose critical eye sharpened as he matured, Jacob seems to be growing both stout and conventional as the novel comes to a conclusion, interesting himself in England, power, and empire: "Why not rule countries in the way they should be ruled?" (JR, 150). Attracted to the vocabulary of heroism but uncritical of its applicability to the war of 1914, Jacob embodies what one critic calls Woolf's suspicions "that the government and the press were engaged in a conspiracy aimed at hoodwinking the unthinking and searching young . . . into becoming players in the drama of war."[82]

In *Jacob's Room*, Woolf wrote a story of the meaningless martyrdom she had witnessed. The novel commemorates both Thoby's death and the death in World War I of her friend, the poet Rupert Brooke. She had bitter insight into the sham efforts to turn Brooke into that war's Byron. Brooke's death in 1915 marked a change in Woolf's attitude to the war, intensifying her pacifism.[83] Certainly, we can see her frustration with the creation of a legacy for Brooke in her review of a posthumous glorification of his life—a review published the very week in 1918 in which she was also reading Byron. She believed that England's hero-worshipping culture encouraged young men to volunteer for war and, thus, that the culture of hero-worship was in some sense responsible for war. The outbreak of a new war in Spain and the threat of its spread across the continent intensified Woolf's pacifism even as it renewed the efforts of others to find "another Byron." Tellingly, Julian wrote to Virginia Woolf from China in 1936 to say that he had been reading Brooke's poetry: "Rupert's far better than I had believed."[84] One can imagine Woolf's unease at that judgment.

Woolf as a young woman saw both Rupert Brooke and her brother Thoby as Byronic. Years later, she came to see Julian as uncomfortably like Thoby. Early in her memoir of him, written just weeks after his death, she links their names when reflecting on her fears for Julian's safety: "I had determined not to think about the risks, because, sub-consciously I was sure he would be killed: that is I had a couchant unexpressed certainty, from Thoby's death I think" (MJB, 256). But later, when Clive Bell suggests Julian's likeness to Thoby, Woolf would not allow it: "For some reason I did not answer, that he was like Thoby. I have always been foolish about that. I did not like any Bell to be like Thoby" (MJB, 256). In the memoir, she expresses regret that she judged his writing harshly, finding it "very careless . . . too per-sonal" (MJB, 256). Nonetheless, she still insists that he never saw him-self as a born writer, and reports his father's judgment that he "did not think he [Julian] was born to be a writer" (MJB, 256), echoing the judgment she had made years earlier about Byron.

In her memoir of Julian, Woolf expresses puzzlement that he could not contribute to the cause intellectually without putting his life in danger, comparing his situation to the conscientious objector (C. O.)

status she and others in Bloomsbury adopted during World War I:

> We were all C.O.'s in the Great war. And though I understand that this
> is a "cause," can be called the cause of liberty & so on, still my natural
> reaction is to fight intellectually: if I were any use, I should write against
> it: I should evolve some plan for fighting English tyranny. The moment
> force is used, it becomes meaningless & unreal to me. (MJB, 258–59)

For Woolf, it was an article of faith that the intellectual life was a form
of resistance to tyranny. During World War II, she wrote "thinking is
my fighting" (D, 5.285). After Julian's death, Woolf wrote several long
letters to Ben Nicolson, the son of her ex-lover Vita Sackville-West,
stationed with the army at Chatham during World War II. These letters
catalogue for a young man of Julian's generation an alternate reading
of Bloomsbury as both highbrow and passionately engaged in political life (L, 6.413–15, 419–22). They depict a Bloomsbury that sympathetic cultural historians now reconstruct: lectures on art for
ordinary people, political activism at all levels (from advising ministers
to small meetings in one's living room), painting, writing, and teaching are all part of a public-spirited liberalism. They make the case that
Woolf must have wanted to make for Julian: that one can fight tyranny
by working for culture.

In the memoir "A Sketch of the Past" (1939), Woolf recounts a
"moment of being" in which she stopped fighting with her brother,
seeing clearly the futility of violence (MB, 71): pacifism, in this
account, has been absolutely fundamental to her character since
girlhood. Although her letters on Vanessa's behalf immediately
after Julian's death adopt the language of purpose that seems to
have comforted her sister, it is clear that Woolf could not understand his choice: "[W]hat did he feel about Spain? What made him
feel it necessary, knowing as he did how it must torture Nessa, to
go?" (MJB, 258). Julian's sense of the soldier as what his biographer calls "his new-found ideal," his admission, in an introduction
to a book by conscientious objectors, that some situations called for
force, and his preference for what Julian himself called "a violent
finish in hot blood" were all alien to Woolf.[85] But for men of Julian's
generation, the lure of going off to Spain to fight for freedom was
strong. It was also, at least in one case, directly linked to the legacy
of Byron: "S. [Stephen Spender] said the C. P. [Communist Party]
which he had that day joined, wanted him to be killed, in order that
there might be another Byron. He has a child's vanity about
himself" (D, 5.57).

When Byron reached his mid-thirties, he became impatient to find purpose and to escape his status as *cavalier servente* to Teresa Guiccioli.[86] In response, he chose a path that led to martyrdom. For generations of English men, Byron symbolized heroism as John Wayne did for generations of American men. In his study of John Wayne, Garry Wills bluntly argues the case that Woolf puts more subtly: Wayne's screen image inspired many American men to join the military. After *The Sands of Iwo Jima*, John Wayne,

> would be the symbolic man who *won* World War II. [The movie's] contagious delusions were registered not only in the lives of Ron Kovic, Newt Gingrich, Pat Buchanan, and Oliver North, but of countless unknown Wayne surrogates who strut about with a need to be tough, to think of life as warfare.[87]

For both Woolf and Wills, the connection is patently clear: a culture full of men who "think of life as warfare" fosters warfare, violence, heroism, and martyrdom. The heroes of World War II inspire the recruits to Vietnam; a martyr for Greek independence inspires volunteers to Spain. For Woolf, it is a mistake to count Byron's death as part of his achievement, as worthy of our admiration.

Martyrdom often brings fame and Woolf returns to Byron's frustration with his own fame as she grew increasingly impatient with the trappings of hers and anxious about the poisonous desire for fame in general. Woolf, whose fame was on a far more modest scale than Byron's, initially enjoyed the prospect of "becoming our leading novelist, & not with the highbrows only" (D, 4.49). Only later did she regret the loss of anonymous and imaginative freedom entailed therein. In her memoir of Julian Bell, Woolf reflected on her sense of fame as a form of egotism:

> But then I came to the stage 2 years ago of hating "personality": desiring anonymity: a complex state which I would one day have discussed with him. Then I could not sympathise with wishing to be published. I thought it wrong from my new standpoint—a piece of the egomaniac, egocentric mania of the time. (MJB, 257)

Woolf writes with a combination of stubborn confidence and wistful understanding about Julian's misguided (in her view) ambition to be a famous poet: this is after all, a memoir of a Byronic young man, her nephew, killed in Spain. She comments that her strong feelings against fame are a hard-won and new attitude, and the context makes clear that, although she "could not sympathise" with Julian, she never had an extended discussion of what it might mean to "desir[e] anonymity." That she counts it as new in 1937, dating the change to just two years earlier, helps explain the shift in her attitude from 1929. In that year, in *A Room of One's Own*, it counts as a shame that we do not know the identity of Anon, who was often a woman. The feminist point of 1929 that women have not received sufficient credit for their creative work becomes, by 1937, a point about the corrupting influence of fame.

In light of her rejection of martyrdom in 1937, her use of Byronic satire in her final novel, *Between the Acts* (1941), is all the more significant. Mr. Oliver quotes Byron. Isa, who yearns to be a poet but is no born writer, has named her children George and Caro, after Byron and Caroline Lamb, his most famous lover.[88] Miss LaTrobe, like Byron, is wounded by gossip, touched by sexual scandal, and, as a result, somewhat rootless. Mrs. Manresa, too, is Byronic. Everyone knows that Mrs. Manresa is putting on a show, but her flamboyant performance is a comfort compared to the stiff, unacknowledged role-playing that traps the other characters. Whereas Giles arrives home and, seeing that there are guests, changes into his flannels (BTA, 46), Mrs. Manresa, gate-crashing, boasts about taking off her stays and rolling downhill and "everybody felt, directly she spoke, 'She's said it, she's done it, not I,' and could take advantage of the breach of decorum, of the fresh air that blew in, to follow like leaping dolphins in the wake of an ice-breaking vessel" (BTA, 41). Her performance not only brings a delicious feeling of freedom and movement to the gathering (they feel like "leaping dolphins"), but it also has moments of sincerity. Listening to the story of rolling downhill, Isa thinks "That's genuine . . . Quite genuine" (BTA, 42). Thus, Byron's legacy is scattered across generations, genders, and sexual orientations. Of all the characters with Byronic qualities, not one is a young man: there is no Jacob, Percival, or Bernard in the novel. Whether such men have, like Lucy Swithin's mastodons, become extinct or fallen prey to war, Woolf does not say. The book does have one prominent and vigorous patriarch in Giles Oliver. But Giles is not Byronic: his masculinity is too brutal, aimless, and suburban. So thoroughly does Woolf separate action from poetry that Giles is the only major character in the book without a feeling for poetry. He, too, more than the other main characters (though like some of the anonymous members of the audience), senses that the impending war threatens this community.

In the end, the strongest Byronic resonance in the novel lies not in the characters but in the form. Some of the best criticism on *Between the Acts* recently has focused on the communal aspects of the novel. But, for me, the village pageant at the heart of the book is not simply communitarian; it dramatizes the tension between the community and the individual. And that tension has a multivalent complexity, for, at different moments, we see the pageant through the eyes of spectators, performers (though we are never in the consciousness of the villagers, the narrator frequently comments on the—always ironic—relationship between actor and role), and artist.

Although Woolf first heard of Byron through gossip and his biography initially helped her navigate her own fame, by the end of her life, she uses literary lessons from Byron in a novel that celebrates anonymous artistic creation. In it, Miss LaTrobe, like Lily Briscoe, Mary Beton, and Bernard, acts as another artist figure who helps Woolf pretend not to be famous or successful.[89] Impersonating an anonymous artist continued to afford Woolf the imaginative freedom she sought, forcing her, with each new book, to push herself to new artistic creations. The scraps of poetry and song throughout do something different. They send out little bits of connection—little gifts from one individual to another. Mrs. Manresa thinks different words to the same tune; Lucy and Dodge trade nursery rhymes; Bart offers a bit of Byron to Mrs. Haines: poetry creates these little, loose, and momentary affiliations. The artificiality of quotation— as in *To the Lighthouse*—creates community by tapping shared memory. It suggests a common tradition.

Though Woolf made few direct comments about Byron's politics, the very different treatment of their political affiliations, in their own day and since, has much to teach us about social class, revolutionary politics, and gender. People read his aristocratic liberalism far differently than her armchair socialism. For decades, critics acceded to Leonard Woolf's offhand remark that she was "the least political creature."[90] More recently, erring in another direction, critics have emphasized her investment in community—especially as manifest in *Between the Acts*. But for Woolf, the community she sought and worked for—be it Bloomsbury, or a group of women, or workers from the local Cooperative Guild—always had to accommodate the needs of the individual writer.

Woolf's care to avoid reading Byron's life retrospectively through his death has its own ironic coda in Woolf's posthumous reputation: her suicide has become the key to her career for many readers. Some hunt for augurs of depression and death. How different that imagery of the freedom in swimming becomes when we insist on reading it as prophetic of her death by drowning. Of course, we need not read an author according to her preferred method of reading. Nonetheless, Woolf's informal study of how fame has kept readers from recognizing the real innovation in Byron's prose offers a cautionary tale. The liberation and joy in her metaphors of swimming, leaping, galloping, and cantering are not just about a death wish. More important than cautions about biographical criticism, however, is the recognition of a deep aesthetic kinship between these two writers: their intense reading within the tradition and their efforts to reshape it to fit their own needs makes them among our least appreciated innovators—innovators of genre, intertextual writers who change the tradition from within. More of an outsider than Byron, Woolf surpassed him with her innovations, finding a purpose in life and writing that he never found, not even in death. For Woolf, the final pathos of her love of Bryon arises out of his dual legacy: his poetry contributed to her literary innovations but his fame and his famous death contributed to her grief. For Woolf, England misplaced Byron's importance. Emphasizing his personality and his death instead of his poetry ultimately does England historical and national harm. It is not too much to say that young male friends and relations died for their misreading of Byron.

# Epilogue: Woolf in Africa: Lessing, El Saadawi, and Aidoo

In *A Room of One's Own*, the narrator muses on the contents of a London newspaper:

> I began idly reading the headlines. A ribbon of very large letters ran across the page. Somebody had made a big score in South Africa. Lesser ribbons announced that Sir Austen Chamberlain was at Geneva. A meat axe with human hair on it had been found in a cellar. Mr. Justice commented in the Divorce Courts upon the Shamelessness of Women. Sprinkled about the paper were other pieces of news. A film actress had been lowered from a peak in California and hung suspended in mid-air. The weather was going to be foggy. The most transient visitor to this planet, I thought, who picked up this paper could not fail to be aware, even from this scattered testimony, that England is under the rule of a patriarchy. (ARO, 33)

In reading idly, Woolf's persona gleans news that has little to do with any single event. She realizes instead with shock that the front page consists of an overwhelming display of masculine bias. Taken individually, each story may present a reasonable claim to be news on a given day, although it is unlikely that a feminist newspaper from the 1920s would lead with cricket scores, the referent, according to newspapers from the time, for "the big score in South Africa." Taken together, however, the dominance of the male perspective is nearly complete. Women are only alluded to twice—once as hussies and once as a damsel in distress. No reasonable woman appears. Only the weather—foggy—offers its barely audible ironic commentary on how the paper passes off patriarchy as universal and normative.

I have singled out this familiar passage because in texts by three African writers—Doris Lessing, Nawal El Saadawi, and Ama Ata Aidoo—the female protagonist experiences a similar "splitting off of consciousness" (ARO, 97) while reading the newspaper. The newspaper, then, serves as a metaphor for an encounter with patriarchy for all four feminists, Woolf and her three African successors. Whereas the

El Saadawi passage sounds most like an allusion to Woolf, her work is a translation, and her connection to Woolf has been the hardest to establish. The Lessing passage almost certainly is not a reference to Woolf; the Aidoo passage may be. Both Lessing and Aidoo have amply documented their engagement with Woolf. In any case, the recurring trope of the newspaper, be it directly Woolfian or a signal of a more indirect sympathy, serves as an opportunity through which to analyze the different Woolfian resonances found in each of these writers.

As the backbone of the public sphere, the newspaper has been credited with creating not only a community, but also a sense of a nation. When Benedict Anderson contemplated the front page of a colonial newspaper, he saw not the alienation of a woman under patriarchy but the unification of citizens: "what brought together, on the same page, this marriage, with that ship, this price with that bishop, was the very structure of the colonial administration and market-system itself."[1] For Anderson, the newspaper becomes the evidence upon which people base their sense of belonging to a nation. Thus, he writes,

> Factory-owner in Lille was connected to factory-owner in Lyon only by reverberation. They had no necessary reason to know of one another's existence; they did not typically marry each other's daughters or inherit each other's property. But they did come to visualize in a general way the existence of thousands and thousands like themselves through print-language.[2]

For Anderson, this is a good and interesting phenomenon: reading the newspaper links men across space; it turns men into citizens. Still, even a moderate feminist might see that singling out the newspaper for criticism is striking and perhaps a little unfair. After all, newspapers are not as discriminatory as most patriarchal institutions: where literacy rates for women lag behind men, newspapers seldom require the superliteracy of a university degree; one need not own property or possess the right to vote in order to read the newspaper; one need not be a citizen. As novelists from Charles Dickens to Ben Okri have shown, the newspaper has often been on the side of the disempowered— representing them and their concerns. But, as these women would remind us, newspapers have yet to represent the concerns of women with the same vigor and criticism as they sometimes have championed the lot of the poor.

Writing about Woolf in Africa is an unusual choice. I am emphatically not writing about Woolf *on* Africa: Woolf's few comments on Africa were limited, racist, uninformed, and disengaged. Furthermore, reading

Doris Lessing, Nawal El Saadawi, or Ama Ata Aidoo, one is unlikely to think first of Virginia Woolf as an influence. And there is something insulting about suggesting it ought to be—as if African writers can and should only be understood in the context of a European tradition. One is not struck, as one is at moments in Jorge Luis Borges, or Anita Desai, or, certainly, in Jeanette Winterson, that the author must have just been reading Woolf. And yet, read Woolf—especially *A Room of One's Own*—each of these women likely did.[3] Their reading of Woolf, in itself, may set them apart from other African writers. For that reason, then, I want to be clear that, just as I do not claim Woolf as the primary influence on any of these women, I no more claim these women as representatives of African literature.[4] Nonetheless, Woolf read her precursors generously, and, having done so, she encourages us to do the same. Just as Woolf was able to make Joseph Addison resonate with a world he could not imagine, so have readers of Woolf from across the globe found things to admire in her and ways to use her that would surprise and maybe even shock her.

If Woolf's narrator in *A Room of One's Own* learns the extent of patriarchy, Martha Quest learns something different in Lessing's *A Proper Marriage* (1952). Returning to reading the newspaper empowers her. It is what shakes her out of her marital and maternal stupor. For Firdaus in El Saadawi's *Woman at Point Zero* (1957), the paper is neither empowering nor devastating. It is profoundly alienating. Looking for confirmation of her own innate pride, she finds marks of the world's indifference. Through the discussion of the heart transplant that Sissie sees splashed across the evening papers in London, Aidoo's *Our Sister Killjoy* (1977) tackles the entrenched racism of even self-proclaimed progressives. That is a rough guide to the scenes of reading the newspaper in each text. The remainder of this brief epilogue sketches the Woolfian resonances therein.

Lessing is the closest in time and culture to Woolf; her debt to Woolf is both enormous and difficult to define. After all, the protagonist of *The Golden Notebook* (1962) is not named Anna Wulf on accident. Lessing, born in 1919, describes herself as a child of World War I:[5] her parents met when her mother, a nurse grieving for her dead beloved, tended to her father, who had lost a leg in the fighting. Lessing and the young women she writes about become adults with a sense of political and social entitlement that Woolf arrives at only late in life. In her first novel, *The Grass is Singing* (1950), the ordinary, passive Mary Turner takes her right to work and live on her own seriously, and only at the age of 30 does she succumb, tragically (and, ultimately, fatally), to the pressures of marriage. Similarly, Martha Quest, the protagonist of the *Children of Violence* novels (which include *Martha Quest, A Proper Marriage,* and three subsequent volumes), takes herself seriously as a modern woman, as smart as her male friends, with a right to dance, drink, and stay out late. (Neither woman, however, has a new vision of marriage.) Lessing would likely not want to be called an African writer, seeing herself as an English one (with Persian roots, perhaps) instead. Yet "the black notebooks" in *The Golden Notebook* detail Anna Wulf's youth in Africa and the red notebooks remind us to turn our gaze to Africa (via multiple newspaper clippings—a Woolfian technique from the 1930s). Furthermore, there are moments of explanation in *The Grass is Singing* that have more in common with African literature than with anything English. When, for example, Lessing writes that Mary Turner "did not know it was part of the native code of politeness not to look a superior in the face," she displays a sure knowledge of the difference between the African world she knows and that of her imagined English audience. In knowing she must explain Africa to her readers if she wants to write to the center, she knows that she cannot write like the insider Woolf was in spite of herself.[6]

In her 1952 novel *A Proper Marriage,* the second in her *Children of Violence* cycle, Lessing plays with the attraction of passivity.[7] When Martha Quest runs into her friend William after 18 months, she admits that she has not been reading the newspapers. In the intervening time, the Soviet forces, still outmatched by the Germans, begin to experience success as they fight the Nazi advance. Lessing writes, "While not reading the newspapers is a practice to be condemned, there are times when it can yield interesting results": her tone suggests a connection with a difference to Woolf. Both women are interested in a kind of documentary prose, defining relevant documents as broadly as Mass Observation did, yet there is a scientific note here— "yield interesting results"—that Woolf seldom has. Lessing notes how the paper marks the change in the newspaper's coverage of Russia's part in the war: "the Russians had become heroes and magnificent fighters. They were no longer a rabble of ill-equipped moujiks fleeing before Nazi hordes."[8] And Martha recognizes the irony and apparent cynicism of the paper's editors: "How did the editor of this same newspaper picture his readers?"[9] Martha wonders, too, at the paper's inconsistency: how could these same soldiers go from "unfortunate victims" to "a race of battling giants" in less than two years?[10]

If international affairs have done an about face, domestic matters "remained static"[11]: Martha notes the "irritable self-satisfaction" of the paper's racist condescension. The newspaper creates "a feeling of stir and excitement" for the restless Martha. Still, she is savvy enough to check her self-aggrandizing fantasies. Her "day dreams of herself going among the people, like a heroine from an old Russian novel" are interrupted by the recognition that "the colour bar made that form of agitation impossible."[12] Martha is aware of the injustice of segregation from the beginning: she notes with discomfort her own assumptions that a young black woman will be a happier or more natural mother than she will be; she visits Solly Cohen at his nascent commune in the colored part of town, and she erupts with irritation that the Contemporary Politics Discussion Circle focuses on England, not Africa.[13] The ironies that Martha sees are complicated by her situation. William dryly notes the number of servants at her beck and call. Martha, it is clear, lives with little hypocrisies of her own. When William's implied criticism discomfits her, she considers inviting him in, "but . . . Douglas [her husband] . . . would be angry."[14]

She has no models of independent womanhood about her and her youth makes her reject literary models as antique. Just a few pages earlier, she thinks back to Ibsen's *A Doll's House*: "There's something so damned *vieux jeu* . . . in leaving like Nora."[15] Lessing connects Martha's personal unhappiness with her growing interest in politics. Restlessness leads her to seek an outlet—and initially politics seems as good as any, a new fad to replace the sundowner parties of her courting days. However, the sense of working toward important social change soon fulfills her in ways that the drinking never did. Like Woolf, Wollstonecraft, George Eliot, and, for that matter, Chekhov before her, Lessing connects having a purpose outside the home with happiness. For Lessing, reading the newspaper is the first step to finding a purpose.

Just as we can imagine Lessing to be a metaphorical daughter of Septimus Smith, a child of violence, born of World War I, we can imagine Nawal El Saadawi to be one of the young women medical students that Woolf wrote about in *Three Guineas*. The resonances between Woolf and El Saadawi emerge most strongly in the intensity of feeling at gender inequity, the frustration of being a daughter in a family where female bookishness is a detriment, a hazard to marriageability, a deep sense that life for a smart girl is unfair. Yet, unlike Woolf's parents, El Saadawi's parents paid for her schooling, even up through medical school, and when she persuaded the dean to give her a scholarship, her father treated her like a hero.[16]

El Saadawi's anticolonial father, together with her girlhood friend who was a communist, taught the young El Saadawi the habit of reading newspapers not as fact but as repositories of hypocrisy. Firdaus, the prostitute whose death row testimony comprises *Woman at Point Zero*, shares El Saadawi's deeply rooted skepticism.[17] Firdaus remembers going to the library to read the paper and stumbling "on the picture of one or other of these rulers as he sat with the congregation attending Friday morning prayers. There he sat opening and closing his lids, looking out through them with an expression of great humility, like a man stricken to his depths. I could see he was trying to deceive Allah in the same way as he deceived the people."[18] She animates the photograph, watching a still photo kneel and blink, pray and abase himself. Here, as in Woolf, all patriarchal figures, from Allah on down, are collapsed into one domineering father to be cleared from the sky.

The most resonant moment comes late in the text, where Firdaus again speaks of her anger at patriarchy, but her anger now comes, terrifyingly, threateningly, from an awareness of truth:

> All my life I was looking for something that would fill me with pride, something that would make me hold my head high, higher than the heads of everyone else, especially kings, princes and rulers. Every time I picked up a newspaper with the picture of one of them in it, I would spit on it. I knew I was only spitting on a piece of newspaper, which I might need to spread on the shelves of my kitchen, yet each time I used to spit, and leave the spit to dry on its own.[19]

In looking for something to fill her with pride, Firdaus seems to be seeking external confirmation of something innate. In *Moments of Being*, Woolf thinks back on her girlhood, on her reflection in the mirror, and her memories of being molested; she wonders at the origins of a deep shame: Firdaus, by contrast, looks at herself as if she were a queen.[20] With the sketch of Professor Von X in *A Room of One's Own*, Woolf recognizes that her anger derives from male anger; here, Firdaus's anger derives from "truth": "When I killed [the pimp] I did it with truth not with a knife. That is why they are afraid and in a hurry to execute me. They do not fear my knife. It is my truth which frightens them."[21] A successful, intelligent prostitute, in prison and sentenced to death, Firdaus rises to operatic magnificence here: she is not poor Mary Beton doodling in a notebook but Antigone or Aida. Moments later she says again, "I spit with ease on their lying faces and words, on their lying newspapers."[22] In spite of claims that El Saadawi is more at ease with people of other classes than Woolf, it is hard, at the end of *Woman at Point Zero*, not to feel uneasy at the narrator's identification with the hanged prostitute.[23] Like Clarissa's moment of communion with Septimus at the end of *Mrs. Dalloway*, El Saadawi's narrator's identification with Firdaus (one she emphasizes in her own voice in subsequent interviews), may overlook the human cost. Septimus and Firdaus pay with their lives for possessing the kind of sensitivity upon which novelists make their living.

Ama Ata Aidoo could never be accused of such a moment of insensitivity. In fact, one of her strengths lies in discovering the callous assumptions of others. The most outrageous of all comes in *Our Sister Killjoy*, her novel about Sissie, an African exchange student who visits first Germany and then London, only to return wiser about the hypocrisies of both Europeans and the "big men" of Africa who have spent time abroad. While in London, Sissie confronts reports of a heart transplant:

> The Heart Transplant. The evening papers had screeched the news in with the evening trains of the Underground. Of how the Dying White Man had received the heart of a coloured man who had collapsed on the beach and how the young coloured man had allegedly failed to respond to any efforts at resuscitation and therefore his heart had been removed from his chest, the Dying White Man's own old heart having been cleaned out of his chest and how in the meantime the Dying White Man was doing well, blah, blah, blah![24]

The paper refers to an operation conducted by Dr. Christiaan Barnard on January 2, 1968, in which the heart of a 25-year-old mixed race donor, Clive Haupt, was successfully transplanted into the body of Philip Blaiberg, aged 52.[25] The London paper goes so far as to suggest that this operation could become an avenue for interracial understanding. Sissie immediately grasps the import of this: the excessive celebration indicates racism so deep and so based in pseudobiology that the transplant is seen as almost across species. Then, the idea that this may amount to interracial understanding or cooperation seems, amazingly, to forget that it depends on the death of the "colored" man. Her observation that the newspapers "screech" is both an apt description of the barbarity of the London dailies and, like her German friend Marija's kitchen English earlier in the book, Aidoo's little revenge on European barbarity. She makes the Dying White Man into an allegory that contains its own ironic undoing, as Woolf does with Professor Von X and Milton's bogey; in contrast, the young colored man remains tragically small, lower case, unknowable, and human. Least willing to see what is so clear to Sissie is her African boyfriend, also studying in London. The men who go abroad are eager to embrace the English rhetoric because they look forward to being "big men" upon their return. Big men are not intellectuals.

They are, in every way, charlatans. But they do have privileges: they have been away, they have drivers, they are on the receiving end of government graft (OED graft n.5: The obtaining of profit or advantage by dishonest or shady means; the means by which such gains are made, esp. bribery, blackmail, or the abuse of a position of power or influence; the profits so obtained). Most of all, they can go to parties hosted by whites and sigh and talk about England like Englishmen.

Part of the power of resonance is that its reciprocal movement has the power to change the writer—Woolf—who has changed us. Reading Lessing, El Saadawi, and Aidoo we find traces of a Woolf who was practical, utterly clear-eyed about the gross gender inequities in everything from family economic decisions about marriage and education to what counts as an interesting and pleasant pastime, to government policy.

It turns out that the negative experience of being alienated by the newspaper connects women. However, this silent connection is not initially felt as community: the daughter of the Lille factory owner does not, when she experiences a "splitting off of consciousness" (ARO, 97) from the paper, immediately intuit a connection to her counterpart in Lyon. When we draw together the fictionalized accounts of women from Europe and across Africa, we begin to see a pattern of alienation that creates a community across national boundaries—one like the society of outsiders that Woolf envisioned in *Three Guineas*. A key text for this community is *A Room of One's Own* for the widely disseminated text confirms the experiences of the daughters of educated men worldwide.

# Appendix

Virginia Woolf wrote over four hundred essays and reviews, but she only oversaw publication of two collections of essays—The Common Reader and The Second Common Reader. Eventually Andrew McNeillie's scholarly edition of her essays, The Essays of Virginia Woolf (now four volumes of a projected six, abbreviated as E below), will prove the definitive resource for scholars. However, copyright questions delay the preparation and publication of the final volumes (covering the years 1929–1941) and have made volume four (which covers 1925–1928) nearly impossible to attain in the United States. Until McNeillie's project is complete, readers have to consult the various collections assembled by others. I have compiled the following appendix to assist those who wish to consult one of the essays, stories, or other short pieces discussed in this book. B. J. Kirkpatrick and Stuart N. Clarke's Bibliography of Virginia Woolf lists the contents of all published collections.

"Addison"—CR1, E 3
"Am I a Snob?"—MB
"Anon"—The Gender of Modernism
"Aurora Leigh"—CR2, WW
"Byron and Mr. Briggs"—The Yale Review (1979), E 3
"Countess of Pembroke's Arcadia"—CR2
"Donne After Three Centuries"—CR2
"Eccentrics, The"—E 3
"Elizabethan Lumber Room, The"—CR1
"Four Figures" (four individual essays: "William Cowper," "Beau Brummell," "Mary Wollstonecraft," and "Dorothy Wordsworth")—CR2, "Mary Wollstonecraft" appears in WW
"How It Strikes a Contemporary"—CR1, E 3, CDML
"How Should One Read a Book?"—CR2, CDML
"Intellectual Status of Women, The"—WW, WE
"Jane Austen" —CR1, WW
"Leaning Tower, The"—M, WE
"Leslie Stephen"—CDB
"Lives of the Obscure, The"—CR1
"London Scene, The" (five individual essays: "Docks of London," "Oxford Street Tide," "Abbeys and Cathedrals," "This is the House of Commons," and "Great Men's Houses")—LS, CDML

"Mark on the Wall, The"—CSF

"Memoir of Julian Bell"—printed as an appendix in Quentin Bell's Virginia Woolf: A Biography

"Memories of a Working Women's Guild"—MWG, WE

"Montaigne"—CR1, WE

"Mr. Bennett and Mrs. Brown"—CDB, WE, E 3

"Mr. Conrad: A Conversation"—CDB, E 3

"Mr. Merrick's Novels"—E 2

"Notes on an Elizabethan Play"—CR1

"Ode Written Partly in Prose on Seeing the Name Cutbush Above a Butcher's Shop in Pentonville"—CSF

"Old Bloomsbury"—MB

"On Being Ill"—M, CDML

"On Not Knowing Greek-"-CR1, WE

"Pastons and Chaucer, The"—CR1

"Patron and the Crocus, The"—CR1, WE

"Phases of Fiction"—GR

"Professions for Women"—DM, CDML

"Reader, The"—The Gender of Modernism

"Reading"—CDB

"Richard Hakluyt"—E 3

"Sir Thomas Browne"—E 3

"Sir Walter Raleigh"—GR, E 2

"Sketch of the Past, A"—MB

"Society, A"—CSF

"Strange Elizabethans, The"—CR2

"Street—Haunting: A London Adventure"—DM, CDML

"Terrible Tragedy in Duck Pond, A"—PA

"Thoughts on Peace in an Air Raid"—DM, CDML

"Trafficks and Discoveries" (1906)—E 1

"Trafficks and Discoveries" (1918)—E 2

"Unwritten Novel, An"—CSF

# Notes

## Introduction: Woolfian Resonances

1. Anyone interested in Woolf's reading will find a wealth of material already collected. Mark Hussey's *Virginia Woolf A–Z* is the starting point. Beverly Ann Schlack's *Continuing Presences* conveniently outlines the major allusions in Woolf's novels. This is especially useful for American readers who may have difficulty—for reasons of copyright—in consulting annotated editions of the novels such as those published by Penguin and Oxford. Elizabeth Steele's two guides to the essays, *Virginia Woolf's Literary Sources and Allusions* (1983) and *Virginia Woolf's Rediscovered Essays* (1986) provide a valuable account of the essays and many of the allusions therein. Brenda Silver's *Virginia Woolf's Reading Notebooks* gives access to Woolf's extensive notes, often made in preparation for review- and essay-writing. For scholarship building on this work, Gillian Beer's work on Woolf, especially the essays collected in *Virginia Woolf: The Common Ground and the essay* "The Island and the Aeroplane"consists in her combined attention to literary and social contexts that my own work takes as a model; however, Beer emphasizes Woolf's Victorian inheritance. This inheritance is a secondary part of my book since Woolf had to discard the preconceived notions of the Victorians in order to arrive at her own fresh reading of earlier texts. Also important to my work has been Brenda Silver's, especially her publication of the reading notebooks (1983); her work inaugurated academic analysis of Woolf's reading. By showing the role Woolf herself played in the construction of her reputation, the present study counterbalances Silver's disempowerment of the literary in her recent work, *Virginia Woolf Icon* (1999). In counterpoint to Silver, my work demonstrates how Woolf's formidable revision of literary history creates a model for writing back to the canon Jane De Gay's *Virginia Woolf's Novels and the Literary Past* (2006) appeared too late for me to consult.

2. Brenda Silver's *Virginia Woolf Icon* offers a comprehensive account of Woolf's posthumous reputation.

3. Rosenberg, "Postmodern Literary History," 1114.

4. Froula, *Virginia Woolf and the Bloomsbury Avant-Garde*, 61. Froula's book, which appeared as I was revising this one, shares a similarly literary vision of Woolf's feminism. Unlike this study, which looks at the literary history of four aspects of Woolf's feminism, Froula's wonderful book proceeds chronologically offering readings of each of Woolf's major novels.

5. This book participates in an emerging trend in Woolf studies, presenting a picture of Woolf as an engaged and engaging public intellectual
who is passionate about her reading, her art, and the world around
her. Melba Cuddy-Keane's *Virginia Woolf, the Intellectual, and the
Public Sphere* definitively argues for Woolf's status as a public intellectual;
Froula's *Virginia Woolf and the Bloomsbury Avant-Garde* offers
readings of the novels that support and extend Cuddy-Keane's claims:
she shows us, as Alex Zwerdling did 20 years ago, the deep and
rigorous philosophical and political commitments in Woolf's fiction;
Julia Briggs finally reverses the trend among Woolf's biographers and
puts Woolf's reading at the center of Woolf's life.

6. Although vastly different in method and style, from a feminist vantage
point, W. Jackson Bate's avuncular, genial account of influence in
*The Burden of the Past* amounts to much the same thing as Harold
Bloom's titanic, fraught, Oedipal model. Be the succession ancestral
(Bate's term) or parental (as Bloom would have it), both critics clearly
imagine literary history in strictly patrilineal terms.

7. E.g., Partha Chatterjee notes how Indian nationalists have used
traditional gender divisions to interesting effect, locating Indianness in
the home, a feminine sphere (perceived as) uncontaminated by colonial-
ism. This, in turn, places women in a complex bind: their role as the keep-
ers of tradition can become yet another justification for failing to educate
them formally. Chatterjee, *The Nation and Its Fragments*, 6, 119.

8. E.g., Joyce's nostalgia emerged from exile; Hurston used folk
traditions to teach people to hear the voices of rural blacks;
R. K. Narayan borrowed the tools of the realist novel to articulate the
challenges of the colonial experience; even Gertrude Stein drew
rhetorical power from the American tradition of experimentation and
exploration and, in one of her greatest and wildest works, found a role
for St. Ignatius and St. Theresa. See my "Modernism and Tradition."

9. For more on the invention of tradition, see Eric Hobsbawm's and
Terence Ranger's collection, *The Invention of Tradition*. Edward Said
makes a similar point in *Beginnings*: "Modernism was an aesthetic and
ideological phenomenon that was a response to the crisis of what
could be called *filiation*—linear, biologically grounded process, that
which ties children to their parents—which produced the counter-crisis
within modernism of affiliation, that is, those creeds, philosophies,
and visions re-assembling the world in new non-familial ways" (Said,
*Beginnings*, xiii).

10. Dimock, "Toward a Theory of Resonance," 1062, 1064.

11. Ibid., 1067.

12. Forster, *Aspects of the Novel*, 9.

13. Gilbert and Gubar, *The Madwoman in the Attic*, 188.

14. Where Gilbert and Gubar see "Lycidas" as a male text, locked away
from women's eyes, I see it as an occasion for Woolf to imagine the
text in the process of being written.

15. Here is the relevant *OED* definition: "bogy,[1] bogey.": "Found in literature only recently; old people vouched (1887) for its use in the nursery as early as 1825, but only as proper name (sense 1). Possibly a southern nursery form of *bogle, boggle,* and *boggard,* or going back like them to a simpler form which, as mentioned under BOG and BOGLE, may be a variant of *bugge,* BUG 'terror, bugbear, scarecrow.' But in the absence of evidence, positive statements concerning its relation to these words cannot be made. (That they are connected with the Slavonic *bog* 'god,' is a mere fancy from the similarity of form, without any evidence.)" *The Oxford English Dictionary.* 2nd ed. OED online. Oxford: Oxford University Press, 1989.

16. Here is the *OED*'s account of the golf term's origins: "bogy,[1] bogey," "Bogey, *golf*.": "The following story reproduces the current account of the origin of the term: One popular song at least has left its permanent effect on the game of golf. That song is 'The Bogey Man.' In 1890 Dr. Thos. Browne, R.N., the hon. secretary of the Great Yarmouth Club, was playing against a Major Wellman, the match being against the 'ground score,' which was the name given to the scratch value of each hole. The system of playing against the 'ground score' was new to Major Wellman, and he exclaimed, thinking of the song of the moment, that his mysterious and well-nigh invincible opponent was a regular 'bogey-man.' The name 'caught on' at Great Yarmouth, and to-day 'Bogey' is one of the most feared opponents on all the courses that acknowledge him (1908 *M.A.P.* 25 July 78/1)." "bogey, *golf*," *OED.*

17. The angled brackets indicate an insertion made by Virginia Woolf to the manuscript of *The Pargiters* (P, xxvii). *The Pargiters,* was not completed; portions of it became *The Years* and other portions informed *Three Guineas.*

18. Froula, *Virginia Woolf and the Bloomsbury Avant-Garde*, 18.

19. For praise of the late Woolf, see especially Brenda Silver, "The Authority of Anger," and Jessica Berman, *Modernist Fiction.* Melba Cuddy-Keane's *Virginia Woolf, the Intellectual, and the Public Sphere* by contrast, emphasizes the 1920s.

20. Rudikoff, *Ancestral Houses*, 1.

## Chapter 1   O Sister Swallow: Sapphic Fragments as English Literature in Virginia Woolf

1. See, e.g., Carlston, *Thinking Fascism*; Carroll, "To Crush Him in Our Own Country"; Froula, *Virginia Woolf and the Bloomsbury Avant-Garde*; Marcus, *Art and Anger*; Silver, "The Authority of Anger"; and Swanson, "An Antigone Complex?"

2. Adams, *Colonial Odysseys*, 183. Though critics have explored the specific feminist lessons Woolf took from her reading of Greek as well

as her aesthetic and rhetorical debt to Greek, no one has explored the wider politics of her reading of Greek, especially how her study of Greek shaped her revision of nationalism and her exploration of the possibility of being an antinationalist English writer. Feminist essays on Woolf's use of Antigone in *Three Guineas* have been central to my thinking on this project. However, they focus on the rhetoric of Woolf's pamphlet, taking her antifascist stand (and, by implication, her attitude to nation and nationalism) for granted.

3. Lee, *Virginia Woolf*, 144.

4. For an account of Woolf's delusion that the birds were singing in Greek, see "Old Bloomsbury," *Moments of Being*, 162. For a skeptical reading of this episode, see Lee, *Virginia Woolf*, 195–97.

5. McNeillie, "Bloomsbury," 2. Although Woolf's brief work with Pater's sister, Clara, who tutored her in Latin and Greek in 1897, suggests the artificiality of distinguishing between Pater and classics.

6. Adams, *Colonial Odysseys*, 184. Adams's chapter emphasizes the development of Woolf's gradual emergence into an anti-imperial consciousness, going against those who see continuity across her career. In place of that interpretation, Adams foregrounds *The Voyage Out*'s many differences from the rest of Woolf's work. Although his is a developmental argument, he does not write about her novels after *Orlando* (1928). He offers readings of a 1903 diary entry, "her boldest declaration of the continuity" (Adams, *Colonial Odysseys*, 184), "Dialogue upon Mount Pentelicus" (c. 1906), and a scene of Rachel Vinrace reading Gibbon to chart Woolf's move from a sense that the English are more Greek than modern Greeks (Adams, *Colonial Odysseys*, 186) to equivocation and confusion. For Adams, inconsistencies in the significance of allusions to Greece in *The Voyage Out* are an "indication of her own lingering Hellenism and youthful confusion" (Adams, *Colonial Odysseys*, 197).

7. For a comprehensive catalogue of allusions and quotations, see both essays by Fowler, "Moments and Metamorphoses" and "On Not Knowing Greek."

8. Guillory, *Cultural Capital*, 96–97. Meanwhile, as Guillory notes, the growing middle class grew increasingly skeptical of the curriculum. E.g., John Locke writes, "Can there be anything more ridiculous, than that a Father should waste his own Money, and his Son's time, in setting him to learn the Roman language; when at the same time he designs for him a Trade, wherein he having no use of Latin, fails not to forget that little which he brought from school" (qtd Guillory, *Cultural Capital*, 96). Guillory continues, "But Locke goes on to concede that a knowledge of Latin is of course the endowment of every gentleman" (Guillory, *Cultural Capital*, 96).

9. Guillory, *Cultural Capital*, 43.

10. For a brief account of the eighteenth-century aristocratic version of the classics, see Colley, *Britons*, 167–70.

11. Cultural histories of Victorian and Georgian England by Linda Dowling, Richard Jenkyns, and Yopie Prins demonstrate how the reading class' engagement with classical Greek literature shaped the notion of nationhood in England.

12. E.g., in the opening pages of *The Woodlanders* (1887), Thomas Hardy writes that the village of Little Hintock "was one of those sequestered spots outside the gates of the world . . . yet where, from time to time, dramas of a grandeur and unity truly Sophoclean are enacted in the real" (Hardy, *The Woodlanders*, 7).

13. Said, *Beginnings*, 10.

14. Her review of Leonard Merrick's novels *While Paris Laughed* and *Conrad in Quest of His Youth* appeared in the *TLS* on July 4, 1918.

15. E.g., Septimus Smith, the young veteran in *Mrs. Dalloway*, reads Shakespeare, Dante, and Aeschylus. His reading, like Woolf's in this letter, marks him both as a traditional and as an ambitious reader, a quality he shares with Woolf.

16. But she is not quoting from *Measure for Measure*, but from *Othello*. Emilia says "Oh she was heavenly true" of Desdemona shortly after her murder (L, n. 2.220). Woolf's carelessness about the source of her quotation is revealing. Her unconscious or buried linking of herself with Desdemona is self-serving but not wholly inaccurate. Like Desdemona, Woolf casts herself here as the good daughter who sees virtue in someone just outside—but not very far outside—her circle's attention, be that Saxon or Merrick.

17. Fowler, "Moments and Metamorphoses," 220.

18. Leonard Merrick (1864–1939) married Hope Butler Wilkins, the daughter of an Anglican clergyman. (Baker, "Merrick, Leonard [1864–1939]," 392.)

19. Sellers, "Virginia Woolf's Diaries and Letters," 118.

20. Beer, "The Island and the Aeroplane," 269.

21. Ibid., 276.

22. Ibid., 281.

23. For a discussion of the class bias here, see Childers, "Virginia Woolf on the Outside Looking Down," 61–79.

24. For more on Case, see Alley, "A Rediscovered Eulogy," 290–301.

25. When Woolf began writing *The Common Reader*, she initially conceived of its first three essays as one (Johnston, "The Whole Achievement," 148). Woolf's initial willingness to lump "On Not Knowing Greek" with "The Pastons and Chaucer" and "The Elizabethan Lumber Room" underscores the way in which Woolf could read Greek literature *as* English literature. As late as 1932, she could still write of contemporary Greece that all remains as it was "in the time of Chaucer or Homer" (D, 4.92), as if Chaucer and Homer were not separated by the continent of Europe and two millennia. In *The Common Reader*, Woolf ultimately divided her essays on Chaucer, the Greeks, and the Elizabethan travel narratives collected by Richard Hakluyt into

three; in each case, a major theme of the essay is a past that is both distant and near. With this theme, Woolf marked out original territory.

26. Jenkyns, *The Victorians and Ancient Greece*, 78.

27. As Linda Dowling shows, this version of the classics was particularly inspiring for liberals, gay men, and also women. One of the remarkable features of Bloomsbury was its inclusion of Virginia and Vanessa in the heretofore all-male Apostolic conversation. In contrast to Bloomsbury, many Oxbridge men dated the decline of Hellenism to the rise of women's colleges, as if the mere presence of women in adjacent institutions weakened their fraternal bonds.

28. See Adams, *Colonial Odysseys*, 192. Following John Mepham, Adams writes, "Woolf admires the Greeks because communal forms of mourning made it possible for them 'to directly express intense emotion.' "

29. Turner, "British Politics and the Demise of the Roman Republic: 1700–1939," 116. See Kenner, *The Pound Era*, 41–53, 61–63, for a discussion of Pound and Sappho in this context.

30. Like most of all her fellow high modernists, Woolf tends to overlook comic figures. Reviewers of *Three Guineas*, on the other hand, were less anxious to appear highbrow, and they used comedy to best her in the game of allusions, linking Woolf not to the tragic Antigone, but to the comic Lysistrata. At first glance, the allusion seems apt. Lysistrata's explicit purpose is the same as Woolf's: persuading men to prevent war. However, unlike Antigone's appeal to principle, Lysistrata persuades the women of Athens to withhold sex from their husbands until there is peace. Linking Woolf's pamphlet to Aristophanes' farce deflates Woolf's serious intent. Calling her "the New Lysistrata" as one headline did, thereby linking her to a famously intelligent courtesan, trades on familiar stereotypes of Woolf and Bloomsbury as sexually deviant. The headline pointedly refuses to engage with Woolf's passionate equation of women thinking under patriarchy with prostitution or with her advocacy of female chastity, moral, intellectual, and sexual. Under the subheading "The New Lysistrata," the author of this *TLS* review writes: "In essence, the question propounded is that of Lysistrata—how can women help to stop war?—but the simple levity of Aristophanes's answer naturally bears no resemblance to Mrs. Woolf's treatment of a matter that brooks no laughter. Humour she uses, but her seriousness is profound." Following suit, K. John's review in the *New Statesman and Nation* the next Saturday took "The New Lysistrata" for its title. Both reviews are reprinted in Majumdar and McLaurin, *Virginia Woolf. The Critical Heritage*, 400–01, 405.

31. Pound, *Personae, 112.*

32. Collecott, *H. D. and Sapphic Modernism*, 10.

33. D. H. Lawrence's *Etruscan Places* expresses a similar love of an ancient, unknowable, and uncorrupted civilization. Though the content of his fantasies differ, Lawrence, like H. D., revels in imagining an idealized ancient world that is not mainstream.

34. H. D., "Eurydice," *Collected Poems*, 55. Collecott's study of H. D. and Sappho includes a comprehensive index of direct allusions to and translations of Sapphic fragments. The lines from "Eurydice" quoted here are neither; instead they are an attempt to capture the Sapphic voice—a move that has closer parallels to Woolf's ventriloquisms than any direct imitation. For an important comparison of H. D.'s more open lesbianism with Woolf's cautious "sapphism," see Collecott, *H. D. and Sapphic Modernism*, 98–102. For another modernist version of Sappho, see Mary Barnard's beautiful imagist translation.

35. Stein, "What are Master-Pieces and Why Are There So Few of Them?" 358.

36. Yeats, "A Prayer for My Daughter," 58.

37. Yeats, "No Second Troy," 6–7.

38. Eliot, *The Waste Land*, 104.

39. Joyce, *Ulysses*, 298.

40. In looking at Woolf as a student of literature, particularly Greek literature, I draw upon the work of Alice Fox and Brenda Silver, both attentive to Woolf's efforts to overcome her girlhood feeling that, as a woman, she had no right to comment on men's writing: "What Right have I, a woman to read all these things that men have done? They would laugh if they saw me" (PA, 178). This sentiment, expressed at the age of 21, took some overcoming.

41. Smyth, *Aeschylus*, 37.

42. Benjamin, *Illuminations* 75.

43. Ibid., 78, 79.

44. Ibid., 82.

45. Ibid., 74.

46. Ibid.

47. Ibid., 75.

48. McNeillie, CR1, 245 n.17.

49. Benjamin, *Illuminations*, 73.

50. DuBois, *Sappho Is Burning*, 37.

51. Benjamin, *Illuminations*, 76.

52. DuBois, *Sappho Is Burning*, 37.

53. Ibid.

54. Ibid., 43.

55. Ibid., 46.

56. Ibid., 53.

57. Rayor, trans. *Sappho's Lyre*, 81.

58. DuBois, *Sappho Is Burning*, 46.

59. Monte, "Ancients and Moderns in *Mrs. Dalloway*," 391.

60. The recitation does not come naturally to Lily Briscoe. Lily's skeptical reaction to Mrs. Ramsay's bow acknowledging the compliment insures that we also see how strangely old-fashioned this elegant performance is.

61. In contrast, though Mr. Ramsay has poems running through his head throughout the novel, when he reads Scott, he finishes the chapter and feels "that he had been arguing with somebody, and had got the better of him" (TTL, 180).

62. And, of course, Mrs. Ramsay's associative reading strengthens the biographical association of the Ramsay's with Woolf's parents, as Leslie Stephen was a renowned Alpinist. For a more critical reading of Woolf's use of this sonnet, see Collecott, *H. D. and Sapphic Modernism*, 230–31.

63. Woolf was writing *Mrs. Dalloway*, a novel that alludes several times to *Cymbeline*, as she wrote "On Not Knowing Greek," so these disembodied eyes may allude to Imogen. In *Cymbeline*, Imogen describes how she would watch her husband voyage into exile: "I would have broke mine eye-strings, crack'd them but / To look upon him, till the diminution / Of space had pointed him sharp as my needle" (Shakespeare, *Cymbeline*, 1.3.19–21, *The Riverside Shakespeare*, 1524).

64. As Gillian Beer writes in reference to *Between the Acts*, in Woolf's work, "Poems do not survive intact in memory but single lines are absorbed and adapted. Past literature permeates the work, but as 'orts, scraps, fragments.' The canon of English literature is no tight island but a series of dispersed traces constantly rewritten in need" (Beer, "The Island and the Aeroplane," 286). Steven Monte takes issue with just this emphasis on revision. Although his remark that Woolf's intertextual moments "are not necessarily tense, or intense" (Monte, "Ancients and Moderns in *Mrs. Dalloway*," 588) is valuable, his subsequent use of the metaphor of "party conversation, from passing greeting to tête-à-têtes" to characterize Woolf's allusions is perhaps too dismissive. I also want to quibble with Beer—for fragments are not rewritten. Rather, they are broken into pieces so tiny that they can fit the new situation. Woolf's use of fragments strikes a balance between preservation and transformation.

65. Guillory, *Cultural Capital*, 43.

66. Beer, "The Island and the Aeroplane," 283.

67. The article "No More Horses" by Jane Marcus (collected in *Art and Anger*) accepts and embraces the description of *Three Guineas* as propaganda. Marcus shows one way in which Woolf tries to reconcile herself to the shift in the essayist's function toward direct political comment: understanding that shift is a temporary response to Hitler and the rise of fascism. Marcus's reading starts from these sentences in one of Woolf's footnotes: "If we use art to propagate political opinions, we must force the artist to clip and cabin his gift to do us a cheap and passing service. Literature will suffer the same mutilation that the mule has suffered; and there will be no more horses" (3G, 170 n.39). Marcus interprets this metaphor—a caution against propagandizing more than an endorsement of it—as if it were

Woolf's nonironic statement of a commitment to use art for political purposes. Furthermore, the sentence on which Marcus bases her argument in "No More Horses" does not appear in the main text of *Three Guineas* but in a footnote. In silently moving these sentences from the margins of Woolf's pamphlet to the center of her own argument, Marcus undoes the complexity of Woolf's use of the footnote throughout *Three Guineas*. Marcus has located one of Woolf's few published concessions that propaganda has a legitimate role at all—but in willfully misreading Woolf's tone and in failing to note the textual role of the footnote, Marcus erases Woolf's deliberate ambiguity.

68. Swanson, "An Antigone Complex?" 33.

69. Harrison, *Reminiscences of a Student's Life*, 11.

70. See Esty, *A Shrinking Island*, 25, 26. Esty documents the increasing popularity in the 1930s and 1940s of a "Little England" outlook that Harrison alludes to here.

71. Gillian Beer notes: "the identification of England with the island is already, and from the start, a fiction . . . Scotland and Wales are suppressed in this description and Ireland is corralled within that very different group, 'the British Isles' " (Beer, "The Island and the Aeroplane," 269).

72. Thus, in Woolf's view Joseph Conrad is not English, but "a gentleman of Polish extraction" (CR1, 214), which, to her mind, explains the presence of "something exotic about [his] genius" (CR1, 234). And "one thing is certain—whatever the American man may be, he is not English" (MB, 115) whereas Turgenev's novels achieve a balance that is "extremely rare, especially in English fiction" (CDB, 57). Elsewhere Woolf writes that she has "no wish to be 'English' on the same terms that you yourself are 'English' " (3G, 101). Erin Carlston argues of this statement on being "English." "Instead of dispensing with the nation, Woolf wants to make it her nation, her civilization, to be English on her own terms," "challenging the assumption that patriotism is equivalent to love of country," proposing an alternate, nonpatriarchal love of nation (Carlston, *Thinking Fascism*, 157, 155).

73. Caserio, "Queer Passions, Queer Citizenship," 171.

74. For lesbians and gay men in the late-twentieth-century United States, e.g., "as long as the official nation . . . police[s] nonnormative . . . sexual practices, the lesbian, gay, feminist, and queer communities . . . do not have the privilege to disregard national identity" (Berlant and Freeman, "Queer Nationality," 154). Though many commentators focus on an antagonistic relationship between insider-citizen and outsider-queers, Benedict Anderson and Partha Chatterjee retain tentative hope in the usefulness of the idea of nation.

75. Pandey, "In Defense of the Fragment," 571.

## CHAPTER 2    THE MEMORY PALACE AND
### THE LUMBER ROOM: WOOLF'S
### RENAISSANCE MISCELLANY

1. The letters, covering three generations, were written between c. 1420 and 1504.
2. Hakluyt, *Voyages and Discoveries*, 31.
3. Beeching, Introduction to *Voyages and Discoveries*, 20. Hakluyt was reprinted by the Hakluyt Society (Glasgow, 1903–05), and by Everyman's Library (London, 1908).
4. In these texts, Professor Walter Raleigh (1861–1922) remains silent on the irony of his academic interest in Elizabethan exploration given that he shares a name with one of England's most celebrated seamen. To avoid confusion between the Victorian professor and the Elizabethan explorer, I refer to the latter as Professor Raleigh.
5. Qtd in Quinn, *The Hakluyt Handbook*, 2.582. Raleigh, *The English Voyages of the Sixteenth Century*, 136. For Jack Beeching, a poet and the editor of the current (1972) Penguin selection, the work has mainly been used "as a source of rattling good yarns" (Beeching, Introduction to *Voyages and Discoveries*, 9): his view of the collection's enduring appeal comes closest to Woolf's.
6. Raleigh, *The English Voyages of the Sixteenth Century*, 29. Leslie Stephen, by contrast, heartily approved of Froude, calling him " 'the best interpreter' of the 'heroic spirit' of the Elizabethan seamen" (qtd in Fox, *English Renaissance*, 33).
7. Raleigh, *The English Voyages of the Sixteenth Century*, 29.
8. Beeching, Introduction to *Voyages and Discoveries*, 11.
9. Greenblatt, *Marvelous Possessions*, 8.
10. Jack Beeching's 1972 selection for Penguin, which I have used here, is called *Voyages and Discoveries*.
11. John S. Rickard argues that Joyce was drawn to Bruno because of Joyce's "hereticophilia" (Rickard, *Joyce's Book of Memory*, 8). Though too agnostic for an explicit interest in heretics, Woolf's love of eccentrics might have drawn her to Bruno. But, with no knowledge of Italian and a strong resistance to the kind of system building to which Bruno—and Joyce—aspired, it is no surprise that she ignored Bruno.
12. Fox, *English Renaissance*, 20; D, 3.271.
13. Bartolovich, "Consumerism, or the Cultural Logic of Late Cannibalism," 228.
14. Ibid., 229.
15. From Woolf's essay "Notes on an Elizabethan Play" (also 1925).
16. E.g., Alice Fox traces Woolf's use of "wood lion" to a narrative in *Trafficks and Discoveries* (Fox, *English Renaissance*, 35).
17. Fox, *English Renaissance*, 22. Fox catalogs additional parallels. E.g., the scene in which Terence and Rachel declare their love "has long been recognized as one Woolf found in Sir Walter Raleigh's

*Discovery of the Large, Rich, and Beautiful Empire of Guiana* (1596), one of the accounts in Hakluyt's *Voyages*. Holtby commented some fifty years ago on Woolf's 'plagiarism' (78–79), and Bazin (52–53) has amplified Holtby's argument by pointing out 'the themes of conquest and virginity' common to Raleigh's account of Guiana and Woolf's treatment of her heroine" (Fox, *English Renaissance*, 30).

18. Fox, *English Renaissance*, 31. Fox is tentative in linking Willoughby Vinrace's name to Sir Hugh Willoughby but, as Woolf mentions Sir Hugh's fate in her 1918 review of Froude and in the 1919 essay "Reading," it seems likely that she intended the allusion in the earlier novel.

19. Fox, *English Renaissance*, 25.

20. Later, looking at a letter from him, Helen Ambrose thinks, "Yes, there lay Willoughby, curt, inexpressive, perpetually jocular, robbing a whole continent of mystery, enquiring after his daughter's manners and morals" (VO, 196).

21. Raleigh, *The English Voyages of the Sixteenth Century*, 9–10.

22. Froude, *English Seamen in the Sixteenth Century*, 3–4.

23. E.g., the leader of one expedition reports that he left one of his men behind: "William Leedes the jeweler [remains] in service with the kind Zelabdim Echebar in Fatehpur, who did entertain him very well, and gave him an house and five slaves, a horse and every day six shillings in money" (Hakluyt, *Voyages and Discoveries*, 258).

24. Fox notes that, in general, allusions are increasingly given to men as the novel gets revised. Fox, *English Renaissance*, 26–29.

25. Ibid., 23.

26. Raleigh, *The English Voyages of the Sixteenth Century*, 94.

27. Hakluyt, *Voyages and Discoveries*, 177.

28. Froude, *English Seamen in the Sixteenth Century*, 88.

29. Hakluyt, *Voyages and Discoveries*, 178.

30. Ibid., 178, 179.

31. Froude, *English Seamen in the Sixteenth Century*, 76.

32. Raleigh, *The English Voyages of the Sixteenth Century*, 83.

33. Hakluyt, *Voyages and Discoveries*, 180.

34. Raleigh, *The English Voyages of the Sixteenth Century*, 94.

35. For a discussion of the transformation of wonder and ignorance into the impulse to possess, see Greenblatt, *Marvelous Possessions*, 9–14, 67–70.

36. These essays are "Sir Walter Raleigh" (1917), "Trafficks and Discoveries" (1918), "Reading" (1919, first published posthumously), and "Sir Thomas Browne" (1923).

37. Greenblatt, *Marvelous Possessions*, 27.

38. Froude emphasizes the centrality of the reformation, as Raleigh notes, and focuses primarily on the defeat of the Spanish Armada, Francis Drake, and John Hawkins. John Hawkins opened up the slave trade. Francis Drake, Hawkins's cousin, made the empire possible by circumnavigating the globe and thus claiming all corners of it as

accessible to England. Alice Fox suspects that Froude's religious fervor and his failure to condemn the slave trade aroused Woolf's distaste, and yet she is rightly careful to note that, at the time of the review (1918), Woolf's politics were not yet what they would become: "I do not mean to overstate the case for Woolf's social consciousness in this review of Froude's book. It is clear, e.g., that she was not yet ready to decry in print the exploitation of the poor of other nations. But her social conscience was sufficiently developed for her to see the value of trade in the rise of a middle class in England. . . . Woolf's emphasis on the common man is not unexpected at this point in her life [1918]" (Fox, *English Renaissance*, 36).

39. Raleigh, *The English Voyages of the Sixteenth Century*, 152–53, 163.

40. Ibid., 37.

41. Professor Raleigh writes, "The single grave charge brought against his [Shakespeare's] competence as a navigator is based on the two allusions in the *Tempest* to the 'glasses' formerly used as a measure of time at sea, and now superseded by bells. From a comparison of these two passages it seems that Shakespeare believed that the glasses measured hours, whereas they measured half-hours" (Raleigh, *The English Voyages of the Sixteenth Century*, 177).

42. Raleigh, *The English Voyages of the Sixteenth Century*, 166. Stukeley, disappointed in not getting a small post in Ireland, offered his services to the pope and died fighting for the Spanish against the Moors in the battle of Alcazar in 1578.

43. Raleigh, *The English Voyages of the Sixteenth Century*, 31.

44. Raleigh, *The English Voyages of the Sixteenth Century*, 107.

45. The story of *Revenge* does not appear in Froude either. His book ends with the defeat of the Spanish Armada in 1588. Woolf did know the story, however; she mentions it in passing in her 1917 review of Raleigh's works: "It is well, perhaps, to begin by reading the last fight of the *Revenge*, the letters about Cadiz and Guiana, and that to his wife written in the expectation of his death" (E, 2.92). In this context, the story is but one item in a list, familiar and perhaps somewhat discredited for being so.

46. Hakluyt, *Voyages and Discoveries*, 237.

47. Ibid., 238.

48. Ibid., 241–42.

49. Raleigh, *The English Voyages of the Sixteenth Century*, 59.

50. Woolf makes a similar distinction in her discussion of Defoe in "Phases of Fiction" (1928). See my "Pleasure and Belief."

51. Hakluyt, *Voyages and Discoveries*, 35.

52. Recent scholars have made the same point. See Timothy Sweet, "Economy, Ecology, and Utopia."

53. Hakluyt, *Voyages and Discoveries*, 38. Some recent scholars have argued that comments on the nakedness of indigenous Americans may

be as much about a potential market for the English wool surplus as Christian doctrine: "The 'nakedness' of the savages was alternately seen as a sign of their barbarity, and an indication of an attractive market opportunity" (Bartolovich, "Consumerism, or the Cultural Logic of Late Cannibalism," 217). See also Timothy Sweet ("Economy, Ecology, and Utopia") and Joan Pong Linton ("Jack of Newbery").

54. Greenblatt discusses the same episode from one of Martin Frobisher's voyages, in which English sailors watch the chaste behavior of a pair of captives (male and female). For Greenblatt, the episode exemplifies the willingness to read signs that cannot justifiably be read, it shows how "the little that the English learn from their captive seems over-whelmed by all that they do not understand" (Greenblatt, *Marvelous Possessions*, 117).

55. As we see not only here and in Miss Julia Hedge's "Oh damn . . . why didn't they leave room for an Eliot or a Brontë" (JR, 106) but also in Mrs. Ramsay's "We are in the hands of the Lord" (TTL, 63).

56. On Woolf's ignorance of the equator, Fox writes, "Leonard's superior knowledge, Virginia's ignorance, were facts of their lives. Although sometimes she could joke about it, her ignorance of rather basic facts made for difficulties (as, for example, when Leonard had to explain the Equator—D. 1 May 1918—to the thirty-six-year-old Virginia)" (Fox, *English Renaissance*, 5).

57. Hakluyt, *Voyages and Discoveries*, 186.

58. Augustine, *Confessions*, 185.

59. Yates, *The Art of Memory*, 18, and Fentress and Wickham, *Social Memory*, 8–15. For an excellent account of Yates, see Hutton, "The Art of Memory Reconceived."

60. Yates, *The Art of Memory*, 161.

61. In "The Art of Memory Reconceived," Patrick Hutton argues that if we see the art of memory as a way to make "paradigms of cultural under-standing," we begin to see "the larger significance of this topic" (Hutton, "The Art of Memory Reconceived," 372). For Hutton, Freud's search for the origins of memory and forgetting share something with the Renaissance magus (Hutton, "The Art of Memory Reconceived," 386).

62. When memory images enter the culture—in habits of mind, books, standardized education, or architecture—they become part of the col-lective memory. Maurice Halbwachs was the first to identify what we now call collective memory, and Pierre Nora's multivolume project connects the collective memory of France to places by way of a term—*lieux de mémoire*—he derived from his reading of Yates. Like Yates and Mary Carruthers, Halbwachs and Nora are naming and identifying as an object of study a phenomenon that has gone on for centuries. In "Between Memory and History," Pierre Nora attributes both the inspiration for the term and his use of the *topos* to his reading of Yates. For an important complementary view of social memory, one more

focused on ritual and body memories than buildings and texts, see Connerton, *How Societies Remember*, 1.

63. In their recent study of social memory, an idea deeply indebted to Halbwachs's study of collective memory, Fentress and Wickham discuss the methodological problems associated with studying the collective memory of women: "it is notoriously difficult even to tape-record women remembering in the presence of their husbands: most men interrupt, devalue their wives' memories, take over the interview, tell their own stories instead, or even, most bizarrely, themselves recount their wives' life stories" (Fentress and Wickham, *Social Memory*, 140). Thus, the idea of social memory, already a difficult one to document, may in fact conflict with or even obscure the memories of women. I.e., social memory may vary along class, race, religious, and gender lines, variations that often put social memory in tension with official, national memory.

64. Yates, *The Art of Memory*, 212.

65. Crook, *The British Museum*, 190; see also Harris, *The British Museum*.

66. Crook, *The British Museum*, 190.

67. Ibid., 191.

68. Knowles, "Virginia Woolf's Dome Symbolism," 89.

## Chapter 3   A Feminist Public Sphere?
## Virginia Woolf's Revisions of the Eighteenth Century

1. McDonald, *British Literary Culture and Publishing Practice*, 53; Rainey, *Institutions of Modernism*, 3.

2. Froula, *Virginia Woolf and the Bloomsbury Avant-Garde*, 2.

3. That first *TLS* piece, "Literary Geography," reviews Lewis Melville's *The Thackeray Country* and F. G. Kitton's *The Dickens Country* and is reprinted in E, 1.32–36.

4. McNeillie, Introduction to *The Essays of Virginia Woolf*, 2.xi.

5. Ibid., 3.xi.

6. McDonald, *British Literary Culture and Publishing Practice*, 129.

7. Ezell, *Writing Women's Literary History*, 37.

8. Qtd in May, *Critical Times*, 125.

9. McNeillie, Introduction to *The Essays of Virginia Woolf*, 2.xi.

10. Leonard Woolf collected many of the essays posthumously in unannotated volumes; feminist critics—notably Rachel Bowlby and Michèle Barrett—have contributed other, more political and feminist collections complementing Leonard's more belletristic selection; Andrew McNeillie has completed four of a projected six volumes of Woolf's complete essays, including all reviews, notices, essays, and journalism. Barrett's selection includes information on the date and venue of the initial publication, as do Bowlby's two volumes. Bowlby also includes ample contextual note. McNeillie's is the only full scholarly edition although it remains incomplete.

11. May, *Critical Times*, 159, 194; emphasis added.

12. Nonetheless, the trend has been for critics to overlook Woolf's journalism. Three notable exceptions offer useful overviews of Woolf's literary journalism: Beth Rosenberg's book on Woolf and Samuel Johnson uses Harold Bloom's model of the anxiety of influence to trace Woolf's connection to Johnson through their shared interest in "the common reader"; Michael Kaufman attributes the difference between Woolf's comfortable, inclusive attitude to her audience and Eliot's combative didacticism to the contrast between Woolf's early establishment in the *TLS* and Eliot's efforts to become a regular contributor; Leila Brosnan examines correspondence between Woolf and her editors to argue that, in fact, the editors did not alter her style or content as much as has been alleged.

13. Kenner, qtd in Sapathy, "Eliot's Early Criticism," 33; Kenner, *The Invisible Poet*, 85–86.

14. Sapathy, "Eliot's Early Criticism," 37. See also Diepeveen, " 'I Can Have More than Enough Power to Satisfy Me.' "

15. Brosnan, *Reading Virginia Woolf's Essays and Journalism*, 61.

16. Ibid., 62, 65.

17. Qtd in Sapathy, "Eliot's Early Criticism," 38. Recent efforts by John Gross (himself the editor of the *TLS* from 1974 to 1981), Sapathy, and others begin to suggest that the *TLS* should be remembered not only for its "prevailing critical inanity" and "impressionistic and fatuous reviews of traditional poetry" but also for editor Bruce Richmond's interest in young modernists, especially Woolf and Eliot (Sapathy, "Eliot's Early Criticism," 33). See also John Gross's *The Modern Moment*, an anthology of reviews by and of the modernists from the *TLS*, assembled in an attempt to rebut charges of the Supplement's resistance to modernism. As Isaiah Berlin notes in an interview, Richmond "was an 'establishment' figure. . . . The paper under him was civilized, decent, informative, but somewhat conventional too. . . . But Richmond did commission such genuine writers as Virginia Woolf." (Sapathy, "Sir Isaiah Berlin Remembers Bruce Richmond, T. S. Eliot and Ezra Pound," 19–20.) While neither Richmond nor Woolf held anything like Addison's cultural position, the centrality of the *TLS* in the 1920s was analogous to that of the *Spectator*. For more on the founding of the *TLS* and Richmond's tenure, see Adolf Wood. Wood's chief source is the *TLS's* fiftieth anniversary number (January 18, 1952).

18. For more on the professional, historical, and theoretical significance of the Hogarth Press, see Cucullu, "Retailing the Female Intellectual."

19. The idea for the press was first mentioned in Woolf's diary on her birthday (January 25) in 1915; their first publication, Virginia Woolf's story, "The Mark on the Wall," and Leonard Woolf's "The Three Jews" appeared in the summer of 1917. Woolf, *Diary*, 1.28, 31 n.90.

20. Habermas, *The Structural Transformation*, 60.

21. Habermas has inspired a group of Anglo-American feminist scholars to explore the relationship between the emergence of the public sphere and gender. These feminists believe that the principles of rational critical debate can be used to justify feminist arguments. For them, Habermas's account of public discourse as "actual, historical, and particular" means that any social norm can be challenged, that its "validation is always contingent upon the outcome of the next round of arguments" (Meehan, Introduction to *Feminists Read Habermas*, 5). Since *The Structural Transformation* fails to take gender into account, feminist critiques have focused on uncovering the gendered implications of its arguments; e.g., in distinguishing between public and private, Habermas fails to acknowledge the extent to which these spheres are interrelated or that "men have always had a legitimate place in both" (Pateman, *The Disorder of Women*, 183). Furthermore, "Habermas's formulation effaces the way in which the bourgeois public sphere from the outset worked to rule out all interests that would not or could not lay claim to their own universality" (Landes, "The Public and the Private Sphere," 97). Habermas was slow to recognize the merits of feminist arguments because he saw them as representing "only" women, a subcategory of the "universal" programs he was interested in. His initial blindness to gender is part of a larger reluctance to recognize the role of social movements and group interests different from those of the bourgeoisie or to look critically at how the term "universal" has tended to mask the interests of the urban male bourgeoisie. Summarizing this general lack, Craig Calhoun notes "the absence of social movements from Habermas' account" (Calhoun, Introduction to *Habermas and the Public Sphere*, 37.) However, true to his professed interest in debate, Habermas responds to these critiques in *The Inclusion of the Other* (1998), in which he writes that "the consistent actualization of the system of rights" will not happen "without social movements and political struggles," a claim he demonstrates through a discussion of the history of feminism. (Habermas, *The Inclusion of the Other*, 208.)
22. Hoberman, "Woman in the British Museum Reading Room," 87.
23. Habermas, *The Structural Transformation*, 87.
24. Stephen, *English Literature and Society*, 3, 30–31.
25. Ibid., 15.
26. Habermas, *The Structural Transformation*, 27.
27. Stephen, *English Literature and Society*, 27, 26.
28. For a comprehensive study of this topic, see Rosenberg, *Virginia Woolf and Samuel Johnson.*
29. Stephen, *English Literature and Society*, 3, 130; for Woolf on Defoe, see Woolf, "Phases of Fiction," *Granite & Rainbow*, 93–145.
30. Stephen, *English Literature and Society*, 42.
31. For a related view of Mary Datchet, see Cucullu, "Retailing the Female Intellectual."

32. Delivered at the Memoir Club around 1922 (MB, 157) and published posthumously in *Moments of Being*.
33. Qtd in McDonald, *British Literary Culture and Publishing Practice*, 129.
34. Brosnan, *Reading Virginia Woolf's Essays and Journalism*, 47.
35. McDonald, *British Literary Culture and Publishing Practice*, 52. Woolf's choice of venues for her publication marked a political difference as well. Woolf did not take the route of the aesthete, as her friend Lytton Strachey did, nor did she take that of Wyndham Lewis and Rebecca West, who built their early reputations as firebrands. The misanthropic, energetic rhetoric of Lewis's manifesto in *Blast* (1914) with its lists of people and institutions to be blasted or blessed, was alien to Woolf. Elitist sentiments pepper Woolf's diaries and letters, but Woolf's public persona did not actively contribute to the attack on mass culture that characterized Lewis's *Blast*, Lawrence's call to bomb the suburbs, or Eliot's shivers at the thought of the "young man carbuncular." Instead, Woolf's ideas of authorship were derived from the eighteenth-century belief that witty sensible criticism could reach, educate, communicate with, and influence a large audience of common readers.
36. For more on Woolf and British *Vogue*, see Garrity, "Selling Culture to the 'Civilized' " and "Virginia Woolf, Intellectual Harlotry, and 1920s British *Vogue*," and Luckhurst, "Vogue . . . Is Going to Take Up Mrs. Woolf, to Boom Her . . ."
37. Spacks, "Introduction," xii.
38. In fact, Eliza Haywood has a lot to teach us about the complexities of writing and spectatorship in the eighteenth century: in the first issue of *The Female Spectator* (1744), Haywood finds herself in the awkward rhetorical situation of having to claim some knowledge of the world without admitting to too much, which would damage her reputation: "whatever Inconveniences such a manner of Conduct has brought upon myself, I have this Consolation, to think that the Public may reap some Benefit from it" (Haywood, *Selections from* The Female Spectator, 8). For an excellent theoretical discussion of how Charlotte Smith turned the fear of publicity into opportunity, see Harries, "Out in Left Field,"
39. Addison, *The Spectator*, 1.3.
40. Ibid., 1.5.
41. Ibid., 1.34.
42. McDonald, *British Literary Culture and Publishing Practice*, 14.
43. See also Tate, "Mrs. Dalloway and the Armenian Question."
44. Schlack, *Continuing Presences*, 90–91, 173–74.
45. Strachey, "Madame du Deffand," 68.
46. Ibid., 74.
47. Ibid., 73–74.
48. Habermas, *The Structural Transformation*, 32–34.

49. Benhabib, "Models of Public Space," 78.
50. By the late 1930s, Woolf foresees in the younger generation the death of the public sphere through the death of the newspaper's influence. There, young Peggy Pargiter thinks, "So she [Peggy] had seen her father crumple *The Times* and sit trembling with rage because somebody had said something in a newspaper. How odd!" (Y, 331).
51. Habermas shares these doubts: "The *salons* were at first places more for gallant pleasures than for smart discourse . . . the unimportant (where one had traveled and how one was doing) was treated as much with solemnity as the important (theater and politics) was treated *en passant*" (Habermas, *The Structural Transformation*, 34). Whereas early Habermas was inclined to suspect the corrupting presence of women, Woolf recognized that the problem lay with social inequality, not women's presence.
52. Stephen, *English Literature and Society*, 15. See Addison's claim, in the tenth number of the *Spectator*, of "Three-score thousand Disciples in London and Westminster," a figure he bases on this calculation: "My Publisher tells me, that there are already Three Thousand [papers] distributed every Day; So if I allow Twenty Readers to every Paper, which I look upon as a modest Computation," the *Spectator* quickly attracted around sixty-thousand readers. (Addison, *The Spectator*, 1.38). While such estimates are clearly impossible to verify, as Brian McCrea notes, they "reveal . . . the commitment of both Addison and Steele to a large audience." (McCrea, *Addison and Steele Are Dead*, 23).
53. Green, *Spectacular Confessions*, 174.
54. Eagleton, *The Function of Criticism*, 12.
55. Ibid., 10.
56. Ibid., 25.
57. Green, *Spectacular Confessions*, 153.
58. Ibid., 155.
59. Habermas, *The Structural Transformation*, 50.
60. Cook, *Epistolary Bodies*, 17.
61. Ibid., 77.
62. Woolf recognizes the fusty spectator in herself, as this exuberant, self-critical performance from a 1930 letter to Ethel Smyth jokes: "And I am only a spectator. I happened, the other day to read an old article of my own, and I said 'Good God, what a prig that woman must be!' I think I must go to some more parties—" (L, 4.281).
63. Habermas, concluding remarks to *Habermas and the Public Sphere*, 475.
64. Habermas, *Structural Transformation*, 96.
65. For a skeptical response to the gendering of the public/private distinction in the eighteenth century, see Lawrence Klein, "Gender and the Public/Private Distinction." Klein, like many social and cultural historians of the eighteenth century, emphasizes the anachronism

inherent in assuming any eighteenth-century space or text could be assumed totally private or solitary.

66. Habermas, *Structural Transformation*, 30.

## Chapter 4   A Very Sincere Performance: Woolf, Byron, and Fame

1. For Byron's posthumous fame, see Andrew Elfenbein, *Byron and the Victorians* and Wilson, *Byromania*; for Woolf's, see Brenda Silver, *Virginia Woolf Icon.*

2. For McDayter, "this is only half of the story . . . he himself began to look at the product of his labor and see neither his ideal self mirrored back to him by his adoring fans, nor the fulfillment of his desires for literary fame. He saw only the evidence of professional degradation brought about by industrialization and the commodification of the poetic image" (McDayter, "Conjuring Byron," 45).

3. Ibid., 48.

4. Here are some additional examples of Woolf's use of "Byronic": Rupert Brooke is "slightly Byronic" (L, 1.495). "Clive has an egg—a turkeys egg—for a head now—quite bald, unashamedly bald; never a hair will grow anymore. . . . What view would I take—about this last phase, for instance, the Byronic?" (D, 2.263). Years later, her 16-year-old nephew "Julian was rather Byronic" (L, 3.103).

5. Surely Vita Sackville-West is Byronic, but Woolf did not call her Byronic in print.

6. London Dotty does sound alarming. Woolf had last seen Dotty in London where Woolf and Vita Sackville-West came upon her in a darkened flat: "She [Dotty] woke up chattering and hysterical. Virginia Woolf Virginia Woolf My god! Virginia Woolf is in the room. For Gods Sake Vita don't turn the lights on. No light you fool!" (D, 3.115).

7. Byron, *Letters and Journals*, 8.114. See also Wolfson, "A Problem Few Dare Imitate."

8. Byron to Lady Blessington, qtd in Marchand, "The Quintessential Byron," 240. Marchand, the doyen of Byron scholars, uses this quotation as the centerpiece of his smart, belletristic essay.

9. Hazlitt, "Lord Byron," 135.

10. Silver, "The Authority of Anger," 204–05.

11. Lauritsen, "Lord Byron Just Keeps Getting Gayer," 34–35.

12. Brenda Silver's *Virginia Woolf Icon* outlines the history of Woolf's posthumous reputation with a careful eye on the implications for feminism. This chapter, indebted to Silver's work, investigates Woolf's reactions to fame in her lifetime.

13. Moore, *Letters and Journals of Lord Byron*, 1.258. Benita Eisler cautions that "Tom Moore is the only source for Byron's remark," so often quoted since (Eisler, *Byron: Child of Passion, Fool of Fame*, 330).

14. St Clair, "The Impact of Byron's Writings," 6. McDayter adds, "*Childe Harold's Pilgrimage* went through ten editions in three years, *The Corsair* sold 10,000 copies in a single day in 1814. *The Lady of the Lake* [1810], which had held the old record, sold a mere 20,000 copies in the space of six months" (McDayter, "Conjuring Byron," 46).

15. McDayter, "Conjuring Byron," 47.

16. Qtd in Rutherford, *Byron: The Critical Heritage*, 411.

17. Ibid.

18. Ibid., 478. Arthur Symons, too, emphasizes the performative: "The life of Byron was a masque in action" (qtd in Rutherford, *Byron: The Critical Heritage*, 497).

19. Stephen, "Byron," 599.

20. Ibid., 594–95.

21. Byron's desire for profit is complicated by his refusal to take the money for himself: for years he sought the profits for his publisher, maintaining an aristocratic distance from paid labor.

22. McDayter, "Conjuring Byron," 51. See note 2 this chapter (McDayter, "Conjuring Byron," 45).

23. Schickel, *Intimate Strangers*, 87.

24. Silver, *Virginia Woolf Icon*, 130–32.

25. Ibid., 132. Silver argues that this particular photograph, reprinted far more often in the United States than in England, "created a version of Virginia Woolf that was far less ethereal and 'bohemian' than those appearing in the British press" (Silver, *Virginia Woolf Icon*, 132).

26. "Internal evidence in this unpublished essay . . . shows that she probably began writing 'Byron and Mr. Briggs' in the spring of 1922" (Hungerford, Introduction to "Byron and Mr. Briggs," 322).

27. That is the speculation of the editors of her diary: "VW was probably reading *The Life and Letters of Lord Byron* by Thomas Moore" (D, 1.180 n.7).

28. For more on interruption, see Kamuf, "Penelope at Work," and my "*A Room of One's Own*, Personal Criticism and the Essay."

29. Woolf records her thoughts on Rosetti in her diary "while waiting to buy a book in which to record my impressions first of Christina Rosetti, then of Byron" (D, 1.178). Rosetti's gift, she notes, might have taken "a far finer form than, shall we say, Mrs. Browning's." Woolf links Byron with Barrett Browning in *Flush*: See *Flush*, 65, 176.

30. Eliot, *On Poetry and Poets*, 232.

31. Christensen, *Lord Byron's Strength*, 160.

32. Ibid., 161.

33. Eisler, *Byron: Child of Passion, Fool of Fame*, 326.

34. Byron, *Don Juan*, 3.626, in *The Major Works*, 507.

35. Byron, *Don Juan*, 3.674–88, in *The Major Works*, 508–09.

36. It thus echoes Byron's many attacks on the changing political views of poet laureate Robert Southey.

37. Byron, *Don Juan*, 3.660–62 in *The Major Works*, 508.
38. Byron, *Don Juan*, 3.704–06 in *The Major Works*, 510.
39. Byron, *Don Juan*, 3.791–92 in *The Major Works*, 512.
40. Byron, *Don Juan*, 3.793–95 in *The Major Works*, 513.
41. Hungerford, Introduction to "Byron and Mr. Briggs," 323.
42. Woolf's comments indicate, as Edward Hungerford notes elsewhere, that, for her, "biography as a craft and an art was unquestionably admired" (Hungerford, "Deeply and Consciously," 105).
43. See Schickel, *Intimate Strangers*, 296–97.
44. Woolf herself makes this (common) point about Shakespeare in "Byron and Mr. Briggs."
45. See, e.g., McGann, "On Reading *Childe Harold*" for distinctions between skepticism and sincerity (48), and between sentimentality and sincerity (51).
46. Earlier in the essay, Woolf seems to be working out her own version of the idea of sincerity her discussion of several short lyrics, one anonymous and three by Robert Herrick. She quotes Herrick's epitaph on his maid, Prudence Baldwin, commenting, "So delightful is it to feel accurately like this that we go on," quoting from "His Grange, or Private Wealth." Immediately following this quotation, she writes simply "and again" and quotes "An Epitaph Upon a Virgin" (B&B, 344 – 45). Woolf's definition of sincerity might well be that writing makes one "feel accurately": the frank pastoral of the lines quoted here are direct, free in their sexuality, and clear-eyed in their acceptance of death. Woolf recognizes the intellectual inadequacy of these long strings of quotations, typical for appreciative criticism even up to this day. These sorts of discussions are "extremely imperfect and highly inaccurate" (B&B, 334), and "the use of metaphors to convey critical judgements is generally an attempt to conceal under artificial flower vagueness and poverty of thought" (B&B, 335), she writes, unable to resist metaphors in her high-handed dismissal of them. In spite of Woolf's professionalism in her attitude to marketing, sales, and reviews, she was ardently antiprofessional in her judgments of literature. In her literary criticism, she strove to read as a common reader and a writer. As such, she sought to approach the ineffable but intense impressions that make some reading so pleasurable: What is it that makes certain lines of Herrick or scenes from Hardy lodge in our hearts? What makes the pleasure of a sincere book different from other kinds of reading pleasure? What do we mean by thinking of a text as sincere?
47. Early on, Jacob is given the chance to choose a remembrance from his tutor's home; he picks "Byron in one volume" (JR, 22). As I discuss below, in the middle of the novel, in a miniessay on letters, the narrator observes, "Byron wrote letters" (JR, 93). And, in the book's final pages, Jacob's tutor sees but does not greet Jacob on a London street, thinking only "I gave him Byron's works" (JR, 173).
48. Byron, *Don Juan*, 1.57–58 in *The Major Works*, 380.

49. Qtd in Levine, "T. S. Eliot and Byron," 532.
50. Jacob and Byron even look alike—i.e., both are curly haired, dark Englishmen and have a Greek beauty. Like Byron, who often dieted, people fear that Jacob may tend to stoutness as he ages.
51. Froula, *Virginia Woolf and the Bloomsbury Avant-Garde*, 63.
52. Ibid., 74.
53. Walter Benjamin makes a parallel distinction between Brechtian irony and Romantic irony. For Benjamin, the latter "demonstrates only the philosophic sophistication of the writer"; unlike Brecht, the Romantic ironist "has no didactic aim" (Benjamin, *Illuminations*, 55).
54. For Christine Froula, Florinda is "an ironic synecdoche of women's sexual enslavement in both ancient Greek and modern European civilizations—an emblem, like ancient Greece itself, of young men's 'dominion' " (Froula, *Virginia Woolf and the Bloomsbury Avant-Garde*, 78).
55. These events have attracted much critical attention of late. See especially Flint, "Virginia Woolf and the General Strike," and Luckhurst "Vogue . . . Is Going to Take up Mrs. Woolf, to Boom Her." For a more critical perspective, see Garrity, "Virginia Woolf, Intellectual Harlotr, and 1920s British *Vogue*."
56. Marchand, *Byron*, 1.345–46. The quotation is from the *Letters & Journals of Lord Byron*, 5.431. Much later, in 1818, Byron briefly considered returning to England to support the trial against Queen Caroline whom he admired; he was relieved to learn that, having missed the first few days of deliberation, he was already ineligible to vote.
57. Garrity, "Selling Culture to the 'Civilized,' " 48.
58. Flint, "Virginia Woolf and the General Strike," 321.
59. Ibid., 322.
60. Thus, for Jane Garrity, "*Vogue* provides us with a prime cultural artifact that documents how, despite Bloomsbury, political involvement and altruistic sympathies with the working class, their real affiliation was with members of their own class. One detail in particular documents this vividly. By sheer chance, Woolf's appearance in the May 1926 issue coincides with the General Strike in England; not coincidental, however, is that the magazine makes no reference to this ten-day conflict or to the ruthless government suppression that ended it." (Garrity, "Virginia Woolf, Intellectual Harlotry, and 1920s British *Vogue*," 48). This coincidence leads to an implied judgment of Woolf that misreads the historical record. It is one thing to hold Virginia Woolf responsible for what she wrote and, with Leonard, published, but to hold her personally responsible for the editorial policies of those vehicles where her work appeared rings of snobbery. As Nicola Luckhurst argues in connection with Woolf's contribution to *Vogue*, "A man might write for both camps [high- and middlebrow] and, tongue in cheek, get away with it; a woman would also risk

compromising herself by such a move" (Luckhurst, "Vogue . . . Is Going to Take Up Mrs. Woolf, to Boom Her," 77).

61. Woolf borrows the name of one of Byron's Cambridge friends, William Bankes (Stephen, "Byron," 587), in *To the Lighthouse*, and much of *Orlando* is Byronic.

62. "The Jessamy Brides" was to be a Sapphic fantasy, and Woolf mentions the "Ladies of Llangollen" in the same entry. Byron, too, seems to have had a fondness for these ladies, aristocratic lesbians who cross-dressed and lived in perfect felicity for 50 years. Of his Cambridge intimate, Charles Skinner Matthews, Byron wrote, "I certainly love him more than any human being, and neither time nor distance have had the least effect on my (in general) changeable disposition. In short, we shall put *Lady E. Butler* and *Miss Ponsonby* [the Ladies of Llangollen] to the blush" (qtd in Marchand, *Byron*, 1.133).

63. For a discussion of the structure and the argument of this long essay, see my "Pleasure and Belief."

64. Woolf's dismissal of "Mrs." Hemans bears note here. Still, the comparison between the supposedly great Byron and a woman is to Byron's detriment even as it assumes Mrs. Hemans's marginality. Woolf links Byron's poetry to the worst of Hemans'. In short, as is often the case, Woolf's assessment is not simple. She does not feel bound by her feminism to speak positively of all women writers.

65. Marcus, "Britannia Rules *The Waves*," 145.

66. Ibid., 154.

67. Robin Hackett concedes the difficulty of reading *The Waves* as a feminist text and a lesbian one: "the lesbianism of the final version of *The Waves* is so subtle as to be almost absent" (Hackett, *Sapphic Primitivism*, 66). Nonetheless, she presents a strong case for Rhoda's lesbianism and its significance to Woolf's larger critique of empire through an impressive accumulation of small bits of evidence. Yet I suspect even Hackett's impressively patient method would not yield an easy feminist interpretation of the final soliloquy. That said, as we have seen, it does not seem right to discount the final chapter as simple parody.

68. Woolf had used this rhetoric before: on completing *Jacob's Room*, she noted with satisfaction that "I have found out how to begin (at 40) to say something in my own voice" (D, 2.186).

69. This distinction between the uncivilized, emotional response and the expected, formal gesture and Bernard's continuing preference for the former are what keeps his relationship with Jinny alive. As tawdry as her life becomes, "she still sought the moment" (W, 275).

70. Forty seems to be Woolf's shorthand for full adulthood. Sandra judges Jacob "credulous as yet. At forty it might be a different matter" (JR, 161).

71. She continues, "But there is no Shakespeare, there is no Beethoven; certainly and emphatically there is no God; we are the words; we are the music; we are the thing itself" (MB, 72).

72. Reading—and being—Byron is central too, to Woolf's 1934 "Ode Written Partly in Prose on Seeing the Name of Cutbush Above a Butcher's Shop in Pentonville." Here, a young butcher's love of Byron fires his imagination, gives him dreams, fuels his reading of Classical literature, inspires his lovemaking, and accompanies him on long swims (Like Byron, Woolf's young man butcher is an accomplished swimmer): "But I swam the Hellespont—he dreams: he had read / Byron in the Charing Cross Road" (CSF, 239). Byron gives us access to Cutbush's inner life as Shakespeare gave us access to Septimus's in *Mrs. Dalloway*. Once again, Woolf's allusion does not entirely work, but the effort is interesting: she forces class-consciousness on her readers, reminding us of the existence of ambitious readers who make their living as shopkeepers. As subsequent literary historians have documented, Byron was especially popular with lower middle-class readers. In spite of her bringing Byron and Cutbush together, Woolf finds it difficult to imagine where Byron lodges in the butcher's imagination. She uses her own limitation in this regard as an opportunity for wonder, tinged, like any sincere performance, with a hint of irony:

> how little we can grasp;
> how little we can interpret and read aright
> the name John Cutbush but only as we pass his
> shop on Saturday night, cry out Hail Cutbush,
>      of Pentonville, I salute thee; passing. (CSF, 241)

73. Flush first understands breeding and distinction in terms of high and low: "Dogs therefore, Flush began to suspect, differ; some are high, others low" (F, 31). What is comic here has a bitter edge in Woolf's essay "Middlebrow," where the high and low join forces against the undefined, unrefined middle.

74. Nicolson, *Byron, the Last Journey*, 83.

75. Woolf and Browning both admired the democratic impulse in Byron, and Woolf especially endeavored to distinguish that political sympathy from her understanding of his death and its effect. Woolf believed that martyrdom—or the transformation of a death into martyrdom—only begets more martyrs. Elizabeth Barrett Browning, in her middle-aged participation in the *risorgimento*, modeled for Woolf the kind of democratic transformation that Woolf wanted to effect. Once Browning had learned enough about Byron to cease admiring him uncritically, she decided not to reject him, but to let his influence on her be selective. For more on Browning and Byron, see Gilbert, "From Patria to Matria."

76. Mermin, *Elizabeth Barrett Browning*, 12, 30, 42, 184; Gilbert, "From Patria to Matria," 205.

77. Gilbert, "From Patria to Matria," 194, 206.

78. See, e.g., "an abstract mystical eyeless book" (D, 3.203); "But who is she? I am very anxious that she should have no name" (D, 3.229–30); "the sense of children; unreality; things oddly proportioned. Then another person or figure must be selected" (D, 3.236).

79. To cite a few other examples: "after Monday comes Tuesday" (W, 271); "Tuesday follows Monday" (W, 283).

80. Nicolson, *Byron, the Last Journey*, 9.

81. Schickel, *Intimate Strangers*, 303.

82. Levenback, *Virginia Woolf and the Great War*, 13.

83. Ibid., 10.

84. Julian Bell, *Essays, Poems, and Letters*, 58.

85. Spalding, *Vanesca Bell*, 294; Julian Bell, *Essays, Poems and Letters*, 196.

86. Wolfson, "A Problem Few Dare Imitate," 869.

87. Wills, *John Wayne's America*, 156.

88. Here are Woolf's infantile George and Caro in action, behaving much as they did in Regency England: "Mabel, with her hand on the pram, turned sharply . . . 'Come along, George.' The little boy had lagged and was grouting in the grass. Then the baby, Caro, thrust her fist out of the coverlet and the furry bear was jerked overboard" (BTA, 9).

89. In writing a novel about a pageant (instead of a pageant *tout court* as Eliot and Forster did), Woolf adds an extra layer of ironic distance. She adds a frame in which she can most effectively transmit her feminist pacifist message: "Seeking to express a troubled half-love for England, Woolf presents an *uncertain performance* of—rather than either a thorough ironization of or a complete identification with—nationalism" (Esty, *A Shrinking Island*, 93). *Between the Acts* presents the English literary tradition as unchanging and shared a common (national) heritage upon which we (English) can all draw (Esty, *A Shrinking Island*, 59). Miss La Trobe offers an alternate, antimartial pageant.

90. Leonard Woolf, *Downhill All the Way*, 27.

## Epilogue: Woolf in Africa: Lessing, El Saadawi, and Aidoo

1. Anderson, *Imagined Communities*, 62.

2. Ibid., 77.

3. I have been unable to find direct confirmation that El Saadawi has read Woolf. For a discussion of links between the two women, see the final chapter of Royer, *A Critical Study of the Works of Nawal El Saadawi*.

4. Alice Walker makes a distinction between feminist (individual, white, first world) and womanist (communal, brown, developing) that we may do well to both invoke and be wary of in a discussion of these three feminist writers, two African (El Saadawi from Egypt and Aidoo

from Ghana) and the third, Doris Lessing, born in Persia to English parents, but raised from the age of 5 to 30 in what was then Rhodesia. (She left in 1949.) Walker's distinction creates an important category of feminism that does not descend from middle-class white women—it is a distinction that Aidoo specifically lauds. Womanism reminds us that these women who read and profited from Woolf are working in a more pluralistic tradition than the one from whence Woolf emerged (Walker, *In Search of Our Mother's Gardens*, xi–xii).

5. See Lessing, *Under My Skin*, 1–10.

6. Lessing, *The Grass is Singing*, 72. There is little that is Woolfian in the language of *The Grass is Singing* and yet Mary Turner is, like Clarissa Dalloway, an ordinary woman of meager education whose lonely marriage forces her into introspection. At the level of theme and in the refusal of a strictly realist or materialist method, both Woolf and Lessing take profound intellectual pleasure in giving depth to the thoughts of a woman whose inner life is haltingly, reluctantly rich.

7. Still, more than any of the others, Lessing can be connected to Anderson and Habermas in implying that by not reading the paper, Martha has abdicated her responsibilities as a citizen. Lessing does not have patience for the kind of "arid feminism" (Lessing, *The Grass is Singing*, 32) that sees injury in all patriarchy and her impatience is such that she might well see the other women author's critiques just that way.

8. Lessing, *A Proper Marriage*, 278.

9. Ibid., 277.

10. Ibid., 278.

11. Ibid., 277.

12. Ibid., 278.

13. Ibid., 37, 194.

14. Ibid., 276.

15. Ibid., 274.

16. While the sense of connection confirmed Woolf in her choice of writing as vocation and contribution, it led El Saadawi to cease wanting to practice as a doctor because the help she was offering did not get at the root political causes of poverty (El Saadawi, *A Daughter of Isis*, 292).

17. The generic status of *Woman at Point Zero* is tricky: a novel based on the testimony of a woman condemned to death as told to the author in her capacity as state psychiatrist, translated from Arabic by the author's husband, it depends on unverifiable testimony: the only other person present is now deceased. In short, it is full of literary devices familiar from both Woolf and prison literature.

18. El Saadawi, *Woman at Point Zero*, 27.

19. Ibid., 101–02.

20. Even letting the spit dry suggests a slower sweeter torture than the gesture of wiping it away; to wipe it might signify an apology. For her

also the newspaper has a pragmatic household function: it lines her kitchen shelves. The revenge she privately exacts on powerful men depicted therein is ineffectual but irresistible.

21. El Saadawi, *Woman at Point Zero*, 102.
22. Ibid., 103.
23. Royer, *A Critical Study of the Works of Nawal El Saadawi*, 143.
24. Aidoo, *Our Sister Killjoy*, 95.
25. "Transplant Case," *New York Times*, 35.

# BIBLIOGRAPHY

Abel, Elizabeth. *Virginia Woolf and the Fictions of Psychoanalysis*. Chicago: University of Chicago Press, 1989.

Adams, David. *Colonial Odysseys: Empire and Epic in the Modernist Novel*. Ithaca: Cornell University Press, 2003.

Addison, Joseph. *The Spectator*. Ed. G. Gregory Smith. 4 vols. New York: E. P. Dutton, 1909.

Aeschylus. *The Oresteia*. Trans. Robert Fagles. New York: Penguin, 1977.

Aidoo, Ama Ata. "The African Woman Today." *Dissent* (Summer 1992) 319–25.

———. *Changes*. New York: The Feminist Press, 1993.

———. "Literature, Feminism and the African Woman Today." In *Reconstructing Womanhood, Reconstructing Feminism: Writings on Black Women*. Ed. Delia Jarrett-Macauley. London: Routledge, 1996. 156–74.

———. *No Sweetness Here and Other Stories*. 1970. New York: The Feminist Press, 1995.

———. *Our Sister Killjoy or Reflections from a Black-Eyed Squint*. 1977. White Plains, NY: Longman, 2004.

———. "To Be an African Woman Writer—an Overview and a Detail." In *Criticism and Ideology*. Ed. Kirsten Petersen. Uppsala, Sweden: Scandinavian Institute of African Studies, 1988. 155–72.

Albee, Edward. *Who's Afraid of Virginia Woolf?*. New York: Atheneum, 1962.

Alley, Henry M. "A Rediscovered Eulogy: Virginia Woolf's 'Miss Janet Case: Classical Scholar and Teacher.' " *Twentieth Century Literature* 28 (1982) 290–301.

Anderson, Benedict. *Imagined Communities: Reflections on the Origin and Spread of Nationalism*. 1983. Rev. ed. London: Verso, 1991.

Armstrong, Nancy. "Literature as Women's History," *Genre* 19 (Winter 1986) 347–69.

Augustine. *Confessions*. Trans. Henry Chadwick. Oxford: Oxford University Press, 1991.

Austen, Jane. *Pride and Prejudice*. Ed. R. W. Chapman. Oxford: Oxford University Press, 1923.

Baker, Nicholson. *The Size of Thoughts*. New York: Vintage, 1996.

Baker, William. "Merrick, Leonard (1864–1939)." In *The 1890s: An Encyclopedia of British Literature, Art and Culture*. Ed. G. A. Cevasco. New York: Garland, 1993. 392.

Bamford, T. W. "Public Schools and Social Class, 1801–1850." *British Journal of Sociology* 12 (1961) 224–35.

Banks, Olive. *The Politics of British Feminism, 1918–1970.* Brookfield, VT: Elgan, 1993.

Barnard, Mary, trans. *Sappho.* Berkeley, CA: University of California Press, 1958.

Barrett, Eileen and Patricia Cramer, eds. *Virginia Woolf: Lesbian Readings.* New York: New York University Press, 1997.

Bartolovich, Crystal. "Consumerism, or the Cultural Logic of Late Cannibalism." In *Cannibalism and the Colonial World.* Ed. Francis Barker, Peter Hulme, and Margaret Iversen. Cambridge, UK: Cambridge University Press, 1998. 204–37.

Bate, W. Jackson. *The Burden of the Past and the English Poet.* Cambridge: Harvard University Press, 1970.

Bazin, Nancy Topping. *Virginia Woolf and the Androgynous Vision.* New Brunswick, NJ: Rutgers University Press, 1973.

Beeching, Jack, ed. Introduction to *Voyages and Discoveries*, by Richard Hakluyt. New York: Penguin, 1972. 9–29.

Beer, Gillian. *Arguing with the Past: Essays in Narrative from Woolf to Sidney.* London: Routledge, 1989.

———. "The Island and the Aeroplane: The case of Virginia Woolf." In *Nation and Narration.* Ed. Homi K. Bhabha. New York: Routledge, 1990. 265–90.

———. *Virginia Woolf: The Common Ground.* Ann Arbor: University of Michigan Press, 1996.

Bell, Julian. *Essays, Poems, and Letters.* Ed. Quentin Bell. London: Hogarth, 1938.

Bell, Quentin. *Virginia Woolf: A Biography.* New York: Harcourt, 1972.

Benhabib, Seyla, "Models of Public Space: Hannah Arendt, the Liberal Tradition, and Jürgen Habermas." In *Habermas and the Public Sphere.* Ed. Craig Calhoun. Cambridge, MA: MIT Press, 1992. 73–98.

Benjamin, Walter. *Illuminations.* Ed. Hannah Arendt. Trans. Harry Zohn. New York: Harcourt, 1968.

Berlant, Lauren. "Intimacy: A Special Issue." *Critical Inquiry* 21 (Winter 1998) 281–88.

Berlant, Lauren and Elizabeth Freeman. "Queer Nationality." In *Fear of a Queer Planet: Queer Politics and Social Theory.* Ed. Michael Warner. Minneapolis: University of Minnesota Press, 1993. 149–80.

Berman, Jessica. *Modernist Fiction, Cosmopolitanism, and the Politics of Community.* Cambridge, UK: Cambridge University Press, 2001.

Bishop, Edward. *A Virginia Woolf Chronology.* New York: Macmillan, 1989.

Black, Naomi. "Virginia Woolf and the Women's Movement." In *Virginia Woolf: A Feminist Slant.* Ed. Jane Marcus. Lincoln: University of Nebraska Press, 1983.

———. *Virginia Woolf as Feminist.* Ithaca: Cornell University Press, 2004.

Bloom, Harold. *The Anxiety of Influence.* New York: Oxford, 1973.

Bolgar, R. R. *The Classical Heritage and Its Beneficiaries*. Cambridge, UK: Cambridge University Press, 1954.

Booth, Alison. *Greatness Engendered: George Eliot and Virginia Woolf*. Ithaca: Cornell University Press, 1992.

Bourdieu, Pierre. *Distinction: A Social Critique of the Judgement of Taste*. Trans. Richard Nice. Cambridge, MA: Harvard University Press, 1984.

Bowlby, Rachel. *Still Crazy after All These Years: Women, Writing, and Psychoanalysis*. New York: Routledge, 1992.

———. *Virginia Woolf: Feminist Destinations*. Oxford: Blackwell, 1988.

———. "Walking, Women and Writing: Virginia Woolf as *flâneuse*." In *New Feminist Discourses: Critical Essays on Theories and Texts*. Ed. Isobel Armstrong. London: Routledge, 1992. 26–47.

Brantlinger, Patrick. " 'The Bloomsbury Fraction' Versus War and Empire." In *Seeing Double: Revisioning Edwardian and Modernist Literature*. Ed. Carola M. Kaplan and Anne B. Simpson. New York: St. Martin's, 1996. 149–67.

Briggs, Julia. *Virginia Woolf: An Inner Life*. New York: Harcourt, 2005.

British Museum. *A Guide to the Use of the Reading Room*. London: By Order of the Trustees, 1924.

Bromwich, David. *A Choice of Inheritance*. Cambridge, MA: Harvard University Press, 1989.

Brosnan, Leila. *Reading Virginia Woolf's Essays and Journalism*. Edinburgh: Edinburgh University Press, 1997.

Browne, Thomas. *Urne buriall, and the Garden of Cyrus*. Cambridge, UK: Cambridge University Press, 1958.

Browning, Elizabeth Barrett. *Aurora Leigh*. Ed. Margaret Reynolds. New York: Norton, 1996.

Burt, John. "Irreconcilable Habits of Thought in *A Room of One's Own* and *To the Lighthouse*." *ELH* 49 (1982) 191–203.

Burton, Richard. *The Anatomy of Melancholy*. New York: Dutton, 1932.

Byron, George Gordon. *Byron's Letters and Journals*. Ed. Leslie Marchand. 11 vols. Cambridge, MA: Harvard University Press, 1973–82.

———. *Lord Byron: Selected Letters and Journals*. Ed. Leslie Marchand. Cambridge, MA: Harvard University Press, 1982.

———. *The Major Works*. Ed. Jerome McGann. Oxford: Oxford University Press, 1986.

Calhoun, Craig. Introduction to *Habermas and the Public Sphere*. Ed. Craig Calhoun. Cambridge, MA: MIT Press, 1992. 1–48.

———, ed. *Habermas and the Public Sphere*. Cambridge, MA: MIT Press, 1992.

Carlston, Erin. *Thinking Fascism: Sapphic Modernism and Fascist Modernity*. Stanford, CA: Stanford University Press, 1998.

Carroll, Berenice. " 'To Crush Him in Our Own Country': The Political Thought of Virginia Woolf." *Feminist Studies* 4.1 (1978) 99–131.

Carruthers, Mary. *The Book of Memory: A Study of Memory in Medieval Culture*. Cambridge, UK: Cambridge University Press, 1990.

Caserio, Robert L. "Queer Passions, Queer Citizenship: Some Novels about the State of the American Nation 1946–1954." *MFS* 43.1 (Spring 1997) 170–205.

Caughie, Pamela. *Virginia Woolf and Postmodernism*. Urbana: University of Illinois Press, 1991.

———, ed. *Virginia Woolf in the Age of Mechanical Reproduction*. New York: Garland, 2000.

Chapman, Alison. " 'In Our Own Blood Drenched the Pen': Italy and Sensibility in Elizabeth Barrett Browning's Last Poems (1862)." *Women's Writing* 10.2 (2003) 269–86.

Chapman, Wayne and Janet Manson, eds. *Women in the Milieu of Leonard and Virginia Woolf: Peace, Politics and Education*. New York: Pace University Press, 1997.

Chartier, Roger. *The Order of Books*. Stanford, CA: Stanford University Press, 1994.

Chatterjee, Partha. *The Nation and Its Fragments: Colonial and Postcolonial Histories*. Princeton, NJ: Princeton University Press, 1993.

Childers, Mary M. "Virginia Woolf on the Outside Looking Down: Reflections on the Class of Women," *Modern Fiction Studies* 38.1 (1992) 61–79.

Christensen, Jerome. *Lord Byron's Strength*. Baltimore: Johns Hopkins University Press, 1993.

Clarke, M. L. *Classical Education in Britain 1500–1900*. Cambridge, UK: Cambridge University Press 1959.

Collecott, Diana. *H. D. and Sapphic Modernism*. Cambridge, UK: Cambridge University Press, 2000.

Colley, Linda. *Britons: Forging the Nation 1707–1837*. New Haven, CT: Yale University Press, 1992.

Connerton, Paul. *How Societies Remember*. Cambridge, UK: Cambridge University Press, 1989.

Cook, Elizabeth Heckendorn. *Epistolary Bodies: Gender and Genre in the Eighteenth-Century Republic of Letters*. Stanford, CA: Stanford University Press, 1996.

Cormack, Lesley B. " 'Good Fences Make Good Neighbors': Geography as Self-Definition in Early Modern England." *ISIS* 82 (1991) 639–61.

Cramer, Patricia. " 'Loving in the War Years: The War Images in *The Years*." In *Virginia Woolf and War: Fiction, Reality and Myth*. Ed. Mark Hussey. Syracuse, NY: Syracuse University Press, 1991. 203–24.

Crook, J. Mordaunt. *The British Museum*. New York: Praeger, 1972.

Cucullu, Lois. "Retailing the Female Intellectual." *Differences: A Journal of Feminist Cultural Studies* 9.2 (1998) 25–68.

Cuddy-Keane, Melba. "The Politics of Comic Modes in Virginia Woolf's *Between the Acts*." *PMLA* 105 (March 1990) 273–85.

———, ed. *Virginia Woolf, the Intellectual and the Public Sphere*. Cambridge, UK: Cambridge University Press, 2003.

Cunningham, Michael. *The Hours*. New York: Farrar, Strauss, Giroux, 1998.

Daugherty, Beth Rigel. "The Whole Contention Between Mr. Bennett and Mrs. Woolf, Revisited." In *Virginia Woolf: Centennial Essays*. Ed. Elaine K. Ginsberg and Laura Moss Gottlieb. New York: Whitston, 1983. 269–94.

Davies, Margaret Llewelyn, ed. *Life as We Have Known It, by Co-Operative Working Women*. London: Virago, 1990.

De Gay, Jane. *Virginia Woolf's Novels and the Literary Past*. New York: Columbia University Press, 2006.

DeJean, Joan. *Fictions of Sappho*. Chicago: University of Chicago Press, 1989.

DeMan, Paul. *Allegories of Reading*. New Haven, CT: Yale University Press, 1979.

Dettmar, Kevin J. H. and Stephen Watt, eds., *Marketing Modernisms: Self-Promotions, Canonization, Rereading*. Ann Arbor: University of Michigan Press, 1996.

DiBattista, Maria. *Virginia Woolf's Major Novels: The Fables of Anon*. New Haven, CT: Yale University Press, 1980.

Diepeveen, Leonard. " 'I Can Have More than Enough Power to Satisfy Me': T. S. Eliot's Construction of His Audience." In *Marketing Modernisms: Self-Promotions, Canonization, Rereading*. Ed. Kevin Dettmar and Stephen Watt. Ann Arbor: University of Michigan Press, 1996. 37–60.

Dimock, Wai Chee. "Toward a Theory of Resonance." *PMLA* 112 (1997) 1060–71.

[Doolittle, Hilda] H. D. *Collected Poems*. Ed. Louis Martz. New York: Norton, 1986.

Dowling, Linda. *Hellenism and Homosexuality in Victorian Oxford*. Ithaca: Cornell University Press, 1994.

Dubino, Jeanne. "Virginia Woolf: From Book Reviewer to Literary Critic, 1904–1918." In *Virginia Woolf and the Essay*. Ed. Beth Rosenberg and Jeanne Dubino. New York: St. Martin's Press, 1998. 25–40.

DuBois, Page. "Antigone and the Feminist Critic." *Genre* 19 (Winter 1986) 371–86.

———. *Sappho Is Burning*. Chicago: University of Chicago Press, 1997.

DuPlessis, Rachel Blau. *Writing Beyond the Ending*. Bloomington: Indiana University Press, 1985.

Eagleton, Terry. *The Function of Criticism: From the* Spectator *to Post-Structuralism*. London: Verso, 1984.

Eisler, Benita. *Byron: Child of Passion, Fool of Fame*. New York: Knopf, 1999.

Elfenbein, Andrew. *Byron and the Victorians*. Cambridge, UK: Cambridge University Press, 1995.

Eliot, T. S. "Byron." *On Poetry and Poets*. New York: Farrar, 1961. 223–39.

———. *Selected Prose*. Ed. Frank Kermode. New York: Harcourt, 1975.

———. *The Waste Land*. 1922. New York: Harcourt, 1934.

Emerson, Ralph Waldo. *Ralph Waldo Emerson: The Oxford Authors*. Ed. Richard Poirier. Oxford: Oxford University Press, 1990.

Engel, William E. "Mnemonic Criticism Renaissance Literature: A Manifesto." *Connotations* 1.1 (1991) 12–33.

Esty, Joshua. *A Shrinking Island: Modernism and National Culture in England*. Princeton, NJ: Princeton University Press, 2004.

Ezell, Margaret J. M. *Writing Women's Literary History*. Baltimore: Johns Hopkins University Press, 1993.

Felski, Rita. *The Gender of Modernity*. Cambridge, MA: Harvard University Press, 1995.

Fentress, James and Chris Wickham. *Social Memory*. Oxford: Blackwell, 1992.

Ferebee, Steve. "Bridging the Gulf: The Reader In and Out of Virginia Woolf's Literary Essays." *CLA Journal* 30 (March 1987) 343–61.

Fernald, Anne E. "A Feminist Public Sphere? Virginia Woolf's Revisions of the Eighteenth Century," *Feminist Studies* 31.1 (Spring 2005) 158–82.

———. "The Memory Palace of Virginia Woolf." In *Virginia Woolf: Reading the Renaissance*. Ed. Sally Greene. Athens: Ohio University Press, 1999. 89–114.

———. "Modernism and Tradition." In *Approaching Modernism*. Ed. Astradur Eysteinsson and Vivian Liska. Forthcoming.

———. "Pleasure and Belief in Woolf's 'Phases of Fiction,' " In *Virginia Woolf and the Essay*. Ed. Rosenberg and Dubino. New York: St. Martin's Press, 1997. 193–211.

———. "*A Room of One's Own*, Personal Criticism, and the Essay." *Twentieth Century Literature* 40.2 (Summer 1994) 165–89.

———. "Woolfian Resonances." *Literature Compass* (2006). <http://www.literature-compass.com>.

Fielding, Henry. *Tom Jones*. Ed. Sheridan Warner Baker. New York: Norton, 1973.

Flint, Kate. "Virginia Woolf and the General Strike." *Essays in Criticism* 36.4 (October 1986) 319–34.

Forster, E. M. *Aspects of the Novel*. New York: Harcourt, Brace, & Co. 1927.

———. *Howards End*. New York: Vintage, 1921.

———. *The Longest Journey*. 1907. New York: Vintage, 1962.

Foucault, Michel. *The Archeology of Knowledge and the Discourse on Language*. Trans. A. M. Sheridan Smith. New York: Pantheon Books, 1972.

———. *Language, Counter-Memory, Practice: Selected Essays and Interviews*. Ed. Donald F. Bouchard. Ithaca: Cornell University Press, 1977.

Fowler, Rowena. "Moments and Metamorphoses: Virginia Woolf's Greece." *Comparative Literature* 51.3 (Summer 1999) 217–42.

———. "On Not Knowing Greek: The Classics and the Woman of Letters." *Classical Journal* 78 (1983) 337–49.

Fox, Alice. *Virginia Woolf and the Literature of the English Renaissance*. Oxford: Clarendon Press, 1990.

———. "Virginia Woolf at Work; The Elizabethan Voyage Out." *Bulletin of Research in the Humanities* 84.1 (Spring 1981) 65–84.

———. " 'What Right Have I, A Woman?': Virginia Woolf's Reading Notes on Sidney and Spenser." In *Virginia Woolf: Centennial Essays*.

Ed. Elaine K. Ginsberg and Laura Moss Gottlieb. Troy, NY: Whitson Publishing, 1983.

Fraser, Nancy. "What's Critical about Critical Theory?" In *Feminists Read Habermas: Gendering the Subject of Discourse*. Ed. Johanna Meehan. New York: Routledge, 1995. 21–56.

Frazer, June M. "*Mrs. Dalloway:* Virginia Woolf's Greek Novel." *Research Studies* 47 (1979) 221–28.

Friedman, Susan Stanford. "Uncommon Readings: Seeking the Geopolitical Woolf." *The South Carolina Review* 29.1 (Fall 1996) 24–44.

———. "Virginia Woolf's Pedagogical Scenes of Reading: *The Voyage Out, The Common Reader*, and Her 'Common Readers.'" *Modern Fiction Studies* 38.1 (Spring 1992) 101–26.

Froude, James Anthony. *English Seamen in the Sixteenth Century: Lectures Delivered at Oxford, Easter Terms 1893–4*. New York: Scribner's, 1895.

Froula, Christine. *Virginia Woolf and the Bloomsbury Avant-Garde: War, Civilization, Modernity*. New York: Columbia University Press, 2005.

———. "When Eve Reads Milton: Undoing the Canonical Economy," *Critical Inquiry* 10 (December 1983) 321–48.

Fry, Paul H. "The Distracted Reader." *Criticism* 32.3 (Summer 1990) 295–308.

Furman, Nellie. "*A Room of One's Own*: Reading Absence" In *Women's Language and Style*. Ed. Douglass Butturff and Edmond Epstein. Akron: University of Akron Press, 1978.

Gagnier, Regenia. *Subjectivities: A History of Self-Representation in Britain, 1832–1920*. New York: Oxford University Press, 1991.

Garrity, Jane. "Selling Culture to the 'Civilized': Bloomsbury, British *Vogue*, and the Marketing of National Identity." *Modernism/Modernity* 6.2 (1999) 29–58.

———. *Step-Daughters of England: British Women Modernists and the National Imaginary*. Manchester: Manchester University Press/Palgrave, 2003.

———. "Virginia Woolf, Intellectual Harlotry, and 1920s British *Vogue*." In *Virginia Woolf and the Age of Mechanical Reproduction*. Ed. Pamela Caughie. New York: Garland, 2000. 185–218.

Gilbert, Sandra M. "From Patria to Matria: Elizabeth Barrett Browning's *Risorgimento*." *PMLA* 99.2 (March 1984) 194–211.

Gilbert, Sandra M. and Susan Gubar. *The Madwoman in the Attic*. New Haven, CT: Yale University Press, 1979.

Gleckner, Robert F., ed. *Critical Essays on Lord Byron*. New York: G. K. Hall, 1991.

Godwin, William. *Memoirs of the Author of* A Vindication of the Rights of Woman. Ed. Gina Luria. 1798. New York: Garland, 1974.

Good, Graham. *The Observing Self: Rediscovering the Essay*. London: Routledge, 1988.

Green, Barbara. *Spectacular Confessions: Autobiography, Performative Activism, and the Sites of Suffrage, 1905–1938*. New York: St. Martin's, 1997.

Greenblatt, Stephen. *Marvelous Possessions: The Wonder of the New World.* Chicago: University of Chicago Press, 1991.

Gross, John. *The Modern Moment.* Chicago: University of Chicago Press, 1992.

———, ed. *The Oxford Book of Essays.* New York: Oxford University Press, 1991.

———. *The Rise and Fall of the Man of Letters: A Study of the Idiosyncratic and the Humane in Modern Literature.* New York: Macmillan, 1969.

Guiguet, Jean. *Virginia Woolf and Her Works.* Trans. Jean Stewart. New York: Harcourt, 1965.

Guillory, John. *Cultural Capital: The Problem of Literary Canon Formation.* Chicago: University of Chicago Press, 1993.

Gutting, Gary. "Foucault's Philosophy of Experience." *Boundary 2* 29.2 (2002) 69–85.

Habermas, Jürgen. Concluding Remarks to *Habermas and the Public Sphere.* Ed. Craig Calhoun. Cambridge, MA: MIT Press, 1992. 462–79.

———. *The Inclusion of the Other: Studies in Political Theory.* Ed. Ciaran Cronin and Pablo De Greiff. Cambridge, MA: MIT Press, 1998.

———. *The Structural Transformation of the Public Sphere: An Inquiry into a Category of Bourgeois Society.* 1962. Trans. Thomas Burger. Cambridge, MA: MIT Press, 1996.

Hackett, Robin. *Sapphic Primitivism: Productions of Race, Class, and Sexuality in Key Works of Modern Fiction.* New Brunswick, NJ: Rutgers University Press, 2004.

Hakluyt, Richard. *Principal Navigations, Voyages, Trafficks and discoveries of the English Nation.* 1589–90. 2nd ed. 1598–1600.

Halbwachs, Maurice. *On Collective Memory.* 1952. Ed. Lewis A. Coser. Chicago: University of Chicago Press, 1992.

Hall, Michael L. "The Emergence of the Essay and the Idea of Discovery," *Essays on the Essay.* Ed. Alexander J. Butrym. Athens: University of Georgia Press, 1989. 73–91.

Hamlin, William M. "Imagined Apotheoses: Drake, Harriot, and Raleigh. in the Americas." *Journal of the History of Ideas* 57.3 (1996). 405–28.

Hardy, Thomas. *The Woodlanders.* Oxford: Oxford University Press, 1985.

Harries, Elizabeth W. " 'Out in Left Field': Charlotte Smith's Prefaces, Bourdieu's Categories, and the Public Sphere." *Modern Language Quarterly* 58.4 (December 1997) 457–73.

Harris, P. R. *The British Museum.* London: British Museum, 1979.

Harrison, Jane Ellen. *Reminiscences of a Student's Life.* London: Hogarth Press, 1925.

Hartman, Geoffrey H. *Minor Prophecies: The Literary Essay in the Culture Wars.* Cambridge, MA: Harvard University Press, 1991.

———. "Virginia's Web." *Chicago Review* 14 (Spring 1961) 20–32.

Hayley, William, *The Life and Posthumous Writings of William Cowper Esquire.* London: Johnson, 1804.

Haywood, Eliza. *Selections from* The Female Spectator. Ed. Patricia Meyer Spacks. New York: Oxford University Press, 1999.

Hazlitt, William. "Lord Byron." *The Selected Writings.* 1824. Ed. Duncan Wu. London: Pickering and Chatto, 1998. 7.134–42.

Heilbrun, Carolyn G. *Toward a Recognition of Androgyny.* New York: Knopf, 1973.

———. *Writing a Woman's Life.* New York: Ballantine, 1988.

Henke, Suzette A. Virginia Woolf's *The Waves:* "A Phenomenological Reading" Neophilologus 73.3 (July 1989) 461–72.

Herman, William. "Virginia Woolf and the Classics: Every Englishman's Prerogative Transmuted into Fictional Art." In *Virginia Woolf: Centennial Essays.* Ed. Elaine K. Ginsberg and Laura Moss Gottlieb. Troy, NY: Whitson Publishing, 1983. 257–68.

Hoberman, Roth. "Women in the British Museum Reading Room during the Late-Nineteenth and Early-Twentieth Centuries: From Quasi-to Counter Public." *Feminist Studies* 28.3 (Fall 2002) 489–512.

Hobsbawm, Eric and Terence Ranger, eds. *The Invention of Tradition.* Cambridge, UK: Cambridge University Press, 1983.

Holtby, Winifred. *Virginia Woolf.* London: Wishart, 1932.

Homer. *The Iliad.* Trans. Robert Fagles. New York: Viking, 1990.

Homer. *The Odyssey.* Trans. Robert Fitzgerald. New York: Vintage, 1990.

Hungerford, Edward A. " 'deeply and consciously affected . . .': Virginia Woolf's Reviews of the Romantic Poets." In *Virginia Woolf and the Essay.* Ed. Beth Carole Rosenberg and Jeanne Dubino. New York: St. Martin's, 1998. 97–115.

———. Introduction to "Byron and Mr. Briggs." *The Yale Review* 48.3 (March 1979) 321–24.

Hussey, Mark. *Virginia Woolf A-Z.* New York: Oxford University Press, 1995.

Hutton, Patrick H. "The Art of Memory Reconceived: From Rhetoric to Psychoanalysis." *Journal of the History of Ideas* 48.3 (1987) 371–92.

Hynes, Samuel. "The Whole Contention between Mr. Bennett and Mrs. Woolf." *Edwardian Occasions.* London: Routledge, 1972. 24–38.

Ibsen, Henrik. *A Doll's House.* New York: Dover, 1992.

Jenkyns, Richard. *The Victorians and Ancient Greece.* Oxford: Oxford University Press, 1980.

Johnston, Georgia. "The Whole Achievement in Virginia Woolf's *The Common Reader.*" In *Essays on the Essay: Redefining the Genre.* Ed. Alexander J. Butrym. Athens: University of Georgia Press, 1989. 148–58.

Johnson, Samuel. *The Major Works.* Ed. Donald Greene. New York: Oxford University Press, 2000.

Jonson, Ben. *Timber, or Discoveries.* Syracuse, NY: Syracuse University Press, 1953.

Joplin, Patricia Klindienst. "The Authority of Illusion: Feminism and Fascism in Virginia Woolf's *Between the Acts.*" In *Virginia Woolf: A Collection of Critical Essays.* 1989, reprinted. Ed. Margaret Homans. New Jersey: Prentice Hall, 1993. 210–26.

———. "The Voice of the Shuttle Is Ours." In *Rape and Representation.* Ed. Lynn A. Higgins and Brenda R. Silver. New York: Columbia University Press, 1991.

Joseph, Gerhard. "The *Antigone* as Cultural Touchstone: Matthew Arnold, Hegel, George Eliot, Virginia Woolf, and Margaret Drabble," *PMLA* 96 (January 1981) 22–32.

Joyce, James. *Ulysses*. 1922. New York: Vintage, 1990.

Kamuf, Peggy. "Penelope at Work: Interruptions in *A Room of One's Own*." *Novel* 16.1 (1982) 5–18.

Kaufman, Michael. "A Modernism of One's Own: Virginia Woolf's *TLS* Reviews and Eliotic Modernism." In *Virginia Woolf and the Essay*. Ed. Beth Rosenberg and Jeanne Dubino. New York: St. Martin's Press, 1998. 137–55.

Keats, John. *Complete Poems*. Ed. Jack Stillinger. Cambridge, MA: Harvard University Press, 1982.

Kenner, Hugh. *The Invisible Poet: T. S. Eliot*. London: Methuen, 1959.

———. *The Pound Era*. Berkeley: University of California Press, 1973.

Kerrigan, William and Gordon Braden. *The Idea of the Renaissance*. Baltimore: Johns Hopkins University Press, 1989.

Ketcham, Michael G. *Transparent Designs: Reading, Performance, and Form in the Spectator Papers*. Athens: University of Georgia Press, 1985.

Kierkegaard, Søren. *The Concluding Unscientific Postscript*. 1941. Trans. David F. Swenson. Princeton, NJ: Princeton University Press, 1968.

Kirkpatrick, B. J. and Stuart N. Clarke. *A Bibliography of Virginia Woolf*. 4th edition. Oxford: Oxford University Press, 1997.

Klaus, Carl H. "On Virginia Woolf on the Essay." *The Iowa Review* 20.2 (1990) 28–34.

Klein, Lawrence. "Gender and the Public/Private Distinction in the Eighteenth Century: Some Questions about Evidence and Analytic Procedure." *Eighteenth–Century Studies* 29.1 (1995) 97–105.

Knowles, Nancy. "Virginia Woolf's Dome Symbolism: *Si monumentum requires circumspice* or Monuments to Patriarchal Infantile Fixation." *Woolf Studies Annual* 4 (1998) 86–100.

Koutsoudaki, Mary. "The 'Greek' Jacob: Greece in Virginia Woolf's *Jacob's Room*." *Papers in Romance* 2.1 (July 1980) 67–75.

Lamb, Charles. *The Works of Charles and Mary Lamb*. Ed. E. V. Lucas. London: Methuen, 1903–05.

Landes, Joan B. "The Public and the Private Sphere: A Feminist Reconsideration." In *Feminists Read Habermas: Gendering the Subject of Discourse*. Ed. Johanna Meehan. New York: Routledge, 1995. 91–116.

Laughton, John Knox. [J. K. L.] "Hakluyt, Richard (1552–1616)." In *The Dictionary of National Biography*. 1900. 21 vols. Ed. Leslie Stephen and Sidney Lee. Oxford: Oxford University Press, 8.895–96.

Lauritsen, John. "Lord Byron Just Keeps Getting Gayer." Review of *Byron: A Life and Legend* by Fiona MacCarthy. *Gay & Lesbian Review Worldwide* 10.2 (March–April 2003) 34–35.

Lawrence, D. H. *D. H. Lawrence and Italy: Twilight in Italy, Sea and Sardinia, Etruscan Places*. New York: Viking, 1972.

Lee, Hermione. *Virginia Woolf*. London: Chatto, 1996.

Lessing, Doris. *The Golden Notebook.* 1962. New York: Harper, 1999.

———. *The Grass is Singing.* 1950. New York: Harper, 2000.

———. *A Proper Marriage.* 1952. New York: Plume, 1970.

———. *Under My Skin: Volume One of My Autobiography, to 1949.* New York: Harper, 1994.

Levenback, Karen L. *Virginia Woolf and the Great War.* Syracuse, NY: Syracuse University Press, 1999.

Levenson, Michael. *A Genealogy of Modernism.* Cambridge, UK: Cambridge University Press, 1984.

Levine, Alice. "T. S. Eliot and Byron." *ELH* 45.3 (Autumn 1978) 522–41.

Linton, Joan Pong. "Jack of Newbery and Drake in California: Domestic and Colonial Narratives of English Cloth and Manhood." *ELH* 59.1 (Spring 1992). 23–51.

London, Bette. *The Appropriated Voice: Narrative Authority in Conrad, Forster, and Woolf.* Ann Arbor: University of Michigan Press, 1990.

———. "Guerilla in Petticoats or Sans—Culotte? Virginia Woolf and the Future of Feminist Criticism." *Diacritics* (Summer—Fall 1991) 11–29.

Low, Lisa. "Feminist Elegy/Feminist Prophecy: *Lycidas, The Waves,* Kristeva, Cixous." *Woolf Studies Annual* 9 (2003) 221–42.

Luckhurst, Nicola. "Vogue . . . Is Going to Take Up Mrs. Woolf, to Boom Her . . ." In *Virginia Woolf and the Arts: Selected Papers from the Sixth Annual Conference on Virginia Woolf.* Ed. Diane F. Gillespie and K. Leslie. New York: Pace University Press, 1997. 75–84.

Lukacs, Georg. "On the Nature and Form of the Essay." *Soul and Form.* Trans. Anna Bostock. Cambridge, MA: MIT Press, 1974.

Majumdar, Robin and Allen McLaurin, eds. *Virginia Woolf: The Critical Heritage.* London: Routledge, 1975.

Marchand, Leslie. *Byron; A Biography.* 3 vols. New York: Knopf, 1957.

———. "The Quintessential Byron." In *Byron: Augustan and Romantic.* Ed. Andrew Rutherford. London: Macmillan, 1990. 240–47.

Marcus, Jane. *Art and Anger.* Columbus: Ohio State University Press, 1988.

———. "Britannia Rules *The Waves.*" In *Decolonizing Tradition: New Views of Twentieth-Century "British" Literary Canons.* Ed. Karen R. Lawrence. Urbana: University of Illinois Press, 1992. 136–61.

———. "Pathographies: The Virginia Woolf Soap Operas." *Signs* 17 (1992) 806–19.

———. *Virginia Woolf and the Languages of Patriarchy.* Bloomington: Indiana University Press, 1987.

Marshik, Celia. "Publication and 'Public Women': Prostitution and Censorship in Three Novels by Virginia Woolf." *MFS: Modern Fiction Studies* 45.4 (Winter 1999) 853–86.

Mason, Nicholas. "Building Brand Byron: Early-Nineteenth-Century Advertising and the Marketing of Childe Harold's Pilgrimage." *Modern Language Quarterly* 63.4 (December 2002) 411–40.

May, Derwent. *Critical Times: The History of the "Times Literary Supplement."* London: Harper Collins, 2001.

McClure, Laura. *Spoken Like a Woman: Speech and Gender in Athenian Drama.* Princeton, NJ: Princeton University Press, 1999.

McCrea, Brian. *Addison and Steele Are Dead: The English Department, Its Canon, and the Professionalization of Literary Criticism.* Newark: University of Delaware Press, 1990.

McCutcheon, Elizabeth, ed. and trans. "Sir Nicholas Bacon's Great House Sententiae." *English Literary Renaissance Supplements* 3 (1977) 98 pp.

McDayter, Ghislaine. "Conjuring Byron: Byromania, Literary Commodification and the Birth of Celebrity." In *Byromania: Portraits of the Artist in Nineteenth- and Twentieth-Century Culture.* Ed. Francis Wilson. New York: St. Martin's, 1999. 43–62.

McDonald, Peter D. *British Literary Culture and Publishing Practice, 1880–1914.* Cambridge, UK: Cambridge University Press, 1997.

McGann, Jerome. "On Reading *Childe Harold's Pilgrimage.*" In *Critical Essays on Lord Byron.* Ed. Robert F. Gleckner. New York: G. K. Hall, 1991. 33–58.

McNeillie, Andrew. "Bloomsbury." In *The Cambridge Companion to Virginia Woolf.* Ed. Sue Roe and Susan Sellers. Cambridge, UK: Cambridge University Press, 2000 1–18.

McNeillie, Andrew. Introduction to *The Essays of Virginia Woolf.* Vol. 1. New York: Harcourt, 1986. ix–xviii.

———. Introduction to *The Essays of Virginia Woolf.* Vol. 2. New York: Harcourt, 1987. 2.ix–xx.

———. Introduction to *The Essays of Virginia Woolf.* Vol. 3. New York: Harcourt, 1988. 3.xi–xxii.

Meehan, Johanna, ed. *Feminists Read Habermas: Gendering the Subject of Discourse.* New York: Routledge, 1995.

———. Introduction to *Feminists Read Habermas: Gendering the Subject of Discourse,* Ed. Johanna Meehan. New York: Routledge, 1995. 1–20.

Meisel, Perry. *The Absent Father: Virginia Woolf and Walter Pater.* New Haven, CT: Yale University Press, 1980.

Mermin, Dorothy. *Elizabeth Barrett Browning: The Origins of a New Poetry.* Chicago: University of Chicago Press, 1989.

Milton, John. *Complete Poems and Major Prose.* Ed. Merritt Y. Hughes. Indianapolis: Bobbs-Merrill, 1957.

Montaigne, Michel de. *Essais.* Paris: Garnier–Flammarion, 1969.

Monte, Steven. "Ancients and Moderns in *Mrs. Dalloway.*" *Modern Language Quarterly* 61.4 (December 2000). 587–616.

Moore, Thomas. *Letters and Journals of Lord Byron, with Notices of His Life.* 2 vols. Paris: Gagliani, 1829.

Nicolson, Harold George. *Byron, the Last Journey, April 1823–April 1824.* London: Constable, 1924.

Nora, Pierre. "Between Memory and History: *Les Lieux de Mémoire.*" Trans. Marc Roudebush. *Representations* 26 (Spring 1989) 7–25.

Oldfield, Sybil. "Virginia Woolf and Antigone—Thinking Against the Current." *South Carolina Review* 26.1 (Fall 1996) 45–57.

Pandey, Gyanedra. "In Defense of the Fragment: Writing about Hindu–Muslim Riots in India Today." Special Issue: Imperial Fantasies and Postcolonial Histories. *Representations* 37 (Winter 1992) 27–55.

Parks, George Bruner. "Chapter XV: The English Epic." *Richard Hakluyt and the English Voyages.* New York: Frederick Ungar Publishing Co., 1961.

Pateman, Carole. *The Disorder of Women: Democracy, Feminism and Political Theory.* Stanford, CA: Stanford University Press, 1989.

Pater, Walter. *Essays on Literature and Art.* London: Dent, 1973.

Phillips, K. J. "Jane Harrison and Modernism." *Journal of Modern Literature* 17.4 (Spring 1991) 465–76.

Plato. *The Republic.* Trans. Allan Bloom. New York: Basic Books, 1968.

Plett, Heinrich F. "Ars Memorativa: Mnemonic Architecture and English Renaissance Literature." *Texte* 8–9 (1989) 147–58.

Pound, Ezra. *Personae.* New York: New Directions, 1926.

Prins, Yopie. *Victorian Sappho.* Princeton, NJ: Princeton University Press, 1999.

Quinn, David B. *The Hakluyt Handbook.* 2 vols. London: The Hakluyt Society, 1974.

Radway, Janice. *A Feeling for Books: The Book–of–the–Month Club, Literary Taste and Middle Class Desire.* Chapel Hill: University of North Carolina Press, 1998.

Rainey, Lawrence. *Institutions of Modernism.* New Haven, CT: Yale University Press, 1998.

Raleigh, Walter Alexander. *The English Voyages of the Sixteenth Century.* Glasgow: James MacLehose and Sons, 1910.

Ramsay, Stephen J. " 'On Not Knowing Greek': Virginia Woolf and the New Ancient Greece." In *Virginia Woolf: Turning the Centuries.* Ed. Ann L. Ardis and Bonnie Kime Scott. New York: Pace University Press, 2000.

Rayor, Diane, trans. *Sappho's Lyre: Archaic Lyric and Women Poets of Ancient Greece.* Berkeley: University of California Press, 1991.

Rickard, John S. *Joyce's Book of Memory: The Mnemotechnic of* Ulysses. Durham, NC: Duke University Press, 1999.

Robinson, Annabel. "Something Odd at Work: The Influence of Jane Harrison on *A Room of One's Own.*" In *Virginia Woolf: Critical Assessments.* 4 vols. Ed. Eleanor McNees. Vol. 2. Robertsbridge: England Helm, 1994. 215–20.

Rose, Jonathan. *The Intellectual Life of the British Working Classes.* New Haven, CT: Yale University Press, 2001.

Rosenberg, Beth Carole. *Virginia Woolf and Samuel Johnson: Common Readers.* New York: St. Martin's, 1995.

———. "Virginia Woolf's Postmodern Literary History." *Modern Language Notes.* 115.5 (December 2000) 1112–30.

Rosenberg, Beth Carole and Jeanne Dubino, eds. *Virginia Woolf and the Essay.* New York: St. Martin's Press, 1998.

Rosenfield, Kathrin H. "Getting Inside Sophocles' Mind Through Hölderlin's *Antigone.*" *New Literary History* 30 (1999) 107–27.

Royer, Diana. *A Critical Study of the Works of Nawal El Saadawi, Egyptian Writer and Activist.* Lewiston, NY: Mellen, 2001.

Rudikoff, Sonya. *Ancestral Houses: Virginia Woolf and the Aristocracy.* Palo Alto, CA: The Society for the Promotion of Science and Scholarship, 1999.

Ruotolo, Lucio P. *The Interrupted Moment: A View of Virginia Woolf's Novels.* Stanford, CA: Stanford University Press, 1986.

Rutherford, Andrew, ed. *Byron: The Critical Heritage.* New York: Barnes & Noble, 1970.

Saadawi, Nawal El. *A Daughter of Isis.* Trans. Sherif Hetata. London: Zed Books, 1999.

———. *Woman at Point Zero.* 1975. Trans. Sherif Hetata. London: Zed, 1983.

Said, Edward W. *Beginnings: Intention and Method.* New York: Basic, 1975.

Sapathy, Sumanya. "Eliot's Early Criticism and the *TLS.*" *The Literary Criterion* [Bombay] 22.3 (1987) 33–40.

———. "Sir Isaiah Berlin Remembers Bruce Richmond, T. S. Eliot and Ezra Pound." [Interview] *The Literary Criterion* [Bombay] 26.2 (1991) 19–22.

Sappho. *Sappho.* Trans. Mary Barnard. Berkeley: University of California Press, 1958.

Schickel, Richard. *Intimate Strangers: The Culture of Celebrity in America.* 1985. Chicago: Ivan R. Dee. 2000.

Schlack, Beverly Ann. *Continuing Presences: Virginia Woolf's Use of Literary Allusion.* University Park: Penn State University Press, 1979.

———. "Virginia Woolf's Strategy of Scorn in *The Years* and *Three Guineas.*" *Bulletin of the New York Public Library* 80 (1977) 146–50.

Scovell, E. J. "Virginia Woolf, Critic." *The New Statesman and Nation* (October 15, 1932) 454–55.

Sears, Sallie "Theater of War: Virginia Woolf's *Between the Acts.*" In *Virginia Woolf, A Feminist Slant.* Ed. Jane Marcus. Lincoln: University of Nebraska Press, 1983. 212–35.

Sellers, Susan. "Virginia Woolf's Diaries and Letters." *The Cambridge Companion to Virginia Woolf.* Ed. Sue Roe and Susan Sellers. Cambridge, UK: Cambridge University Press, 2000. 109–26.

Shakespeare, William. *The Riverside Shakespeare.* Ed. G. Blakemore Evans. Boston: Houghton Mifflin, 1974.

Showalter, Elaine. *A Literature of Their Own: British Women Novelists from Brontë to Lessing.* Princeton, NJ: Princeton University Press, 1977.

Silver, Brenda R. "The Authority of Anger: *Three Guineas* as Case Study." *Signs* 16.2 (1991) 340–70.

———. "Virginia Woolf and the Concept of Community: The Elizabethan Playhouse." *Women's Studies* 4 (1977) 291–98.

———. *Virginia Woolf Icon.* Chicago: University of Chicago Press, 1999.

———. *Virginia Woolf's Reading Notebooks.* Princeton, NJ: Princeton University Press, 1983.

Smyth, Herbert Weir, trans. *Aeschylus: Agamemnon, Libation-Bearers, Eumenides, Fragments.* 1926. Cambridge, MA: Harvard University Press, 1995.

Solomon, Julie. "Staking Ground: The Politics of Space in Virginia Woolf's *A Room of One's Own* and *Three Guineas.*" *Women's Studies* 16.3/4 (1989) 331–47.

Sophocles. *Three Theban Plays.* Ed. Bernard Knox. Trans. Robert Fagles. New York: Penguin, 1984.

Spacks, Patricia Meyer. "Introduction." *Selections from* The Female Spectator. New York: Oxford University Press, 1999.

Spalding, Frances. *Vanessa Bell.* New Haven, CT: Ticknor, 1983.

Squier, Susan. " 'The London Scene': Gender and Class in Virginia Woolf's London." *Twentieth Century Literature* 29 (Winter 1983) 4.488–500.

St Clair, William. "The Impact of Byron's Writings: An Evaluative Approach." In *Byron: Augustan and Romantic.* Ed. Andrew Rutherford. New York: St. Martin's, 1990. 1–25.

Steele, Elizabeth. *Virginia Woolf's Literary Sources and Allusions: A Guide to the Essays.* New York: Garland, 1983.

———. *Virginia Woolf's Rediscovered Essays: Sources and Allusions.* New York: Garland, 1986.

Stein, Gertrude. "What Are Master-Pieces and Why Are There So Few of Them?" In *Writings, 1932–46.* Ed. Catharine R. Stimpson and Harriet Chessman. New York: Library of America, 1998. 355–63.

Steiner, George. *Antigones.* Oxford: Oxford University Press, 1984.

Stephen, Leslie. "Byron, George Gordon, Sixth Lord (1788–1824). *The Dictionary of National Biography.* 1900. 21 vols. Ed. Leslie Stephen and Sidney Lee. Oxford: Oxford University Press. 3.584–607.

———. *English Literature and Society in the 18th Century.* N.P. 1903.

———. *Hours in a Library.* London: Smith, 1909.

Sterne, Laurence. *Tristram Shandy.* Ed. Howard Anderson. New York: Norton, 1980.

Strachey, Lytton. *Eminent Victorians.* New York: Harcourt, 1918.

———. "Madame du Deffand." *Books & Characters, French & English.* 1922. London: Chatto and Windus, 1934. 67–92.

Strychacz, Thomas. *Modernism, Mass Culture, and Professionalism.* Cambridge, UK: Cambridge University Press, 1993.

Swanson, Diana L. "An Antigone Complex? The Political Psychology of *The Years* and *Three Guineas.*" *Woolf Studies Annual* 3 (1997) 28–44.

Sweet, Timothy. "Economy, Ecology, and Utopia in Early Colonial Promotional Literature." *American Literature: A Journal of Literary History, Criticism and Bibliography* 71.3 (September 1999). 399–427.

Tate, Trudi. "Mrs. Dalloway and the Armenian Question." *Textual Practice* 8.3 (Winter 1994) 467–86.

Tillyard, E. M. W. *The Elizabethan World Picture.* London: Chatto and Windus, 1943.

Torgovnick, Marianna. "Discovering Jane Harrison." In *Seeing Double: Revisioning Edwardian and Modernist Literature.* Ed. Carola M. Kaplan and Anne B. Simpson. New York: St. Martin's, 1996. 131–48.

Tratner, Michael. *Modernism and Mass Politics: Joyce, Woolf, Eliot, Yeats.* Stanford, CA: Stanford University Press, 1995.

Tremper, Ellen. *Who Lived at Alfoxten?: Virginia Woolf and English Romanticism.* Lewisburg: Bucknell University Press, 1998.

Trilling, Lionel. *Beyond Culture.* New York: Viking, 1965.

Turnbull, Mary. "Virginia Woolf's 'Noble Athena': Miss Janet Case." *Hatcher Review* 3 (1986) 95–104.

Turner, Frank M. "British Politics and the Demise of the Roman Republic: 1700–1939." *Historical Journal* 29. 3 (September 1986) 577–99.

Vanita, Ruth. "Bringing Buried Things to Light: Homoerotic Alliances in *To the Lighthouse*." In *Virginia Woolf: Lesbian Readings.* Ed. Eileen Barrett and Patricia Cramer. New York: New York University Press, 1997. 165–79.

———. *Sappho and the Virgin Mary: Same-Sex Love and the English Literary Imagination.* New York: Columbia University Press, 1996.

Walker, Alice. *In Search of Our Mother's Gardens.* San Diego: Harcourt, 1983.

Wills, Gary. *John Wayne's America: The Politics of Celebrity.* New York: Simon & Schuster, 1997.

Wilson, Francis, ed. *Byromania: Portraits of the Artist in Nineteenth- and Twentieth-Century Culture.* New York: St. Martin's, 1999.

Wolfson, Susan J. " 'A Problem Few Dare Imitate': *Sardanapalus* and 'Effeminate Character.' " *ELH* 58.4 (Winter 1991) 867–902.

Wollstonecraft, Mary. *A Vindication of the Rights of Woman.* 1792. New York: Penguin, 1985.

"Women in a World of War, A 'Society of Outsiders': Mrs. Virginia Woolf's Searching Pamphlet," *TLS* (Saturday, June 4, 1938) 379. Represented in Robin Majumdar and Allen McLaurin. *Virginia Woolf: The Critical Heritage.* London: Routledge, 1975.

Wood, Adolf. "The Lure of the *TLS*." In *Adventures with Britannia: Personalities, Politics, and Culture in Britain.* Ed. Wm. Roger Louis. Austin: University of Texas Press, 1995. 135–44.

Woolf, Leonard. *Downhill All the Way: An Autobiography of the Years 1919 to 1939.* New York: Harcourt, 1967.

Woolf, Virginia. "Anon." In *The Gender of Modernism.* Ed. Bonnie Kime Scott. Bloomington: Indiana University Press, 1990.

———. *Between the Acts.* New York: Harcourt, 1941.

———. "Byron and Mr. Briggs and Other Essays." Ed. Edward A. Hungerford. *The Yale Review* 68.3 (March 1979) 321–49.

———. *The Captain's Death Bed.* New York: Harcourt, 1950.

———. *The Common Reader.* 1925. Ed. Andrew McNeillie. New York: Harcourt, 1989.

———. *The Complete Shorter Fiction.* Ed. Susan Dick. New York: Harcourt, 1989.

———. *The Crowded Dance of Modern Life* and Other Essays. Ed. Rachel Bowlby. London: Penguin, 1993.

———. *The Death of the Moth.* 1942. New York: Harcourt, 1970.

———. *Diary.* Ed. Anne Olivier Bell. 5 vols. New York: Harcourt, 1977–84.

————. *Essays*. Ed. Andrew McNeillie. 6 projected, currently 4 vols. New York: Harcourt, 1986–94.

————. *Flush: A Biography*. New York: Harcourt, 1933.

————. *Granite & Rainbow*. New York: Harcourt, 1958.

————. *Jacob's Room*. 1922. New York: Harcourt, 1923.

————. *Letters*. Ed. Nigel Nicolson and Joanne Trautmann. 6 vols. New York: Harcourt, 1975–80.

————. *The London Scene*. New York: Random House, 1975.

————. "Memoir of Julian Bell." In *Virginia Woolf: A Biography*. 1936. Ed. Quentin Bell. New York: Harcourt, 1972. Appendix C. 255–59.

————. "Memories of a Working Women's Guild." *Life as We Have Known It*. Ed. Margaret Llewelyn Davies. New York: Norton, 1975.

————. *The Moment and Other Essays*. New York: Harcourt, 1948.

————. *Moments of Being: Unpublished Autobiographical Writings*. Ed. Jeanne Schulkind. New York: Harcourt, 1985.

————. *Mrs. Dalloway*. 1925. New York: Harcourt, 1981.

————. *Night and Day*. New York: Harcourt, 1919.

————. *Orlando: A Biography*. New York: Harcourt, 1928.

————. *The Pargiters: The Novel-Essay Portion of* The Years. Ed. Mitchell A. Leaska. New York: Harcourt, 1977.

————. *A Passionate Apprentice: The Early Journals, 1897–1909*. Ed. Mitchell A. Leaska. New York: Harcourt, 1990.

————. *A Room of One's Own*. 1929. New York: Harcourt, 1989.

————. *The Second Common Reader*. 1932. Ed. Andrew McNeillie. New York: Harcourt, 1986.

————. *Three Guineas*. 1938. New York: Harcourt, 1966.

————. *To the Lighthouse*. 1927. New York: Harcourt, 1989.

————. *The Voyage Out*. 1915. New York: Harcourt, 1926.

————. *The Waves*. New York: Harcourt, 1931.

————. *A Woman's Essays*. Ed. Rachel Bowlby. New York: Penguin, 1992.

————. *Women and Writing*. Ed. Michéle Barrett. New York: Harcourt, 1979.

————. "Women Must Weep—Or Unite Against War." *The Atlantic Monthly* 161.5 (May 1938) 585–94; 161.6 (June 1938) 750–59.

————. *The Years*. New York: Harcourt, 1937.

Wordsworth, Dorothy. *Journals*. Ed. Mary Moorman. London: Oxford University Press, 1971.

Wordsworth, William. *William Wordsworth: The Oxford Authors*. Ed. Stephen Gill. Oxford: Oxford University Press, 1984.

Yates, Frances A. *The Art of Memory*. 1966. London: Pimlico, 1992.

Yeats, W. B. *Collected Poems*. Ed. Richard Finneran. New York: Scribner, 1996.

Zwerdling, Alex. *Virginia Woolf and the Real World*. Berkeley: University of California Press, 1986.

# INDEX